No. 1 *New York Times* bestselling author **Christine Feehan** has had over ninety novels published and has thrilled legions of fans with her seductive Dark Carpathian tales. She has received numerous honours throughout her career, including being a nominee for the Romance Writers of America RITA and receiving a Career Achievement Award from *Romantic Times*, and has been published in multiple languages.

Visit Christine Feehan online:

www.christinefeehan.com
www.facebook.com/christinefeehanauthor
@AuthorCFeehan

Praise for Christine Feehan:

'After Bram Stoker, Anne Rice and Joss Whedon, Feehan is the person most credited with popularizing the neck gripper'
Time magazine

'The queen of paranormal romance'
USA Today

'Feehan has a knack for bringing vampiric Carpathians to vivid, virile life in her Dark Carpathian novels'
Publishers Weekly

'The amazingly prolific author's ability to create captivating and adrenaline-raising worlds is unsurpassed'
Romantic Times

By Christine Feehan

CHRISTINE
FEEHAN
Dark memory

PIATKUS

PIATKUS

First published in the US in 2023 by Berkley,
An imprint of Penguin Random House LLC
First published in Great Britain in 2023 by Piatkus

1 3 5 7 9 10 8 6 4 2

A CIP catalogue record for this book
is available from the British Library.

ISBN HB: 978-0-349-43818-4
TPB: 978-0-349-43821-4

Printed and bound in Great Britain by Clays Ltd, Elcograf S.p.A.

Papers used by Piatkus are from well-managed forests
and other responsible sources.

Piatkus
An imprint of
Little, Brown Book Group
Carmelite House
50 Victoria Embankment
London EC4Y 0DZ

An Hachette UK Company
www.hachette.co.uk

www.littlebrown.co.uk

For Rachel Powell, with love.
Everyone has demons to slay, but no one does it better.
No matter what is happening in your life, you manage
to stand up under the worst possible circumstances
and keep fighting on.

FOR MY READERS

Be sure to go to ChristineFeehan.com/members/ to sign up for my private book announcement list and download the free ebook of *Dark Desserts*. Join my community and get firsthand news, enter the book discussions, ask your questions and chat with me. Please feel free to email me at Christine@ChristineFeehan.com. I would love to hear from you.

ACKNOWLEDGMENTS

Thank you to Diane Trudeau, Sheila English, Brian Feehan and Skyler Cline. I would never have been able to get this book finished under such circumstances. I especially want to thank Anaruz Elhabib, who graciously answered so many questions for me and made this book possible.

Thank you all so very much!

Dear Readers,

There are times when I'm writing a book that I get very caught up by the research I'm doing. In this case, I found the Amazigh people fascinating. The more I learned about them, the more I wanted to know. I was fortunate enough to come across a man by the name of Anaruz Elhabib, a translator who was absolutely wonderful to me. He not only did translations for me but answered questions about culture and history and anything else I pestered him about. He went out of his way to assist me when I asked him what I am certain he must have considered strange questions.

Anaruz Elhabib represented everything I read and studied about the Amazigh people. He was kind and giving and patient with me. I wanted to do the people justice in writing about them as a whole, even while writing a fictional book that fit in with my Carpathian series. I hope that I did so and that he will find this work respectful of his people. Any mistakes I've made are strictly mine.

I want to thank him for his patience and understanding and for the time he took explaining so many things about language and customs to me. If anyone needs translations, he is fast and efficient and goes that extra mile.

I hope you enjoy the story. I love the family, the setting and, most of all, the couple.

Best regards,
Christine

THE CARPATHIAN FAMILIES

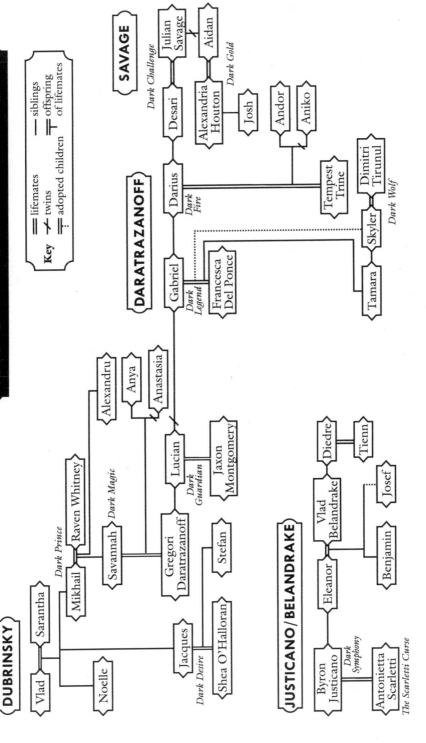

Key
≡ lifemates
⋏ twins
⚏ adopted children
— siblings
⊤ offspring of lifemates

DUBRINSKY

Vlad ≡ Sarantha
Mikhail ≡ Raven Whitney *Dark Prince*
Noelle
Jacques ≡ Shea O'Halloran *Dark Desire*
Savannah ≡ Gregori Daratrazanoff *Dark Magic*
Alexandru
Anya
Anastasia
Lucian ≡ Jaxon Montgomery *Dark Guardian*
Stefan

DARATRAZANOFF

Gabriel ≡ Francesca Del Ponce *Dark Legend*
Darius ≡ *Dark Fire*
Tamara
Skyler ≡ Dimitri Tirunul *Dark Wolf*
Tempest Trine

SAVAGE

Julian Savage ≡ Desari *Dark Challenge*
Aidan ≡ Alexandria Houton *Dark Gold*
Josh
Andor
Aniko

JUSTICANO / BELANDRAKE

Byron Justicano ≡ Antonietta Scarletti *Dark Symphony* *The Scarletti Curse*
Eleanor ≡ Vlad Belandrake
Diedre
Tienn
Benjamin
Josef

THE CARPATHIAN FAMILIES

Key
= lifemates
≠ twins
∽ triplets
= of lifemates
— siblings
⋎ cousins

⋎ parents not lifemates
∼ lifemates
∽ offspring
* monastery ancients
^ converted male
◊ other species

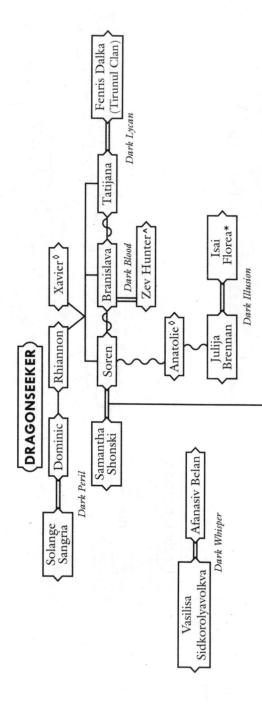

DRAGONSEEKER

Solange Sangria

Dominic ∼ Rhiannon ⋎ Xavier◊

Dark Peril

Samantha Shonski ∼ Soren

Branislava = Tatijana

Dark Blood

Zev Hunter^

Fenris Dalka (Tirunul Clan)

Dark Lycan

Anatolie◊

Julija Brennan ∼ Isai Florea*

Dark Illusion

Vasilisa Sidkorolyavolkva ∼ Afanasiv Belan

Dark Whisper

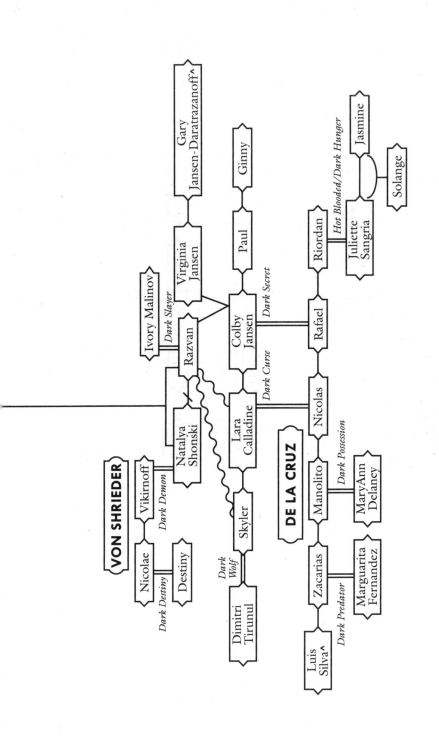

OTHER CARPATHIANS

Key

═══ lifemates	∿ offspring
⋁ parents not lifemates	* monastery ancients
─── siblings	∧ converted male
╤ offspring of lifemates	◊ other species

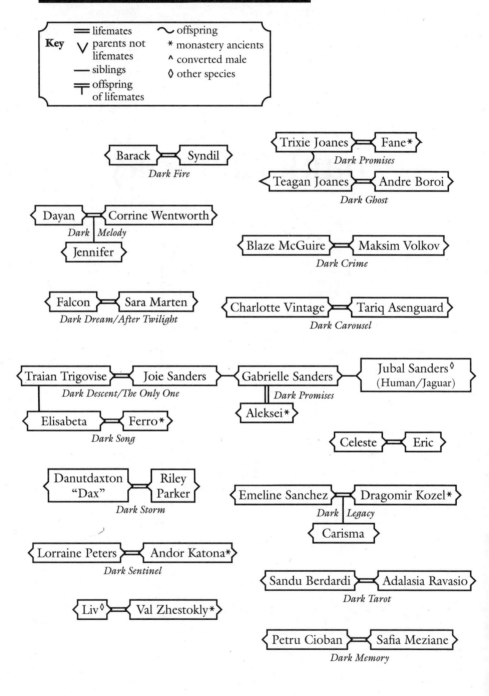

Barack ═══ Syndil
Dark Fire

Trixie Joanes ═══ Fane*
Dark Promises

Teagan Joanes ═══ Andre Boroi
Dark Ghost

Dayan ╤ Corrine Wentworth
Dark | *Melody*
Jennifer

Blaze McGuire ═══ Maksim Volkov
Dark Crime

Falcon ═══ Sara Marten
Dark Dream/After Twilight

Charlotte Vintage ═══ Tariq Asenguard
Dark Carousel

Traian Trigovise ═══ Joie Sanders ─── Gabrielle Sanders ─── Jubal Sanders◊ (Human/Jaguar)
Dark Descent/The Only One | *Dark Promises*
Elisabeta ═══ Ferro*   Aleksei*
Dark Song

Celeste ═══ Eric

Danutdaxton "Dax" ═══ Riley Parker
Dark Storm

Emeline Sanchez ╤ Dragomir Kozel*
Dark | *Legacy*
Carisma

Lorraine Peters ═══ Andor Katona*
Dark Sentinel

Sandu Berdardi ═══ Adalasia Ravasio
Dark Tarot

Liv◊ ═══ Val Zhestokly*

Petru Cioban ═══ Safia Meziane
Dark Memory

dark memory

BETRAYAL.
SACRIFICE.
LOSS.

Seven of Swords

XII

The Hanged Man

Five of Cups

The breeze blowing in from the Mediterranean Sea brought a hint of the coming storm with it. Safia Meziane stood at the very top of the hillside overlooking the turquoise water, which was now beginning to grow choppy as little fingers of wind touched the glassy surface. The knots in her stomach tightened as she watched the water begin to churn. Ordinarily, she loved storms, but she was uneasy, certain the weather heralded something much more sinister than lightning and thunder.

"I will never tire of this view," Amastan Meziane said, his gaze on the sea. "As a young man, I would stand in this exact spot with my father and feel fortunate to live in this place."

"Just as I do," Safia admitted, looking up at her grandfather.

Safia's family was Imazighen. Outsiders sometimes referred to them as Berbers. Her family owned a very prosperous farm located up in the hills outside the town of Dellys. They had extraordinary views of the sea and the harbor. The farm kept a variety of animals, mainly sheep and goats, and harvested the wool, spinning and dying it for clothes and rugs they sold at the local market or sent with Safia's oldest sister's family across the Sahara to markets. Some of the family members made jewelry and others pottery. All contributed to the success of the household, farm and tribe.

Her grandfather Amastan was the acknowledged head of her tribe. Like her grandfather, Safia had always felt very lucky to have been born into her family. To live where she lived. To be raised on her family farm. She had two older sisters who doted on her and three older brothers who always treated her as if she were a treasure, just as her parents and grandparents did. They all worked hard on the farm. When her oldest sister, Illi, married and left with her husband, Kab, no one resented the extra work. They were happy for her, although Safia missed her terribly and looked forward to the times when she returned from her travels.

Beside her, Amastan sighed. "Our family has had centuries of good years, Safia, and we can't complain. We've always known this time would come."

He felt it, too. It wasn't her imagination. Evil rode in the wind of that storm. It had quietly invaded their farm. She had known all along but had done her best to tell herself it was her wild imagination. The number of invasive insects had suddenly increased. Three weeks earlier, she had begun to note the tracks of an unfamiliar predator. One week ago, several predators had eviscerated a goat near the cliffs. Whatever it was seemed to disappear into the ground when she'd tried to follow it. There had been more than one, but she couldn't determine the number or exactly what it was.

"I love the way Dellys looks, *Jeddi*, day or night. The blend of beautiful modern structures built so close to the ancient ruins and the way the ruins are on the hillside facing the sea. I love the sunrises and sunsets, and the sea with its colors and ever-changing mood, the markets and the people. Dellys is so modern, and yet our history, our culture, is right there for everyone to see. And on the hillside, evidence of our history remains. We're like that. Our family. Like Dellys. So modern on the outside. Anyone looking at us would believe we're so progressive." She loved her life. Mostly, she loved the huge tribe she called family.

Safia didn't look at her grandfather; she kept her gaze fixed on the beauty of the sea. The women in her family were well educated, unlike many females in other tribes. They spoke Tamazight and Arabic, but along with that, they had learned French and English. Safia had been required to learn an ancient language that none of the others had to master. Her grandmother and mother were able to speak it, and she had one friend, Aura, who was an expert in the language, so she was fortunate to be able to practice with her. Safia never questioned why she had to learn such an ancient language that no one spoke in modern times. When her grandfather or grandmother decreed anything, it was done, usually without question.

Her grandfather not only believed they should expand their thinking, he insisted his daughters and granddaughters learn how to use weapons and to fight in hand-to-hand combat just as well as the males in the family. The women took care of the house, but they also worked on the farm. They learned to do everything needed and were always treated as valued members of the tribe. Their voices were heard when it came to solving problems. It was all very progressive and different from tradition in many other tribes.

Her grandfather arranged marriages in the traditional way. His word was law. He held the men they married to a very high standard. She couldn't imagine what would happen should he ever find out his daughters or granddaughters were mistreated. Amastan appeared stern to outsiders, but he was always soft-spoken and fair. No one ever wanted to upset him. It was a rare event, but when it happened, he had the backing of the entire tribe, not that he needed it. He was a force to be reckoned with.

"We must go inside, Safia. I told your father to call a family meeting. We can't continue to put this off. You will read the cards, and I'll consult with the ancestors tonight. We need to know exactly what we're facing and how much time we will have to prepare." He placed his hand on her shoulder as if he knew she needed encouragement.

Her heart sank. All along, she had told herself the tales she'd been raised with were simply fictional stories handed down for hundreds of years. They weren't real. Demons and vampires didn't belong in a modern world any more than the myths and legends that had sprung from the area where they lived.

"I tried not to believe it, *Jeddi*," she confessed. "I've trained from the time I was a baby to fight these things, and I read the cards daily, but I still didn't believe."

"You believed, Safia, or you wouldn't have trained so hard. You're very disciplined, even more so than your mother and grandmother ever were. You worked on the farm and at home with your mother, but you never once shirked your training. You believed. You just hoped, as we all did, that evil wouldn't rise in our lifetime."

She turned her head to look at her beloved grandfather. For the first time, she truly saw the worry lines carved in his face. There was unease in the faded blue of his eyes. That alone was enough to make all the times her radar had gone off and the knots in her belly very real.

"When you were born," he continued, "we knew. Your grandmother, your mother and father. I knew. I consulted the ancestors just to be certain. None of us wanted it to be true, but the moment you came into this world, all of us could see you were different. You were born with gifts." There was sorrow in his voice. "You were born with green eyes."

It was true, she was the only one in her family with green eyes, but why would that make a difference? Still, she didn't question him. "I did prepare," she whispered. "But it feels as if it can't be real, even now, when I feel evil on the wind. When I know the accidents on the farm were actual attacks on our family. I *know* these things, yet my mind doesn't want to process the reality."

She turned back to look at the town of Dellys, spread out in the distance. "All those unknowing, innocent people living there. The restaurants. The shops. The market. I love the market. Everyone is so unaware of the danger coming. It isn't as if soldiers are attacking them and they can see the enemy coming. No one would believe us if we warned them. I wouldn't even know what to tell them."

"You don't know what you're facing yet," Amastan pointed out, his voice gentle. "I've told you many times, Safia, prepare, but do not worry about something you have no control over—something that may or may not happen. That does you no good. If you have no idea who or what your enemy is and you dwell on it, you will make him much more powerful than he is."

She knew her grandfather was right. She trusted him. Throughout her years growing up, she hadn't known him to be wrong when he gave his advice. He was always thoughtful before he spoke, and she'd learned to take what he said to heart.

Once more she looked at the harbor. The port of Dellys was small, located near the mouth of the Sebaou River and east of Algiers. Many of the men permanently living in Dellys were fishermen, sailors or navigators. The fishermen provided their fresh catch daily to the local restaurants. The harbor was beautiful with the boats and lights, so modern-looking. Everything looked contemporary—so this century. Just by gazing at the beauty of the harbor and the town, one wouldn't imagine it had been around since prehistoric times.

"We must go in," Amastan reiterated. "The others will be waiting. Hopefully, Amara will have fixed dinner for us, and it will be edible."

Amara was married to Safia's oldest brother, Izem. She really liked Amara. Who could not? She didn't understand how the match worked, yet it did, perfectly. Amara was a tornado moving through the house and farm, one disaster after another. Through it all, her laughter was contagious. She was bright and cheerful, always willing to pitch in and help, eager to learn every aspect of farming. Clearly, she wanted to be a good wife to Izem, but her youth and exuberance coupled with her total inexperience and clumsy energy were sometimes recipes for disaster.

At the same time, she was an amazing jeweler. One would think when she was so clumsy around the farm, tripping over her own small feet, she wouldn't be able to make the fine necklaces and earrings she did. Her artwork was exquisite and much sought-after. She was an asset to their family for that but also, most importantly, because she made Izem happy.

Despite the two appearing to be total opposites, Izem was extremely satisfied with Amara. He was a very serious man. He took after Amastan in both appearance and personality. His name, meaning "lion," epitomized who he was and what he stood for. He was always going to be the head of his family. He was a man to be counted on, and maybe that was exactly why the match worked so well. Amara needed the security of Izem, and he needed the fun and brightness she brought him.

Safia loved watching her oldest brother and his wife together, because she was a little terrified of her grandfather choosing a husband for her. She knew several offers had been made for her, and he'd turned them down, stating she was already promised to another. He'd never explained to her what he meant. She'd never met a man she'd been promised to in marriage. Her father seemed to accept her grandfather's decree, as did her brothers. No one ever questioned her grandfather, and for some reason, even on such an important subject, she couldn't bring herself to, either. Seeing Izem and Amara so happy made her feel as if there were a chance she could find happiness with a man, a stranger, her grandfather believed would be the right choice for her.

They walked together side by side through the field and toward the house. "Your leg is hurting," Amastan observed. "You were injured today."

She wasn't limping. She'd been careful not to show any signs of pain. Instantly she felt shame. How could she possibly be ready to protect her family if Amastan could so easily read her discomfort? Her enemies would be able to do so just as easily and take advantage during a battle. All those years of training, and she couldn't cover a simple injury?

"I'm not ready, *Jeddi*," she whispered. "If I can't hide a simple injury from you, how can I defend the farm? Our family? How can I defend the people in the town?"

He spoke in his gentlest voice. "*Yelli*, I observed the tear in your trousers along with the dirt and bloodstains. You have not given anything away by your actions or expression. It is the condition of your clothes that tells me something happened."

"I did have a little accident today when I was herding the sheep in from the back pasture. They were far too close to the cliff and very uneasy." It had been in the same area where those strange tracks had been. She had been searching for them.

She didn't look up at him, but she felt her grandfather's piercing eyes on her, drilling into her, seeing right past her casual tone to the truth.

"Safia?" He stopped abruptly in front of the house.

More than a question, it was an order. Reluctantly, she halted as well and forced herself to look up at him, holding her gloves in front of her as if the thin leather could protect her from his close scrutiny. His gaze moved over her, examining her inch by inch.

"It was no accident, any more than what happened to me or any of the others, Safia. We can't pretend this away any longer. How badly were you injured?"

She pressed her lips together, reliving the terrifying moment when the dirt gave way on the cliff and she went over. She had clawed at the dirt, rock and scraggly tree roots as she slid over the side. It seemed to take forever before her fingers dug into the mud and roots, and she gingerly found a grip with her fingertips. She clung there, legs dangling, heart pounding, head resting against a tough rope of knotted wood.

Insects began to emerge from the mud, crawling toward her from every direction. Stinging bugs flew around her hands and face. A hawk screamed and rushed out of the sky straight at her. In that moment, she knew exactly what she faced, and calm descended. She forced air through her lungs, calling on her training to keep from panicking.

Evil had come to her family's farm. She couldn't deny it any longer, as much as she wanted to. She had known for the last three weeks the small "accidents" happening on their farm were attacks against their family. She felt guilty that she hadn't been able to protect the animals or her family members from the escalating violence. It was just that she had no idea how to stop it, because she wasn't certain how to fight what she couldn't see. Right at that moment, evil was striking at her as if it knew she was the primary defender.

"I was more frightened than anything else. A few scrapes and bruises." She had dug her toes into the rocks for purchase and reached with her mind for the hawk. She had gifts—incredible gifts she'd been born with. Before that moment, she had thought it was just plain cool that she had an ability to connect with animals, but the hawk turned away from her at the last moment, pulling up sharply at her command.

"Lacerations," her grandfather corrected.

She nodded. "When I was climbing back up the cliff, there were a few jagged rocks poking out. It really was more the scare of feeling the dirt give way under me and then having to admit to myself that all these little accidents haven't really been accidents at all."

Her grandfather continued to look at her.

She sighed. "I'm sore, shaken up, but really, nothing broken or sprained, so I got off easy."

Her grandfather remained silent far too long, thinking over her revelation. There had been too many small accidents lately. Both had become aware over the last few weeks that something was very wrong. Her father, too, had become suspicious. Even her brothers had grown quiet and exchanged worried looks between themselves.

"You're certain all the animals are in for the night?" Amastan asked.

Safia nodded. "Usem and Farah brought in the sheep."

Her brother, Usem, and his wife, Farah, were fast at moving the sheep. She was certain Usem had his own gift with animals. They always seemed to respond to him, especially the sheep. Usem was the third oldest and, like Izem, was steady and a hard worker, but much more inclined to laugh and take time to play pranks on his siblings. Farah was quiet and sweet, her gaze following Usem lovingly. She was a very good cook and did her best to help Amara learn. She treated Amara like a younger sister, welcoming her with open arms.

"Badis and Layla took care to round up the goats and get them into the shelters," she continued, turning to survey what she could see of their land.

Layla was nearly as tall as Safia's brother, Badis. Layla was confident and beautiful. There was very little she couldn't do. She excelled in combat, just as she did in keeping house and making rugs. She was also kind and showed endless patience toward Amara. Badis and Layla were a wonderful match and were never far from one another, especially now that Layla was pregnant.

Her grandfather laughed unexpectedly. "That left your sister Lunja and Zdan to round up the chickens with their children."

Despite the gravity of the situation, Safia couldn't help smiling, too. Her two nephews and her niece loved the chickens. They spent quite a lot of their day chasing after them, naming them, collecting eggs, finding new nests—whatever they could do to interact with them. The chickens were given free range over the farm for the most part, being brought in only at night, when predators would attack and eat them. The children were very enthusiastic about their jobs.

Zdan, Lunja's husband, was a great bear of a man, the largest in their family. He certainly looked intimidating, or he would to an outsider. It was difficult to think of him as scary when his children clung to his arms and legs, winding around him and riding on his shoulders every chance they got. Lunja looked at him as if the sun rose with him every morning, and for her, it most likely did.

"I love my family so much, *Jeddi*," she whispered, more to herself than to her grandfather. "I'm so afraid I can't protect them. My brain refuses to really acknowledge what's happening because I worry I'm not up to the task. If something happens to any of you because I failed to train hard enough . . ." She trailed off.

Throughout the years, she had considered her training fun. It was extremely difficult and demanding, but she had fast reflexes that only sharpened as she got older. Every muscle and cell in her body sang when she ran or climbed or when she picked up weapons or fought hand-to-hand.

"You are ready, Safia," Amastan confirmed. "You must have faith in yourself and in your training. You were chosen. You have two older sisters, but the gift was not given to either of them. It was given to you. You were born with the talents you have, Safia. You must know, when you train with your brothers and father, when you did with your mother and grandmother or with Aura, no one is faster or more intuitive than you are."

She took a deep breath and let it out before she nodded. "I just never believed it would come to this."

"None of us wanted it to come to this, not in our lifetime, but it has, and we'll do whatever is necessary to defeat our enemies, just as our people have done for over two thousand years." He opened the door and waved her inside.

At once, Safia's stomach reacted to the delicious aroma filling the house. Amara had been busy in the kitchen, and her efforts filled the house with the inviting scent of one of the staples the family often relied on. Tajine was a delicious stew Safia particularly enjoyed after a long day working in the field. She was suddenly very, very hungry. She knew Amara had been trying hard to get the tajine just right.

Tajine was slow-cooked with lamb or poultry as a rule. Vegetables, nuts and sometimes even dried fruits could be included. Spices such as ginger, cinnamon and turmeric, along with a host of others, were used, depending on whether it was a vegetable, poultry or lamb tajine. Amara had trouble with the spices, sometimes dumping all kinds into the stew, or trying to make it first sweet and then savory, but she hadn't given up, determined to master the craft of cooking.

Amara had made loaves of bread to go with the tajine, and the one thing she was very good at was baking bread. Couscous was the dessert—her grandfather's favorite. Amara often struggled with couscous as well. Safia knew it was important to her that she get that right. Amastan never said anything when the dessert was doughy or overly sweet. Although Amara laughed at herself, it was obvious to Safia that she was disappointed if the meal wasn't good. Safia hoped this would be the one to turn things around for Amara.

Family members washed up and gathered to eat together. After prayers, there was much laughter as the hot stew was served up in bowls of clay their ancestors had made. This was one of Safia's favorite times of day. She knew it wasn't the same for all other families, but in hers, they were encouraged to talk to one another, to laugh and share their day.

She recognized Amastan's wisdom in encouraging family members to give input on the farm, the gardens, livestock and even the children. Her brothers had secured land around the original farmland handed down through generations, adding to the flourishing tribal business. The livestock was healthy, the soil was rich, and every member of the family meticulously worked to produce beautiful rugs, carpets, pottery, jewelry and clothing to sell. Many of their items were sent with her eldest sister, Illi, and her husband, Kab, across the Sahara to the markets in the Middle East. Kab's family was one of the few very familiar with the Sahara Desert and the places one could find water.

Kab's family were also artisans. Illi had been welcomed into their family, not just because she had caught Kab's eye but because she knew the old ways of making pottery, and her work was sought-after. Their grandmother had handed down the history and designs that went back centuries. Illi not only had the skills but could pass along those skills and her knowledge to new generations.

Safia realized just how difficult her grandfather's job as head of the tribe and head of the family really was. Choosing others to bring in when they had so many secrets had to be extremely challenging. She looked around the table and realized just how carefully Amastan had chosen those he had allowed into their inner circle.

The newcomers had to be loyal and willing to keep secrets. They had to train every day to fight as both modern and ancient warriors. Anyone coming into their family would have to fit their personality into a unit that was already tight-knit and learn to accept their very different ways. It wasn't an easy ask. Every one of the chosen brides had done so, as had Zdan, Lunja's husband.

It was unusual for the man to choose to come to his wife's family rather than for her to go to his. Zdan's family had become very small. His two sisters had married and left home. His parents were dead. One aunt remained, and he offered to bring her with him, but she had adamantly refused. He checked on her daily. She was very set in her ways. Safia knew Zdan's aunt would never have accepted Amastan as head of the family. He wasn't traditional enough.

Safia couldn't help noticing how anxious Amara looked as everyone began eating the tajine. Twice, Amara's gaze went to Izem's, and he shifted slightly toward her, giving her a reassuring smile. Deliberately, Safia took a spoonful of the stew, expecting it to be a little better than the last time Amara had made it, but this time it was far, far better. The blend of spices was nearly perfect.

Safia looked across the table at Amara, unable to keep the huge smile from her face. She didn't want to make a big deal about the fact that the tajine was so good, because that might embarrass Amara and point out all the times she had failed.

"Charif," Amastan said with a false frown. "Are you already finished with your first serving? Leave some for your elders."

Charif looked up at his father, puzzled, with a spoon halfway to his mouth. Zdan ruffled his hair and leaned down to whisper in an overly loud voice. "I have a much longer arm, Charif. I'll get you extra helpings."

Pretending to fight over the stew was the perfect way to convey to Amara that she had gotten it right and that everyone was devouring her efforts gratefully. Safia once again noted the exchange between Amara and Izem. This time there were tears in Amara's eyes, which she hastily blinked away, and pride on Izem's face. He smiled at her lovingly. The look her eldest brother gave his young wife was enough to make Safia wish, just for that moment, that she wasn't so alone, especially now, when she faced something evil and her family depended on her to lead the defense against it.

She felt her father's gaze on her, and she sent him a small smile, which she hoped was reassuring. When Safia's mother was alive, Gwafa Meziane had laugh lines around his startling blue eyes and a ready smile for his six children. He teased his wife continually, and she was his constant companion and adviser. He worked harder than any other on the farm. He was loving toward his children, but when it came to teaching them to wield weapons and defend themselves, he was every bit as fierce and demanding as Amastan, her grandmother and mother, and even her friend Aura.

Since the death of Safia's mother, Gwafa's laugh lines and smile had faded. Several of the "accidents" on the farm seemed to have been directed at him and Amastan, but the majority were definitely aimed at Safia. He'd grown even quieter, and he and Amastan had taken to staying up and talking for long hours into the night. She lay in her bed and stared up at the ceiling or paced back and forth in her room, wondering if she should reach out to her closest friend, Aura, while her father and grandfather were whispering in the other room.

She couldn't talk about her fears to her family, not when they would have to depend on and look to her for guidance. It didn't matter that she was the youngest of the six siblings. She had been born with the gift. Amastan had decreed it was so. Her grandmother and parents concurred. That meant she carried the burden whether she thought she could or not.

"We have many things to talk about before night falls," Amastan announced once the dishes were cleared. "Everyone needs to gather close."

Dread filled Safia as they adjourned to the wide-open room they preferred, where they could sit in front of the open fire on the carpets woven by their ancestors. There was a connection always felt from past to present. Safia found it comforting to be in the room with her family, sitting on the carpets surrounded by other keepsakes from those who had gone before her. She felt their presence stronger than ever, as if they were there to give her courage.

Amastan waited until everyone had settled comfortably and looked up at him expectantly. So many nights, this had been storytelling time. This had been a favorite time for everyone as they gathered together to hear stories that had been handed down for generations. Children sat on laps and listened with wide eyes. Safia remembered sitting on her mother's lap and snuggling close to her father's side when Amastan regaled them with tales of brave men and women defending their lands from invaders.

They were Imazighen, free people and very peaceful, but they would defend themselves fiercely when needed. They were proud of who they were and, with their last breath, would always declare to the world they were Imazighen.

"All of you studied the history of our country and are aware that many wars have taken place here. One of the most significant for our family started with the continual political wars as one faction after another invaded Algeria. In AD 17 to 24, the Romans invaded. They cut a road right across the migration route. Where there was once wild grass to feed livestock, there were fences to keep out the nomads' flocks from wheat the Romans needed for their supplies."

Safia knew a little of the history of that war, but there had been so many invaders.

"An entire way of life was disrupted. The Romans sought to take the tribal lands and divide them up for settlers," Amastan continued.

"The free people rebelled. The fighting became quite fierce, and those living here refused to bow down to outsiders. As Imazighen, we do not accept the dictates of any other."

Amastan paused for a moment and looked around the room at his family. "Had the tribes been fighting only humans, the battle would have been won very quickly, but that was not the case. It was not mere mortals our ancestors fought. The underworld chose that time to enter our world and turned neighbor against neighbor, sending an army of vampires and demons mixing with the invaders from Rome."

An icy shiver crept down Safia's spine. She glanced out the window. The sun was beginning to sink, and small fingers of fog began to drift in from the sea. The gray fingers looked like bones long dead and pointed straight at their farm.

"Our male ancestors have gifted us with their presence and wisdom. They share, through the elders, advice and knowledge. Through the female side, handed down for centuries, we have been given the wisdom and direction of the cards. The gift of reading is given to only one female in the family. She not only holds the power and responsibility of the cards, but should the demons rise to attack again, she must lead us to slay them. Without her, this will be impossible."

All eyes turned to Safia. She heard Amara gasp and then hastily cut off the sound. Glancing up, she could see that Amara had her hand over her mouth and was leaning into Izem.

Amastan's sharp gaze was on her as well. "Amara." His voice was gentle. "You have known of this almost from the day you married Izem."

She nodded. "That is true, *Jeddi*, but it wasn't real to me. Lately, I've felt the presence of evil, but even with that, I've done my best to ignore it. I often spoke to Izem, urging him to speak with you and *Emmi* about finding Safia a husband. It didn't seem right that we were happy and she had no one. She loves children, and she works harder than any of us. Because fighting something we can't see and the fact that the family would send her out to fight unknown evil entities didn't seem real to me, I just wanted someone very special for her. Now it feels like we're all abandoning her. Forgive me, *Jeddi*, but I don't understand."

Amastan's expression remained gentle. Safia loved him even more for the way he had always allowed every family member to ask questions and share opinions. That had been a difficult concept for Amara, and Safia knew it had to have been very hard for her to express her concerns, especially in front of the entire family and Safia.

"It's natural for you not to understand completely, Amara. You weren't raised from childhood with the knowledge those born into this family have. Perhaps it was already imprinted on us for our family to accept these ideas so easily. I have never asked the ancestors this, but it is a good question. I admire you for caring so deeply about Safia, but I assure you, she is spoken for."

It was Safia's sister, Lunja, who questioned their grandfather next. "*Jeddi*, I have heard you express this on more than one occasion, that she is promised, and you would never say this unless it is true, but we are now in a dire situation, and she will need all the help she can get. If that is so, where is he?"

"He will come, Lunja. You must have faith. He is a great warrior."

It was Izem, her oldest brother, who brought up what Safia worried about the most. "Is this wise, *Jeddi*? Bringing an unknown into a complicated battle and having Safia get used to a relationship that will need time to develop? She is used to coping on her own with just us. If this man decides to take over and has his own strategy, it may well throw her off-balance."

Ordinarily, Safia would have had several questions of her own, but it was nice to have family members addressing the concerns for her. Her heartbeat stayed steady, under control, a win for her. She'd trained hard to keep her heart and lungs functioning under every circumstance. The accident in the afternoon that had sent her plunging over the cliff had shaken her confidence in her abilities for a brief period of time. She'd lost that control, sending her brain into chaos. She had to be able to always think, no matter what was going on around her.

"You raise a legitimate concern, Izem. Gwafa and I have worried about the same thing many times. We prepared Safia as best we could. She knows many of the customs of his people, and she speaks his language."

The breath caught in Safia's lungs. A stunned silence filled the room. She pressed a hand to her throat in an effort to stay grounded. For a moment, she couldn't feel her own flesh.

"He doesn't speak our language? He has different customs?" Izem echoed. "Are you saying this man you have chosen for our sister is not a member of our tribe? He is not Imazighen?" He looked to his father and then back at his grandfather. "You would have Safia leave our family? Our tribe?" He was shaking his head even as he spoke, rejecting what his grandfather implied.

He wasn't the only one. Her brothers and sister were also indicating a strong disapproval of the choice selected for her. It was extremely rare for anyone to disagree to such an extent with Amastan, and never over an arranged marriage.

Safia had never considered that she would be sent away from her family, especially since she had been trained to protect them. She had the family cards. She had spent her entire childhood, her teens, her early adulthood, training to fight, to hone her skills. She'd been devoted to her family. She couldn't believe her grandfather would arrange a marriage to an outsider. It felt like a betrayal.

"Jeddi." It came out a choked whisper. She turned to her father, knowing she wasn't successful at hiding the shocked horror on her face. She did feel as if her father and grandfather had deceived her all these years. They had known they were going to send her away, and yet they had demanded the long, grueling hours of training from her. They had forced her to accept her fate as the defender of her family, and she had done so willingly.

This felt like sheer treachery. Disloyalty. It didn't just feel that way; it *was* betrayal. Her parents and grandparents had treated her as if she were special to them, and yet they would send her away with a perfect stranger, someone not even of their tribe, not of their people. Worse, they would do so after she risked her life to save them.

Even Illi's marriage was closely monitored to ensure she was treated with kindness, acceptance and love. Her husband was Imazighen. Once Safia was married to this stranger, her family would have no say in how he treated her. If he took her away from them, they would never know if he beat her or even murdered her.

Still, with all that, she had the years of love and kindness her father and grandfather had shown to her. Could they really have betrayed her in such a terrible way? Amastan stated plainly that she was to marry outside their people. She had to get away from everyone, go somewhere to think. She couldn't breathe properly. She had to leave. Pushing up with one hand, she managed to get to her feet. All the years of training made her look good, calm, steady. "I can't stay here right now. I must leave."

2

As Safia rose, Izem stood as well, suddenly looming larger than life. Amastan regarded them both without changing expression.

"You cannot leave, Safia. I must consult with the ancestors tonight and will need you to stay in the cave and guard my body."

Izem's breath hissed out in an angry stream, but he refrained from speaking. Safia lifted her chin at her grandfather. If this was a test to see if she would stand by her family, she had no intention of failing.

"I know my duties, Grandfather," she said. "I have every intention of protecting my family against any who attempt to harm them. I ask for one night to process the news you've given me. I had no idea you had arranged a marriage for me with a man who is not Imazighen, and I would no longer be able to be with my family once he claimed me. I just need a little time for myself."

"I did not choose this man for you. I did not arrange the marriage," Amastan said. "Nor did your father."

Safia caught at her brother's arm to steady herself. The crackle of the fire was overly loud in the room. Her brothers, her sister and their spouses all exchanged looks of astonishment.

Izem wrapped his arm around Safia's shoulders. "Who other than you would dare promise my sister to a man?"

It was a fair question. Amastan was the sole, unchallenged leader of their tribe. He was well respected by every other tribe in the area. He appeared fearless, as did her father, yet both seemed resigned to her fate. That made no sense. Safia found herself more afraid than she had ever been. It took tremendous control to keep her heart rate the same. To control the air moving in and out of her lungs. Who was this mysterious man? How was it possible for him to have so much power over her grandfather and father?

Amastan waved his two grandchildren toward the carpet, clearly wanting them both to sit down. "This promise goes all the way back to the time of the war two thousand years ago. Without the intervention of the men and women known as Carpathians, an ancient race, no one would have survived the slaughter. They took the brunt of the war, and many of them were lost. There are very few left, and those losses were a huge blow to their people as a whole."

Izem put a little pressure on Safia's shoulder and they sank to the carpet once again. She leaned into her brother just as his wife did. On the other side of her, her father placed a hand on her arm as if to comfort her. The knots in Safia's stomach tightened. She couldn't quite accept comfort from her father yet. She was willing to hear the explanation, but she felt she should have been warned years earlier, not now, when they were on the brink of war. Still, she didn't pull away or let on that she was upset with her father. She owed it to her grandfather and father to hear the explanation before she passed judgment. She could tell her brothers and sister felt the same. They were all very quiet, their attention fixed on Amastan.

"I can only tell you what has been handed down from mother to daughter and what has been confirmed when I questioned our ancestors. One of the warriors fought valiantly. He lost every one of his relatives in the battle. Apparently, and I don't know how this works, the daughter of one of our ancestors was meant for him. It was determined that these monsters would rise again, but no one knew when. From what I understand, everyone present knew they could not defeat the enemy should that army rise again if they did not have the help of this warrior. They needed him to commit to returning."

Safia and Izem exchanged a long look before she confronted her grandfather. She believed in evil. She even could stretch things and believe in vampires. But a two-thousand-year-old man coming back for a bride? "They withheld his woman and made him wait two thousand years? He's two thousand years old? I don't understand what you're saying. How can I be promised to him, *Jeddi*?"

"This race is nearly immortal. They can be killed, but it is extremely difficult, and they live for centuries. Their lives are not pleasant, especially when they do not have their partners. I don't know much more than that they are experienced warriors, and they hunt these demons and other evil all over the world."

"If the woman two thousand years ago was the one promised to him, why is he coming for Safia?" Badis asked. "How does he even know of her? Or that evil has risen here?"

"I don't have the answer to that. I know he is on the way because I feel him getting closer." Once again, his gaze met Gwafa's. "I will go tonight to consult with the ancestors. I wish Safia to consult with the cards. We must honor the word of our ancestors and give him the price of a bride should he defend our people against our enemy. Our people, our family, have always kept our word. At the same time, we must determine if this man is worthy of Safia."

"If we don't give him Safia," Layla qualified, "he might not fight with us, and the war will be lost. That's what you are saying?"

Amastan nodded. "I am only going by what little I have determined from the stories and bits and pieces given to me by the ancestors. I could have parts or all of it wrong. Unfortunately, I know evil is rising. It is close and it is attacking our family. In particular, evil is striking at Safia. I don't know if it is striking at her because she will lead us in battle or because she is important to this warrior. It is possible evil strikes at him through her."

"He doesn't know me," Safia pointed out. "I wasn't born two thousand years ago. He might have been, but I wasn't. This still doesn't make sense." It didn't, but she was very uneasy. She had been having horrific nightmares of a terrible battle—one she had feared was her future. Now she was afraid she might be looking at the past. More and more, the dreams keeping her awake were beginning to invade her mind at odd hours, seeming all too real to her, as if they were memories and not delusions created by her mind.

Amastan clearly agreed with her. "I go tonight to consult with the ancestors. It must be tonight, Safia. You know there isn't much time. I feel evil closing in on us. Also, I know this man is very close, coming toward us fast."

She had known her grandfather would deem it necessary to consult with their ancestors, but she'd hoped he would give her a reprieve. She had a bad feeling things wouldn't go well in the caves where he would spend the night. It would be her job to protect him from all harm. Now she was more worried than ever. She would call on her childhood friend, Aura, a young girl who had grown up with her, her closest friend and companion, more a sibling than a companion. Aura was as steady and loyal as Amastan himself, yet as elusive as the water in the sea. No one knew where she lived unless Safia's mother or grandmother had known, and they had never said. She had come to their home for as long as Safia could remember, raised nearly as a sibling, a constant companion, but she came only at night.

As they grew, Aura would help with her studies. She was particularly knowledgeable in languages, especially in the ancient one Safia's brothers and sisters were not required to learn. It was a fun, secret language Aura and Safia shared from childhood. Now it felt as if something comforting and fun had taken on a sinister connotation, as if everything familiar was somehow just shifting slightly, like sand, and slipping out from under her.

Aura had superior fighting skills and was faster than even Safia's mother and grandmother, although both had amazing reflexes, even better than her father and grandfather. As a child growing up, practicing those skills seemed fun, an art form, like dance, and then getting faster and stronger became a matter of pride.

The four women would often train through most of the night. In the morning, Aura would be gone, and Safia's family would allow them a couple hours of extra sleep time before they woke them to help on the farm. That was a period in her life Safia had loved. She'd bonded with the women in her family and loved Aura, counted on her. Now she didn't know what to think.

Was it possible that Aura was a member of this ancient race? Was that the reason she was never seen with her family? Safia had met Aura's mother once or twice. She always seemed distant and sad. She appeared ill to Safia, as if she were already gone from this world. That made Safia feel bad for Aura, but she didn't say so, because Aura never commented on her mother.

If Aura wasn't human, why hadn't Safia's mother just come out and told her? Clearly her father and grandfather didn't know. She wasn't going to stay in the dark. She'd ask her. They would have several hours with no one around, and hopefully Aura would answer her questions. She planned on asking a lot of them.

"Nothing about this makes sense." Usem agreed with Safia's assessment. Her brother, usually so good-natured, looked like thunder.

"When Illi was born, we thought the cards would go to her in the natural order of things." Gwafa took up the commentary. "She was the firstborn and female. Your grandmother and mother were prepared for her to be chosen to be trained as the defender of our people. One is born into that position. Chosen before birth. The cards are normally passed to the firstborn female. She has the sight. The moment we realized Illi wasn't chosen, our hearts were heavy. That was the first clue that this time might be one when evil would rise. It is why we pushed all of you to learn to defend yourselves from such an early age."

The sorrow in her father's voice made the situation even more real.

"How did you know?" Safia asked. "When Illi was first born, how could all of you tell right away that she wasn't the one chosen?"

Again, Gwafa and Amastan exchanged a long look. Amastan frowned. "It was obvious to your mother and grandmother. We are men, and this gift is handed down mother to daughter. Your mother knew immediately Illi wasn't the one. And she was born with blue eyes."

"It was . . . unsettling," Gwafa said. "The boys were born, three in a row, before we had Lunja. Again, the expectation was that the gift would be passed to her. Her birth was very tense, with all of us waiting. When your mother announced Lunja was not chosen, there was relief that she was safe, and yet it only reinforced our belief that evil was going to rise in our time, and we would have to be prepared to fight it. How could we have two female children and yet neither was chosen to read the cards?"

Amastan turned his loving gaze on Safia. "You were born two years later. The moment you came into the world, it was very apparent you were our little warrior. There was not a single doubt in your mother's mind or your grandmother's. Without even seeing the beautiful jade of your eyes, I knew. There was something different about you, a light that clung to you, and even as a newborn, when I spoke to you, you looked directly at me, as if you understood every word I said."

"We concentrated on training you," Gwafa added. "Morning, noon and night. Your mother, grandmother, little Aura—every single person we knew with skills helped train you. It wasn't until the first man approached your grandfather and offered for you that we remembered the old stories of the promises made to the warrior."

"I immediately went to the cave of our ancestors to consult,"

Amastan said. "I knew we couldn't make any mistakes. It was difficult to get the exact answers I sought. You were promised. I asked the ancestors, was he a good man? They answered that he was the warrior sent by the moon, unmatched in his abilities to fight these demons and vampires. He would come and bring others with him. If he did not, all hope was lost, and every man, woman and child would die." He cleared his throat. "They used the words in the song honoring the moon knight: *Ayur uzend aghzen addigh imagh.*"

Moon sends the monster to fight with us. There was a long silence. Safia let out her breath slowly. She could see that her grandfather had felt he'd been trapped. She understood. Their people had to be saved. This man—this monster—was necessary. He must be a superior warrior. But what kind of man was he? Maybe he wasn't even a man.

"But you didn't tell me what to expect," Safia pointed out, trying to rein in the hurt and sense of betrayal. Everything they said made sense. She could see that they hadn't known about the ancient man making a claim on her for very long. She needed time to process before meeting a man who would take her from her family and everything familiar to her. How could she possibly embrace him, knowing she might never see the ones she loved again?

"We felt it would be better to gather more information before we talked to you," Gwafa said. "We have no choice but to honor the word of our ancestors, but you are my beloved daughter, and I refuse to blindly hand you over to a man whose character I know nothing about."

Amastan nodded. "We set about attempting to find out more about this race of people and, in particular, this warrior you are promised to."

Safia studied first her grandfather's set features and then her father's. It came to her what they had planned to do, and she had to blink back tears at the enormity of their intended sacrifice. She'd questioned their loyalty to her, and all along they had planned to challenge this warrior for her, a man reputed to be so skilled in battle they could not win the war without him. Still, once she was properly handed over to him, they were willing to fight his claim if they determined he would not make a good husband to her.

She shook her head. "You can't. If he's as good as he's reputed to be, you would be throwing your life away."

"I don't believe in worrying about things we have no control over," Amastan reiterated, as he had so many times in the past. "It is best to gather as much information as possible and be prepared."

"They would not be alone in fighting for you, Safia," Izem reassured. "I would make it known that he would not walk away with you without challenge."

She shook her head. "You have a wife. If I'm promised to him and he fights with us and defeats our enemy, I will honor the word of our people." Even making the promise was terrifying, but the thought of such a fierce man fighting and killing her brothers or father or grandfather and taking her anyway was too much for her to bear.

"We will meet him before he is judged," Amastan declared. "Safia must read the cards tonight, and then we will go to the caves for more answers."

The cards her grandfather referred to had been handed down from mother to daughter for centuries. They were hand-drawn and hand-painted by an ancestor in vivid, vibrant colors that never seemed to fade. For Safia, the cards came to life and revealed answers when the right questions were asked. She always carried them with her, and they seemed to have a life of their own. One card in particular, the one she referred to as the goddess card, she carried against her skin next to her heart.

The cards had their own secrets. The deck could disappear and be flat under any clothing she wore, hiding the large stack. The goddess card was never shown to anyone else, not ever. It held tremendous power, and over time, Safia had noticed that the image looked very much like Aura, as if Safia's ancestor had known Aura's and had drawn her on the card. Once Safia's mother had given her the cards to read, they never again responded to her mother. They would only "speak" to Safia.

She wasn't certain she wanted to read the cards and see what was in store for her family. It wasn't just her family, but the entire tribe. Not even just the entire tribe. The people innocently living their lives in Dellys had no idea a terrible threat was approaching their small city.

Safia couldn't stall any longer, not with her family, who were all staring at her expectantly. They were just as uneasy as she was after the revelations Amastan and Gwafa had disclosed. She rubbed her temples, her head beginning to hurt. Once more, she stood, moving to sit in front of a small table that was carved from ancient wood and polished lovingly by every one of her female ancestors. Various rocks were embedded in the wood, each a different shape, all quite unique in composition.

She took the pouch from beneath her shirt and pulled the deck from it. At once she felt the cards tuning themselves to her. More than anything, she wanted to ask the cards about the mysterious man she was promised to. She was filled with such trepidation and even resentment. At the same time, her family was facing a terrible crisis. The evil creeping toward them was very real. She had to acknowledge it, whether she wanted to or not. Every weapon in their arsenal had to be utilized. The cards were one of the most powerful tools her people had.

Safia had been brought up almost from the time she was born with the idea that she would lead in a crisis. That she would sacrifice. Her time was now, and she knew, no matter the circumstances, she would rise to the occasion, even if that meant she would eventually leave her family. If this man saved her people, he would be owed everything.

She laid out the cards as she thought carefully about what she would ask. She had to know how real the danger was, not only to her family but to her people, and if there was a war, how important the stranger's participation in it was. That was a lot, but if all those questions were answered, she would try a second layout to see if the members of her immediate family would be safe.

Taking another deep, cleansing breath, she cleared her mind of everything but her questions for the cards as she shuffled, divided and then laid them out in a simple pattern, turning them over carefully. Her heart stuttered. Knots gathered in her stomach. She felt sick. Clammy. The cards always told the truth. There it was, laid out in front of her. She had to open her mind to accept the whispers of all the revelations the cards were willing to give to her.

Everyone dead. Everyone she loved. The city destroyed. The animals dead. Everything gone. The soil saturated with blood. A black acid destroying every wildflower, the trees, crops, their world. Vile creatures taking over and spreading mayhem and hatred, reaching to extend their foothold into other places. The danger was very real. It was right there in front of her. No getting around it.

She had believed in the cards all her life. Each time she'd read them, the predictions had come true. The path the cards had put the one asking on had always been correct. She couldn't very well ignore the warning.

Safia forced herself to continue the reading. There he was—the stranger and his traveling companions. He brought five men with him. Seeing the enormity of what they faced, she didn't think five men, her family and Aura were going to be nearly enough to turn the tide. Quickly, she pushed that thought from her mind. She had to be open to whatever the cards would tell her. This wasn't about her fears or ego, only about gathering information and being grateful for whatever the cards would show her.

She kept her mind and her heart open to the impressions and whispers of the cards. The stranger was dangerous beyond anything she had ever conceived. A fast, experienced fighter of demons and vampires, things she only had nightmares about. Creatures she'd trained to fight but had never seen. She had the impression of terrible battles, hideous wounds, more battles, but always he returned undaunted, unswerving.

She sat back in the chair and took another deep breath as the images in her mind faded. Very slowly, she looked up from the cards to meet her grandfather's eyes. He knew. She saw the knowledge on his face. Her gaze traveled to her father. That same awareness was there and then on the faces of her brothers. Comprehension slowly dawned on her sisters-in-law.

"We must train harder than ever," Amastan decreed. "Starting in the morning before light. Before the chores. Everyone, even the children."

"Perhaps it would be best to send the children and Layla to Illi and Kab," Izem ventured. "Layla is a great asset to us, but she is with child. Kab and Illi can protect them while we fight here in Dellys. If we succeed, they can come home. If not, at least a part of us still lives on."

Layla drew in her breath and shook her head, leaning close to Badis. She looked up at him. "I would rather be with you. I feel if we're together, we have a better chance. It's a strong feeling, Badis. Very strong."

Safia's heart ached for her. She couldn't imagine how her sister Lunja felt. At the moment, Zdan had the children on his lap, with Lunja cuddled close to him. Her sister's face was pale under her normally golden skin.

The family looked to Amastan as Safia gathered the cards and placed them in the pouch. She had to cleanse them before she packed to spend the night guarding her grandfather in the cave.

"I will think on this question and ask the advice of our ancestors." He turned his attention to Safia as she stood. "I take it the cards decreed that we need this man to win this war."

She nodded. "Without him, it is clear to me there is no hope. It appears he is extremely skilled. Even with him and those he brings, it will not be easy. We will need every fighter, and I fear there will be losses." She couldn't keep the sorrow from her voice.

Safia didn't look at her family as she left the room to go to her own little space where she kept her things. She donned a long coat that her grandmother had made for her. There were loops and pockets inside where she could shove the many weapons she would need. She'd practiced removing each of them hundreds of times so she could get to them without looking. The draw was natural after so much practice, and she knew exactly which weapon was where on her body.

She took her time cleansing the cards and thought about the friend she'd known all her life. She'd accepted Aura and her strange ways because her grandparents and parents had. It had been normal for Aura to arrive in the evening and to leave before dawn. She'd grown up with Safia and had been part of their family for the last twenty-three years.

Of course, Safia had asked about her parents, especially after meeting her mother. Aura had said that her father had died and her mother was ill. Was waiting. When Safia had asked what that meant, she simply said, "For the promise to be kept." Recalling those words made her pause. *The promise to be kept*. Was *she* the promise? More and more, it seemed as if Aura had answers to questions—unless, like Safia, she hadn't been told anything. Why keep them in the dark? Why hadn't her mother told her things she should know instead of allowing her to be afraid of the one man who would be coming to aid them?

Aura had told her she wouldn't be able to be reached until after sunset. The sun was sinking into the sea, and the wind was bringing the fog into the harbor. She began to feel a sense of urgency. If her grandfather was going to spend the night in the caves, she wanted to be far down in them and not outside, exposed to the elements.

Slinging the backpack onto her shoulders, she caught up her bow and the quiver of special arrows as well and hurried out into the family room. Amastan was waiting. She should have known he would be ready. He always seemed one step ahead.

Once on the outskirts of the hillside leading to the entrance to the cave system, Safia's grandfather led the way up the narrow stairway hewn out of the earth and formed with rocks. The rocks felt old and solid, sacred to her, beneath the soles of her boots. To the thousands of others who had walked over those rocks, she knew they were just old stones to be used as a staircase up the hillside, but she felt the difference each time she made the journey to the caves.

Amastan Meziane was close to six feet tall and on the slighter side, although strong and wiry. He walked with deliberate steps, neither fast nor slow, as was his way. Safia had been following him from the time she was a toddler, and she could shadow his every step, anticipate his every move. She did so now, checking to make certain he wouldn't fall on the steep stairs.

Bats flew overhead, seeking insects in the light, wheeling and dipping, snatching them with practiced ease. Safia connected with them, easing into them, making herself part of their circle, their family, so that they accepted her. They had grown used to her presence over time and thought nothing of her joining with them.

In northern Algeria, there were six principal species of bats. Although not all were close, Safia could call them to her when needed. From a very early age, Aura had insisted she practice until she had command of birds, bats, insects and reptiles. When she was able to successfully bind those to her and keep them under her command, Aura had her go on to larger farm animals and then wildlife. Aura had told her the point was to ensure that if an evil creature took command of any of the raptors, insects or whatever she'd practiced connecting with, they would be so familiar with her, she could easily take them back.

The process became second nature to her, and every morning when she went outside to do chores on the farm, she greeted the sheep and goats. Even the chickens. She would look for hawks and other birds in the sky and communicate with them. The practice became a ritual, and it kept her mind and abilities sharp. She particularly made certain she worked with insects until she wasn't afraid of them. When she'd been very little, stinging bugs had really frightened her. Aura had insisted she let them land on her and fly all around until she didn't even flinch when they flew at her face.

Now she sent a request to the bats, putting them on alert, letting them know that she would be down in the caves all night and that she would need them to be alert to anything that felt wrong. She wanted sentries when she was in the cave of their ancestors with her grandfather.

"You didn't tell us what the cards said," her grandfather pointed out, walking without missing a step.

"I didn't have to. You knew. You always know. Everyone knew. There was no need to scare the children any more than they already are."

"I want to know exactly what you saw and felt."

Amastan never raised his voice when he issued his commands, but she knew better than to disobey him.

"Without this man coming, everyone will die. Everyone. Not just us, *Jeddi*, but our entire tribe will be wiped out and everyone in the city of Dellys. The harbor, the fishermen. The world as we know it will be gone. Even our soil will no longer be the same. There will be blood and death everywhere. More than the horror of war. Torture and cruelty beyond measure. One can't imagine the depravity. The images were not to be seen, and I only glanced for a moment."

"What did you see of this man who is coming?"

"The stranger has battled these vile creatures for centuries, sometimes winning and sometimes losing, but always gathering more information. He appears very knowledgeable and battle savvy. He brings with him five men, fighters such as he is. There is no chance without him, and truthfully, after seeing what is coming at us, even with him and the others, I don't see how we are going to make it through this."

She gave him the strict truth. A strange calm had descended now that she knew the reality of the situation. She was no longer terrified. She accepted that they would be facing an enemy far beyond anything she'd imagined, yet she'd trained her entire life to defeat it. She'd trained hard, and she had to put her faith in those who had gone before her. They had done their best to prepare her.

"I know you think we should have told you about all this, Safia," Amastan said as he reached the entrance to the labyrinth of caverns. He paused and looked back at her. "You have to remember, we were not alive when these battles took place or these promises were made. They were simply stories to us, just as they were to you. They were told around campfires and handed down mother to daughter and father to son. We honor the traditions, and we follow the old ways, but we were not alive during those times."

He turned back to the entrance, the doors that allowed entry when guides were present to take others through so as not to disturb the beauty inside. He was Amastan Meziane, and he merely nodded to any guarding the sacred caves as they would him. No one would think to prevent his entry.

She didn't know if her grandfather was apologizing to her, but she hoped not. She was slightly ashamed that she'd doubted him. She had needed time to process that she'd been promised to a man outside her people. She loved being Imazighen and took great pride in her identity.

Safia followed her grandfather through the doors. Most tourists interested in seeing the caves used this entrance, eager to see the interior, with a guide explaining the formations inside. Her family followed the old tradition and beliefs of their people, choosing to worship as they had for thousands of years. The caves were very important to them.

They followed the well-marked pathway through the columns of stalagmites. The twisted spikes were beautiful formations of various colors and sizes, depending on the way the ceiling had dripped. Overhead, the ceiling had formed long, gorgeous stalactites. The colors were beautiful. Every time she entered the cave and viewed the creations nature had formed over thousands of years, she was awed.

Hidden behind one long rounded configuration that looked very much like a series of flowers on a vine was a slim crack that allowed the two of them to slide into another corridor. They were extremely careful to leave no tracks. The corridor was narrow and led steadily downward. There were no sconces or twinkling lights to add to the wonderland of what could pass for a fairy-tale world above them.

Safia had been on this narrow path many times in her young life with her grandfather. The stones beneath her soft-soled boots were familiar and felt sacred to her. When they came to the fork in the passageway, her grandfather led them to the right, the path that took them even deeper underground.

"I will find out as much as I can about this man you are promised to, *Yelli*." her grandfather said as he continued walking along the uneven stones.

"There is no need. We already know he is a man of honor willing to sacrifice for others. We have no idea if any of us will live through this war. If we do, we can deal with that later. What we need is as much information as possible on our enemy. The more we know, the better the chance we'll have of defeating them."

Her grandfather tossed her an approving smile over his shoulder. In the dim light from the headlamp she wore on her forehead, he looked eerie.

"I knew you would choose the right way, *Yelli*. You always do."

She couldn't help but warm at his praise. Her grandfather had a way of making all his family feel special to him. His gift. "You're going to be a target, *Jeddi*. You are too important to our people, and while we are attempting to gather information on the leader, I would bet he or she has been gathering information on us for some time."

Amastan nodded slowly. "I believe you are correct. You must outthink them, Safia. They think you're weak because you're human, but you're not. You've been trained by the best. Your ancestors insisted we prepare for this, and by doing so, each generation improved, not only in our ability to fight these creatures but in our reflexes and our thinking."

Safia had to agree with him. When her brother-in-law, Zdan, joined them, he already had a reputation as a good fighter. He played in the games at the fairs and nearly always won. There were few that could match his abilities with weapons or in hand-to-hand combat, yet when he tried his skills against any of the family members in private, even his wife, he was easily defeated. They were careful to keep their proficiencies within their tribe.

"We are more prepared than ever, and yet the cards said we have no chance without this man and those he brings with him," Safia said. She couldn't help the speculation in her voice. "I wish he had come sooner so we had time to learn from him. I doubt we will have the time now. I have this feeling, and when I have such a strong intuition, I am nearly always right."

She wished that weren't the case, but she wasn't even certain the stranger was going to make it in time before evil rose to claim them.

A sense of urgency had taken hold of him, and Petru Cioban had learned over the endless centuries never to ignore those warning signs of impending danger. Once again, he had awakened early, before the sun had set, leaving him locked in the earth, paralyzed and unable to rise when every single cell in him demanded he streak toward his destination before it was too late.

Already he knew there had been delaying tactics, useless battles, sacrificial pawns thrown in his way in an effort to prevent him from reaching Dellys—and his lifemate. *She* was the target. He was certain of it now. That certainty had been growing in him from the moment he set out toward Algeria.

He was Carpathian, a race near extinction, powerful and yet vulnerable, existing on the blood of others, sleeping beneath the ground during the day, considered powerless against their enemies at that time. He was one of the oldest in existence, never a good thing, having lost his ability to see in color or feel emotion after his fiftieth year, when he was still considered a child. As time passed and he relentlessly hunted vampires, century after century, even the whispers of temptation to kill while feeding faded until there was nothing at all.

He had grown more dangerous than the vampires he hunted. He'd held on to honor—the code he had scarred into his skin—for her, his lifemate. She held his soul, such as it was, and she was alive in this century. He had searched for over two thousand years for her, and now that she was close, enemies had risen in an effort to keep him from reaching her.

Petru knew his lifemate was alive because, twice now, two women he trusted had read from ancient tarot cards. *Alive and well in the century with him. Danger surrounding him. Betrayal. A terrible sacrifice.* That had been the first reading by Adalasia, Sandu's lifemate. Danger nearly always surrounded him. He only cared that his lifemate was alive and in the same century with him.

The second reading had been given by Vasilisa, Siv's lifemate, and that reading had been more in-depth. There was transition, moving from one situation to another, hopefully a better one. Not surprisingly, she had predicted action and again danger. She had also predicted that the love connection with his lifemate would be successful. He wouldn't allow anything less. He'd waited centuries for her. He'd locked himself away from the population to keep them safe.

It had been the last part of the reading that had been the most valuable to him. She had asked him if he had scars from a particular battle. She told him those scars were a map. "That battle, those scars, show you the way."

His heart, a dead stone in his chest, had reacted to her revelations. Carpathians rarely scarred, only if the wounds they acquired had been mortal—ones that should have killed them. He had a road map of scars on his body, evidence that he had come very close to succumbing to deadly wounds. The strange thing was, the battle was such a distant memory, he couldn't recall it. There had been so many over the centuries, so many times he'd gone to ground for indefinite lengths of time to heal. One didn't measure time. Hunting the undead was his way of life.

The scars on his back were deliberate—he and his fellow ancients living in the monastery had tattooed their oath to their lifemate in the only way they could, scarring their backs deliberately so their creed would stay permanently. The process had to be repeated over and over until the scars stayed. He had never considered that the scars on his chest were anything but a distant memory of his battle with the vampires he had hunted down through the centuries. The moment Vasilisa had told him they were a map to his lifemate, a door had creaked open in his mind. Each time he touched those scars, the memories of the past came closer. None of them were good.

Once he recognized that the scars on his chest were actually a map, he knew exactly where his lifemate resided. Algeria. To be more precise—Dellys. It was a small but important harbor. He had been there in the past. Long ago. The memories seemed shrouded in a dark gray veil that was slowly lifting as he neared his destination.

He was beginning to puzzle out the pieces, and, darkness take him, it wasn't pretty, if he was on the right track. Betrayal and sacrifice weren't necessarily about the present. Adalasia had warned him. She'd stated it very plainly. He didn't like where his thoughts were taking him, but unfortunately, Petru was a man who viewed problems from every angle. It was what had kept him alive for centuries.

Benedek. He reached for one of his traveling companions. Benedek Kovak was also an ancient Carpathian. Lethal. Extremely dangerous, a fierce fighter with midnight black eyes and long flowing salt-and-pepper hair. He'd lived in the monastery for well over two hundred years before once again setting forth to look for his lifemate. He had agreed to join Petru, along with four others, on the journey to Algeria. Now that his memories were returning, Petru was more than grateful for the five Carpathians accompanying him.

Are you going to continue to make it a habit to rise before the sun has set?

Benedek was not a man with a sense of humor. Ancients had no emotions, but he had traveled so often with Petru and knew him better than any other. There might have been a hint of Adalasia's humor in that one brief comeback. They had traveled long distances with her and spent time sharing her mind and emotions. That had given them a brief respite at times from the bleak world they existed in. The emotions weren't really theirs, they were Adalasia's, but it was something besides the gray world they had known for far too long.

I woke knowing an attack is imminent.

Seriously, Petru? Clearly Benedek thought that was a poor reason to miss out on an hour of sleep. *The undead are always planning our demise.*

I do not believe we are the targets. These persistent attacks on us are only to slow us down. We are not the true targets. Petru was certain he was correct. He'd had a lot of time to think over what had been occurring every step of their journey toward Dellys.

It was difficult to move his arm. His body was in a state of paralysis, and his limbs were heavy and felt as if they were made of lead. Still, he managed to bring his hand to his chest and lay his palm over the scars there. How could he never have noticed the map scarred into his skin just as the code of honor had been scarred into his back?

Benedek was silent for a long moment. *Who do you believe is the true target?*

My lifemate. I believe they delay us so they can kill her before we get there.

How would they know you travel to find her?

It was a good question. Petru had asked that question quite a few times when he was attempting to put the pieces of the puzzle together. His palm rested over the scars on his chest. Those scars were partially made from mortal wounds sustained in battle, yet they were too precise to have been unintentional. Someone had helped to build the scarring up where needed to form the map.

The door in his mind creaked open a little wider. Bats. Hundreds of them flew toward him, an army of them. They were small, with tiny, very sharp teeth. Voices rose in his head, speaking in his ancient language. Human voices speaking in their native language. Everyone calling out at once. The master vampire high on his kills. The army of demons pausing in the bloodbath to capture the moment when he abandoned his family and the humans to their fate. The child. The little girl in the master vampire's arms, looking up at him with her startling green eyes. Waiting. Certain he would do what was right—what every Carpathian was sworn to do.

The memory seeped out from under that partially open door in his mind and crept beneath that twisted gray veil before he could shut it down. There was a reason he hadn't remembered his past—a reason it had been locked away. A reason those scars on his body hadn't meant anything to him.

Betrayal. He whispered the truth to Benedek. *How can there be forgiveness?*

Benedek was again silent, but Petru had his complete attention. Petru didn't continue, didn't look further into those memories. The sun would sink soon, and they would be streaking toward Dellys and his lifemate. If he was going to get to her in time to save her life, he would have to use every means possible to get around the vampires seeking to delay him.

Petru? What is wrong? I have been scanning around us, and I do not feel danger near.

That was Nicu Dalca, another constant companion now, grim-faced, gray-eyed, with long black hair tied back in leather cords. He had a scar that ran from his left temple to his eye. His muscles were sleek and powerful. Lightning-fast in a fight, he had an affinity with animals. He would spend long periods of time off in the wilds with them. They would spy for him and always guarded him if he was close.

Petru? Benedek prompted.

What was the use of holding back? His traveling companions were risking their lives to help him. They deserved to know everything. He had a code of honor. He held himself and those around him to a high standard. He refused to shrink from telling them the truth of what he found disturbing in the memories returning to him.

As you are aware, Vasilisa read the tarot cards for me before we set out on this journey. She said the scars on my chest were a map to my lifemate.

Once she said that to me, each time I passed my palm over the scars, I began to have disturbing memories. Bits and pieces of past battles. Far in the past. Creatures such as those we fought with Adalasia and Vasilisa, only far more aggressive. Humans fought valiantly, but those creatures tore through them.

Benedek broke into the explanation. *Perhaps it would be wise to include the triplets in the conversation if you believe this will change our course of action.*

I believe someone knows my lifemate exists in Dellys and wants to destroy her before I can get to her. I have been remembering a terrible battle that changed the course of my life. Someone else survived that battle and is rising once again. They are aware of my return and seek to prevent me from interfering with their plans.

Nicu stirred in their minds. *I am catching glimpses of this dark battle in your mind, Petru. I agree that you should share the information with Mataias, Tomas and Lojos. You are the best of us at outthinking any enemy. If you talk out the details of what we will face and what you expect now, before you claim your lifemate and emotions interfere, we will have a solid plan to defeat him.*

There was wisdom in Nicu's advice. Nicu was a man who spent a great deal of time alone, away even from the other ancients he traveled with, and he rarely spoke, but when he did, Petru always found he made sense. He put out the call to wake the triplets. They were never far from one another. They had not spent time in the monastery with him, but he knew them.

They were scary predators, disappearing into the mist, not as molecules but as fully formed Carpathians. The three of them moved in complete synchronization, as if they were one person, in utter silence, cunningly intelligent and eerily frightening in their abilities to fight the undead.

They shared the same body type: tall, with broad shoulders, long chestnut-colored hair at odds with their brilliant aquamarine-colored eyes. Each had their own scarring from the battles they'd fought over the centuries. Tomas had strange tear-shaped scarring on the right side of his face from his hairline to his jaw. Lojos had a web of scarring running from his left shoulder, down his arm, all the way to his hand. Mataias had no visible scars on his face or arms, but Petru had seen his back and chest where vampires had done their best to carve through his chest to extract his heart. It said quite a lot about him that he had survived.

Petru shared with the three the concerns he'd conveyed to Nicu and Benedek. *The more I am able to trace the scars on my chest, the more the door in my mind opens and allows me to remember more details of the battle in the past. I was in Dellys centuries ago. I was not alone. My family was with me. My father and mother. Two brothers. There were three other families with us.*

It was odd that he could remember those details and even see their faces now, yet not feel emotion. Not feel the love he knew Adalasia would tell him she felt was in his heart for his family.

At first, when we set out on this journey, voices haunted me while we traveled, rising at unexpected times as that door in my mind creaked slowly open, again and again. I tried to sort through the memories to determine how real they were. In the beginning, the various battles were so dim and vague, I could barely make out any details. Eventually the specifics began to emerge.

Petru felt the memories weren't his alone, and that was partially what made him uneasy.

There appeared to be a war going on between human factions, something not entirely unusual. In the middle of that, at night, vampires appeared, a coven of them, as if a great nest were concealed underground in the labyrinth of caves. They fell on their human prey, gleefully ripping them from limb to limb. As they did, grotesque creatures I was unfamiliar with clawed their way through the ground to devour the humans even while they lived. No one was spared—man, woman, child or even animal.

Benedek interrupted. *It would be good to share as many impressions as possible so we can get an idea how these battles are fought.*

Nicu agreed. *If we face the same kinds of enemy, the knowledge of their technique will give us aid in defeating them.*

We will face them, Petru said. *I could not return to this place, nor would my lifemate be born again, until I was needed.*

The moment he uttered the word *again*, there was a foul taste in his mouth. His lifemate had been alive during those horrific battles. That memory was there as well.

Again? Tomas echoed. *She died and you survived her passing without turning?*

The truth is far worse than you can imagine, Petru said. He couldn't conceive of it. Were the memories even true? Could they be? If so, he would be the only Carpathian in all of history who had ever done such a foul deed.

He pressed his palm tighter over the scar that represented the Dellys harbor, needing to know if those details emerging were real or not. Had someone planted them? Instinctively, he knew the Carpathians in the battles were his family. He might not feel the loss of them now, but he knew they were his. He had known the others who had fought so valiantly to save humans and Carpathians alike, to stop the rise of evil, and had fallen.

Afanasiv's lifemate, Vasilisa, read her tarot cards for me. These are cards that were handed down mother to daughter for hundreds of years. The blood of a Carpathian woman gave them power and longevity, and provided the ability to see into the seeker's heart and character. He could ask a question and the cards might answer. In my case, I wanted to know if my lifemate was alive in this century. The answer was yes.

Petru paused, this time sliding his palm over his heart. It was beating, but very slowly, as if his body knew he had no business being awake yet.

While giving me this reading, she said there was betrayal and sacrifice. I thought the cards warned me of a betrayal once I reached our destination. I was prepared for such an eventuality as disloyalty and deception. We have dealt with such treachery on many occasions. As these memories have re-turned to me and I see the war raging between the human factions and then the vampires and demons joining in, I realize the betrayal and sacrifice happened in the past. I was the one who committed the ultimate betrayal. I betrayed my own lifemate.

Even as he told his traveling companions, his heart felt as if it were being ripped from his body. The pain was real, all-encompassing. The moment it happened, there was a stirring in his mind, as if someone shared his pain, if only for a brief second. That someone felt feminine.

Who was that? Benedek demanded, confirming that all of them had felt that piercing pain along with that other person sharing his mind for that fleeting moment.

Petru didn't feel pain. He didn't feel emotion. Who had managed to slip into his mind for just that brief instance? Had he connected with his lifemate? Was it her pain? He'd felt it before. Then she'd been a child. A little girl with intelligence shining in her bright green eyes. She had looked at him and then at her parents and grandparents, knowing . . . all too knowing when he hadn't even known.

Betrayal. Sacrifice. Just as Vasilisa told me in her reading, but it was in the past. I was the one to betray my lifemate.

His lifemate had died once before. The memory surfaced fully. The choice had been his. Not only his but her mother's. Her grandmother's. Her family. His family. They had made that terrible choice with him.

There was an impossible choice put before me, and I had to decide in a split second. We had battled the worst of the demons and hellhounds for several risings, losing far too many humans and Carpathians. There were so many—armies of demons coming from beneath us. It took me far too long to figure out how to stop them. I had no experience with such things. No one had. We knew we could not allow them to win. We had to drive the demons back and seal them underground, and we had to wipe out the vampires, even if it took every last one of us to do it.

You had to have been a young warrior, Petru, Mataias protested. *Why was it left to you to figure out how to stop them? Surely there were other, much more experienced hunters present.*

Even then, given time, I could envision the entire layout of a battle and how best to defeat the enemy. Knowing my lifemate was in the center of danger and I could not get her out had been distracting.

Petru could feel the puzzlement in the others.

It was Lojos who voiced the question they all had. *You had not claimed this child. How is it you were not wholly centered on the battle? You should have been able to ignore the child.*

I should not have been able to feel anything, Petru agreed. *I had lost my abilities centuries earlier, but I could feel her emotions. Her fear. Her sorrow when her sisters and brothers were killed in front of her. When she lost aunts and uncles. Each loss she felt, I felt. She was barely five, yet she had such knowledge and awareness.*

All of us saw Val with Liv. Tomas mentioned another ancient they all were very familiar with. *They are lifemates and she is still a child. He stays close to her, protective, yet he cannot claim her. He is affected by her and knows when she is in danger.*

That is true, Nicu agreed. *And what of Skyler and Dimitri? They are legendary. Lifemates for years, and yet he could not claim her. Still, she saved him even from across an ocean once, when his wounds were severe. She held him to the earth. She was far too young, but she still felt his pain even from such a distance.*

The takeaway seems to be, Benedek said, *if the couple both have superior strength—and we know you do, and maybe your lifemate does, as well—it is very possible they can connect even at that young age, perhaps unknowingly.*

Petru considered the possibility. The child had looked at him with those too-intelligent eyes. He hadn't had time to get near her, not while learning to destroy the various demons preying on the humans in the fierce fighting. The worst was, they didn't just come out at night. Many of the demons were able to influence the humans at war with one another so that the crimes they committed against each other were even more vicious than they might normally be.

Whoever was orchestrating the war, sending the demons and driving the vampires to do their will, realized that one tribe of the Amazigh people and the Carpathians were slowly turning the tide and were possibly a real threat to their plans. They concentrated on wiping out both.

The silence that followed meant his traveling companions considered what that might mean. Nicu and Benedek had already been in two major battles with the demons and, like Petru, had grown skilled in fighting them. Each type of demon had to be destroyed differently. Some were far more difficult to kill than others, just as vampires were. Experience counted. It was a common practice for the ancients to share information on their enemies and how best to defeat them. Without emotions, they had no egos, and it didn't matter who was the most skilled hunter; it only mattered to rid the world of evil.

Did you get a sense of who was orchestrating the war? Benedek asked.

At first, I believed the oldest master vampire was behind the attacks, but I realized over time that whoever had sent the demons from below was the true commander. I began to get a feel for how they communicated with their army and who their generals were. When they began to concentrate their forces on Carpathians and the Amazigh people, I countered.

Tomas understood immediately. *You used the common path of communication all Carpathians use while orchestrating a defense. Vampires were Carpathian before they chose to give up their souls, so they heard and understood you were the one directing the others.*

Yes. They sent as many at me as possible. My family stood in front of me, although I did not want them to. I didn't mind that they all came at me. I welcomed the battles. It was my duty to destroy the undead. I felt the same about the demons. They were just as evil.

Petru paused once again, allowing the memories into his mind and then finding a way to convey them to his companions. The slow, insidious assault of emotions that had crept into his mind and heart had been a shock. He wasn't supposed to feel *any* emotion. He saw no color, but still emotions crept in despite the fact that he hadn't claimed his lifemate. She was a mere child. He'd barely gotten close to her and only on one occasion, enough to know she existed. She had been whisked away when the demons had erupted all around them and vampires had attacked as well.

I became very aware of my lifemate's emotions. She was a little girl and couldn't control her feelings. Everywhere she looked was death and horrific scenes of torture. Her relatives were dead or dying. The people defending them were pulling hearts out of chests and calling down lightning. For her, there was no telling the difference between us and the monsters we were fighting. To her, that was what Carpathians appeared to be—monsters. Demons were eviscerating beloved cousins. She was young, but she understood that if we didn't win this war, it would happen elsewhere—maybe everywhere.

Petru knew that the ancients couldn't possibly understand how it would feel to have a lifemate in need and not be able to get to them, because he hadn't—not until that moment. He attempted to share the overwhelming need with them.

Amid the most important battle for the continuation of humanity, every cell in my body, every instinct I had, urged me to go to my lifemate. In that brief moment, there was no logic, no thought other than to get to her. I did the unthinkable and turned toward her before I realized what was happening to me, and experience took over. I knew what I was feeling was illogical. I couldn't comfort her. I couldn't go to her. I could do nothing but fight for her.

While the emotion was difficult to deal with, he was an experienced ancient and could compartmentalize.

There is no betrayal in that, Petru, Mataias assured him. *You were fighting for humans and Carpathians alike. We are sworn to destroy every evil that walks the earth. It is a matter of honor. Every lifemate should understand that, even at five.*

She was not Carpathian, Petru reminded him. *I wish there had been no betrayal in what I had done, but in that moment of distraction, I gave her existence away. It was a brief second, no more, but it was enough; the damage was irreversible.*

Again, there was a moment of silence as his companions attempted to comprehend the magnitude of the damage of what he was saying. He shared the fierce battles that followed. The Carpathians had known that they had to succeed in defeating the enemy that very night if they were to prevail. By now, Petru was aware of how his opponent's mind worked. He anticipated where the demons would strike next and had his army ready and waiting to counter every move.

There were so many to fight on every front: the invading humans, the vampires, and hordes of demons, even hellhounds. We lost so many valuable warriors. The battles took a toll on our fighters. We couldn't afford the losses, but even with that, we were gaining ground.

Once the demon leader became aware the tide was turning against them, she went into a fury. There were other children, both human and Carpathian, and the vampires and demons suddenly targeted them, rushing those guarding them, sending the hellhounds at them, burning them alive.

Sickening, but typical of a vampire tantrum, Tomas pointed out.

I retaliated, driving a wall between the remaining families and the army trying to get to the children. All the while, I was concentrating on locating the leader. It was difficult when there were so many humans around and their grief and terror were amplified by my lifemate. It was a fight to keep her emotions at bay while I concentrated on staying ahead of each strike to position my army.

It was strange that her terror had suddenly broken through again when I'd had it under such control, but I pushed it aside. I was so close to tracking the leader of the demon army, and my concentration couldn't be broken. I was still directing attacks, all the while fighting battles of my own with vampires and demons.

Benedek had fought many battles through the centuries with Petru against master vampires and their pawns. He knew Petru could multitask easily, so it wouldn't occur to him that there might be a problem even with a young child pouring her emotions into his mind. But he had known Petru for so long that the break-off signaled something bad was coming.

You need to tell us, Petru. Whatever occurred was two thousand years ago. This cannot matter now.

It does matter. I have inadvertently dragged you into an old war. One of hatred. And I did betray my lifemate. I did not remember these things, or I would have told you before we set out. If you wish to turn back, I will not hold it against you. I was not to come back and my lifemate was not to be reborn until evil was rising again. I will be facing my greatest enemy. This time my lifemate will be fully grown, and she will have knowledge that I betrayed her.

Petru felt Benedek sigh in his mind. *Really, my brother? You would deprive me of a fierce battle with both demons and vampires? You know I have fought at your side for centuries. I will do so again.*

Nicu, who had stayed mostly silent, as was his way, agreed. *I go with you.*

The triplets murmured their agreement.

Finish your explanation before the sun sinks and we must rush to beat your enemies to your lifemate, Benedek counseled.

His brethren. He could count on them the way he could the cycles of the moon.

I found that the outpouring of loathing and vile glee at those being attacked, tortured and killed was a direct pathway leading back to the one giving the orders. It was feminine and cruel. Sadistic. Gloating. I could read her in the same way all of us read the undead when they are before us. She longed for power over all things. She had long been plotting for this opening gambit in her takeover of the world aboveground.

She had her eyes on me. She realized I was the one standing in her way, and she had found my greatest weakness—my lifemate. That little girl. I didn't even know her name, but I had exposed her to my enemy in that one unguarded moment when I felt her emotions and I responded.

When the hellhounds rushed the children, and the demons and vampires attacked the families, burning most alive, Nicu guessed, *your lifemate was taken.*

That is so, Petru told them. *She was brought to the master vampire. His name was Eduardo, and he was repulsive. He enjoyed such cruelties as I have not seen in many centuries. Between the female leader beneath the earth and the master vampire, the human race and Carpathians were in trouble. We had few defenders left. We had to end the war before it was too late.*

But then Eduardo gave her family and me an ultimatum. We must put down our arms and walk away with her. We had to leave everyone else to their fate, but she would live and so would we, or she would have her heart ripped out right then, on the spot.

I had a split second to weigh the consequences. I knew Eduardo had spoken to the leader below and assured her no Carpathian would allow his lifemate to die. In our history, I had never heard of a single instance.

My parents and two brothers still lived. Her parents, grandparents and some of her tribe still survived. There were two surviving Carpathian families and a small female child from one of them. They would all die, as would everyone else. We knew that. I saw her mother and grandmother look at me as Eduardo held her high. There was sorrow on their faces. The battlefield had gone quiet. My father and mother looked at me with compassion. Even my lifemate was looking at me. She made no sound, just stared at me with her green eyes as if she could see into my soul. Her mother nodded her head very slowly, one hand going to her heart. I knew what she felt I had to do. All of that happened in a split second.

Through the battles, I had been following the trail of venom and hatred back to the exact location of the leader beneath the ground. I made the decision to kill the leader and then the master vampire, even knowing the child would die. She would be reborn, but if I didn't shut this war down that night, it would not matter. The world would not ever be the same.

My family had a private path we could communicate on, and we did so. We gathered energy, as much as possible, and as my father opened the earth over her head, I slammed a lightning bolt straight down on top of her.

She screamed hideously, and black blood erupted from the ground. The demons shrieked and moaned and went into a frenzy of killing, but they were without direction. Eduardo clearly couldn't believe his eyes and just held the child in the air for a second, giving me time to take flight. He was halfway across the valley, surrounded by his lesser vampires and several demons.

Petru felt as if he were there in that valley all over again, staring into his lifemate's terrified eyes. She was so little, but she refused to scream, refused to give the hideous vampire the satisfaction of hearing her cry out.

He shook her. "Look at him." The sound grated, booming across the valley as Eduardo's army of lesser vampires attacked, coming at Petru from all directions. Demons leapt on him, ripping at his legs and arms with teeth, clawing at his belly to eviscerate him.

"Look at your mother and father. Your grandparents. Your own lifemate rejected you when no Carpathian has ever done such a thing. They betrayed you. No one wanted you enough to save you. You are nothing to them. You are unworthy. Always remember that. Remember that in the end, they will always sacrifice you, because you are truly nothing to them." The vampire drove his teeth into the child's neck and deliberately drank from her.

Still the child made no sound, her eyes on Petru as he fought, slashing with his shocking speed and calling down lightning when he extracted hearts with blurring swiftness. Petru didn't tell the others that part of the battle—he couldn't. He allowed himself to feel her emotions. It was the only thing he could do for her. He stayed with her as he fought to get close. He stayed with her as Eduardo took her blood. Fighting vampire and demon alike, slick with his own blood and covered in wounds, he drew close, knowing it was too late.

Eduardo waited until he was nearly staring right into those baby jade eyes before he dug his talons cruelly into the child's chest and slowly, as painfully as possible, extracted her heart.

4

Aura Zeroual was one of the most striking women Safia knew. She was tall and slender, with dark flowing hair and very intelligent vivid blue eyes. She always arrived in the cave of the ancestors silently, so that even the bats, Safia's sentries, didn't seem to notice her entrance. Safia knew she herself moved with grace, but Aura took it to an entirely different level. She seemed to flow across the ground, no matter how uneven it was. Safia did her best to emulate her, practicing for hundreds of hours in the hope that she could achieve Aura's level of expertise.

"The time has finally come," Aura said softly. "The moment you were born, I knew you were the one."

Safia regarded her best friend, the woman she loved as a sister, and tried not to allow hurt to show on her face. "Yet you said nothing to me."

"There was no point, Safia," Aura responded. "No one trained harder than you. You're nearly as fast as I am, and that should be impossible. I didn't want anything to get in your way, especially your head. Worrying about reality would have done that."

"What we're facing is terrifying. For the first time, I caught glimpses of the past. I seem to be having more and more memories of them, almost as if I were there myself."

Aura's blue eyes regarded her steadily, coolly. "You were."

Safia's heart accelerated for a moment before she could slow it down and keep it under control. The nightmares that had crept into her bedroom despite all the preventions she'd taken to keep them at bay might be all too real. She'd been getting little bits and pieces of demons and vampires ripping at a child's body while a man fought desperately to come to her aid. She would force herself to wake up because the nightmares were terrifying and left her nearly paralyzed with fear.

Sometimes her chest had hurt. Not just hurt but was horribly painful. She would rub her fingers over the strange birthmark she'd been born with. It was a whitish-blue star shape right over her heart.

"I need to explain to you about my people in order for you to understand," Aura said. "We live very long lives and have extraordinary gifts. It isn't as if we can't be killed—we can—but it is difficult. When a male child is born, his soul is split in half. All the light goes into a female soul, and he has all the darkness. There is only one woman for him, the woman protecting the light of his soul. He must search for her, and when he finds her, the ritual words, imprinted on him before his birth, are spoken, binding the two together, weaving their souls back together so they're complete."

Safia struggled to understand what Aura was telling her. "Like a marriage ceremony?"

Aura shook her head slowly. "It is more than that. Once the binding is done, it cannot be broken. The two cannot be apart."

"What if one of them isn't happy?" Safia couldn't imagine being happy away from her family.

"Let me keep explaining our people to you, Safia. I know being promised to this man must be frightening, especially since he's not only a complete stranger but an entirely different species. Let me tell you about us—and about him."

Safia knew that was only fair. She shouldn't be so resistant. This man deserved courtesy, and so did Aura after all the time she'd spent training Safia to fight. The truth was, she wanted to know about these people.

"We call ourselves Carpathians because we settled in the Carpathian Mountains," Aura continued at her nod. "The men have extremely difficult lives. After some fifty years, which is our childhood, we are beginning to go into adulthood. At two hundred for the men, the ability to see colors begins to fade, along with emotions. For some, it can happen much earlier. Some a little later. Because of the length of time we live, it is very difficult to live without feeling anything at all for anyone or to see anything but gray year after year."

Safia tried to picture what Aura was telling her and had to admit it sounded pretty bleak.

"Vampires are Carpathians who choose to give up their souls, refusing to wait to find their lifemate. They kill to feel the rush when feeding. They prefer adrenaline-laced blood because it makes them high. Fear makes them high. The hunters are continually tempted with whispers to feel, just for a moment, that rush after centuries of nothing."

Safia stepped back, her mind nearly refusing to comprehend what Aura had just revealed. She'd used the terms "feeding" and "adrenaline-laced blood."

"Aura, you're clearly Carpathian. Does that mean you take human blood to survive?"

"Yes." Aura didn't hesitate.

"This man I'm promised to—does he?"

"Yes. It is what we live on. We don't kill as the vampires do. We are respectful, and those who provide for us generally aren't aware they are donating. It was different in your family for many reasons."

Honesty rang in Aura's voice, but Safia needed a little time to process the things she was telling her. Vampires and demons were one thing. She could believe they existed, because not only had she been raised on the stories about them, but she'd been taught how to destroy them. But to think about Aura drinking someone's blood turned her stomach. Or did it? It should. She thought about it. Why didn't it?

"Are you able to control how I think or feel?"

Aura shook her head. "I can influence most people, but it is impossible with you. No one can. You were born with a shield too strong to penetrate. I believe it is protection for you against demons and vampires. Two thousand years of genetics has a way of preparing you for what you need to be. That's why you learn so fast and have astonishing reflexes. The things you can do, no other human can do, Safia."

Safia considered what Aura told her. Who else could control insects, reptiles and raptors? Or use the bats as sentries? To her, it was normal, but it really wasn't. She had accepted that ability because she'd grown up first trying to connect with creatures as a game and then later developing a stronger and stronger link with them.

"If this man must drink blood in order to survive, will he expect to drink my blood?"

"Lifemates exchange blood on a regular basis, Safia. It is part of their ritual, but let's move away from that for now and get back on track. You need to know how this all came about. We don't know how your family, specifically you, could possibly become intertwined with our species the way it did. This was two thousand years ago. How is it possible that you are his lifemate? That's the question. That was always the question. You're human and he is Carpathian. It didn't seem possible, and yet you're the proof."

"Could there be a mistake?" Safia couldn't repress the hopeful note in her voice. She didn't want to insult Aura. It wasn't that she didn't have respect for other cultures. She did. She'd been raised to appreciate other nations and their beliefs, even though they weren't her own. It was just that she wanted to stay with her family. She was Imazighen. In her heart, she always would be.

"This man, the one you are promised to, his name is Petru Rares Cioban. He was not the oldest or most experienced fighter, but very quickly it was apparent he was the one who could assess the battlefield and lead. We were losing until he took charge. Not just losing; everyone was dying. The losses were not to be sustained. Once he took charge, it was like a wave of hope. I was a child, but I still felt it. He was our *only* hope."

Safia had impressions of bodies on the ground. It felt as if doors creaked open in her mind. Ugly whispers. A harsh, scraping voice that dug into her memory and pulled out visions of horror. Or maybe Aura shared them with her. However it happened, she was suddenly on the battlefield from so long ago, watching with a child's terrified heart as friends and family died right in front of her.

She became aware of one man the fighting seemed to be centered around. Every demon and every hideous vampire fought to get to him. That didn't deter him from directing the others as he ripped through those attempting to destroy him. She realized some of the other fighters were doing their best to protect him, but he continually broke out of the circle because he was trying to get closer to the families, which meant closer to her.

He had silvery white hair pulled back to hang thick and long almost to his waist, corded tightly with leather. His eyes were a slashing silver as he cut through demons and vampires alike. He was covered in blood, some of it black, some of it red, but flashes of lightning lit up the sky continually all around him. He exuded power and sheer confidence. He was mesmerizing—terrifying in the way he faced his enemies so fearlessly. Head-on. Directly. Without flinching. They tore him open, ripped and bit at him, attempted to eviscerate him and tear his heart from his chest, but nothing deterred him. He mowed his enemies down as if they were paper dolls.

Around her, coming at the families with children, were vicious hellhounds, animals with two heads and foul breath, their red eyes fixed on the screaming babies. Automatically, she reached out to try to soothe the creatures. Their brains were chaotic, filled with rage, determined to kill everything in their path. She felt the presence of another, someone cruel driving the beasts onward toward the families, demanding death.

Fires broke out. Hideous monsters with sharp teeth fell on the

women and children, tearing at them as flames engulfed the sanctu-
ary. Talons grasped at her, digging into her shoulders, dragging her
against a rotting body. She looked up into a gaping mouth with jagged,
dark-stained teeth. Rotting flesh sloughed from his face as maggots
crawled from beneath his skin, and his hair came off his scalp in bloody
patches.

"Let me introduce myself, my dear. I am Eduardo."

She couldn't help the little shiver that went through her body, but
she didn't reply. She didn't look at the bodies trapped in the fire, although she wanted to know if Aura had gotten away. Everyone had
tried to run, but the hellhounds and those terrible creatures were round-
ing them up and throwing them back into the flames to burn them
alive. She expected the disgusting creature raking at her shoulders and
arms to hurl her into the flames as well, but he didn't.

His breath was so foul she thought she might pass out. He caught
up a baby and handed her the infant. "Throw the baby into the fire.
Tell him you want to see him burn."

The words beat at her mind like a bird might chip away at the trunk
of a tree with its beak—an obnoxious, repetitive sound. She glared at
the hideous creature, shook her head and tried to hide the crying infant behind her.

At once, fury filled the bloodshot eyes, and he yanked the little
boy from her, ripping at him with his claws and then tossing him into
the flames. "How dare you disobey me."

He dug his nails into her and shook her before taking to the air,
heading to a high point across the valley, where he could see the fighting below.

The child remained silent, partially out of fear and partially because there was no getting away from or reasoning with Eduardo. She
decided to wait to see how everything played out. She knew, like everyone on the battlefield, he was watching the fighter.

"Aura, how did you get away from the fire?"

"Most of the families were Imazighen. I am Carpathian. I simply changed my composition and took to the air. I was so little, the vampires and demons didn't pay attention to me. They were mostly interested in acquiring you. All along, that was their goal."

"Why? The child had been about four or five. What good would it do to take her and keep her alive?"

"As I said, there is only one lifemate. That child—you—held the other half of Petru's soul. They all seemed to know it. If she'd been a grown woman and he'd claimed her, if she died, he would have suicided or gone into a thrall, which would have made him very dangerous. He could have turned vampire. As she was a child, he couldn't claim her, but all Carpathian males protect their lifemates. They can't do anything else. It's instinctive. Their mind and soul demand it. Vampires know this."

"So by taking the child, they essentially held Petru prisoner."

"They trapped him, yes. Not only him but her family as well. Her grandfather was head of the tribe. As you know, Imazighen are a peaceful people, but they are fierce fighters when defending themselves and the ones they love. Her parents were alive. Her grandmother and grandfather. There were still Carpathian children alive, but without Petru, no one was going to live through the next few hours, and all of us knew it. The leader directing the war knew it, too."

Safia placed her palm over the bluish-white star over her heart. "I remember," she whispered. "I had nightmares."

"It wasn't a nightmare," Aura said. "As evil began to rise, your memories began to return, just as his did. Two thousand years ago, you had an ancestor by the name of Kahina. She was a seer, a true one. When she spoke, her family listened. She was a brilliant woman. You come from a long line of extremely intelligent people."

Safia found herself abruptly sitting on the mat she'd placed on the floor in the outer chamber out of respect for her grandfather. She would never disturb him while he was consulting with the ancestors unless it was an emergency. She would have to trust her instincts. If there was trouble, the bats would warn her—or her internal system would raise an alarm. Now was the time to rely on her training.

The candlelight flickered and glowed, throwing eerie silhouettes on the walls of the cave. Sometimes the shapes looked like people bent over or crouched low, other times they appeared to be inky 3D shadows climbing out of the pitted dirt. The continual sound of water trickling, cutting a path through dirt and rock, could be heard.

Safia pressed her hand tightly to her heart. "There was such triumph in the vampire. It radiated from him. He kept whispering that he had no choice, that the fighter would have to save me, and in doing so, he would condemn everyone else to death. My parents, grandparents, his parents, everyone. His voice was terrible, and he kept repeating the same thing over and over—that he had no choice."

"The last thing anyone expected was for Petru to attack the leader beneath the ground. He did so with pinpoint precision and turned the tide of the battle," Aura reiterated. "But no Carpathian male can trade the life of his lifemate for others, no matter how right the decision is."

For the first time, Safia made herself look at Aura. "You said he wouldn't turn vampire because he had not claimed his lifemate."

"That did not mean there wouldn't be severe consequences. In the history of our people, no male had ever done such a thing. There was no precedent set. We all knew it would be bad, though. He hadn't expected to live through the coming battles. Watching him hurtle himself into one fight after the next, I don't think anyone expected him to live."

Aura paused, and Safia could see she was lost in the memories of that long-ago war. Aura's large dark eyes met hers. There was always something fierce about Aura, but right then, she looked vulnerable, almost childlike in the dim lighting of the chamber. Safia couldn't imagine what it would have been like for her all these years.

"Do you have a lifemate?"

"Somewhere. He still lives. He has not found me, but I have duties, responsibilities that tie me to this place. I cannot go out into the world and leave a trail for him to follow."

Was there sorrow in Aura's voice? Safia's heart felt heavy, as it often did when she was in the presence of others and felt their emotions.

"As I said, there were severe consequences for Petru's decision to sacrifice his lifemate in order to save the rest of us. Her parents and grandparents, his family, my family, every single member of our tribe—we all knew if he did as the master vampire said and took the child and left with a guaranteed safe passage, all of us were dead. They were so smug and superior, Eduardo and the one beneath the ground running everything. They were so certain he would do as all Carpathian males are programmed to do. He would just take the child and go, leaving us to be slaughtered. It had to be a horrific split-second decision for him."

Once again, Safia pressed her palm tightly against the scars over her heart. She had shared that moment with him. She remembered now. The door had cracked open, and the memories seeped inside her whether she wanted them to or not. She felt his sorrow. His regret. The knowledge that those in the valley had no chance without him—that he was their only chance. She felt his apologies to her. She gave him her permission. As young as she was, she knew it was the only decision.

He didn't hesitate. That wasn't his way. He struck at the leader of the war with everything he had, focusing his enormous power on the destruction of the unknown entity and leaving the child to her fate.

Safia's heart pounded in trepidation. She didn't ever want to go through that again, not in her nightmares, not in her memories. Aura was speaking again, and she concentrated on listening, blocking out the emotions crowding in that gripped her, holding her prisoner of those childhood memories.

"He tried to get to you, but it was too late, and the vampire brutally murdered you right before his eyes. He went berserk. Nothing could stop him. They sent everything they had at him, but no matter how torn up he was, he went after that vampire, going through everything in his path to get to him. The battle raged through most of the night, and just before dawn, we knew we were the victors."

Again, Aura paused, and Safia could feel her deep sorrow. She couldn't help reaching out to her, putting her hand gently on her wrist. They exchanged a long look, and for the first time, Safia felt as if she could truly see the real Aura, the one who had been hidden all the years they'd grown up together.

"They brought him from the battlefield with the most horrific wounds I'd ever conceived. The few remaining Carpathians tried to save him. They put soil in his wounds and sang the healing chants while those that knew their healing ways worked on him. That was when Kahina stepped in to help. No one thought a human would be of assistance. We were a different species, but the dawn was on us, and we had to go to ground. We could not save Petru. He was too far gone, and after the grave sin he had committed, he did not want to be saved."

"If he had died, what would have happened to me?"

"You would have been born and could have married in your world. You wouldn't have been as happy, would have felt as if something were lacking, but you wouldn't have known why. At least that is what I'm guessing would have happened. It is possible you wouldn't marry, but in your culture, your grandfather arranges marriages, so most likely, you would have been given to someone."

Safia had often wanted to have a partner when she observed her brothers and sisters with their spouses, yet when she tried to envision herself with someone, a part of her always rebelled. Now she realized it could have been because she was already attached to the man she was promised to.

"Kahina saved him," Aura continued. "She was a very wise woman, and she had the ability to see into the future. She knew that evil would rise again. She didn't know when, but she knew it would return. She said that Petru's sacrifice was shared by all of us and therefore so were the consequences. Petru would be long in the ground healing before he could rise. She had time to think of ways to make her plan work."

Safia thought about the woman of long ago who brought two species together to form an alliance in the hope of defeating evil in the future. Everything depended on one man—Petru, the man she was promised to. They knew he was a man of honor.

"Kahina had no way of knowing that two thousand years would pass before evil would rise. She had been told he couldn't survive, that he would succumb to the temptation of the vampire after what he'd done if he carried those dark memories, so she devised a way to remove them until the time when he would need them to return. Even so, for a Carpathian male to live two thousand years and remain with honor is a feat beyond all expectations. It is rarely done. Only a very few have managed to do so."

"You know I can't possibly live up to this man." Safia whispered her confession. "He's a legend. If he's coming for me thinking I'm something special, he's totally wrong. I don't want to leave my family. My first reaction when I found out about him was that my grandfather and father had betrayed me. I'm not a heroine, Aura."

"He will not think he's a hero. If anything, he believes he has betrayed you and has much to make up for."

There was some relief in hearing Aura say that, although Safia knew it wasn't the truth. Petru wasn't the one who had done anything wrong. He had saved countless lives that night. But if he felt he owed her, he would give her time to adjust to their relationship, time she would need if she was going to leave her family.

"Tell me the things Kahina did to ensure Petru would return." Safia needed a distraction, anything to get her mind from thinking about Petru coming. She should be more concerned with evil rising than her partner coming to claim her, but she couldn't help seeing that terrible warrior fighting his way toward her across the valley, his eyes a slashing silver, as turbulent as the lightning as it forked across the night sky.

"Carpathians don't scar unless the wounds are mortal, and he had several mortal wounds on him. She manipulated the scars into a map to the Dellys harbor, to guide him to this exact location. Then she implanted a suggestion to be triggered by a phrase to open the door to his memories. She was so brilliant and wise. She drew and colored the cards your family handed down from mother to daughter. I donated my blood so the cards could live and be aware."

Aura again paused for a moment and then shrugged. "I told you about the gate I guard with the beast behind it. When it was first set up, there were four gates and four of us guarding them. The other three guardians were in other countries. The ones they were befriending, like you, were human or another species. At that time, I asked the grandfather if he would consult with the ancients, specifically Kahina, to see if we could use the cards to aid us in guarding the gates and staying in touch. I had this strong impression it was the right thing to do, but they were her cards. Her idea."

The tarot cards were such a part of her. "Others have the same cards?"

"Not the same. Kahina agreed that others could use the idea, but they had to design them, and they could not be traced back to her. Nothing could give Petru the idea that he was part of their makeup. The first person to actually design the next cards could take the credit, and that would help with Petru's journey of natural discovery."

"The others holding the cards are demon fighters?"

"Yes," Aura nodded. "Like you. They keep the demons from slipping through. And they help the one guarding the gate. I never fully explained the beast and the gate to you because I knew evil was going to rise here and we would have to make a stand. Your training took precedence over everything else."

"And you think I'm ready."

"I know you're ready. I believe Lilith is the one attacking us, and she waited all these years, believing your family would give in to the modern ways. She thinks you would have grown lazy over time and forgotten the war. My guess is she is attacking Petru with everything she has in order to slow him down or stop him from getting here. She will try to kill you before he can make it. With the two of you out of her way, she believes she will have an easy victory."

"The cards say she is not wrong."

"She *is* wrong. She's wrong in that your family has taken these centuries to prepare yourselves. Generation after generation, you've improved your fighting techniques."

"But we still can't succeed without Petru."

"She won't believe you can succeed even with him. She won't believe for one moment the skills you or your people have when it comes to fighting her demons or the vampires. You are no child, Safia. That is what you are in her mind. That five-year-old. But you're a warrior, one very skilled. You have command of the creatures she thinks she controls. You can take them away from her, and you can do it with ease."

That was true. She was very skilled, and she did connect with all kinds of reptiles and raptors, Aura had seen to that. She'd drilled it into her that she had to practice every day.

"You trained my grandmother and then my mother."

Aura nodded. "As well as all who came before them. The interesting thing was each generation became more skilled than the one before them. It was as if your mother would pass what she learned on to you before you were born so that you had the reflexes and skills. I had the feeling that as time progressed, the true fighter was emerging." She smiled at Safia. "And then you were born."

"You paid a very steep price, having to be a child over and over again," Safia pointed out.

"I had the privilege of living with your family at night and getting to know the way of your people. They are so lovely and honorable. They accepted me despite my differences. My parents had the most difficult time, not me. My father suffered an injury that should have killed him. He stayed in this world for as long as possible because my mother couldn't leave me alone when I was portraying to the human world that I was a child. She'd made that promise when Petru won the war for us. Carpathian couples do not leave one another. When one goes, the other follows to the next life. Eventually, my father had no choice. He said to her those were their consequences, and he would wait for her in the land of shadows."

Again, Safia heard the sorrow in Aura's voice. She really didn't fully understand what her friend was trying to tell her, but she knew Petru's choice to save so many people rather than her had caused a huge ripple effect on so many others. She might never really comprehend why, because she didn't really know or understand the Carpathian culture, but she had great empathy for Aura, and her parents' separation weighed heavily on her.

"I begged my mother to follow my father, but she said she wouldn't leave me alone until she was certain it was safe for me to be in the world without her. She was so . . . diminished. It hurt to see her that way. At the same time, I was in awe of her and loved her even more for her tremendous sacrifice for me."

Safia knew that Aura had lost her mother recently. What did all that mean? Had her mother not really been ill but instead pining away for her spouse? What had Aura said about lifemates? Once the binding words were spoken, they could not be far from one another.

"I would have liked to have gotten to know your mother better. I only was able to meet her that one time. She was lovely and very welcoming."

Safia had been fifteen. She and Aura, who appeared fifteen as well, had been night-training on the narrow footpaths on the cliffs with swords and then with bows and arrows. When they were coming back down the steep path to the main trail, they met a small group of men. Immediately, they knew they were in trouble. Most of the time, they would have been safe, but women didn't travel unescorted at night. Both girls were wearing trousers and would be considered inappropriately dressed. At that time of night, their appearance without an escort was scandalous.

Without a sound, Mirabelle was there, emerging out of the shadows, dressed in a long robe with her hair covered by a hood, her cape flowing gracefully from her shoulders and down her back. On either side of her paced Amastan and Gwafa. Both men paused to greet the younger men while the women continued down the path to the main road.

"Amastan and Gwafa weren't with us that night," Aura informed her. "She created an illusion."

"That was why we were asked not to speak of that night to anyone," Safia said. "Because she didn't want me to find out Amastan and Gwafa hadn't been there."

"Exactly."

Safia should have been upset, but she found herself laughing. "Did your mother always come along when we went out for night-training on the cliffs?"

Aura nodded. "Your mother and grandmother were in charge most of the time, but the cliff training was so dangerous, my mother would go in case of an accident. She could have stopped you from going over the cliff into the sea."

"Aura, I'm really sorry that growing up, I had no real idea how difficult it was for you. You're a sister to me, closer even, and I knew there were times you were hurting, but I couldn't find a way to reach you and make things better. You've always been there for me. Always. I want to be that way for you."

"You always have been. I could feel the way you would reach out to me when I was particularly distressed over the gate. Or over my parents."

"I wish you could have talked to me."

"I can now," Aura said. "I really wanted your input about the gate. It was built of ancient wood and set up with the strongest interwoven safeguards. The wood is resistant to any kind of destruction, including fire, yet lately, I've felt weakness in it, almost like a thinning in places. It doesn't make sense."

"Have the other guardians mentioned the same phenomenon?"

Aura nodded. "When I brought it up to them, they did. They didn't put it the same way, but there was something different taking place. Also, more and more, the smaller demons seem to be finding ways to escape to the surface around the gate."

Safia frowned. "Wouldn't I be the one to stop them from doing that?"

Aura's smile widened so that a dimple revealed itself. "Yes, I believe that is so, now that you mention it. As soon as your grandfather is finished talking it up with his ancestors, I will be more than happy to show you the gate and where these little demons have been escaping. Hopefully, you can figure out a way to plug the dam and keep the intruders on their side."

"That is my level of expertise," Safia assured. "At last, all that training isn't just to show off my excellent fighting stances."

"You do have an aesthetically pleasing form, especially when you're holding your sword, if I do say so myself," Aura confirmed.

Safia burst out laughing again. "I reflect well on my teacher, is what you're saying."

The candles flickered and then burned hot and bright for a moment, making the shadows on the cave walls come alive with an ominous foreshadowing. Within a minute, bats filled the cave, flying in tight formation like the long tail of a comet. The lead bat flew straight toward Safia, only at the last possible second pulling skyward before it collided with her head. All the other bats followed suit.

The communication was quick, the sentries reporting the rise of evil beings in the chambers below—two of them heading straight to the women. Along with two of the undead was a covey of demons, five total, horrid little creatures, according to the bats, the kind that tore at entrails and ate people alive.

"They are coming," Safia announced. "Are you certain the safeguards surrounding my grandfather will hold up against the vampires?"

"Absolutely, they will," Aura confirmed. "Their mentor never touched one strand of these weaves and wouldn't recognize any of the safeguards. They would never be able to unravel them. He can walk out freely, but they cannot enter."

"I guess we're about to see just how skilled I really am," Safia said. She hoped she was as prepared as everyone thought she was.

5

nsects burst through the chamber walls, clawing their way to the surface from deep within the bowels of the earth. They were small, the size of dung beetles, but had a bright orange stripe across the dull brown of their backs. Safia had never seen them before, which meant she had no prior connection with them. That mattered little.

She had been required to study every species of insect before she worked with them. Aura had insisted she start when she was very young, around two or three, playing a game. Who was faster? Who could get the insect to turn away from them? Come to them? Fly away? Land on them? They would shout out commands, each taking a turn trying to get the new bug to cooperate. She'd enjoyed the game, and she became adept very swiftly.

The key was finding the way they communicated with each other. Usually, communication was through scent. Pheromones. That had been difficult to understand as a child, trying to figure out how to manufacture the right scent and send it to the insect. Aura had laughed at her a few times when she got it *very* wrong. It had been a good thing they were outside when they were doing their first trials. Like any child with a new toy, she'd practiced in secret on her brothers, producing awful new scents to drive them out of their rooms until her mother caught her and she got in trouble. It had been *so* worth it.

The whispers came next. Grating voices that preyed on nerve endings. Strangely, she remembered the voice. It triggered that long-ago memory of a child's terror. Her chest ached beneath the white scar.

You think he will come for you, but he deems you worthless. He betrayed you once. He will again.

The voice could have scraped her raw, played on weaknesses. The memories could easily have conjured up exactly what they were meant to: hurt and feelings of worthlessness. A child's terrible insecurities. But Safia had a brilliant ancestor—a seer by the name of Kahina. She had made certain Petru's lifemate would be prepared this time, that the sacrifice he'd made wouldn't have been in vain. She didn't react at all to the voice or what he said. She was no child, and she knew exactly what Petru had done. She totally condoned his choice. She would not be trapped in the past by a trauma, hiding from the truth, afraid to face reality.

She didn't bother to respond to the voice she knew to be a vampire. It wasn't Eduardo. He was long gone from the world. Petru had destroyed him. Aura had shown her how he followed the trail of the master vampire relentlessly, no matter how many lesser vampires attacked him.

Petru never faltered. His injuries didn't matter; he continued until he cornered the one who had murdered his lifemate, and he fought him without mercy. His body was torn beyond comprehension, but it didn't slow him down. He didn't seem to notice. He simply continued as if he were a machine, not a man. It was only after he called lightning from the sky and incinerated Eduardo's heart that he staggered and went down. Aura had witnessed him killing the master vampire and the great hunter's fall.

Safia didn't falter. She didn't look to see if Aura took up her position just as steadily—she knew she did. She counted on her just as she did the sea. Candles flickered and spat; shapes on the wall changed to greedy claws reaching for the two women. Safia merely spread the scent of the beetles over Aura and herself, covering their bodies in the pheromones so they would be part of that large group of beetles invading.

She let herself be consumed by the feel of the beetles as they swarmed into the room. What drove them? Hunger? For what? Flesh? The flesh of humans? No, Carpathian flesh and the flesh of Amazigh people. *Her* people. They had been fed on the living flesh of both species and craved it. Her stomach turned.

She probed further, ignoring the screech of anger as vampires scraped and clawed at the door, trying to get past the safeguards woven by Aura. The safeguards kept them out of the chamber the women were in. It sat just above Safia's ancestors' chambers. Safia tuned out all noise, everything distracting, becoming one of the beetles, moving like one, thinking like one, feeling like one.

Safia sought to find the one programming the beetles. She needed to have a very delicate touch. There was no doubt in her mind that the leader of the army would be monitoring this first foray into battle to see what kind of results she would get. Already she knew the general was feminine. She recognized the same cruelty and need to feel others' pain in the torment she caused the beetles in programming them. There was no doubt it was the same woman who had led the war two thousand years prior.

Once again, she studied the beetles to ensure that they were nutritious and not at all poisonous to the bats. It hadn't occurred to their mistress that anyone would take control of the creatures surrounding her army, and she hadn't made provisions to protect from natural things like predators.

Safia slipped away from the beetles and reached for the bats. They hung along the ceiling and down the walls, staying out of the light of the candles. The flames had burned low now, so only the very floor of the cavern could be seen. The stirring on the ceiling sounded like a low fluttering of wings. As if disturbed by the continual scratching and demands at the entrance to the cave, the bats suddenly took to the air, wheeling and dipping, darting at the beetles, all the while calling to the others outside the chamber to come and join the feast. It would be impossible once the safeguards were in place, but Safia knew Aura was about to allow the demons to slip through next. With them, some of the bats might glide through quickly enough before the guardian of the gate would once again close the barrier.

Are you ready for this? Aura asked. *We don't have much time. It won't be much longer before the vampires decide to target your home.*

Vampires could take to the air. So could Aura. That was one thing Safia couldn't do. There was no flying for her. She could run like a gazelle—fast, faster even for a short amount of time. They would rely on the preparations her family had made. All of them had weapons to fight and destroy the vampires. The weapons had been perfected over the years. Using the various instruments was like second nature to them after practicing with them so many times that they didn't miss.

You've reached out to them to let them know to be ready. That we are under attack. The children are safeguarded—if they stay where they are supposed to.

That was always the worry. This was their first big test. They had stressed over and over to the children that they had to obey orders, that it was life or death. That didn't always mean a child understood the grave consequences. Seven-year-old Charif, Lunja and Zdan's son, was his father's shadow. He was the one Safia was most concerned about. Maybe she should have been tougher with him, stricter with his training.

She shook off her worries. It was too late now. As the underground leader was testing them, they were testing their defenses. She had to concentrate.

Yes, I've let Baba know that the vampires will retaliate soon by coming at them. Aura sounded matter of fact. *He will direct everyone there. They are prepared. I will allow the demons access when you are ready. Five seconds only, or the vampires will slip through as well.*

Safia loved that Aura called her father the affectionate *Baba*. She loved him the way Safia did. It also meant that Aura felt like part of their family circle. Safia wanted that for her, especially now, when danger surrounded them.

Now then.

Safia stayed in control of her heart rate. She drew a short sword from the inside of her hooded coat. The blade was crafted from the crystals of vanadinite. When one looked at it, the weapon looked harmless, like a child's toy. The blade appeared beautiful but looked as if it could shatter easily. Made of vanadinite, there seemed every possibility, but it was as hard as any diamond. The weapon had been crafted by her ancestors close to two thousand years ago with the aid of the Carpathian people. The sword reacted only to the one meant to wield it.

From another loop she drew a vial containing water that had been taken from the sacred waterfall. Each weapon she carried on her was placed exactly where she could get to it easily. She'd gone over what she would need, including emergency supplies, in case she was wounded and needed to stop the bleeding fast.

Ready. She was as ready as she would ever be. They could do this in a controlled environment, or they couldn't do it at all. It wouldn't take long before their adversary realized they had hijacked her initial strike at them, turning the tables on her and hopefully learning as much about her and her tactics as she did about them.

With the bats flying around the cave, it seemed natural to ease up on the safeguards just for a moment in the walls and underneath them to allow a few more in to clear out the flesh-eating beetles. The general beneath the ground had been waiting for just such a mistake and sent her demons in quickly. They were very small, tiny enough to ease through the slots the bats could fit into.

Claws appeared first, little hands with sharp hooked nails. Heads popped up—red glowing eyes, a wide slashing mouth with jagged, serrated teeth. Instantly, their gazes riveted on Safia as if they were robots and saw only her. Not even one of them glanced toward Aura. They dragged themselves through the narrow openings, coming at her from all sides of the walls and from beneath the ground. At the five-second mark, the openings closed abruptly, slicing anything still emerging in half. Black blood sizzled and bubbled up in a few of the holes. Noxious smoke rose into the air.

The creatures screamed and shrieked, the sounds filling the chamber of the cave as half their bodies were cut off. Still, they continued to drag themselves to the surface of the cave until what was left of them flopped onto the dirt. The other creatures rushed to them, falling on them, raking at their bodies with their long, hooked claws, tearing deep gouges in the strange, mottled fur. It wasn't fur exactly, Safia decided as she studied the demons. Hair grew in patches over reptilian scales. Armor that wasn't armor. Not fur. Not armor. These demons had been manufactured, just as the beetles had been.

She had a book of demons and could identify all of them. The drawings had been painstakingly made over centuries, along with as much information on each type as could be collected. There was a hierarchy of demons. Some were much more powerful than others and extremely difficult to kill. These little creatures were disturbing, and she'd seen the evidence on the farm of what they were capable of. Now she was seeing what the demons would do to their own if they were injured.

She reached out in the way she had to the beetles, touching the frantic chaos of their minds. It wasn't as if they were thinking creatures. A red haze seemed to be where their brains should have been. Slashes of deep weeping wounds that bled acid into the craniums caused even more pain. Their skulls were too small to hold the leaking fluid, so they shook their heads back and forth in a useless effort to relieve the agony. The slashing smile wasn't because they were grinning on purpose; their mouths were cut wide open to show their teeth and allow them to drag larger prey inside.

She pushed down the bile rising along with compassion. The woman below was twisted and evil. Excruciating pain, fear and the need to consume flesh drove these demons, just as they had the poor beetles. The bats couldn't eat these horrid demons. They were hers to dispose of. She couldn't imagine them let loose on the city.

She lifted the sword in the air an inch higher and began to chant. The moment she did, the blade blazed into a bright yellow-orange, casting an eerie flame-like shadow ringing the wall. At once, the demons began to crawl toward her as fast as they could, abandoning the dead or dying demons on the chamber floor.

Safia spun in a circle so that the blade burst into a brilliant light bathing the chamber in scarlet. The blade pulsed with life, causing the glow of red to illuminate the cave in that strange eerie glow. She had trained her entire life for this one purpose—to defeat demons. She was the defender, keeping demons from coming through a vent, a tear in the earth, any means of entry at all. That was her job. She had to destroy them or send them back.

She was aware of the position of each of the dreadful creatures in the cave. Where they were, how close to her, how close to Aura. They thought themselves good at utilizing the scant vegetation growing in the cave. The rocks and stubby shrubs. They skittered fast across the dirt and rolled behind the thin brush to conceal themselves from her. They had no idea of her connection to the earth. How she felt the heartbeat like her own. How it gave her information and told her exactly where her enemies were at any given moment.

As the creatures circled the two women, coming up on them like a pack of hungry wolves, she spun again, her crystal sword pointed toward the ceiling, the light spreading outward, glowing brighter and brighter as she chanted in a low, very sweet voice. Concealed in the other hand was the small vial of water. As she spun, droplets sprayed outward and mingled in the red light. The drops caught in the tempest—a mini tornado she created with her spinning sword. She was the calm in the center, barely moving while all around her the deluge was pouring down. A force of nature hurtled itself on the demons that were desperate to rip her apart.

"Hear me, demons from the underworld, sent by your queen and the commander of her army. You cannot have my lifemate. You cannot have any member of my family or my people." She didn't raise her voice or change her tone. She continued to speak in as angelic a tone as she was capable. It had been one of the things her mother had worked with her most on.

Safia plunged the blade of the sword into the ground of the cave. It was shocking how easily the vanadinite slid right into what should have been hard, rocky ground. As the crystal blade sliced through the soil, the earth shivered and moaned. The creatures shrieked and cried out. Rocks jolted forward, and the shrubbery shook as if having a seizure.

"This ground is lost to you. This form is lost to you. This shape is lost to you. Each form she sent this night is now locked in this consecrated earth." She scattered more drops of liquid from the vial in the four directions, and then above her head and onto the ground.

The remaining beetles the bats had not yet managed to catch smoldered with foul smoke. They emitted high-pitched screeches and leapt from where they were trying to burrow into the walls or climb to the ceiling along a wooden root. Trying to avoid the merciless red wash of light, they flung themselves into the air and burst into blue flames. All around the two women, gray ash began to rain down.

The demon creatures grew frantic to get to Safia, dragging themselves with their claws, trying to get to their back feet to stand upright so they could better run at her. Unlike the beetles, who did target Aura, the demons centered their attention wholly on Safia.

They are programmed to destroy the lifemate of Petru.

Before Aura had told Safia that she protected the other half of Petru's soul, she had no knowledge of such a sacred duty. And it *was* sacred. She was entrusted with a man's honor. These terrible creatures devised in hell would not be able to wrest Petru's soul from her and give it to their mistress. Whatever use the woman had for it was not anything good. He would suffer greatly if the underground ruler was ever able to get her hands on his soul.

These will not meet their goal this night, Safia assured her.

The rain continued to fall, each large drop hissing, a liquid fire, as it sank into the flesh right through their armor. Holes formed, and orange-red flames began to spring up from the inside like tiny lit candlewicks. The slashed mouths gaped open even wider, and streams of white saliva poured from them in the form of venom, only the white was slowly turning reddish from the fires burning inside them.

Despite the sickening stench, Safia continued to chant, using her sweetest, most angelic voice, as if she had been called from the heavens to sing the creatures a lullaby. They fell to their sides and writhed and moaned, attempting to dig their way back into the earth, but it was sealed against them. They were locked aboveground and could not return to their mistress. The woman could not send any other demons in that form to the surface. Safia smoothed the crystal blade sideways, and the red flames encompassed all bodies left on the ground, incinerating them, leaving nothing but ash behind.

Once again, Safia let a few drops of the water touch the ashes, and then she nodded to Aura. "That should get her really angry."

Aura waved her hand to clear the stench from the room. Safia was eternally grateful.

"The vampires have grown quiet. They aren't gone yet. I can feel them sniffing around outside. They know you aren't Carpathian and therefore can't move through the air," Aura said.

"I'm the rabbit, the bait," Safia said, refusing to allow her heart to pound. They were sticking to the plan. So far, they had done fairly well, but then the underground queen hadn't been trying that hard. She was only testing them. "Run, little rabbit."

"It won't be long," Aura assured. "Vampires are not patient."

"Open this door," a voice demanded.

"I don't know who you are," Aura answered. "We are unaccompanied. Our grandfather fell ill, and we cannot open the door to a man. That would be unseemly. You are not a member of my people, or you would know this."

The vampire made every effort to keep the impatience from his voice. "Your grandfather sent me, child."

Aura sent a quick grin toward Safia. *I'll bet he'd like to pull out what little is left of his hair.* The smile faded from her face, and she pointed to the ceiling. *His partner is up to something. Do you feel him up there? You must get used to feeling their presence.*

Safia did her best to expand her senses in the way Aura had taught her. Evil had a slimy feel to it. Vampires sometimes simply had a blank space where living energy should be. In this case, above their heads, she caught the trace of something twisted, like a tree branch that might have grown wrong. It was very subtle, but she felt the difference.

What is he doing?

Trying to see into the chamber. He can't get through my safeguards or your sacred binding spell. The vampires are locked out of the ground. They aren't aware of that yet, but they will be the minute they try to burrow into it. You consecrated it, and they can't rest or travel in consecrated ground.

Oh dear. I am going to be on their hit list.

At the very top, Aura confirmed, *at least with these two.*

Give me a minute, and I think I can manage to do a direct strike on Mr. Meddlesome. The crystal can penetrate the guards. You weren't guarding against light.

Aura sent her another quick grin. *I think the generations gave you just a little too much sass. Vampires are very egotistical. He won't live down whatever you do to him, and he'll remember and come after you until he's destroyed. The others will make fun of him relentlessly.*

Isn't that a good thing? He'll be focused on getting me and not my family.

You will have to be very careful, Safia. We controlled this environment and defeated the beetles and demons easily because we were prepared, and

*she had no idea that we would be. But vampires have immense power, and
when you face one, there is no room for error.*

Safia had witnessed the battles Aura had shown her over and over,
studying the various techniques the hunters had used to slay vampires.
She studied each vampire and the way he had approached the fights
with the hunters. Most preferred talking. They were vain and wanted
to distract their adversary. At the same time, they wanted to talk about
their exploits and be admired and feared. They used delaying tactics if
they had others with them so that their pawns could circle around and
get in place to attack from behind or above. Sometimes poisonous vines
would shoot from beneath the ground to wrap around prey and lock
them in place so the vampire could more easily strike down the hunter.

Safia had forced herself to replay the battles night after night as she
grew up, watching them as one might movies, studying them from
every angle. She'd had little time to watch how Petru had fought his
battles with the vampires, she was just recovering those memories, but
they were inside her mind, imprinted on her brain. They were *her* memories and were very vivid when her mind allowed them to slip through.

Petru's technique was far different from any of the other hunter's
styles Aura had shown her. He didn't speak. He didn't engage at all
with his enemy. He was direct, grim, like the grim reaper of death, a
shocking, powerful instrument of justice clearly striking terror in his
enemies. They tried to hide the fact that they feared him, but it was
impossible. In the end, they almost always tried to flee.

He never retreated. It mattered little how abused his body was or
even if they were close to tearing his heart out. He stood toe-to-toe
with them, looking them in the eye, never so much as flinching. It was
no wonder he struck terror in them. He seemed invincible, even surrounded by his enemy.

*The one scratching overhead is called Bumbus. I heard the other address
him. The one at the door is Larriot. He seems in charge, although Bumbus is
obsessed with making his way through the ceiling and has assured Larriot
that he has made progress, even though it is not so. He lied.*

Shocking that he lied to his boss. Who would ever believe a vampire could lie to another vampire?

Aura laughed softly. *Vampires never actually admit another one is over them, even if they are choosing to follow that vampire for a semblance of protection.*

Safia frowned. *Do vampires protect one another?*

Not really. The newly made ones think they have protection with the older ones, but they're used as pawns, fed to the hunters first in battle to slow the hunters down and hopefully wound them. If they lose enough blood, the vampires have a better chance at killing them. The lesser vampires mean nothing to them.

The scratching overhead became frantic. Safia allowed her senses to spread out and pinpoint the exact location. Her focus zeroed in on the vampire, allowing her to visualize him bent over, digging at the surface of the floor in the chamber above them. He continually sniffed the ground and peered into the hole he was attempting to enlarge.

She timed his next look, and as he bent to see how thin the layers were, she thrust the crystal sword upward, straight toward his eye. The red light burst in a stream through the surface directly into the orb. The fiery blaze was pure and contained sacred water held within the stream of light. The moment it touched the twisted abomination, the flames detonated outward like a starburst, spreading through the vampire's skull.

He fell back, howling, shrieking, trying to hold his head on his shoulders as it lurched sideways off his neck. Red light poured from the holes where his ears should have been, and the gaping holes where his mouth and nose should have been. Pinpricks of red streamed from breaks in his neck and the top of his skull. Parasites poured from his body, dropping to the earth in scorched, blackened, twisted shells.

Harsh laughter echoed through the caves, the sound grating and demeaning. Abruptly it was cut off, and a chill crept down Safia's spine.

They've gone, she whispered to Aura.

Aura didn't bother to state the obvious. She caught up Safia and whisked them both from the safety of the chamber to the surface, following the vampires back to Safia's farm. The plan was for Aura to take Safia most of the way there and then put her down on the familiar track where Safia would begin her run, the beacon to draw the vampires straight to her, away from the farm and her family.

They had chosen their first battleground with care, giving themselves every advantage. This was an important opening in the gambit between the opposing parties. Safia had to know she could defend her family and that her strategy against her opponent was a solid one. As she learned more about her enemies, she could be fluid and change her approach when needed. For now, she'd built these first forays in the hope of gathering as much information as possible.

The moment Aura disappeared, Safia was running alone in the night, her stride long, arms pumping for speed, her rhythm steady. She ran like the gazelle, moving along the trail knowing she was a beacon of light and all eyes would turn to her quickly. There was trepidation, fear even, but this was what she had trained for her entire life. Either she was up for the task or she wasn't. She believed she was. There was no room for failure, because if she failed, her family would die, and that was unacceptable to her.

So yes, she was afraid. She would be less than human if she wasn't afraid. Fear was good because it kept her sharp. Every one of her senses flared out into the night, seeking to find her enemies. She was alone as she ran the familiar trail toward her farm, her heart staying at that steady beat, although it wanted to thunder in her ears and demand she reach out to Aura for reassurance that the safeguards hadn't been penetrated—that the vampires didn't have access to her family, and Charif had stayed where he'd been told.

The fog shrouded the entire area in a gray veil of thick mist, muffling sound. It was eerily quiet, as if she were the only living creature in existence. Her soft-soled boots made no impact on the loose dirt trail as she ran, leaping over the occasional obstacle, knowing it was there almost by a peculiar radar imaging in her head.

She had run nearly a quarter of a mile and the familiar peaceful euphoric endorphins had slipped into her veins. A tingling of alertness crept down her spine, icy fingers of awareness. She still had another quarter of a mile to go to get to the designated target area. She pushed her speed just a bit, not wanting to alert the one watching her. One? Or two? Had she drawn both vampires off the house? Or had there been a third one the two women hadn't spotted lurking in the shadows?

Safia pushed speculation from her mind. Amastan was right when he'd told her repeatedly not to waste time on worrying about things she couldn't control or that might never happen. She just had to get to the battleground and draw the vampire to her. Hopefully, he would watch her, making certain she was foolishly alone.

It was much more difficult to control her fear and her heart rate when she knew a vampire was drawing closer and she was alone on the trail. She kept her arms loose and pumping as she ran with long, even strides, keeping her form as she raced over the uneven dirt as if she were trying to get to her family.

The vampire struck at her mind just as she rounded the wide sweeping curve that ran along a set of misshapen boulders jutting out of a field of wild grasses and flowers. Her defenses were far too strong for him to break through her barriers. Generations of forming that protection had been put in place, and then Aura's patient teachings, along with her mother's and grandmother's instructions, had aided in building a wall so strong it was impossible for a vampire to compel her to do his bidding.

Safia abruptly broke from the trail and entered the field, racing across it to reach the next set of boulders. These were even larger than the ones by the trail and shaped into a loose circle. She tried to appear as if she were going to hide in the rocks from her adversary.

Taunting laughter erupted around her, coming out of the fog from every direction. She stood still for a moment, catching her breath in the middle of the sphere of rocks, where she'd already formed a consecrated circle of protection. She looked out cautiously to see what she faced.

Around the rocks, coming out of the fog, were a dozen vampires, all looking the same. Heads tilted to one side, as if their necks were broken, and flopped obscenely with every movement as they shifted from one foot to another. Their skulls were blackened as if they'd been through a fire. Inside, through the gaping holes, small red flames could be seen occasionally flaring brightly and then receding. When the flame rose, the vampires would shudder and shriek in unison and then lift their arms to their heads and try to rock the flames loose.

"You will suffer a thousand deaths for this," Bumbus snarled. When he spoke, all the vampires spoke at the same time.

Safia recognized the tactic. The vampire had replicated itself, making it nearly impossible for the hunter to find the real vampire in the midst of all the impostors. She had to discover the true vampire and isolate him from the others. He would be the one she would have to destroy, no matter if the others attacked her. They would be illusions. She knew illusions could seem very real and be terrifying. That was what could get her killed.

She took a deep breath and watched carefully as the vampires placed their feet in a complicated dance pattern meant to mesmerize. The footwork was exact. She studied the drag marks in the dirt. The soil appeared blackened and in places withered, shrinking from contact with the undead's rotted flesh. Bodies were the same. Movement the same.

"Go away." Her voice trembled. She shooed at the ring of vampires with her fingers as if waving them away from her. She sounded scared because she was. Inside, where it mattered, she was pure steel. Ready. She had planned out every move. She just needed to find the right vampire.

His broken neck and scorched skull had to be her answer. She assessed each vampire as if they were paper dolls and she had to find the one thing different about them. She was aware of the ticking clock. If she didn't hurry, his partner was certain to join him. She didn't want that to happen. She needed to face one vampire at a time to test herself.

The moment she spoke, the vampire's mouth widened into a slashing, ghastly smile. She barely caught a glimpse of jagged teeth in the blackened maw. It was only that low red light flickering that lit up the stained, serrated, spiked teeth enough for her to make them out.

She tapped the crystal sword gently, and immediately, the fiery light leapt like a flame throughout the skull, bursting through every gaping hole in the vampires. That brilliant red light shot a greater distance in every direction from one vampire than from any of the other vampires. As he swayed with the others, rocking back and forth, moaning, adjusting his head to fit it back on his shoulders, she targeted him.

"Come to me." The vampires all beckoned to her, lifting their arms and using their fingers to gesture to her to go to them.

She took a reluctant step out of the circle of boulders as if she couldn't help herself. The vampires grinned evilly.

"Yes, that's it. Come here. Kneel before us."

Safia thought that was a little dramatic. She made a show of stopping and starting, as if she couldn't help herself, always angling toward the real Bumbus.

PERSONAL POWER.
ENTRAPMENT.
SUFFERING.

Strength

Three of Swords

The Devil

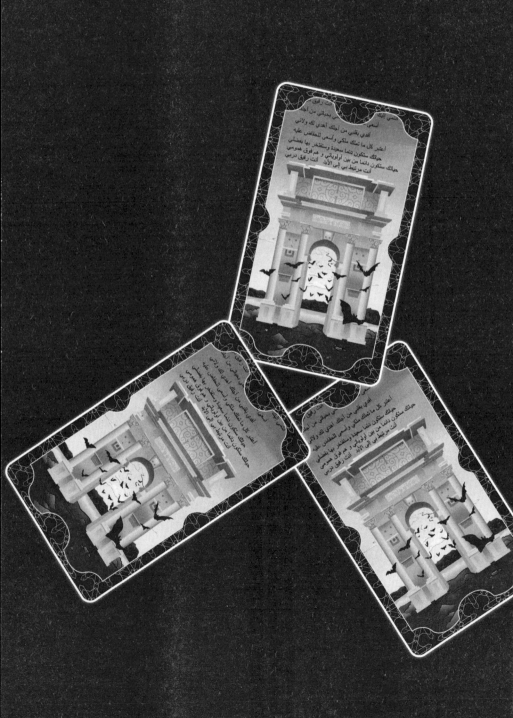

H urry, girl. I haven't all night to wait for you." The circle of vampires looked cautiously around the night sky, attempting to pierce the veil of thick gray fog.

It was obvious to Safia that Bumbus didn't want to share her with Larriot, the vampire over him. She shook her head as she continued to slowly stumble forward. "I don't want anything to do with you."

"You should have thought about that before you played with your little light." His voice grated harshly on her ears.

The small veneer of civilization was fast disappearing. Spittle began to run down the sides of the mouths of all the vampires. Maggots wiggled in the stream and hit the ground with the drops of poisonous saliva.

Safia concentrated on one thing only. The target. The chest where the undead's heart lay like a stone. She had to incinerate his heart in order to destroy him. That was the only thing that mattered to her.

She took another step closer to Bumbus, and the circle of vampires tightened around her. Their foul breath made it difficult to breathe. She felt their triumph. They began to clack their talons together in eager anticipation. She slipped her hand inside her coat, sliding the crystal sword back into the loop and drawing her long sword with the spiral blade. She kept the sword concealed in the folds of the coat while she once more sent her senses reaching out into the night to test for other vampires or demons that might be hidden from her. It had been drilled into her not to take anything for granted. Bumbus could very well be used as a decoy.

Again, she found nothing else to alert her. Taking a breath, she wasted no more time and went on the attack. She knew it was the last thing Bumbus would expect. She used her speed and the energy of the vampire to thrust the sword deep into his chest, straight into the heart, triggering a blast of white-hot fire to incinerate it on contact.

Bumbus shrieked and ripped his talons down her arm, tearing through her flesh to the bone as she withdrew the sword and plunged it into his chest a second time. Her aim had been good on the positioning of a normal heart, but his was askew, and she'd only managed to burn part of it.

He clawed at her throat, bending his head to bite into her shoulder with savage teeth. She had seen the same thing happen dozens of times to hunters fighting battles, but nothing could prepare her for the shocking pain of the acid blood burning through her flesh to the bone or the tear of those cruel serrated teeth biting through muscle to get to her blood.

Still, she was Safia Meziane, the defender of her people, keeper and guardian of Petru's soul. She would not be less than Petru. Stoically, she endured the pain as she used the vampire's momentum against him, thrusting the sword through his chest once again and twisting so that every part of the fiery blade incinerated what was left of the heart.

Bumbus stared at her with his soulless eyes, his mouth gaping open in horror. His body slowly crumpled to the ground as the flames began to lick at his rotted flesh from the inside out. Safia stumbled back to the consecrated circle and sank onto one of the flatter rocks, breathing deeply to keep from passing out.

She had known there was a huge possibility that she would be injured, but in her wildest dreams, she had never imagined the pain would be anything like it was. She pulled out her emergency kit and continued to breathe deep as she once more drew her crystal sword. It was the only weapon she had against the parasites she knew the vampire had injected into her bloodstream when he had bitten her.

Her stomach lurched as she tipped her head to one side and held the blade of light against the torn flesh. At once, white dots began to spin behind her eyes. She knew she was going to faint. There was no way she could hang on.

Aura. I'm in trouble. I destroyed Bumbus, but he tore me up, and I'm not able to stay conscious. I'm crashing.

She slid off the rock and landed on the ground. Fortunately, it was soft dirt. Her stomach lurched again at the jarring. Her arm was useless where the acid had torn through her flesh. She could see the white of her bone. How did the hunters endure such pain and keep going? She had the will, but her body refused to continue functioning.

No, no, you must stay alert. I can't get to you yet. There was genuine alarm in Aura's voice. *She will know you're injured. They will send everything they can to kill you. If they can kill you, they will win before the war even starts.*

How was she supposed to stay on her feet when she could barely lift her head up? She took a breath, forced air through her lungs and took another one. Tried to shut out the pain. Once more, she did her best to let her senses reach out into the night to ensure she was alone in that fog-enshrouded, consecrated circle.

Safia's heart jerked hard. Not only was she not alone, but she was surrounded by silent predators. She had no idea exactly where they were; she just knew they were close and creeping closer. Determinedly, she pressed her palm to the flat surface of the rock and tried to lever herself up. She needed to be on her feet. She didn't make it the first time. She felt their eyes on her and found that gave her added resolve to push to her feet. She couldn't use one arm, and it hung uselessly at her side, but her good hand gripped her sword. She had the presence of mind to stay solidly within the consecrated ground, where demons and vampires could not enter.

As soon as she stood, a figure strode out of the fog. At first, it was almost impossible to make him out. He blended with the blues and grays, his long gray coat falling nearly to his ankles and swirling around his body. He moved as fluidly as the fog itself, as if he were a part of the night. His eyes were glacier cold, a kind of piercing silver, turbulent like the lightning forking in the bottom of the low-hanging clouds. His hair was platinum and silver, thick and pulled back from his very masculine face. This was not the face of a boy. Every line was carved deep. Those eyes slid over her, taking in everything, seeing everything, then moving over the ground around her, clearly reading what had taken place there.

Safia's breath caught in her lungs. She fought to stay on her feet. This was her lifemate. She would not fall facedown in the dirt and humiliate herself. He was just so . . . intimidating. She wasn't prepared for the reality of him. He looked like a being sent from another realm—half dangerous predator, half avenging angel.

He didn't smile, nor did he slow down even when she froze, clearly nervous at his approach. When he continued to stride toward her, she brought her hand up to indicate for him to stop. Unfortunately, the sword was still in her fist, and she supposed she looked as if she might be threatening him.

"Stop."

"You are injured, *päläfertiilam*." He continued to stride toward her as if the sword meant nothing.

The consecrated ground didn't slow him down in the least. He stepped right into the circle, pushed the sword aside and caught her around the waist with both hands to lower her onto the flat surface of the rock. His touch sent a series of electrical shocks tripping through her body. The way he lifted her shouldn't have felt in the least personal, and yet it was more intimate than he could have meant it to be. Her body slid against his as he lifted her onto the rock; he was that close to her. It was just the briefest of contacts, but his body felt as hard as the African blackwood, a tree renowned for its density.

The moment he touched her, the pain was gone from her shoulder and arm. He hadn't done anything to rid her of it, yet immediately, when his hands touched her waist, it was as if he'd blocked her ability to feel all pain. She had no idea how he managed to block it when the pain had been excruciating, but she wanted to learn.

"I am Petru Cioban, your lifemate. Tell me your name." He leaned over her to inspect her torn shoulder.

She closed her eyes against the warmth of his breath as he bathed the terrible wound in heat. Just the contact of his breath seemed too intimate, as if it connected them, establishing an unbreakable tie between them.

"Your name," he repeated.

His voice was soft, like the brush of velvet against her skin, yet there was a command there, one she couldn't ignore. She lifted her lashes, knowing it was a mistake, but she couldn't stop. She found herself looking directly into his odd-colored eyes. Instantly, it felt as if she were being drawn into a turbulent storm.

The fog enfolded Safia and Petru like a gray cloud, cutting them off from the rest of the world and setting them adrift. She began to think she was hallucinating just a little. Maybe the wounds were making her delusional. She couldn't seem to think clearly with Petru so close to her.

She made every effort to pull herself together, but she felt dizzy and disoriented with the fog swirling around her and memories that weren't all her own crowding too close. The past and present seemed to be colliding when she was weak and vulnerable. She hung on to reality by concentrating on the images of those she loved most. Her family was still in danger.

"I'm Safia Meziane. There are other vampires attacking my family home. I'd prefer you go to their aid. I can take care of these wounds."

Petru's eyes had settled to a strange mercury color, but at her suggestion, they once again blazed into twin streaks of silvery turbulence. "The health of my lifemate comes first. The vampire leaves behind parasites that multiply quickly in the bloodstream. They must be removed. I have traveling companions with me. Three will go to your residence and aid those there. The other two will stay here to guard us while I heal your wounds. You can never allow any wound a vampire inflicts on you to go unattended."

His voice was very mild, but she felt reprimanded. It wasn't as if Aura hadn't given her those instructions. Training to fight a vampire and talking about them or replaying battles in one's mind wasn't nearly the same thing as fighting one. They hadn't been real to her, and this had been her first time. She'd been alone. Terrified. And she'd managed to destroy him.

"I must go outside my body to heal you from the inside. I will drive the parasites from your bloodstream and any organ they have lodged in."

As Petru spoke, the pad of his thumb moved over the top of her shoulder and her neck where the tears were the worst. It was the lightest of touches, barely there, but was a caress all the same, felt through her body like a ripple of pleasure. The idea of physically reacting or, worse, her soul reacting to this stranger over such a small gesture when no man had touched her and she was alone and unguarded and so vulnerable, was very disturbing. She had lost too much blood, and she was very susceptible to him. She didn't want to be alone with him and his friends. All along, when she'd thought of meeting him, it had been in a position of equality, not weakness, not like this.

"Nicu Dalca will guard my body and give me blood on my return."

She tried not to wince when he so calmly explained that his friend would give him blood. She appreciated that he was taking the time to clarify each step for her, instinctively aware she was nervous, but she wanted to go home, not hear about what was normal for him.

Needing blood was a fact of his life. It was just that the information was very new to her, and she hadn't had that much time to process what he was and what he would need. She was Imazighen and she always would be. As his lifemate, she would embrace his culture and his family, but it would not be easy for her to give him blood in the way Aura had explained he would expect. The thought of it had her mind shutting down again.

A second man emerged from the fog. He was leaner than Petru but clearly strong, extremely handsome, with blazing gray eyes and black hair. A deep scar curved from his left temple to the corner of his eye. He nodded to her, his gaze moving over the horrific wounds on her neck, shoulder and arm. Like Petru, his gaze moved over the ground, reading the battle that had taken place. His brows drew together.

"Where are the others?"

"Others?" she echoed, not understanding. She was swaying, even sitting there on the rock with Petru's hand supporting her. The fog was warping time for her, the way it swirled in patterns of blues and grays. The pain might be gone, but she was definitely not at her best.

Nicu and Petru exchanged a look she couldn't interpret. Petru gestured toward the scorched soil. "It is clear you fought this vampire on your own. Where are the others? Did they return to your farm when it was clear there was need, leaving you alone and wounded?"

She couldn't exactly detect a change in Petru's tone, but icy fingers crept down her spine. Something dangerous swirled in the air. Suddenly there was menace, a sinister promise of retaliation. It didn't just come from Petru but also from Nicu and the unseen watcher beyond the fog bank.

She raised her chin and looked Petru straight in the eyes. It was much easier without the excruciating pain, although she was weak from blood loss and the dizziness persisted, making her feel sick. "I am the defender. It is my duty to destroy demons and vampires and anything else that preys on my people."

There was silence. She knew instantly the three men were talking telepathically in the way she did with Aura. Alarm spread through her, and she did her best not to jerk away from under Petru's hands. He continued to move the pads of his fingers over her scorched shoulder in a soothing touch, but now, she didn't feel caresses. The sensation was more one of being his prisoner.

Were they talking about her behind her back? Belittling her? "If you have something to say, say it where I can hear it. I know I made mistakes, but it isn't like I kill vampires every night. It was a trial run." She couldn't keep the defiance from her voice—or the hurt.

Petru took her injured arm, the one that hung uselessly at her side, and brought it up for his inspection. He bent down, examining the damage to her arm, so she could see the wild mass of silvery white hair inviting her to sink her fingers into the thickness. It was such a temptation even when he'd hurt her with his careless words.

She'd worked hard to learn how to slay a vampire, and she'd been very scared. He didn't seem to admire her efforts at all. His lips moved over the blackened ruin of her skin, and her stomach clenched at the sheer intimacy he invoked. He was throwing her senses into complete chaos. Her mind was already far too disoriented with the fog, her wounds and the strange way she was beginning to feel.

"*Pelkgapâd és Meke Pirämet,*" he murmured in his language, and she struggled to interpret the phrase. The words were unfamiliar to her and sounded more like an affectionate endearment, especially the way the low whisper of his voice swept over her.

"You misunderstand. What you did here is extraordinary and unheard of. The question is, why were you fighting a vampire without aid of any kind?"

"There is no one else. Aura and me. My family. That is all. We spent years training, but this is the first time any of us has ever crossed paths with an actual vampire. Aura has, but she's Carpathian. She's the only one left though."

His mouth continued to move over her blackened ruin of an arm. Everywhere his lips touched, her arm tingled, came back to life. Nerve endings she didn't know she had began to wake up, coming to attention.

"There are no Carpathians in this area at all?" Nicu asked.

"Just Aura. Her mother followed her father in death several weeks ago. She was the last." A little shiver went through her body. "I need to get to the farm."

"They are in good hands. My friends will take care of any vampires daring to attack your family. I am going to remove the parasites and heal your body. We can talk about how you fought this vampire alone after. I am very proud of you, although it is disturbing to me."

She watched as he suddenly was simply gone, shedding his body as if it were no more than a shell. She caught a glimpse of a brilliant white light, and that was gone as well. She blinked several times, wondering if she was beginning to hallucinate from blood loss. It was possible. Maybe none of this was real. She'd seen Aura heal small wounds before, but she'd never left her body behind.

Warmth moved through her insides. Heat. Then it was hot, very hot in places. Tiny drops of blood leaked from her pores to the ground, each containing several wiggling parasites. The sight turned her stomach. Those had been inside her. Now she hoped she was hallucinating.

Each time the maggots touched the surface, Nicu aimed a streak of fiery lightning at them, incinerating them instantly. "You never want to give them a chance to burrow back into the soil. If you pull them out of you, burn them right away," he said.

The easy, casual way he called down lightning through the blue-gray fog added to the weird way she was feeling. At the same time, she liked that he was treating her with enough respect to give her advice. She also wanted to examine everything Petru was doing. She was very good at learning how to do things once she was shown the way. He'd shed his body so quickly, she couldn't figure out how he'd done it, but she could ask Aura. If it was possible for a human to do it, Safia had confidence that she would be able to learn.

She did her best to keep her senses alert for trouble and at the same time be aware of what was happening inside her body, trying to follow the healing process. There was no doubt that Petru was meticulously repairing the bones, organs and muscles the vampire had shredded.

Three dictators have arrived to tell me how to conduct myself properly as a female Carpathian. Aura's amused voice slipped into her mind. *They would have made very short work of Larriot, but your father and oldest brother managed to lure him right where we wanted him. It was perfect, Safia. He went just like you said he would go. Your strategy was exact.*

There was not only elation but admiration in her voice, something that made Safia feel much better. She'd worked hard on tactics to divide the vampires and lure each one to a different site where they could be destroyed. Things hadn't gone perfectly on her end, but she'd managed to kill the vampire and incinerate his heart. Yes, she'd been wounded, but that had been expected. Maybe not quite as severely as it had occurred.

Was anyone hurt? What if she'd been wrong? She had studied their adversaries, but there was no way to target individuals. She had no idea how many her family would be pitted against.

Everyone is fine. Well, apart from me. I have a few ruffled feathers. I had forgotten what Carpathian males could be like. Again, amusement flooded Safia's mind. Aura didn't seem as upset as she indicated.

Abruptly, Petru was back in his own body and looking up at her with eyes the color of mercury—eyes that seemed to penetrate her shields. He couldn't possibly hear her conversation with Aura, but there was no doubt that he knew she was talking to someone, and he didn't like it any more than she had.

"If you are going to converse with another, you can loop me in."

Nicu casually made a straight cut in his wrist. Blood welled up instantly, and he offered it to Petru as if he'd done so a million times. Petru brought the laceration to his mouth. Safia looked away. She couldn't do that. Not in a million years. She could give him blood. But take it from him? Hadn't Aura said there had to be an exchange?

"Why are you shaking your head?" Nicu asked. "Stay still. You've lost too much blood and you are weak."

Her gaze jumped to his. "If you're planning on giving me blood, I require a transfusion the normal human way, not . . ." She broke off, gesturing toward Petru without looking in his direction. "I know that's your custom, and I respect whatever it is you do, but it isn't my way." She was swaying again, her body definitely weak. She *had* lost too much blood. She needed to get away from them. She needed to be home, where her grandfather, father and family would surround her with love and care.

Aura, I might be in trouble again. I don't like being alone with these men. One is Petru, the man I am promised to, but I feel too vulnerable. He healed my wounds, but I'm dizzy and weak. I want to go home.

Safia was reaching out to someone else for aid again. Petru could read her fear. He detested finding her torn up by a vampire, in such a dire circumstance. His lifemate. Two thousand years ago, a promise had been sworn to him. They would protect her, keep her safe, guard her. Instead, he had come across her, drawn by unbearable pain.

She was human, not Carpathian. What did they expect her to do after being ripped to pieces by a vampire? She clearly was afraid of him and the situation she found herself in. She feared receiving blood from him, even though she needed it desperately. That didn't make sense. She'd been taught to fight a vampire but not taught the ways of her lifemate?

Petru closed the laceration on Nicu's wrist and lifted his slashing gaze once more to meet Safia's directly, refusing to allow her to look away from him. He had to take charge immediately before it was too late. He'd wanted to start off their relationship on as equal a footing as possible, but she needed blood, and she needed it immediately.

He stood, keeping his movements fluid and nonthreatening. "I'm going to give you the blood you need, Safia, and at the same time, create a link between us so we can speak telepathically. That way, we will be better able to support one another during every battle with our enemies."

He was careful to tell her exactly his intentions so there would be no surprises, but he didn't give her the opportunity to protest. She had a strong barrier in her brain, but fortunately, when the door had opened to both their memories, they shared that path, leaving him an entry-way into her mind.

Petru was an ancient and extremely powerful. Very gently, he pulled her into his arms, cradling her on his lap as his mind took complete control of hers. She would have resisted, fought him, but she had no chance when she hadn't a clue to his intentions. He'd told her, but she still hadn't read his resolve in his gentle, almost tender touch.

He didn't waste time but immediately slashed a line in his chest and pressed her mouth over the welling blood. His blood was rich and ancient and would heal her fast. It would also tie them together. Just the touch of her lips on his bare skin had his body reacting unex-pectedly.

He'd deliberately refused to see in color after the initial shock of hearing her voice, when those colors had exploded around him in bright, vivid, dazzling light. Then he had to push all emotion aside so he wouldn't feel a berserker's rage at the idea that his lifemate had been left alone like bait for vampires to kill. Now his body was responding physically to her touch, another new sensation when she was scared and feeling vulnerable, surrounded by strangers.

Why was he considered a stranger to her? To give himself some-thing to concentrate on other than the way his body was reacting to her, he examined her memories. He didn't need to look at the ones from their shared past but at the recent ones, from her birth to pres-ent day.

"Nicu, she was not told of me until this rising. She knew nothing of having a Carpathian lifemate. She believed she was promised to one of her people."

Above their heads, lightning forked in the dark swirling clouds, barely seen through the thick fog. Thunder rolled and boomed, spread-ing across the sky in all directions. The sound waves traveled like a dark, brooding foreshadowing of what the ancient had become.

Nicu glanced up at the sky and then at the man he had traveled with on and off for hundreds of years. "You have every right to ask questions of these people, Petru. I can see why this woman was frightened of us. She slayed a vampire on her own and faced the three of us when she was wounded and in a very weakened condition. I have nothing but respect for her. She is worthy of you."

When Petru knew Safia had taken enough blood to replace what she had lost and also for a full exchange, he stopped her feeding and closed the laceration over his chest. Taking her blood would establish a blood bond between them and give them their first step toward her coming into his world. It would take three blood exchanges to bring her into the Carpathian world. He planned on bringing her in as quickly as possible. This time he was taking no chances with his lifemate. She would be close to him, under his protection at all times. He would never survive her death without succumbing to a thrall. He was too old, and there were far too many scars on his soul.

"It is very disturbing to me that her family has done this to her when promises were made. You are right, there is no point in speculating, but she is the one to pay the price, and it is a steep one."

Petru swept his palm down the back of her head, feeling soft dark hair as he shifted her in his arms and nuzzled her throat. There was a distinct scent to her. He inhaled, taking her into his lungs. Jasmine mixed with a hint of pine and the sea. There was something else, a scent he remembered from meadows of flowers too many years ago, the memory faint, tiny little white stars staring up to the sky at night. They had a subtle perfume unlike anything he'd ever smelled.

He sank his teeth into her without any expectations. The results were nearly overwhelming. Her blood burst into every one of his senses like an aphrodisiac, a spice created only for him. Addicting. It would be difficult to ever want anything other than the taste of her blood. The rush was hot, every nerve ending coming alive, making him acutely aware of her as a woman and him as a man. Blood pounded through his veins, settled low and wicked with urgent demands, something he had never experienced. She was giving him too many firsts all at one time when he needed discipline and control to find a way to best handle their relationship. More than anything, he wanted her to feel like an equal partner, which wasn't going to be easy.

Very reluctantly, he stopped himself from taking more than just enough for their first blood exchange. "Safia, when you wake, I want you to remember just enough, keeping emotions at a distance so you aren't afraid, but we can discuss what was necessary."

Her lashes lifted instantly, and he found himself staring into her wide, very intelligent green eyes. She took a moment to examine what he'd done. He expected fear, but what he got was more like fury. She made a move to jerk out of his arms, but he didn't so much as rock back or act in any way as if he'd noticed.

He continued to stare into her eyes, partially mesmerized by her. He hadn't considered he would be awestruck by her.

"I didn't give you permission to give me blood that way. In fact, I specifically told you I needed to be transfused the human way."

Her voice trembled with temper, but she made every effort not to raise her voice at him.

"I am a Carpathian male, Safia. We have no choice but to see to the health of our lifemate. You were in need, and I provided for you. It is that simple. Arguing was pointless. Allowing you to be frightened over something that was necessary and easy was unacceptable."

"It was taking my free will away."

He didn't respond. "I will take you back to your residence. My understanding is I must meet with your grandfather to make my claim on you official."

For one moment, her heart accelerated, and then she was able to get it under control. "I thought we could take a little time to get to know one another before we proceeded with your claim."

"That would be too dangerous. Your family was to prepare you in advance. I'm sorry they did not. War is inevitable and we must be ready."

She nodded, her green eyes searching his. "Exactly. That's why it's important we spend some time getting to know one another before we agree to become husband and wife. You don't want to make a mistake. You could be wrong about me."

He reached up to trace the full curve of her lower lip. It was soft and inviting, a temptation he had never noticed on any woman in the long centuries of his existence. "There can be no mistakes with a Carpathian male, *Pelkgapâd és Meke Pirämet*. I know this is frightening for you and is happening too fast. I would want to slow time down to give you whatever you would need, to give you the extra weeks to understand my ways and customs, but we do not have that luxury."

Safia didn't argue with him. He almost wished she would. It wasn't as if she accepted what he said. She only regarded him with her jade green eyes and then looked around her at the thick fog.

"I think it best we go to the farm. My grandfather is consulting with the ancestors this night. He's protected by Aura's safeguards, but I will have to go back to the cave after I check on the family. It's my duty to guard him through the rest of the night. I doubt any demon can slip through the safeguards, but I must be there just in case."

Petru's gaze met Nicu's over her head. She would be guarding her grandfather in the cave of the ancestors, waiting for demons to surface after the ugly ordeal with the vampires. What next? "Do you plan on traveling to the very gates of hell and taking on the mistress, Lilith, and her hellhounds tonight?"

Her fingers had been loose on his shoulder, but they curled into his shirt at his question, and for the first time, a slow smile touched her mouth. It was very slow in coming, but when it did, he noticed at once that she had a small dimple near the left corner of her mouth. The green in her eyes deepened to an unbelievable shade of emerald. She was beautiful. Her beauty came from inside her. An indomitable spirit. She would need that in the coming weeks.

"It did occur to me that taking the war to her might throw her off her game, but I don't quite have that confidence yet."

"Thank the stars for small favors," Nicu said. "The underworld does not seem to be a place I wish to experience, and no doubt if you go there, Petru will insist on the rest of us following you."

"No doubt," Petru agreed. He stood, an easy, fluid motion, keeping Safia in his arms. "If you still must go to the caves this night, then let us get you to your farm to check on your family."

"Don't sound so grim. And don't give them lectures," Safia said.

"I plan on having a talk with your grandfather, father and brothers, Safia, but I will wait until your grandfather is available. It is important that they understand you are under my care, and I am very exacting on how that will be done."

She raised an eyebrow, her gaze moving over his face with a hint of haughtiness. "I believe you missed the part where I told you I am the defender. I was born into that role and trained for it my entire life. Don't think you are going to come here and dictate to me or my family something different, because that is what is going to be."

"We shall see," Petru said complacently. He didn't believe in arguing.

7

The market in Dellys was a familiar place that always gave Safia comfort. She loved the sounds and smells. The way people spoke various languages, laughed and bargained, interacted with one another and showed off their best wares made her smile. She enjoyed haggling and trading. She was good at it. The family stalls were always busy. Amara's jewelry was especially sought after. Farah's clothing was a big success. The pottery was a huge seller, but the rugs were their top moneymakers.

Amara sat behind the table while Safia did the actual bargaining. In the produce section, Lunja and Farah were selling the farm eggs and vegetables. Layla was home tending to the children and the farm itself with the men.

Amastan was resting after a long night consulting the ancestors. He hadn't said a word when he woke. That was his usual way. He'd simply returned with her to the farm and retired to his room to rest. Safia hadn't been so lucky. She'd been up all night, but she was expected to train and then work several hours on the farm before accompanying the other women into Dellys to sell their wares in the marketplace.

For the first time that she could remember, the market didn't soothe Safia. She found herself exhausted and on edge. Her mind kept trying to find Petru. She considered herself a very disciplined person— she had to be when she was the defender—yet she couldn't stop herself from wondering if he had already deserted her. If he found her lacking.

He had stayed close during the rest of the night, keeping the vigil, waiting for her grandfather to awaken, but he had gone out on patrol, continuing to familiarize himself with the area. He didn't attempt to talk to her again. He didn't talk to her family about her. The more she thought about his behavior, the more she convinced herself he thought she wasn't the right one for him.

"Safia, what's wrong?" Amara asked when there was a lull in the customers around their table. "You look very sad. This is not like you. You're always very animated and draw people to us. If you're tired, I set up a cot behind the curtains. You can lie down for a little while. We have a couple of hours before we must return to the farm. I can handle the customers, and if there are too many, I'll wake you."

It was a generous offer. Safia could see Amara was genuinely concerned. Just hearing Amara make the offer made her feel a little better. "I'm fine. Just tired."

"It's him. The man who has made the claim on you." She lowered her voice. "He came to see *Emmi* last night."

Safia's head jerked up in reaction. She went very still. If Petru had gone to her father, that might explain a lot. "He did *not*. When? He went to see *Baba*? Petru never said a word. You saw him? What did he say?"

At first, Petru's mind had stayed in hers. She resented that, afraid he'd see things in her she wanted to keep hidden. She was still so unsure of him. She had no desire to commit to a man outside her tribe. She feared that would make her less than honorable in his eyes. It wasn't that she didn't intend to follow through; she just needed more time. But she wanted those thoughts private.

On the other hand, there was an intimacy she'd never known,

sharing her mind with him. He kept his touch very light, almost a sliding velvet caress, as if he were simply making certain she was safe and comfortable while he was patrolling and learning the city and surrounding countryside.

Amara shook her head. "I tried to see him, I even tried to listen to what he was saying to *Emmi*," she confessed, having the grace to blush. "But then I caught a glimpse of another man, but only his back, and he looked ferocious. I retreated immediately."

Safia laughed. "Amara, how could he look ferocious from the back?"

"Trust me, he did. And I think he growled. And snarled. He had a lot of black hair. Lots of it. Very long."

"That had to be Nicu." Safia tapped her fingers against her thigh, trying to repress a smile. "He might have growled."

Amara nodded solemnly. "No way was I going to put my ear against a door with that man standing around in the hallway."

"Do you make a habit of putting your ear to the door?"

Amara grinned unrepentantly. "Yes. That was the only way to learn anything at all when I was growing up. Izem says I should just ask him anything I want to know, but it's a habit and kind of fun to see if I can get away without being seen."

"One of these days, you'll get caught," Safia warned.

Amara laughed. "I've been caught dozens of times by *Jeddi*. He just shakes his head and asks me if there is anything I particularly desire to know. If I say no, he has me sit down with him and talk about my day. I love that most of all."

Safia knew it was the time Amastan spent with each family member that made them feel important and needed. Amara hadn't had that growing up the way Safia and her siblings had. Amastan and Izem recognized her needs before any of the others had and immediately saw to them. The rest of the family followed their lead, and Amara had thrived in her new environment.

The smile faded from Amara's face. "If this man isn't good to you,

Safia, we can find a way to sneak you away to Illi and Kab. They can take you across the desert. I know our family owes him, but trading your life for his services is wrong. I talked to Izem and he agrees with me. It's not just Izem that feels that way; all of us do. The entire family owes him, not just you. You shouldn't have to pay the debt for all of us."

Safia loved her family even more. Tears burned behind her eyes. They were wonderful. How could she ever contemplate leaving them? Amara might seem very young and reckless at times, but she had a serious side, and she was extremely loyal and very courageous.

"His name is Petru Cioban, Amara. He came to me last night when I was wounded. I'd fought a vampire and the wounds were terrible."

Amara's eyes widened and she pressed her hand over her mouth. "Izem didn't tell me. Does he know? Does anyone in the family know? Because Aura talked of you battling beetles and demons, but she didn't say a word about vampires. Izem and *Emmi* destroyed a vampire, and we were celebrating that your plan worked. Not one word was said about you being injured."

"I also sustained rather severe blood loss. I was very dizzy and weak and vulnerable to another attack. It is an understatement to say he was not happy to find me in that condition."

Amara's gaze ran over Safia, inspecting her, trying to look for injuries. "Where?" There was anxiety in her voice and eyes.

Safia glanced around the busy marketplace and stepped closer to Amara. She tugged at the colorful purple top she wore, pulling the material from one side of her neck and shoulder. The fabric was a beautiful ombré, starting with a vivid shade of deep royal purple and fading into a much lighter purple toward the bottom hem. It was one of Farah's designs, and Safia particularly loved it.

Farah loved fashion and aspired to be a fashion designer. She'd gone to school for that purpose but stopped abruptly just before graduating and returned home. She was an amazing talent. Safia hoped one day she'd share why she decided against continuing forward with her dream. If she had told Usem, he kept her secret. She saved her skills for the family business, contributing her beautiful creations with her own label. They sold very well.

"Petru is also a healer," Safia explained. "The vampire ripped through my skin and took my blood. It was a ghastly wound. My arm was black to the bone. I'd never felt pain like that in my life. He took that away, too. I can't see a mark on my skin. The vampire leaves behind these vile little parasites in the bloodstream." She couldn't help the shudder that ran through her body. "He got rid of them as well. I'm not sure I can learn to do that."

A group of female customers came down the aisle, laughing and talking in French, pointing excitingly to several of Farah's beautiful shirts. Two of the women admired Amara's necklaces, and one of the older women studied Illi's teapot from every angle, clasping her hands together and nodding as what appeared to be a relative—her sister, most likely—nodded and agreed that the teapot was the nicest they'd seen.

Safia always engaged with her customers, finding out about their lives. Where they were from. What they were doing in Dellys. She was genuinely interested, and that always came through. This was three generations of women vacationing together, and they were clearly having a wonderful time. They had taken a walking tour of the Casbah already and loved it. They'd seen the lighthouse and planned on visiting the harbor. They had heard of the various myths surrounding the area and wanted to see the ruins.

Safia cautioned them not to go out unattended at night but gave them recommendations for various places to eat. They got down to serious negotiations on pricing. The two older women definitely wanted the teapot and two of Illi's vases. They were not inexpensive. Her custom work was nothing short of artwork, and her family didn't allow it to be undervalued. Safia would come down only so far, and the women seemed to sense her bottom line and capitulated. Amara wrapped the pottery very carefully for them.

The three youngest girls loved Farah's clothing and couldn't make up their minds on which tops to buy. They consulted their mothers and grandmothers and ended up purchasing two each. There wasn't much in the way of bargaining, but there was a lot of laughter.

The two women admiring Amara's jewelry took their time, going over every piece. It was clear they were mostly interested in the necklaces rather than the earrings. They did look at the earrings, but only to see which ones matched the necklaces they really wanted to purchase. Amara was doing her best to look very businesslike, but the way the women were exclaiming over the jewelry was bringing in more customers, making Amara's face light up. Safia couldn't help but be proud of her.

This was a great day for the farm. Business was brisk. Not only did they do amazing sales with just the ladies on vacation, but more and more people stopped by. That always seemed to be the way. Safia should have been ecstatic. She told herself she was, but as time passed, she found it harder to concentrate.

Safia found her mind continually reaching for Petru despite being occupied with bargaining, which was one of her favorite things to do. Meeting new people and learning about them was always fun, yet a part of her was uneasy, concerned that Petru had decided he didn't want her after all, or worse, what if he had run into a vampire during the night and was injured? She wouldn't have known. He had left her to guard her grandfather, and she had fallen asleep there in the cave, as she often did. When she woke, it was morning, and Petru, like Aura, was nowhere to be found.

Her brain couldn't seem to settle but bounced all over the place until her skull felt too tight and her head pounded. At times, she felt physically ill, worried that Petru was hurt and needed help. She had never been out of control. She'd always been capable of discipline, and yet she couldn't rein in her runaway thoughts, even though she felt they were illogical.

A tall man with stern features but kind dark eyes approached their booth. Behind him, an older couple walked, both dressed in the more traditional clothes worn by some of the Imazighen. Safia smiled in welcome, but her stomach knotted even more.

Aabis Kalaz owned the most successful restaurant in Dellys. He was a good man, a good businessman. He was a good son and treated his parents with respect and love. He had made an offer for her on two occasions. She knew he would make an offer for her again and that he didn't understand why Amastan had refused him. She detested hurting the man. She wasn't the least bit attracted to him. It was strange, now that she thought about it. He was a very handsome man, kind and successful. Most women would have been thrilled to have his attention.

"*Azul*, Safia. *Azul*, Amara. You seem to have had a brisk business today," Aabis greeted.

"*Azul*, Aabis," Safia responded. She looked past him to his parents and gave them a friendly welcome. "I hope you have been well."

Aabis nodded as his parents indicated that they were going to move on to the produce section of the market. He took his time before answering, his gaze moving over her the way it often did when he encountered her. There was always a slight hint of disapproval. She knew he didn't like her modern clothes. He would have preferred she dress in the traditional robes his mother wore, and if Amastan accepted his offer for her, she would have to embrace his beliefs and his practices. The women in her family had been accepted and loved for who they were, but it seemed that she didn't quite come up to the standards of the men interested in making her their life partner.

"My family has been well, and business is very good."

There was a *but* in his voice. Safia waited to see if he would disclose whatever worried him. Aabis was a man who believed men handled business. It would be rare for him to share anything with a woman, but she knew he was doing his best to entice her to accept his proposal, maybe enough to talk to her about things he might not normally discuss with her.

"Have you heard the news of the ships in the harbor? I thought it might be the talk here in the marketplace."

Safia shook her head, a sudden chill creeping down her spine. Inside her body, every cell, every fiber, tuned to Aabis and his every gesture, every expression. She listened to the tone of his voice, took in the exact way he worded his sentences.

"Three days ago, right before my fishing boats set out to sea, my captain discovered someone had sabotaged our vessel by drilling holes in it, a hundred of them, very small. If they hadn't been found before they put out to sea, the boat would have gone down, and we could have lost lives. I had them examine our other vessel, and it also had been tampered with. The holes were so well placed it was nearly impossible to see them. According to my men, it looked as if someone had come from under the water and done the damage."

Alarm spread through Safia. A hundred holes in each of Aabis' fishing boats? His rivals wouldn't do such a thing. They might be rivals, but they were still friends. This was the beginning of spreading dissent.

"I bought fish from my competitor, thinking it was possible they had been the one to sabotage my fishing boats."

Safia frowned and shook her head.

Aabis nodded. "I am afraid it did cross my mind. I talked it over with my father. He didn't agree. He thought it unlikely. Why now, after all this time? There has always been enough business to share."

The chill had turned to an icy freeze. Safia forced back the need to rush down to the harbor. Information was key. She was the defender. Aura had spoken of a gate she guarded, one she had hoped she could rely on Safia to help her with. She had worried that something was happening to it, and lately, there were thinning spots close to it that demons might be able to slip through. That gate was somewhere in the ruins near the harbor.

Safia felt guilty for falling asleep instead of insisting Aura tell her about the gate and what was behind it. She should already know the location of it.

"I think it natural to worry about every possibility when the people's lives you're responsible for are on the line, but I'm also grateful you concluded your friends weren't conspiring against you. We've been having problems at the farm," Safia disclosed. "Little things, but damaging. Amastan checked with the neighboring farms, and some of them have been having problems as well."

Aabis rubbed his jaw. "It is good he checked. Just today, Kadin Merabet, my friend who owns the fishing boats and sells most of the fish to the markets and other restaurants, had one of his vessels sink. Two more began to sink but in the harbor, so his crew was safe."

"Aabis," Amara whispered. "Was everyone rescued?"

"Two crew members drowned. Kadin blames himself. I had sent word to check his boats, and they had the day before and found nothing. They hadn't checked them this morning. He believes he should have ordered the captains to check them every morning."

There was a wealth of sadness in Aabis' voice. He was really a good man. Safia had never understood why she wasn't in the least attracted to him—and she wasn't. Petru had been the only man she had physically responded to, and that upset her even more now. She'd known Aabis nearly all her life. Seeing him so vulnerable when he was so strong made her feel as if she had failed her people. These were demons wreaking havoc, and she was the defender. She hadn't done her job, and two men had lost their lives. Aabis and his friend blamed themselves, when in reality, those deaths were on her.

"This is the way every war has started," Aabis stated. "Unrest, turning neighbor against neighbor. Did Amastan send an escort with you to ensure you reach home safely?"

"We are leaving the market early," Safia assured.

"Tell your grandfather that my parents and I will come by tomorrow for tea." He maintained eye contact with her, indicating he was once again serious about asking for her hand in marriage.

"You are always welcome to visit, Aabis, as are your parents. You know I am promised, and he has arrived to make his official claim." She managed to get the announcement out as casually as she could. She knew it would hurt him, even though he'd been told by her grandfather both times he'd come to the house asking to marry her.

Aabis stared at her for a long time, almost as if he didn't believe her. "Have I met him?"

"He comes from a different land." She was reluctant to admit it. Safia did her best to keep her expression as placid as possible. She didn't want Aabis to see her insecurities in the matter of her promised husband.

His eyebrow shot up, but he didn't respond to her comment. "I trust you will be home before sunset."

"Yes, thank you for your concern. I'll send for the others and ask them to close the stall early so we can leave." She wanted to go immediately. She needed to get her family home safely and then get down to the harbor to see if she could locate where the demons were slipping through. She had to close and seal those portals. As soon as Aabis left, she signaled to Amara to start closing the stall and texted Lunja and Farah to close so they could leave immediately.

Safia led Izem into the maze of caves through the small side entrance they used when no one was close to see them slip inside. She moved down the stone steps going steadily toward the harbor. Each stair brought her closer to the demons she knew she would have to face. It also took her farther from the man she knew she had let down.

She felt that distance. Strangely, when she didn't really know him, the feeling was gut-wrenching.

"I understand Petru came to see you last night," she ventured. What was the use in not asking her brother? She couldn't discipline her mind from turning to the Carpathian, and it was making her feel bad about herself. She needed confidence, not the mindset of failure, before going into battle with demons.

"Yes," Izem said, his voice noncommittal.

She sighed. "I've never been like the others, Izem. I never dreamt of being a wife with a family of my own. I wasn't attracted to the men who came around me. And I always knew I was found"—she paused, searching for the right word—"lacking," she finally said. "Even the ones making an offer for me always wanted to change me. I would never have had what you have with Amara. I wouldn't be loved for me."

"Safia, that isn't true."

"It is. I can see into people, the way they look at me, and it's very clear to me, and really, it's all right. There's never been a man I wanted to be with." She hesitated. "If Petru doesn't want me, Izem, it is better I know it now than having to worry about it while I am fighting demons. I need to be able to concentrate wholly on what I am doing. He was disappointed in the way I fought the vampire. I could tell he thought I was inadequate, not fit to be his partner. If he withdrew his claim on me, please tell me. Don't wait for *Baba* or *Jeddi* to tell me. It might be a blow to my pride, but you know I was unconvinced it was going to be a good match."

Instinctively, she knew it was going to be more than a blow to her pride. It was going to hurt; she just didn't understand why. She didn't want to go off with him to a foreign land. She wasn't even certain she liked him. She was physically attracted. That was the first time in her life she'd ever had butterflies around a man. The first time her body had responded. That was as much as she would admit to herself. She'd wanted to explore that. And she wanted him to respect her.

"Safia, stop for a moment." Izem laid a hand on her shoulder.

She didn't want to face him. She had discipline, tons of it, but for some reason, when she thought of Petru, tears burned behind her eyes. She felt shame that she hadn't done better fighting the vampire. Shame that she wasn't good enough for the man. She told herself it was because she represented her people, but she knew it was more than that. She just didn't know why she wanted Petru to look at her—to see her. To think she was special.

She took a deep, steadying breath and turned to face her older brother, forcing her gaze to meet his.

He frowned at her, but his expression, his eyes, were gentle as only Izem's could be. "Petru Cioban has no intention of giving up his claim on you. He made that very clear to *Baba* and to me."

Safia had prepared herself for Izem to let her down gently, to tell her that Petru didn't want her after all. For a moment, she could barely process what he was saying. Then she didn't know what to feel. Elated? Scared?

She touched her tongue to suddenly dry lips. "What did he talk to you about? He had been very attentive, and suddenly, he withdrew. He left me completely alone with *Jeddi* in the cave of the ancestors. He said he was patrolling, familiarizing himself with the area."

Izem nodded. "He has to know the battlefield, Safia."

That was true. "What did he want to talk to you and *Baba* about?" she persisted.

"He explained that there were some things that he had no choice about, that he had to do to keep everyone safe. He had to claim you immediately. He regretted not being able to give you time to get to know him, especially since you were not told of him until recently. He wanted to know our ways. To learn the things that mattered to you. He asked if we would guide him to be a better husband to you and make the transition easier for you."

Heat blossomed low in her stomach. "He did?" She couldn't imagine a man as strong and powerful as Petru humbling himself to ask for help and guidance from her father and brother just to make her passage into his life easier. He seemed . . . omnipotent. As if he wouldn't notice lesser mortals and their struggles, although why she thought that after the way he'd healed her wounds, she didn't know. Her own insecurities?

"He did. He said he wasn't used to talking with others so much. He was a hunter of the vampire and spent most of his time alone. He didn't think he knew the things a woman would like, and he felt he had already hurt you with careless words. He didn't want to make that mistake again."

"He said that?" she whispered, her fingers stroking over the pulse in her neck where it suddenly burned, sending fiery licks of heat through her body.

"He did. There was no doubt he was sincere. He had a strange method of obtaining the information. I wasn't certain I was comfortable with it at first, but he took his time explaining that it was the way his people communicated during a battle and the way they shared information."

"Blood."

He nodded. "Although he said if we were uncomfortable with giving and receiving a small amount of blood, he could read what we were willing to share with him."

"Did it bother you to give him blood?"

Izem shook his head. "I don't know why, but it seemed natural. I don't remember him giving us blood if he did. But he could speak in our minds after that."

That did make Safia feel a little less special. The entire ritual had felt intimate between Petru and her. The way he spoke in her mind had been almost sensual, as if it had been for her alone. Knowing he did the same with her father and brother, preparing them for war, let her know she had misread what Petru had been doing.

Color swept up her face. Had he known her thoughts? Had she given herself away? Probably. He seemed to be able to read what was inside one's mind. She immediately became determined to strengthen the barrier in her mind. She didn't need him to read every little thought she had about him.

She turned back to the path determinedly. "We'd better hurry. If I'm right about what is attacking the fishing boats, I need to find where they're slipping through and consecrate the ground so they can't return to the underworld and no others can come through, and then go after the ones that are here."

"You have an idea where the demons might be getting through?"

"Aura told me of a place close to the harbor but very deep. She said there is a gate she guards. Lately she's been worried that there were places thinning in the ground. She feared something might slip through. I was going to come with her tonight to check it out."

"But you don't know exactly where it is?"

"She left a map in my mind. She does that sometimes. It isn't the easiest to follow because the caves have quite a few twists and turns, but I think I'll feel the way." She knew she could. If she was close to demons or anywhere they had traveled, her body reacted like a tuning fork. Already she could feel a pull to the left, and when she rounded a slight bend, there was a fork. She took the left tunnel that dropped steeply downward.

She not only smelled the sea but the foul stench of the demons. She had a bad feeling she knew exactly what had made those small precise holes in the decks of the ships. If she was correct, they were lucky the demons hadn't taken the ships down, crushing them, because they were certainly capable of it. They could grow to the size of a whale if they were in the water long enough.

She didn't tell Izem what she feared. There was no sense in having him worry until she knew for certain what they were dealing with. She hurried through the narrow dripping tunnel. It was damp and unpleasant, mud on the walls and overhead. The rock floor was slippery. She was sure-footed, every step placed with care, the defender in her taking over.

The tunnel opened into a grotto overlooking the harbor. The grotto turned abruptly at a right angle, narrowing in that direction. The pull on her body was just as strong as the foul stench. She set her dive pack down carefully and removed her crystal sword from her long coat. Before she turned toward the dark shadows harboring evil, she stepped to the edge of the grotto to look down at the sea.

The water in the harbor glistened like glass on the surface, the colors turquoise and deep blue mixed with purples and sapphire. In places where the sun shone directly on the water, Safia could see all the way to the brightly colored rocks on the bottom. Despite the time of day, people were swimming in close near the little lagoon a circle of rocks created. Most of the fishing boats were anchored or in the slips out of respect for Kadin Merabet's deceased crew members.

The tourists had no idea of what had occurred, and no one shared the bad news. They wanted the tourists to come and spend their money at the various shops and restaurants. It kept their city thriving. Little by little they had established tours. Found beautiful locations that would interest outsiders. By working with each other, they had thrived. The last thing they wanted to do was drive everyone away with fear.

Safia glanced up at the sun. She needed to seal the ground and get into the water before the demons had aid from vampires. She had no idea how many vampires were in the vicinity, but she wasn't yet adept at dealing with them. She spun on her heel and walked straight back into the darkness. At once, her crystal sword glowed a bright amber, gleaming off the walls and ceiling and lighting up the floor like a beacon.

Farther down, she could see the edge of a thick gate made of ancient wood. She didn't have time to examine it. She could see the thin places in the mud where something had punched through and dirt had trickled back into the hole. There was only one open hole, but two other places were thin enough that, given time, the same thing could happen. She had no idea how many of the creatures had slipped through. Hopefully only two or three. If Aabis' fishing vessels had been attacked three days earlier, that gave the demons that many days to grow larger. She released the droplets of sacred water as she spun, creating a turbulent storm so that the water became a cyclone, wind howling through the small chamber, pushing the rain so that it fell chaotically in every direction from the ceiling, bouncing off the walls, to flood the floor.

The water began to form a pool, whirling around and pouring down the hole that had been opened between the two realms. The hole glowed with an orange-red flame, and then it abruptly went black, leaving only the amber crystal glowing.

Safia plunged the blade into the ground. Immediately, the earth rolled under her feet. She didn't so much as sway. She sealed the portal, closing off all ability to use the ground to any caught above. They could not reenter. Any below could not use the portal to come above ground. No more could whatever form the demon had been given be sent above ground. She was careful to ensure that weapon would no longer be in the army of the underground.

When she was certain she had sealed every possible entry, she returned to her brother and her diving gear. To her dismay, Izem was already changed.

"Izem," she began.

"We spoke of this already, Safia. I will not allow you to go alone. You are the defender, and I will follow your lead, but you will not go into the sea without me."

She narrowed her eyes suspiciously. "Is this *his* decree?"

"You are my sister," he answered. "If we are to do this before the sun sets, we must hurry." He gestured for her to put on her diving gear.

Safia was absolutely certain Petru had insisted her brother go with her if she had to hunt and destroy demons. Not insisted. He would do more than insist. Petru was the type of man who would command. He was a dictator. Why had she thought sweet things about him? Why had she secretly harbored romantic fantasies about him? Because he was the most sensual man she'd ever met in her life. She'd been captivated by him. He was intelligent. Worldly. Okay, sexy. His voice. The touch of his fingers on her skin. But he was a dictator, and she wasn't having any of that. She never had and she never would.

She glared at her brother, slid her equipment into her bag, anchored it to her waist and indicated for him to do the same.

"We're going to be facing the worst kind of nightmare, Izem. I'm sure this is a sea centipede." She delivered the bad news in a matter-of-fact voice. "If you're going with me, we might as well come up with a plan."

8

A man could have every noble intention in the world and then end up with a lifemate such as Petru had. He didn't need to fight armies of vampires to find himself in a grave. Safia Meziane was going to do that all by herself. The moment the sun sank from the sky and he was released from the paralysis of his kind, he burst from the ground, taking to the air, streaking toward the harbor.

He had awakened knowing she had once again placed herself in harm's way. Not just harm's way; the woman was maddening. It was going to be a full-time job just keeping her alive. Knowing he had a lifemate was one thing; being obsessed with her was another. The little he'd shared her mind, he'd learned a great deal about her in a short amount of time.

He found her intriguing and courageous. She was giving and compassionate. Emotional. She practically ran on emotion. She was everything he was not. He was a man with no emotion—until it came to her. She brought out the worst in him. Or maybe the best. Perhaps a combination of both. He only knew the world was better with her in it, and if it was going to be a safe place, she had to stay alive. If he lost her . . . well, that wasn't even going to be considered.

What was she doing right now? Going after the Algerian sea serpent. Naturally, his woman wouldn't think twice about diving into the harbor and confronting the demon of the sea. The centipede-like crab could grow to the size of a whale, given time, and was amphibious. The pincers were lethal. It could crush ships once it reached its full size. The fins ran from head to tail and could propel the creature at great speeds. Those fins were legs when on land, so the crab could run at an astonishing rate as well. More, the teeth inside that round mouth were jagged and dripping with venom. It was a nasty demon any way one looked at it. The last thing Petru wanted was for Safia to be anywhere near it.

Petru knew his woman hadn't hesitated, and she wouldn't again. She had been trained to fight demons no matter how dangerous or how many there were. He cursed in his language and signaled to his brethren as they took to the sky with him. They needed to feed. It would be bad enough that he was going to follow her without first feeding, but he wouldn't take a chance on losing her.

Is it possible that she knows what she's doing, Petru? Benedek asked.

She has been training for this since she was a babe, Nicu added. *Adalasia and Vasilisa both were demon slayers. I did not see you lose your mind when they sought to kill the creatures.*

They didn't understand that Safia was soft inside. All jasmine and honey. Not that he knew anything about jasmine and honey, but he imagined that was what she was like inside.

You have lost your mind, Tomas announced.

He has, Lojos agreed.

Go feed before you make an utter ass of yourself, Mataias added.

I never thought I would see the day when Petru Cioban would be besotted by a woman, Benedek crowed.

It is impossible for me to be besotted. I have no feelings. No emotions. No heart or soul, Petru denied. *It is my duty to look after her. She is my lifemate and I betrayed her once. I cannot do so again.*

Perhaps his brethren were correct, and he needed to feed before he plunged into the harbor and took on the sea centipede, interfering with Safia's position as the defender. He should at least be a silent watcher in the background, waiting to see what skills she possessed before he interfered. The last thing he wanted was to make her think he didn't believe she could slay a demon.

He groaned, continuing toward the harbor, already slipping carefully into Safia's mind. He had to use a delicate touch. If she was fighting off the demon, he couldn't distract her, but he couldn't waste one more moment wondering if she was hurt or about to be. He wasn't about to leave his lifemate unguarded. He didn't care how well trained she was or if his brethren thought he was out of his mind. She was his woman, and his code of honor demanded he protect her.

She moved through the water without a sound, and she didn't seem to displace the water itself. There was a slight ripple as waves moved with the breeze stirring on the surface. Fortunately, the draft was moving in the direction she wanted to go, so as the current gently carried the water, it carried her along as well. She swam fast, propelling herself with speed, like a little rocket, and still she seemed a part of that underwater current.

Petru found a little spot in her mind to adhere to as he slipped beneath the water right behind her. Izem followed her, but there was no way for him to see Petru when the ancient Carpathian didn't want to be seen or felt. He was a phantom, as were his companions.

Tomas and Lojos had broken off from the rest of them and gone to feed. The two had been given the task to take enough blood to share with the others if it became necessary after the battle with the sea centipede. They might give Petru all kinds of advice, but they would follow him into the deepest recesses of the underworld, face the worst of the master vampires, and never, under any circumstances, leave his lifemate unprotected.

Like Petru, they were little more than molecules in the water, impossible to detect. They weren't in Safia's mind, but they had taken care to stay close to her brother, aware of the two sea centipedes swimming against the current on the surface of the water, heading his way. Unlike Safia, who hid her presence, Izem wasn't as adept in the water.

Petru was very aware of Izem drawing the two demons closer to his lifemate. It wasn't that her brother was clumsy; he swam with great proficiency. He moved like he was part of the sea, but he still disturbed the water, alerting the creatures to his presence. Petru stayed very still in her mind as she processed calculations so fast. Her brain was fascinating, never resting.

Someone named Aabis had his ships sabotaged three days earlier. She was determining how large the first demon to come through had been able to grow in three days' time. The ones coming through the second day, if any—which she doubted, as no fishing boats had been harmed—and any that might have come through this day. The small holes cut in the fishing boats indicated to her that at least two of the demons had come through that morning and cut the circles in the vessels with their claws, not only to do mischief but to sharpen them.

As the information raced through her mind, Petru realized she knew her brother would draw the sea centipedes to them. She counted on it. She had a plan, and Izem was fully aware of it. He was the bait just as if he were a fish on a hook. Petru touched her brother's mind. The man was just as cool as she was. He seemed to have complete faith in his sister.

There was so much to admire about these people. Petru had stayed away from humans for the better part of his life. He hunted vampires. Lately, demons had been added to the evil he destroyed. He was often the general running the war, but he was direct when he killed. He'd been alive far too long, far beyond even what was considered ancient for his kind. There was danger in living so long. Making kills long after there was nothing at all, not even the whisper of temptation to take a life while feeding just to feel a rush.

The rush came now with every battle he participated in. A kind of euphoria. A berserker's ice turning to blue flames that raced through veins and burned in the belly. Feeling. Something. Those smoldering flames left behind scars that were permanent in their souls. In their hearts and minds. They weren't the tatters a lifemate could mend. These were scars so deep inside, never meant to be. Rough, blackened and developed over time with battle after battle and kill after kill until they knew it was far too dangerous to even keep hunting vampires.

In an effort to keep their code of honor for their lifemates, the ancients—Petru included—had retreated behind monastery walls for over two hundred years. In other words, Petru had lived far longer than he should have. The danger to those around him, even his brethren, was extremely high should he give in and lose what remained of his soul. He had more need of his lifemate than most.

Safia. She was right there, and the compulsion to claim her was overwhelming. Being in her mind and seeing her in action, no matter the distance he put between them, drew him to her more. He had come to Algeria knowing he would make his claim on her, as all lifemates did. But because he could so easily shut down emotion, it hadn't occurred to him that his need of her would turn into an obsessive hunger, and the desire to protect her would be so acute, it would remove all good sense from him.

She was slowing just a little, veering to her right, making the decision to go after the first sea centipede. It was a bit faster and smaller than its partner, angling its long body toward Izem's right side, the crablike pincers extended in front of it. The demon had already grown significantly. The sea centipede wasn't yet the size of a whale, but certainly it was a good ten feet long and thicker than a shark.

Benedek inserted his body between the fast-swimming creature and Izem, while Mataias protected his left side.

Safia has a plan, Petru forced himself to advise them. *She is the demon expert here. Mataias, keep watch for the other one. We are going to allow her to show us how she kills this thing. I have never seen one before. Nicu, have you?*

Nicu could reach any animal form and connect with them. When he was with them, it was a rarity for creatures to attack them.

No, these are new to me as well. I have tried to reach them, but their brains have been tampered with. They are demons, not real fish. There was a pause. *That is not exactly correct, either. At one time, they belonged to the sea, but they were mutated and twisted into something else, something very evil.*

Petru stayed quite still in Safia's mind, hidden but examining every brilliant strategy speeding through. Her serenity amazed him. She held that calm tranquility even as her brain worked at warp speed. Her body seemed to be tuned, like a radar system, sending signals into the water and getting so many back, all feeding her necessary information, much like the bats in the air or the whiskers on the large cats in the jungle.

Nicu hadn't been able to connect with the sea centipede, but Safia slid easily into the brain of the mutated creature. First, she matched a pulsing, disjointed rhythm that felt like a drumming off-beat heart. Petru found it disturbing. The sound resonated through his nonexistent body, producing a pain in the region of his heart.

That sent an alarm shooting through him. He had no physical body to worry about, but Safia did. If the demon produced a sound affecting him with potential consequences, what would it do to her, particularly underwater? Examining her mind, he could find no change. There was no alarm, no thought of abandoning her mission. Only that calm serenity. Tranquility. Her heartbeat remained steady, although very faint. Nearly soundless.

Petru forced down all emotions. He was an ancient and extremely disciplined. He'd managed to push color from his vision unless he was looking directly at his lifemate. He had to do the same with emotions. As far as he could see, feelings were useless and hindered men greatly. He turned his complete attention back to his lifemate and how she planned to destroy the demon swimming straight toward her brother.

She matched the disjointed waves in the chaotic brain of the demon. Agonizing pain shot through her and was cut off in much the same manner that a Carpathian hunter shut down pain. He found that fascinating. Safia eventually would have been able to overcome the wounds the vampire had inflicted on her once she managed to overcome the trauma of the attack. The first time was always shocking. The blood loss had been severe.

Safia's training had been extensive in demon hunting. She took each separate step in stride and was methodical about it. Exploring the mutation came at an excessive speed. She learned where the weak points were. Where the venom was stored and how it was delivered. The pressure the pincers could inflict and the bite that could be delivered via the jaws. She had the information from her studies, but she confirmed it quickly and filled in every unknown fact. All her studying of the creature took place in seconds. She was that fast.

The sea centipede drew closer. The body glided, propelled by the multitude of fins dipping fast in the water, the crablike claws open and the beady eyes fixed on Izem.

Safia shot straight between her brother and the centipede, the crystal sword in her hands, the light not in the least diffused beneath the water. If anything, it was more brilliant than ever. The streak of light broke apart, dividing into two streams of white-hot then bluish flame, simultaneously piercing both eyes of the creature. It lifted its head, the cavernous mouth opening in a silent scream as it lunged forward toward Safia. The deadly claws snapped in the water, surrounding her as if they were trying to hug her.

Petru's heart was in his throat. It was all he could do not to throw a shield around his lifemate, but he managed. This was who she was. He had to allow her to be who she was and accept her for it if he expected the same in return. What he would be asking of her—no, demanding of her—was not going to be easy. She would be giving him far more than he would ever be giving her. He was uncertain he even had much left in the way of a heart or soul to give her. Just his protection and a promise that he would do everything in his power to make her happy.

In the grand scheme of things, that didn't seem a fair trade to him, but he didn't know much in the ways of women. This one . . . She was magnificent. Unflinching. Moving with the streaming light from her crystal sword, now twin blue-hot flames sliding into the open mouth and pouring down the throat of the centipede, she drew even closer.

The creature's armored skin began to glow a bluish color from the inside out. Blackened holes began to break through. The sea centipede thrashed, churning up the water all around it. Safia dropped beneath the hapless demon, running the crystal sword straight along the length of its belly. All the while, Petru could hear a soft chanting, her voice in her mind, speaking not just to herself but also into the mind of the creature.

The Carpathian hunter realized her brother had continued swimming straight ahead as if nothing were happening. Safia had intercepted the first sea centipede and taken it off course, away from Izem. He was still the bait for the second demon. When Petru touched his mind, Izem had that same tranquility he had earlier. He believed his sister would be there in time before the sea centipede reached him. It seemed an impossibility, but Petru was no longer going to think anything was impossible for his lifemate.

In the time it had taken for Petru to observe that the sea centipede was breaking apart and dissolving, Safia was gliding through the water at an unbelievable speed, on course to intercept the second creature closing in on Izem.

She kept the crystal sword in her hand, but the bright light was off. Her mind tuned itself to the creature's. Now that she knew the way and what to expect, she was ready, slipping into the mutated brain to start veering it off course slowly. She took care not to alert it that she was directing the demon away from her brother.

Nicu, do you see what she is doing? She has taken command of the sea centipede. She has actually stolen control from its mistress. He had known she was inside the brain of the creature, but he had been so caught up in how she destroyed the demon that he wasn't aware she controlled its actions.

Lilith will not be happy with this one, Nicu said. *She is a vindictive, cruel woman.*

Lilith is the one who directed the first war here. When I struck at her, she ordered the vampire to rip out the heart of the child and make it as painful and as memorable as possible. She wanted me to feel that pain just as Safia felt it. She also wanted Safia to always remember that her people and the Carpathian people and, most of all, her lifemate chose life over her. That she was tossed aside as fodder for the vampire, the sacrificial lamb, so they could live.

How was it possible to feel her pain, Petru? You were incapable, and you were not bound to her, Benedek reminded.

Petru allowed the darker memories to overtake him, remembering the moment when Eduardo, the master vampire, had sunk his teeth into the child, deliberately hurting her, terrifying her, as he took her blood. The little girl had remained stoic, refusing to cry out. Then he held her up so Petru could see, so everyone in the valley could see. Her grandparents, her parents. His parents, her little friends. Humans and Carpathians alike. All stared, transfixed by the sight of that little girl and the master vampire. Only Petru was in motion, streaking toward the two, knowing he was too late.

At every turn, he was surrounded by the master vampire's pawns. Eduardo had newly made vampires and far more skilled fighters. There were some close to becoming master vampires. All of them flew at Petru to prevent him from getting near their master and the little girl he held.

Petru didn't care who was in his way or what wounds they inflicted on his body. Nothing mattered but getting to the child. He mowed everyone down who dared to get between them. He barely noticed the damage to his torn flesh. Eduardo laughed hideously, the sound taunting as he tore into the child's chest. Petru was merged with her, and for that one moment, he felt the horrific pain. Then suddenly it was gone.

The truth came to him. *The child. She connected with me. She held the connection all along between us. Just like she does now with the animals. She touched my mind and I felt what she did. We shared information. That was how I knew she was my lifemate even though she was so young. She held the connection,* he told his brethren.

The revelation shouldn't have surprised him, but it did. The child had been no more than five, yet she'd been so powerful even then.

As the vampire ripped out her heart, I wanted to stay with her, shoulder the pain, comfort her, but she broke the connection, refused to let me share it. I couldn't even give her that. I fought my way to her, but I was too late. I hunted Eduardo and slaughtered his army, but that didn't bring her back or comfort her in any way. She was already gone and couldn't know what I did for her.

Lilith will try for her again and again, Benedek warned. *She will never forget that you bested her. It matters little how many years have passed. And the fact that Safia has wrested her demons from her will make her furious. She will do everything she can to make her suffer and then kill her.*

From his past encounters with Lilith, Petru knew Benedek was right. The woman was mad. She was determined to rule the underworld as well as those above it. She wanted to best her mate. Mostly he looked on her and her antics with amusement and did little to rein her in, so she became more and more bold. Petru was grateful he had forgotten about her until those memories had been triggered by an unknown event.

Now he watched as Safia put herself in harm's way a second time, bringing the sea centipede to her and repeating the same ritual of destroying the creature. This adversary was slightly larger, and Petru could see Safia was tiring. That didn't make her movements any less graceful or self-assured. It did take her longer to dispatch the demon, but the sea had grown rougher as the wind picked up.

Petru eased the rough waters around her, doing what he could to help her without interfering. The moment the sea centipede was dispatched, Safia swam to her brother and the pair surfaced slowly. She scanned quickly.

"The sun is already gone, Izem. You must get out of the water. There's still the giant one left. I was able to read the others, and it was just the three of them. I closed off the portal and she can't send any others. But you're exhausted, and the tanks are almost out of air. I'm tired. The water is getting rough, and with the sun already down, we don't know if the vampires will come out. I can't watch over you. You can't argue, it's just wasting time."

Izem glanced back toward the harbor. It was a distance away. "You can't face that thing alone, Safia. You're too tired. Wait for tomorrow."

"It will continue to grow. If it comes on land, we don't know how much damage it will do. Just go, Izem. Let me get this done."

Petru was in her mind, and for the first time, he saw that she was uncertain of how she was going to defeat the gigantic demon. She was resolved, just not sure how. Very slowly, so as not to frighten her, he allowed himself to shimmer into her sight.

"*Ku Tappa Kulyak*, perhaps my brethren and I can be of some assistance to you. Mataias will help Izem to shore and wait with him while Benedek, Nicu and I will do as you order. We can build the illusion of a ship, and you can lead the demon farther out to sea, away from people. That way, no one will have the chance to be harmed."

Petru drank in the sight of her. Her hair was sleek, shiny and dark from the water. It hung thick and long down her back. The moon seemed to spotlight her beauty, the oval of her face with her dark lashes framing her large, jeweled eyes. It was impossible to keep from looking at her full lips and not imagine kissing her, which was a little shocking to him. He didn't have thoughts like that, not in the middle of a crisis.

Safia wore a royal blue one-piece bathing suit that hugged her figure like a second skin. Petru had dulled the brightness of colors to keep from hurting his eyes, but even with keeping them blurred, it was impossible to stop the vivid beauty of her from nearly blinding him. She shone like the brightest star. More, she had a natural sensuality in every line of her body that appealed to him.

There was no way to stop himself from putting his hands on her hips to hold her steady in the rough water. The moment his palms settled around her and his fingers pressed into the contours of her feminine shape, his body reacted. Discipline was gone. Unexpected fire swept through his veins every bit as hot as the blue flames in her crystal sword. Her green gaze jumped to his, confusion mixed with reluctant desire.

"Have you been here all along?" Her gaze didn't leave his.

He realized he had to be very careful. "Yes, we have no knowledge of these demons or how to best fight them. You are the expert, and we thought it best to learn from you. We did not give away our presence for fear of distracting you." He hoped it didn't occur to her that he could just pull the knowledge from her mind the way he did from everyone else around him.

Benedek and Nicu both made some disparaging sound in his mind, which could have been a snicker on their private ancient path established in the monastery.

Petru thought it best to ignore the brethren and concentrate on his lifemate. Evidently, he'd given her the best answer possible. Her eyes lit up briefly despite the wariness she was exhibiting.

"I think it best, Safia, if we allow Petru and these men to help," Izem said. "I have little air in reserve, and if the last sea centipede is a giant, you'll need to rest and regain your strength before you take on that large of an opponent."

Carpathian males never allowed interference when it came to their lifemates, but Petru had gone to Safia's father and oldest brother to ask for their advice. He was aware he knew nothing of relationships or humans. He had hurt her feelings once already through careless words. He knew she felt less than confident around him, even though those emotions were buried deep. He knew the vampire had planted those seeds in the child for Lilith. Now he kept quiet and was grateful for Izem taking control.

"But Izem . . ." Safia gave a halfhearted protest.

Izem gave her a stern look. "I don't wish to argue over this. I will wait with Mataias for you. Rest on the boat while the demon is led farther from the harbor. Gain strength and then destroy it. Hopefully vampires stay away this night." He leaned over, gripped his sister's forearms and then looked at Petru. "I leave her in your care."

As if he were the one protecting his sister, Benedek said.

He didn't leave her, Petru pointed out. *There is true honor and courage in these people.*

That is so, Nicu agreed. *And loyalty. He would have slit that demon's belly if Safia had been in trouble. He would never have left her behind, even if he knew it meant his death.*

Lojos and Tomas have returned, Mataias announced. *Lojos will assure the safety of Izem. I will seek blood and Tomas will go to aid you, Petru, to free Nicu to feed.*

It was a good plan. Without further explanation, Mataias plucked Izem out of the sea and took him toward the shore. Safia gasped, her body jerking, and Petru drew her closer to him. She didn't need her brother for comfort or protection, not when she had him.

"Will the demon go after a fishing vessel rather than a yacht?" he asked to distract her. "We can create the illusion of either."

"I think a fishing vessel."

She was trembling. Whether from cold or fear, he didn't know. He wrapped his arms around her, stripping her of her tank as he took them from the water and built the illusion of the fishing vessel beneath them. Once on board in the cabin, he wrapped her in blankets, sinking into a plush chair, but keeping her on his lap.

"What are you doing?"

Her voice was a whisper, but she'd turned her face up toward him, and her breath was warm on his bare throat.

"You don't seem to realize it, Safia, but you're very cold. Your skin is like ice." He began to rub her right arm gently between his hands. "You expended a tremendous amount of energy destroying the demons. Physically, anytime you use that much energy, it takes a toll on your body."

She relaxed a little more against him. "The sea, swimming and concentrating adds to it as well. I have a couple of energy bars in my pack. I need to drink water. I'm dehydrated."

He handed her the water and watched her drink it. "I must give you more blood, Safia. That's the most efficient way to give you strength. At the same time, it will be our second exchange."

She frowned at him, pulling back to meet his eyes. "I needed blood before because of my wounds. I don't need it now. I can eat my energy bars."

"It isn't the same thing." Petru tried to be patient and explain. She deserved an explanation. "Just as there are certain rituals you have in your world, there are certain ones in mine. They must be adhered to. The blood exchange is one of them. In this case, it will benefit you and make you stronger and faster when you fight demons." He kept his voice even, refusing the temptation to use compulsion.

She was silent, studying his expression while he switched to her left arm, gently massaging to warm her up. Her lashes were incredibly long. He was very glad he'd wrapped her in a blanket because just touching her silky skin and inhaling her scent was wreaking havoc on his discipline.

"Are you going against your tradition by sharing this information with me rather than just forcing your will on me?"

"Lifemates do not lie to one another. Not ever. If you ask me a question, Safia, be certain you want to know the answer. I do not wish for you to fear me."

She again was silent, studying his expression. He knew she wouldn't be able to read much there. He didn't telegraph emotion because he didn't feel emotion—unless it concerned her, and he was just beginning to sort through those confused feelings, so he'd shoved them down and just allowed the physical to rise to the surface. If he was honest with himself, he had no choice in that matter. Looking at her brought his body to life. Touching her turned him into pure hunger, a roaring fire of need.

"I think it best if you explain things to me, since no one else has."

He would give her the short version, be as matter of fact and casual as he could. "Carpathian women grow up knowing they hold the other half of a man's soul. They know that one day that man will find them, and the two will unite. The binding words are imprinted on the man before he is born. It is our marriage ritual. Once said to his woman, they cannot be taken back. Those words weave the two halves of the soul back together, and she becomes his wedded wife. Blood, in our world, is life. Between the man and woman, the exchange is . . . erotic. She gives him blood should he need it if he is wounded. He gives it to her for the same reason, or if she needs to be fed and cannot find food for herself."

Her green gaze hadn't left his for a moment. Twice, her long lashes had swept down and then back up while he gave her that explanation. Each time, his stomach muscles had clenched, and his cock had jerked hard in reaction. She couldn't fail to notice, not with her rounded bottom sitting on his lap. It mattered little that the blanket separated them. She didn't pull away, but faint color had slipped under her skin.

Safia moistened her lips. "I'm not Carpathian."

He switched his hold from her arm to the nape of her neck, massaging with his long fingers. "No, you aren't. There are times when a special woman outside the Carpathian species is born with the other half of a Carpathian male's soul, as you were. When that happens, he must find her and bind her to him. I have searched for you for two thousand years. There are stains on my soul that even you cannot remove. I kept to the code of honor. I etched it into my skin so I would never betray you. I stayed alive and continued far past the time I should have left this world but knew I had to find you."

One arm slipped out from under the blanket, and she traced his jaw with the pads of her fingers. It felt as though a butterfly skimmed along the golden shadow that never quite left his skin, even when he commanded a clean shave.

"Tell me about why, when I am not Carpathian, I must share blood."

She wasn't objecting. He was in her mind, and she was struggling to understand. She had accepted that she was his lifemate. The biggest part of her feared him, but she was willing to learn his ways. She hoped for the best between them. She was attracted to him, and that was a big part of the battle. She wanted time to get to know him. Petru wanted that for her, but it was the one thing they didn't have.

"It is one of the most important rituals we have." He shook his head. "It isn't just a ritual. As I said, should I be wounded while battling a vampire, for you to save my life, you would have to be able to feed me. I require blood to survive. At times, it would be a great deal of blood. You would have to be able to take blood from someone else to provide for me."

He stayed in her mind, prepared for her to be horrified and repulsed. She was not. She absorbed what he told her quickly, the way she did all information. It made sense to her.

"It will take a little time to get over my inhibitions, but I can see, especially now, when we are surely going to war, that I should be able to provide you with whatever you should need."

"I can shield you completely or distance you from the taking and receiving of blood at first so you can slowly get used to it." Petru made the offer as gently as possible.

A hint of amusement lit up her eyes, turning the jade into a mysterious shade of emerald. Her dark lashes swept down, showing the incredible length and curl, and then she was looking at him solemnly. "I think it best if I know what is going on. I'm quite unexpectedly attracted to you. If I were unaware of what I was doing and I found this practice . . . um . . . erotic, it is possible I could take advantage of you."

Her lashes swept down and back up again, two thick fans giving the impression of innocent demureness when she was teasing him.

Another first for him. He liked that she was willing to try with him. Even admit she was attracted to him physically.

He did his best to appear stoic and yet give her the impression of amusement, so she knew he was entering into their game together. "I can see how that would be a problem, especially since you are scandalously without proper attire now, and I am equally if not more attracted to you."

"It's good to know I'm not alone. It's unfamiliar territory for me," she admitted. "I haven't been exactly wild when it comes to men."

He caught a note in her voice that gave him pause. She was conveying something important to him, something that she worried and feared he wouldn't like about her.

"I would be disappointed if you were wild about other men. I have never been wild about other women. In fact, *Ku Tappa Kulyak*, I have never noticed other women. My oath to you is carved into my back. When our soul is one, I will show it to you."

Again, her smile came slow, but when it reached her eyes, it changed the jade into that beautiful jeweled color that sent heat pounding through him. A strange roaring, like the heavy rush of the tide, rolled in his ears.

"I think it best if we get on with it," he murmured, finally, *finally*, giving in to the temptation to slide his lips just once over her silky hair.

He had long since dried her to make her more comfortable. Safia hadn't appeared to notice. The pads of her fingers stroking on his jaw were driving him beyond the brink of all rational thought. He was growing desperate for her and had to do something before his brain completely short-circuited.

P etru shifted Safia in his arms, allowing the blanket to pool at her waist. Without material covering her feminine form, the firm muscles played beneath the satin skin, showing the definition easily.

I had no idea a woman could be so beautiful. I noticed your beauty be-fore, when I held you after the vampire had attacked you.

She shook her head, her eyes on his. *I was a horrible mess.*

You were beautiful then and you are now.

He ran his palm down her arm again and then locked his fingers with hers to bring her hand to his mouth. *I do not think I have ever felt anything softer than your skin. Carpathians do not dream, yet I dreamt of you.*

Speaking telepathically with Safia was shockingly intimate. That was unexpected as well. He'd been communicating that way with his brethren for hundreds of years and never once had it felt anything but normal and mundane. Being so close to Safia, breathing in her scent, touching her skin, was dangerous to both of them.

Her fingers smoothed back his hair. *What did you dream?*

My dreams are not fit for your ears, sívamet. Not yet. I will tell them to you when we are bound together properly.

Faint color stole up her neck and into her cheeks. Her jeweled gaze drifted slowly over his face as if committing every detail to memory.

Ku Tappa Kulyak, you must stop looking at me like that.

His thumb of its own accord slid over her tempting lower lip. A knot the size of his fist suddenly developed low in his belly, and his blood began to run very hot, rushing to pool wickedly in his groin.

How am I looking at you?

Her tone was sultry, brushing over his skin like the touch of her fingers on his jaw, producing that same butterfly effect. The knot in his belly grew larger, pushing deeper. She was lethal. Dangerously lethal.

That I belong to you, and you like what you see.

That little smile of hers caused the intriguing dimple to appear on the side of her mouth, a sensual enticement that drew him like a magnet. He bent his head to hers and traced the little indentation with his tongue. A shiver went through her body and goose bumps broke out.

If you are claiming me and the lifemate thing is real, then you do belong to me. I already told you, I very much like what I see.

Once again, her fingers brushed him, this time in his hair, sending flames flickering through his scalp, her touch sinking deep into his skull and making its way into his bloodstream. She was so honest with him, trying to connect. He saw the determination in her mind to meet at least halfway for him. She was courageous, his woman.

I assure you, the lifemate thing is very real. Can you not feel the pull between us? He kissed her chin. Waited for her answer.

Yes.

Did you think of me when I was away from you? Did you worry for my safety?

For the first time, she hesitated and looked down. He cupped her chin very gently, forcing her head back up. *That is what happens between lifemates. It becomes more and more difficult for us to be apart. It isn't something to be ashamed of. It is natural.*

I have always been independent.

He could see the confusion in her eyes. He kissed first one dark

eyebrow and then the other. *Do you think me less independent than you?*
I am a hunter of the vampire. I have been all over the world, yet I dreamt
of my lifemate. I woke early, before sunset, on my journey here to claim you,
restless and concerned for you, disturbed that we were apart and I hadn't
seen or claimed you yet.

She frowned as she absorbed the information he gave her, but then
she gave a little shake of her head. *That's true, but it isn't at the same*
time. You have a way of shutting down your emotions. You can stop yourself
from feeling. I can't do that.

He stroked a caress over her hair and then down her throat and
shoulder, needing to touch her. *You do, Safia. When you work, you are*
completely absorbed in what you are doing, and you block out emotion.

I do?

He found himself enamored with her frown. *Yes, you do.*

He leaned into her again, unable to stop himself. Very gently, he
cradled the back of her head in his palm. It fit so perfectly, as if she'd
been made just for him. He lowered his head, shaping his lips to her
frown, tracing the lower one with his tongue and then the upper one,
that full tempting bow. The lightest of pressure, barely tasting her, yet
the flavor of her filled him. Her lips were so soft. Very sweet. So *his.*

He felt the warmth of her breath like sunshine. Like moonlight.
He took his time. One breath after another. Savoring each moment,
feeling the loss of years, of separation, knowing the true miracle he
held in his arms. Each kiss, as gentle as he kept it, was more sensual than the last, sending flickering blue flames throughout his body.
Branding him with her. There was no getting her out of him. Not her
scent. Not her taste. Not the courage or soul of her. That wasn't enough.
He wanted her heart to belong to him.

A small moan escaped her, the sound resonating through his entire
body. He tugged gently at her lower lip with his teeth and then kissed
his way to her dimple. He claimed that as well, spending a moment
lavishing attention with his tongue before moving on to her chin and
then down to her throat.

Deliberately, he dragged the bristles on his jaw gently along her skin, bringing alive nerve endings, keeping her acutely aware of him. He kissed his way down the fragile line of her throat to her vulnerable neck and the pulse throbbing out of control there. Wild—for him. He ached for her. *Hungered.*

I heard that.

He did hunger for her. His hands soothed her while his strong teeth nipped and teased over her pulse, making her gasp. He scraped back and forth.

I could spend hours devouring you. I am already addicted to your taste. He paused for a moment, barely lifting his head. Letting her feel the heat of his breath against her skin. Against her pulse. *Do you remember what I taste like?*

His voice, even in her mind, was a temptation to sin. To remember the erotic taste of him. The one that was meant only for her.

Safia's bottom ground down on his hard cock while her legs shifted restlessly, and another helpless moan escaped her throat. She seemed boneless, her head tilting back against his shoulder and her body leaning into the support of his arm.

Yes, she whispered.

He took great pleasure in using his hands to slide the straps of her bathing suit from her shoulders. His knuckles were rough against the smooth satin of her skin. She inhaled raggedly but didn't protest when he dragged the suit from her breasts, letting it fall to her waist, revealing the rounded globes with the dusky nipples rising and falling in rhythm to her breathing.

So incredibly beautiful.

I think you're seducing me.

It didn't sound like a protest to him.

No, sívamet, you are seducing me. It was the truth. He couldn't look at her or touch her without wanting more.

He indulged himself for one brief moment, sucking her nipple into the heat of his mouth, stroking with his tongue, giving her the edge of his teeth. He used his fingers to produce the same rhythm, kneading and tugging on her other breast. She gasped and arched into his mouth, her body growing hot and flushed.

He kissed his way to the thundering pulse just on the upper curve of her left breast. Without hesitation, he sank his teeth deep, hooking into that vein. She cried out at the piercing pain that instantly gave way to erotic heat.

Both hands came up to cradle his head as he shared with her the near ecstasy he was feeling as he took her blood.

Is it always like this?

She was panting, her breathing ragged, body on fire.

Only with you. Your blood is special to me, as mine is for you. He stroked her breasts, traced her ribs, slid his calloused fingers lower to her belly. She had such a perfect feminine form. It was pure hell forcing himself to take enough for a second blood exchange and stop. He swept his tongue across the twin holes in the swell of her breast and lifted his gaze to hers.

He knew his eyes were blazing hot. He was all male Carpathian in that moment, claiming his mate. It took every bit of discipline he had not to utter the binding words that rose from the darkness in what was left of his soul. He let her see two thousand years of need. Of hunger. Of relentless pursuit. The determination that he would never let her go.

It is your turn. Remember my taste. It is already on your tongue, Ku Tappa Kulyak. You are so courageous. His chest was bare to her. They were skin to skin. His fingernail lengthened and he drew a line over the heavy muscle precisely where she had taken his blood before. Drops of crimson instantly beaded up.

He didn't force her mouth toward those tiny ruby drips. Instead, he collected several on his finger and put them on his tongue and then bent his head to hers. Instinctively she leaned against the cradle of his arm, parting her lips for him. His tongue teased hers, stroking and caressing, transferring the taste of him right down her throat and straight to her bloodstream.

Safia moaned and then swallowed convulsively. Even the delicate motion of her throat was arousing to him. He lifted his head, breaking the kiss, eyes glittering down at her. He knew she couldn't fail to see him as a full Carpathian. A dangerous, merciless predator, ruthless beyond all means.

He didn't try to hide from her because he belonged to her. He would use every trait he had to keep her safe. He gave her as much of himself as he could without frightening her. The more often she saw him as the ruthless predator he was, the more quickly she would be able to accept who he truly was.

Safia blazed a trail of kisses from his mouth to his throat using that same butterfly touch that sent his body into overdrive. It was the lightest of caresses, the whisper of wings brushing against his jaw and under his chin, down his throat, over the heavy muscles of his chest. Everywhere her soft lips touched him, she left behind flickering flames on sensitized nerve endings.

Like colors and emotions, his physical reaction to her was overwhelming, but he didn't want to blunt that. He wanted to feel every sensation. Savor it. Lock it into his memory and hold it close to him. When he was with her, there was no thought of anything or anyone else. She filled him with emotions he hadn't known existed. If he'd felt them in his youth, he didn't remember them.

Her lips made their way to the line of ruby beads, her silky tongue tentatively touching the corner of the laceration. The touch was like a torch burning a brand through skin, muscle and bone.

He cupped the back of her head with his palm. *I will help you, sívamet. Another feeding and you will be able to do this yourself without my aid.*

She preferred to do things by herself, his independent woman. She was tentative, but willing to try. The moment the taste of him was on her tongue, she hadn't resisted.

Yes, please. Help me.

The sultry note in her voice was nearly his undoing. He was proud of her courage. She hadn't pulled away, hadn't showed fear or repugnance. And she'd asked him for help when that wasn't her nature. A man could find himself worshipping a woman like her.

He lengthened her teeth and helped her hook them into his vein. The moment she connected them together, the white-hot flame shook them both. Flames raced up his spine, ran from his chest where she drew his blood into her hot velvet mouth, spread downward straight to his groin, fueling him with fire.

He flung back his head and silently roared his need of her to the world. He would not lose her this time. Nothing. No one would stand in his way. If Lilith and her army thought they could take her from him, they were very wrong.

Two thousand years I have waited for you.

Holding Safia steady in one arm, he stroked her right breast with his large, calloused fingers. He had slain hundreds of vampires with his hands. Torn their hearts from their chests and incinerated them. He had never thought he could be gentle, but everything was different with his lifemate. He was different.

Like he had, she found the taste of him an aphrodisiac. Wildly addicting and wholly erotic. He shared her mind, and as his blood filled her, she writhed on his lap, unable to hold still, urgently reaching for something she had no real knowledge of.

Petru. Her soft pleading was impossible to resist. *I'm burning up.*

I can help. Touching you intimately is dangerous. He would do anything for her, even this. Already, his palm slid down her feminine form, committing it to memory until he rested it on her smooth inner thigh. *Spread your legs wider for me.*

The combination of her mouth on his chest, the sensual feel of her breasts against his body and the sight of her added to the pleasure he shared with her. *Trust me, Ku Tappa Kulyak, I will relieve this burning for you, if it is what you want.*

It would only increase his hunger for her, but he could block the sensation if it came down to it, where she could not.

Yes, please.

That voice of hers, working its way into his chest, making his heart ache. She was getting to him, no doubt about it.

He slid his palm beneath the edge of her swimsuit, closed his fist and then rubbed along the tight curls. She didn't pull away. A soft little groan escaped, and in their shared minds, he felt the fever of desire grow in her.

Very gently, he dragged his knuckles back and forth over her soft curls and then cupped her mound lightly with his palm. He had a large hand, and he covered her completely, absorbing the shape and heat of her. His heart pounded irrationally, matching the beat of hers. He slid two fingers lower to find her slick heat. She moaned softly and shifted restlessly. Burning. Her veins were liquid fire. His veins infused with those same flames.

Do something. There was a plea in her voice. Low. Trembling.

She had no idea what she was asking of him. He might not survive this when he survived a thousand battles with vampires. He smoothed his fingers between her most intimate lips, stroking caresses gently petting her, tugging, soothing, heightening her pleasure. She didn't pull away, only moaned a second time and moved her hips restlessly.

Petru stroked the pads of his fingers across her slick entrance. Her feminine scent called to him. Faint notes of jasmine, moonflower and the sea. When he took her blood, the addicting taste of jasmine and moonflower was subtle, but it was there. All Safia. All his. He circled her clit, little caresses, driving up the sensations she was feeling.

Very gently, he slid one palm up his chest to bridge between her mouth and his bare skin while he allowed her teeth to retract, releasing the vein.

Slide your tongue over the laceration. Just that small sensation of velvet brushing over the spot where she'd taken his blood when she obeyed him was highly erotic. All the while, he continued to make little circles around her clit, never touching where she wanted or needed most.

Spread your legs wider for me. He whispered the temptation intimately.

Her head fell to his shoulder, her long lashes veiling her eyes. Her hips lifted toward his stroking fingers. Petru slowly inserted one finger into her wet entrance. Her tight muscles fought him, but he was patient.

Relax for me. He kissed her ear, tugged on her earlobe with his teeth.

Safia immediately followed his instructions, taking a deep, shuddering breath and letting it out. The moment her tight muscles yielded, he moved his finger deeper into her silken sheath. She was burning hot, liquid fire. His cock burned and jerked in reaction as her muscles clamped around his finger.

He moved his finger gently, finding the sensitive bundle of nerves, stimulating them, adding to the burn slowly until she was in a fever of need. Only then did he stroke the pad of his thumb over her clit. A featherlight sensation at first. Just enough to add to the feel of elusive release she needed so desperately.

Petru.

There was not only a little plea in her voice but the tiniest demand that told him she was going to be a little wildcat in bed. She was a passionate woman. Adventurous. Just the fact that she was on his lap allowing him such intimacy told him that.

So impatient, sívamet.

He kissed the side of her neck. Stroked his tongue over her pulse while he began to tug on her clit, tap gently and circle with his finger and thumb. He stroked his fingers inside her silken channel, feeling her surrounding his cock the way she was his finger.

Her breathing was ragged, her hips lifting to follow the rhythm of his finger as she drew closer and closer to her release. Petru didn't want this to end, but he knew he had no choice. His only compensation was that she was his lifemate, and he would have her for an eternity. He tapped on her clit and sent her flying over the edge.

She bit down hard on his arm to muffle the sounds of her broken cry. He wanted those sensations for himself, so he caught her chin and lifted her face to his to catch those glorious sounds in his mouth. He licked at her lips, sucked the jasmine and moonflower from her tongue, claimed her moans and soft cries, absorbing them internally so that they were forever etched into his mind.

Everything about you is so beautiful, Safia, he whispered into her mind, meaning it. He held her tightly to him, stroking caresses down the back of her head, his fingers tangling in all that thick silky hair. *Thank you for trusting me.*

She buried her face in his chest. *I had no idea you could make me feel like that. But you must be . . .* She trailed off.

Do not worry about me. I want to show you so many things, Ku Tappa Kulyak. That is only the beginning. There is so much more between a man and his woman. So many ways I can make you feel good. Far more pleasure than that.

She lifted her head, her green eyes still a little hazy as they searched his, as if she needed to read him to see if he was telling her the truth. "More than that?"

He didn't want to, but he gently lifted each breast into the bathing suit as he pulled the material up and then slid the straps over her shoulders. "I detest hiding such beauty. And yes, *sívamet,* there is far more pleasure to be had. I intend to show you as soon as we are bound together."

The little frown appeared once again. He was growing fond of that frown. He leaned forward and tugged at her full bottom lip with his teeth, nipping just hard enough for her to give a little yelp. He soothed the sting with his tongue. Then, because he couldn't resist, he traced the dimple that appeared when she gave him a half smile.

"I think you're going to be difficult," she said.

"Probably. But why were you frowning?" He bent his head again and nibbled on the sweet spot between her shoulder and neck. Immediately, endorphins flooded her system, and little electric sparks jumped from her skin to his.

"I know you said there are certain things you can't change. I know customs are different in other lands, but surely we can get to know one another better before you bind us together."

"War is imminent, Safia. It could start at any time. Hopefully we will have a little time, but you see the signs. Lilith—and it *is* her stirring things up—is trying to pit neighbor against neighbor. That's our only hope of having a few days. Not weeks but days. We can't take the chance that we are not bound."

"I still don't understand."

"I promise I will explain it to you, but I must first speak to your grandfather. It would be disrespectful of me not to talk to him."

Safia sighed. Petru knew she couldn't argue with that. Her grandfather arranged the marriages in their tribe. He would have been insulted if Petru didn't discuss arrangements with him first.

Petru tucked a strand of hair behind her ear. "It will work itself out, Safia. I'll talk with your grandfather tonight, after you show us how to destroy this demon."

"I've locked the portal. Lilith, or whoever, shouldn't be able to send any other demon in this form to us."

"The more knowledge we have of destroying them, the more we can share with other Carpathians. If Lilith sends this form against them somewhere else, they will know how to slay the demons."

"That makes sense," Safia said. "I'd better get to it."

Petru didn't want to let her go for many reasons. He didn't want her in harm's way. And he didn't want to release her feminine form with all the soft skin and silky hair. That fragrance that belonged only to her. He wanted to spend all the time they had together before it was too late and they were in the fight of their lives.

She slid off his lap, her bottom inflaming his cock all over again when he'd just managed to get it under control. She steadied herself by placing her hands on his shoulders, leaning down, giving him a view of her full breasts and just a brief glimpse of nipples. It was all he could do to keep from taking one into his mouth.

She couldn't be deliberately tempting him, could she? He looked into her jeweled eyes, and her dark lashes swept down, veiling them immediately, but that dimple of hers was very much in evidence. She straightened and turned toward the stairs.

"I need my bag."

"It is on the deck." Petru followed her, admiring the way she walked easily on the boat. The water was rougher, and yet she had no trouble balancing, as if she were used to being out to sea.

Once on deck, he pulled her bag out from behind a chair where Benedek had placed it and indicated for her to tell them what she needed. The others were waiting to give him blood, and he gratefully accepted their offering. They waited for Safia to take over.

Safia found that the vessel the Carpathians had duplicated was an exact replica of one of Kadin Merabet's fishing boats. She'd seen the boats many times in the harbor when they'd returned from sea. She stood for a moment, there in the dark, her face turned up to the night sky, welcoming the breeze. Hopefully, it would cool the hot blood surging through her veins and calm the raging fire that Petru had started in her.

She'd never been so aware of herself as a woman. She hadn't known her body could ever feel such intense sensations. He'd used his fingers, and she'd soared so high. He'd told her there was so much more between a man and his woman. She wanted to know everything, experience everything with him. If she were honest, while she was a bit embarrassed that she'd allowed such liberties, she wasn't in the least sorry. At least physically, she was more than compatible with Petru. There was no doubt in her mind she would enjoy that aspect of their relationship.

She needed to clear her mind, something difficult after what she'd just experienced with Petru. The things she'd allowed him to do to her made her blush, and it was hard not to anticipate what might come next. She liked that he explained things when she asked him. He never seemed to look down on her for asking questions. She was used to being able to voice her opinions and being taken seriously. She had always been encouraged to ask questions and seek knowledge.

It was a little disconcerting that she hadn't remembered his friends were aboard the fishing boat. Had she been loud when she was moaning and crying out in such pleasure? She couldn't remember, and she couldn't think about that now. She had work to do, she told herself sternly.

Right at this moment, she had to clear her mind and call on every ounce of discipline she possessed. There was still one sea centipede she had to dispose of. It wouldn't be an easy task, but she was the defender, and this was what she did. Once she made up her mind, she felt her armor slipping into place, the warrior pushing out the woman.

She took another deep breath and raised her arms to the sky, seeking to connect with the sea creature. She already knew the brain pattern she was searching for, since she had connected with two of the demons prior to this one. The giant sea centipede would be throwing off far more energy than the smaller ones had.

Once she located him several miles to the east, she searched for protections. The demon, like the others, had no safeguards she had to unravel. Lilith hadn't expected opposition so early. Using a very delicate touch, Safia entered the creature's brain, flowing in on the chaotic pattern. She had no idea if being larger meant he was more sensitive or less so. She took her time, patient as always, reading the intent in the demon.

As with the smaller demons, he was in pain. The cruelty of his mistress knew no bounds. Lilith had mutated this creature. She forced his hearing to be so acute that when he was submerged, the amplifying effect caused so much pain he was driven into a rage. If he went to the surface, the burning on his outer shell drove the creature insane. No matter where he went or what he did, he couldn't get away from what she'd done to him.

His orders were to crush the fishing boats. If he did this to his mistress' satisfaction, she would take away the pain. The demon didn't believe it, yet it was his only hope, and he intended to carry out the order.

"Take us farther out to sea, away from any other ship," she instructed. She was used to giving orders to her family when they simulated demon attacks. She did so now without thinking.

The ship began to move at once. She stood on the edge of the deck and began a singsong chant, calling to the giant sea centipede, enticing it to follow them. Her hair was unbound, flying like so much silk in the wind. She gathered information that way, the long strands of hair receptors of every detail the wind gathered for her. She was aware of the precise moment the sea centipede locked onto them and changed course.

From her bag she pulled a wicked-looking three-pronged fork. The handle sprang up tall and spiraled.

Petru drew closer to look at it. "A trident?"

She nodded. "You are probably aware the trident was forged in fire and given to the sea. But the prongs represent fire, water and metal, all of the earth. This weapon was developed for warriors of the earth who keep evil from spilling into the world. The sea centipede walks on land and swims in water. The crystal sword burns the small ones from the inside out, but the giant one requires far more to destroy it."

Petru's eyes went from liquid mercury to pure silver. He regarded her coolly. She felt a shiver go down her spine. He could be very intimidating, more so even than a giant sea centipede.

"Far more? What is far more?"

"That is what you're with me to find out," she retaliated. She was the defender. This was her field of expertise, and she wasn't going to allow this man, who had a claim on her, to stop her from doing her job.

Petru continued to study her for a few more moments, and then he nodded abruptly and stepped away from her. Safia turned back to the dark water, her mind already dismissing Petru and the others. She was immediately consumed with her task.

The demon was coming toward them at a high rate of speed. He swam on the surface, propelling himself along with his many fins. At night, there was no burning the way there was during the day, so he took advantage by staying on top of the water, just as she'd known he would.

She turned the three prongs upward to face the stars and shifting clouds, setting the long spiraled staff in her palm. Balancing it, she spun the trident so that it whirled fast. It came alive. The prongs each began to glow a different color. One end took on a brilliant shade of lavender. The opposite end was deep dark purple. The middle prong was royal purple.

As Safia spun the trident, the colors deepened and climbed higher and higher into the night sky. The colors reached a cloud and began to tangle together, forming a hollow, round net of shades of purple. The purples were shimmering as if made of millions of stars. The net seemed to have tangled with the cloud itself, infusing the white with darker colors. Immediately, low flashes of lightning began to fork through the cloud as if the trident had awakened an angry dragon.

Safia wasn't looking up at the colors or cloud; she was looking down at the fast-approaching sea centipede. She needed to turn his approach by a few degrees to ensure his claws didn't touch the fishing boat. It took concentration to keep her trap in the air precisely where she wanted it and steer the massive demon off course by slowly fouling his sense of direction just enough to put him where she wanted him.

The net descended, opening wider and wider as it did so. It looked as if it were made of fragile filaments as it blossomed open. The centipede was as big as a whale, but when the net dropped, it completely surrounded the centipede without touching it until Safia snapped the trident closed. The net pulled tight beneath the centipede, trapping it inside.

The demon threw its head from side to side and shrieked its rage and hatred. It tried to leap out of the water and cut the net with its lethal pincers. Lightning forked in the dark purple-filled cloud and then traveled down the streaming bright strands of the net to slam again and again into the creature. The jagged bolts of lightning didn't stop but continued to rain down on the pointed armor of the hapless creature. The centipede smoldered from dozens of places throughout its enormous body.

Safia deftly pulled the crystal sword from the tool belt she had fashioned around her waist and pointed it at the demon's open mouth. The blue flames began to lick inside along the jaws and tongue. The flames leapt, the wind catching them and spreading them throughout the centipede, driven through the holes made by the lightning. Now the blue flames rolled as they burned the demon clean. She chanted, closing the sea and harbor to Lilith.

The giant sea centipede rolled over as the outside structure of the beast collapsed in on itself. She waited until the creature was completely eaten by the flames before she released the net and freed the cloud.

10

P etru is talking to my grandfather right this minute, Aura," Safia said. She put both hands on her hips and glared at her friend. "I ought to strangle you. I wasn't in the least prepared for him."

Aura smirked. "I don't think it's possible to be prepared for one's lifemate. You see the others. They have the same traits."

"Not exactly," Safia denied.

Aura kept looking at her, and Safia couldn't help the blush stealing up her neck and into her face. "Will you stop?"

"I haven't said a word," Aura denied.

"He's very different than I thought he would be. He was with me when I went after the demons, but he didn't try to take over."

Aura's eyebrow shot up. "He didn't?"

Safia shook her head. "No. He stayed quiet in the background and so did his friends. They didn't interfere at all. He said they were learning from me."

Aura narrowed her eyes suspiciously. "Did he take your blood?"

Safia's heart skipped a beat. "Yes. Isn't he supposed to? Maybe you should explain to me the customs so I don't get myself into trouble, Aura. I don't like surprises."

"I need to check the gate. Why don't you come with me? I've

wanted to show it to you for some time. I've been guarding it alone, and it would make me feel easier if you checked it over. We can talk there."

Safia had wanted to examine the gate. "I was there and closed the portals where the demons were slipping through. I also consecrated the ground. Lilith can't send any demons through from there even if she tries. Same with the harbor itself. I'll let my brother know I'm going with you."

"Are you going to let Petru know?"

Safia frowned. "I don't have to answer to him yet, and I'm not looking forward to it. I've had freedom for most of my life. It's going to be a difficult transition trying to fit into his world. Fortunately, he disappears during the day like you do, and that will give me some freedom."

Safia told her youngest brother she was going with Aura to do some training and they'd be back in an hour. Aura was waiting just outside the door to lift her easily and whisk her through the air to the caves near the harbor. Before, Safia had closed her eyes. Now she took in the way Aura traveled, impressed by the efficiency of covering ground so fast.

The cave looked exactly the way it had when Safia had left it. She examined the floor and walls to ensure she hadn't missed any thin places in the dirt, but everything looked intact. There were no fresh scratches. Her safeguards had held against Lilith's invasion. Aura led her farther down the corridor toward the partially hidden gate.

The fencing was tall, as if a giant resided behind it. The wood was very dark, solid and thick, from an ancient tree, without any insect holes or cracks. The gate was quite beautiful, although very plain, but it didn't need any adornments. Safia could see thick weaves of safeguards shimmering around the gate and across the fence. She recognized Aura's weaves. This was far more complicated than the ones Aura normally used, even to guard Safia's family farm.

"Do you see those thin places in the wood? It's a pattern, every few feet in the safeguards, as if someone has been picking at my weaves. It can't be a vampire because they wouldn't know my work. Under the safeguards, if you look closely, you can see the wood has little indentations. This is ancient wood. It's impervious to almost anything." Aura sounded very anxious, when few things worried her.

Safia moved close to the gate and inhaled deeply, taking in the various scents. "Aura, this leads directly to the underworld. What exactly are you ensuring is staying behind that gate?"

Aura nodded. "He was once a great Carpathian hunter. Maybe the greatest we've ever had. When a Carpathian has been too long in this world and continues to hunt the vampire and make kills, something happens to him. He changes."

Safia heard that little warning note in her voice, and icy fingers crept down her spine.

"Don't get me wrong, all the hunters are dangerous. They live under harsh, brutal conditions, but they can live too long. The ancients . . ."

"Such as Petru and the ones he travels with," Safia interrupted. She wanted clarification. She wanted everything out in the open. Answers.

Aura nodded. "Petru has lived far too long. This beast behind the gate would be nearly impossible to destroy. It would take many of our greatest hunters to kill him should he escape. He is there because he sacrificed his life in order for his family to escape the underworld. He had not yet found his lifemate and was looking for her, holding out hope. Some of the ancients refuse to suicide, believing they are betraying their lifemates in doing so. But if they stay alive too long, they risk becoming what this Carpathian ancient became."

Safia heard the clear warning in Aura's tone. "You're saying Petru could turn into a monster."

"Absolutely he could. Even those traveling with him would not be able to stop him easily. He would kill many before, or even if, he could be destroyed. I don't know what happens to these ancient hunters, but I do know it is very hard on them to be without their lifemate."

"Is there a way to stop it from happening?"

"He must bind you to him. That is the only way," Aura explained.

"You hold the other half of his soul. He is all darkness. You are his light. Once your souls are woven back together, he cannot turn. In our culture, when that ritual is performed, and you consummate what you refer to as a marriage, he is safe unless something happens to you."

"That's why he says we have no time to get to know one another." Safia stepped even closer to the gate, looking under the safeguards to examine the thinning wood. It was a very systematic thinning.

"He doesn't dare wait. He cannot afford to. Should something happen to you, he knows he would scorch the earth."

"This wood hasn't been touched by a tool, yet it's pitted every few feet."

Aura moved up beside her to peer at the gate. "I thought maybe demons were digging at it, but there aren't any scratch marks."

"If the beast you guard against was once Carpathian, is it possible he uses his mind to wear down the wood?"

Aura peered down at the pits in the wood and slowly nodded her head. "Yes. He could do that. He isn't a vampire. He's not wholly Carpathian. He's more beast than man now, but I've heard him speak the Carpathian language. Not to me. He doesn't converse with anyone but Gaia. She was a young Carpathian child given to Lilith by Xavier, a mage, in exchange for something foul. She grew close with the beast and stays of her own free will with him. They aren't lifemates, but she tries to keep him from getting any worse than he is."

"Why does Lilith want control of him?"

"Like I said, he is very powerful and dangerous. If she could make him do her bidding, she would have the ultimate weapon. Even she fears him."

Safia turned to face her friend. "What else should I know about the Carpathian culture? I can tell you're withholding something important from me."

"I didn't say anything about your lifemate because I didn't know what I was supposed to say. There was so much mystery. I was a child when the seer set everything up, and my mother wasn't that forthcoming with information, especially once my father died. She stayed with me, but she was only half in this world. I didn't know if I was supposed to educate you on Carpathians or not. I wasn't told. When I realized you hadn't been told anything, it was very alarming to me."

"It wasn't fair."

"No, it wasn't. But if I interfere between lifemates, that wouldn't be right, either."

"Why would talking to me about your world be interfering?"

Aura moved away from the gate, back up along the narrow corridor toward the larger chamber. "Now that Petru is here, he will expect to be the one to answer your questions."

"Am I to have no other friends or family to talk to? Is that the way it works in your world?" Safia trailed after her much more slowly.

Aura half turned to send her a small smile. "Honestly? I've lived with your family far longer than I've lived in the Carpathian world. I'm more Imazighen than Carpathian. At least in my heart. Maybe in my mind. The grandmothers and mothers in your family have shared more wisdom with me than my mother ever shared."

Safia heard the note of sadness in Aura's voice, and it wasn't the first time. Her life had to have been very difficult and at times extremely lonely. Aura had lived one lifetime after another without any of her people other than her mother around. By Aura's admission, her mother had lived her life with one foot in another world.

"I'm sorry I wasn't there for you more, Aura. I should have paid more attention. I did think of you as one of the family. My best friend, my sister. You always seemed happy, but I should have made sure. It was selfish of me not to think about you." She was genuinely upset with herself. She loved Aura, and the thought that she hadn't considered her more disturbed her greatly.

"Don't be so distressed, Safia. I know you love me," Aura said. "You've always shown me that you do, more so than anyone else ever has." She turned fully around, hiding her expression. "In the end, even more than my mother."

Safia's heart ached for Aura. As a rule, Aura closed off her emotions from everyone, but she was sharing with Safia, making herself vulnerable. Safia pressed a closed fist to her chest where her heart felt so painful, a physical reaction to the empathy she felt for Aura.

Azul, Safia.

Petru's warm masculine strength poured into her mind, filling her with him. With his essence. He felt like velvet brushing at the walls of her mind intimately. She hadn't realized how many times she had tried to tune herself to him and stopped. How many times she had wanted— no, *needed*—to feel him close until he was there.

You are distressed. Have you need of me?

His voice was gentle. Kind. She had the feeling that if she answered in the affirmative, he would instantly stop whatever he was doing and come to her. She had often felt lonely, even in the midst of her family. In those moments, with the intimate way Petru communicated with her, she felt she belonged with him. What had Aura felt all those years? She had to have been so lonely.

Thank you for asking, but I am fine. I am talking with a close friend of mine, and she is upset. I didn't realize I was broadcasting my reaction. I will be more careful not to disturb you.

No one else caught the slightest hint of your feelings, sívamet. I am your lifemate. Although we are not bound, we are connected. Reach for me if you have need.

He was gone before she could react, and she felt . . . bereft. She took a moment to process the feeling and why she would feel that way. Her emotions when it came to Petru made no sense at all. She thought of herself as a logical person, but with him, more often than not, she was just plain confused.

"I wouldn't want you to leave, Aura, but would you if you were given the opportunity? Had you shown me the gate and asked me to guard it for you so you could go, it would be heart-wrenching to lose you, but I would have taken that task for you. Now I have no idea what is going to happen to me in the future. I am uncertain if I have a say in where I will go."

"It is my responsibility to guard the gate, just as yours is to destroy demons and aid me if necessary. You protect the cards. The duty of the cards increased when the gates were built."

"Aura, do you think Petru plans to take me away from my family?"

Aura hesitated, and Safia's heart skipped a beat and then accelerated. There was something she was missing. Petru was like a giant puzzle. She was collecting pieces, but she didn't have them all. She didn't understand the undercurrent, but she felt it coming at her from every direction.

"What is it?"

"Only Petru can answer that question. I would directly ask him about his intentions, Safia. Don't wait until he binds you together. Ask him to explain everything he's doing and how he intends for the two of you to live together."

Once in the larger chamber, Aura made her way to the grotto. She rested her hands on the railing and looked out over the sea. "I'm Carpathian, and every sunrise I sleep beneath the ground. The soil welcomes and rejuvenates me. If I have the least little cut, or a broken bone, the rich minerals will heal me. But during that time, I am very vulnerable. I lay as if dead, in a state of paralysis. If you found my body, you would believe me to be dead."

"I understand."

She told Aura she understood, but it wasn't the truth. Perhaps she did in theory, but in practice, the Carpathian culture was an extremely difficult concept to understand. She had studied cultures. Amastan had insisted every member of the family respect the way others lived; however, the thought of drinking human blood and sleeping beneath the ground conjured up the idea of vampires. She tried to get that vision out of her head, but now that she'd met one, it was impossible.

But then there had been the exchanging of blood with Petru. She struggled with where to place that experience in her mind—how to understand the strange, erotic desire that had stolen over her. She secretly hugged that experience to her. She didn't just want to repeat it—she needed to repeat it. She found it took tremendous discipline to keep her mind from reaching out to him, as if she needed constant reassurance that he was alive and well.

"Petru will sleep beneath the ground during the day and come to you at night, as I did. Once you are bound to him, it is nearly impossible to be separated in that way."

Safia's chin came up, and she studied her friend's face. There was a note in her voice that was cautionary. Worried. Aura was in the shadows, but Safia had always had superior vision. She seemed to have even more so now. She could see Aura quite clearly, and for the first time, Safia could see the worry lines around her eyes and mouth. Again, she had that strange premonition, the crawling of icy fingers down her spine. She was missing something huge.

"Why would it be impossible to be separated that way? Aura, you want to tell me something, but you're dancing around it. I am certainly not going to sleep in the ground with him. I would die. Even if, by some miracle, I wouldn't, the idea doesn't appeal to me. And if I were in the ground during the day, who would be here with my family to watch for demons? That's my job, what I'm trained to do. If the war really is pending, I can't take time to go to sleep when Lilith would take advantage and send demons that can come out in the daytime."

She made her case as logical as possible because she had the feeling Aura might reveal something to her that would be devastating.

"Do you crave his touch?" Aura asked bluntly. "His mind in yours? When he's away from you, does your mind seek his?"

Safia nodded slowly. "Yes. And it's gotten worse since our first encounter. I allowed him to take . . . liberties I would never have dreamt of."

"Did you exchange blood? Do you remember? I know he gave you blood the first time because you were in need."

"Yes, but he took my blood as well. He said it would establish a connection between us, that we would be able to communicate on a private path." Safia continued to watch Aura closely for the slightest sign that Petru had been deceiving her, because something wasn't quite right.

"Yes, he's right about that. We can do that because I took your blood and gave you mine. When you've been wounded, I've given you blood."

"I don't crave seeing you, Aura. I miss you when I haven't seen you for a couple of days, but I don't feel as if I have to use every bit of discipline I have in order to keep my mind from seeking yours like I do his."

"There's a difference between me giving you a small amount of blood to establish communication between us and a true blood exchange," Aura explained. She tapped her fingers on the wide railing that ran along the end of the grotto overlooking the harbor.

Aura didn't exhibit nervous behaviors. Twice, Aura looked around the grotto as if suspicious that they weren't alone. Safia hadn't detected the presence of any others, but Aura was very good at sensing vampires.

What do you think is here with us?

Not what. Who. I doubt your lifemate would leave you without protection. I am suspicious that one or more of his traveling companions are close.

Aura would naturally be reluctant to talk to her in front of them. Safia opened her mind and sent out a call for the bats to aid her in mapping out the cavern and grotto. She expanded the search, taking care not to give off the slightest bit of energy.

Petru's friends had been with her several times. Growing up, she had learned to automatically recall every detail about those around her. She absorbed their habits, the way they moved, breathed and, in this case, the preferred images they took when they shifted. They were ghosts, fading into whatever the background was, or becoming molecules, part of the air itself.

For Safia, Nicu would be the easiest to find. His mind was more like that of a feral animal, a dangerous predator, and she was drawn to low energy that was entirely different. It would be one thing for Petru to send his men to aid her or look after her during a fight with vampires or demons. She would understand that, but not during a private conversation with one of her friends. Aura rarely allowed herself to be so vulnerable, and she would be very embarrassed to know that these strangers had heard every word she'd said to Safia.

Safia had lived a life of freedom. She'd been trusted. She couldn't live with a man who was so controlling he needed to know where she was every single moment of the day or night. Who she was with, what was said.

"Tell me what the difference is between what we did and what I shared with Petru." Safia encouraged Aura while she sought out any intruders. She was more than convinced they weren't alone, but she had to find the evidence. She wasn't going to jump to conclusions.

Aura shook her head, fingers creeping toward her throat, her gaze darting around the grotto. *We should leave this place.*

Safia found Nicu, a tiny bat tucked into a crevice. The one they called Lojos was a few feet from him, a transparent cave spider. Benedek was scattered through the air right above them. She raised her arms and sent wind crashing through the grotto.

"How dare the three of you stalk me like some madmen. Aura, take me home, please. I have a few things to say to that horrid man who thinks I will honor a claim from someone who believes he has the right to control me. On the way, we can continue our conversation without eavesdroppers listening to every word we say."

She was furious. *Furious.*

All three men materialized, startling her, their size filling the grotto. They looked menacing, intimidating her more than she wanted to admit, but she didn't step back. They were looking beyond her to Aura. Each of them pinned her with steely eyes.

Benedek spoke. "It is best that you allow Petru to explain blood exchanges to Safia. You know better than to interfere between life-mates. You do not want to earn his ire."

Safia hissed her displeasure. "His *ire*? Are you threatening her because she was answering questions I asked? In my world, we're allowed questions, and we answer them for one another. I definitely won't fit into your narrow little world. Don't you *dare* threaten her. I don't care how big and bad you are. I don't even care how much we need you in a war against Lilith. You don't get to bully us because you're supposed to be such great fighters."

Deliberately, she turned her back on them. "Aura, please take me back to my house."

Aura caught her up and sped through the opening in the grotto straight into the air. Safia allowed herself to be dazzled by the harbor and city lights. The night air felt cool on her skin but didn't quite soothe her temper.

They will report to Petru.

Let them. I'm not going to accept his claim. I refuse to live under a dictator's rule.

Aura hesitated, then sighed. *I know you're very independent, and you were raised to speak your mind. You deserve to, especially when you're expected to destroy demons and defend your family. But these men are not like the men in your family. They aren't even like the men in other tribes who seem arrogant to you. These men are ancients, and they command the lightning, the earth. They are used to obedience. They don't interact well with other species, because if they meet resistance, they simply take over. They can command obedience.*

Safia stared down at the lights, colors blurring together because they were moving so fast over the harbor and then the city as Aura circled around rather than flying directly across the bluffs toward the farm. She clearly was delaying their return.

You mean they force obedience, making people into puppets.

Aura sighed again. *I suppose it can be interpreted that way. They see it as avoiding useless arguments.*

Because they believe they know best, so everything should be done their way, Safia translated.

I guess. They are two thousand years old. They have great wisdom, Safia. They've seen things we will never see. They know things we have no knowledge of. It would get old to know the answers and have continual arguments when you're aware of what will work and what won't. Imagine having to explain why you must kill a demon a certain way over and over. It would be so tedious.

Don't defend Petru's actions. There was no need for him to send those men after me when all I was doing was talking to my friend. I even told him I was having a private conversation with you. He had no right to eavesdrop. I refuse to live that way. He can't force me. It isn't done in our culture. He'll find that out soon enough.

If you are his true lifemate, Safia, and he has a prior claim on you, then yes, he can force you. It is done in our culture. He can bind you to him, and nothing will be able to tear you apart. Not your will or his. If you are not his true lifemate, the words imprinted on him will do nothing at all. You can challenge him if you don't believe you belong to him.

Even just Aura's choice of words annoyed her. Safia didn't belong to anyone. She was her own person. She had been prepared to learn what she could about Petru's culture and do her best to respect him and be a partner to him. But she couldn't tolerate being controlled or having her friends threatened. That reduced Petru to a bully in her eyes. Just thinking about it made her furious all over again.

Has it occurred to you that you've been looking for an excuse to get out of your commitment, and this provided you with the perfect out?

You don't think this is a good reason? Safia valued Aura's opinion, but she couldn't imagine her friend putting up with Petru's controlling behavior.

I think you need to be very careful. You don't know how powerful or dangerous he is. I believe if you push him, he will retaliate, and in a way that you won't be able to come back from. Go slow, Safia. Don't be reckless.

Choose every word you say carefully and try to get him to give you all the facts.

That frustrated Safia even more. *All the facts? So, you are holding something important back from me. Are you afraid of those men? Clearly Petru is withholding information that is vital to me, and they don't want you to disclose it.*

I'm sorry. Petru must be the one to reveal what you should know. He's your lifemate.

What if he's not, Aura? Does it feel to you that I'm compatible with him? I will admit that, physically, we have powerful chemistry between us, but nothing else. Not one single thing.

Was that the truth? She didn't know. She thought something had been growing between them, but now she knew she didn't know him at all. He was capable of turning humans into puppets.

Is he capable of making me feel things I wouldn't normally feel?

Aura hesitated again before answering. *These are unfair questions. What he is capable of doing and what he does may be two very different things.*

In essence, that meant that Petru could plant suggestions or emotions in her mind. What in the world was she supposed to do with that knowledge?

If I left, went to my older sister and her husband, and asked them to take me across the Sahara, would he be able to find me?

He can find you anywhere in the world, Safia. He has taken your blood. You must be calm when you face him. I can't keep flying in circles. His brethren have grown restless, which means he has. If we force him to come after us, he will have the upper hand.

Safia wanted to laugh, but she was afraid she would turn hysterical. Petru Cioban already had the upper hand. There was no question about that. He'd made her his prisoner. It was one thing to know you were raised to have an arranged marriage with a member of one's tribe. She would have done so willingly.

Now she was told there was a prior claim by a man outside her tribe, and her family owed him a debt of honor. She still would have been willing to marry him and learn his customs. It would have been heart-wrenching to leave her family, but she would have fulfilled her duties with honor. But this was too much for anyone to ask.

I will do my best not to punch him in the face when I see him. You can take us home.

You've always had an atrocious temper.

She did sometimes. Rarely. Only when it was really warranted. Mostly, she kept her anger to herself while she worked at trying to understand the other person's point of view. Maybe that's what she needed to do. Ask questions. Get answers. See if there was something in his culture that would make him think a woman should have three men spying on her when she was having a private conversation with her friend.

Aura's soft laughter slipped into her mind. *You're making yourself angry all over again. Using the word* spying *isn't helping.*

Safia's sense of humor kicked in. Aura always found a way to make her laugh. *I suppose you're right. I swear, I'll try to listen to him. Do you know a reasonable explanation?*

I don't know Carpathian ways. My mother wasn't very forthcoming. I told you, I know more about your culture. I have picked up a few things from the other guardians, mostly things pertaining to the beast behind the gate, but not a lot.

Aura set the two of them down right at the front door. They both smoothed their clothing, Aura making certain they looked their best before opening the door.

Amastan, Gwafa, Izem and Petru were inside the family room waiting for them. Benedek, Nicu and Lojos sat at the back of the room, each beside a window. The rest of the family were nowhere in sight, which didn't bode well as far as Safia was concerned.

"*Azul, Yelli. Azul,* Aura," Amastan said. "It is good you are home."

Both murmured the customary greeting back to him and the others. *Azul* meant "close to the heart" and was the way they welcomed those coming into their home.

"Aura," Petru said. "Lojos will see you safely back to your home. There is much to be discussed this night, and then I must speak to you."

His voice was gentle, but there was an underlying note of command one didn't dare disobey—or at least Aura didn't. He was clearly dismissing her. She gave a short nod of her head, spun around and left without another word. Lojos rose much more leisurely and followed her out.

Safia's nails bit into her palms as she curled her fingers into fists. Petru didn't have the right to tell her friend to go when this had been Aura's home her entire life. She knew her eyes blazed fire at her grandfather and father. What was wrong with them that they permitted such a thing?

You are angry with me.

How very perceptive of you.

"Come sit, Safia. We have been discussing the wedding and marriage. Petru has explained that certain rituals must take place immediately in order for everyone to be safe."

"That's just the thing, *Jeddi*," Safia said, keeping her tone even. She crossed to the chair closest to the fireplace and as far from Petru as she could get. "I have some concerns that haven't been addressed. From what I understand, each male has only one lifemate. That lifemate must be compatible with him. I'm terribly afraid a mistake has been made. I'm not in the least compatible with him. I don't think we can go through with a marriage when I know it's wrong."

She kept her gaze fixed on her grandfather. She was absolutely careful to sound logical and firm.

What do you think you're doing?

"Why have you come to this conclusion, Safia?" Amastan asked. "You were willing to try. You said you would learn what you could of his culture and of him."

She nodded. "I certainly intended to. At first, I believed we would make a good match. I believed him to be respectful and a man who would answer my questions and consult with me before he made arbitrary decisions. I have since found that is not the case at all. My understanding of lifemates is that one makes the other happy. That happiness of their lifemate is always put above their own. I would never be happy with a man who sends spies to listen to private conversations. Or one who dictates to me. I believed we would have a partnership. That is not the case."

She made more of an effort to keep her voice perfectly even. She didn't want any of the men in the room to regard her as angry, although Petru knew.

Amastan rubbed the bridge of his nose thoughtfully, switching his gaze to Petru, who sat with an expressionless mask on his very masculine face. He looked as if he could have been carved from stone. His eyes had gone pure silver, a molten liquid heat that threatened retaliation.

"Is it possible there is a mistake, Petru?"

Petru looked only at Amastan, regarding him as the ultimate authority and dismissing Safia as if she were a child not capable of understanding the negotiations taking place.

"It is impossible to be wrong about one's lifemate. There is only one. After two thousand years, I can once again see color. I must tone it down and sometimes blur the colors to be able to endure it; otherwise, the brilliance can affect my vision. Only a lifemate can restore color. I have not felt emotion in two thousand years. Nothing. Not until I heard the sound of my lifemate's voice. Handling unfamiliar feelings is a trial I wish on no man. Only a lifemate can restore emotion."

"Safia." Amastan sounded compassionate, too much so. She felt the burn of tears behind her eyes.

"For all we know, Aura restored these things to him, not me. I don't believe I'm his true lifemate because I am not in the least compatible with him. We have always had the right to refuse a marriage, *Jeddi*. I wish to invoke that right."

She lifted her chin at Petru when his slashing silver eyes jumped to meet her defiant gaze.

"I will not relinquish my claim." There was absolute resolve in his voice. "I told you I will fight to the death for you. If you have doubts, there is one more way to know for certain that you are my lifemate. I was waiting for your family to be here with you in the traditional way, but we can do so now and see what happens."

"What is this test?" Gwafa asked.

"It is not a test. It is the ritual marriage, binding the two of us together. If Safia is not my true lifemate, the words won't work. She holds the other half of my soul. The words will weave our soul back together, uniting us, forming an unbreakable bond. If she is not my lifemate, nothing will happen."

"This is the marriage ceremony of your people?" Izem asked.

"Yes. Once the words are said, Safia will be my wife, but only if she is my true lifemate. If she is not, then I will remain here to aid you in the war with Lilith and then continue to search for the woman who guards the other half of my soul."

He was so calm about it. Not just calm; utterly certain. Arrogant even. Smug. Ruthless. A merciless predator who had easily cornered his prey. Safia was terrified she'd walked right into his trap. Aura had even warned her, but she was every bit as arrogant as he was, thinking she could outmaneuver him.

COMING TOGETHER.
REVELATION.
BALANCE.

S afia took a deep breath. "Honestly, *Jeddi*, I don't think it's necessary to go so far as to perform a marriage ritual. That's sacred to me, and I assume it would be to Petru as well. It should be intimate and personal, not a test."

Petru stood, a fluid motion that centered all attention on him. "*Ku Tappa Kulyak*, for me it will be intimate and personal, as anything to do with you always is. It is necessary to bind you to me. From the moment I first saw you and heard you speak, the compulsion has weighed on me. The ritual binding words are imprinted on our souls long before we are born."

He crossed the room with slow, measured steps, footsteps that were impossible to hear. Her heart accelerated out of control. His shoulders looked far wider than she remembered. His chest was thicker and heavily muscled, waist narrow, arms pure defined muscle. It was his eyes that were frightening. They didn't blink but remained on hers, a slashing silver that pierced right through her, seeing far too much.

He held out his hand to her. "Come to me, Safia. Let us try this."

She couldn't look away from his gaze, trapped in that liquid heat. Drowning in it. She swallowed her protest and put her hand in his.

Was it a compulsion? Or obsession? She honestly couldn't say, only that she needed someone to save her because she couldn't save herself.

"What are you going to do?"

He shackled both wrists by wrapping his fingers around them, settling his fingers over her pulse, beating so hard. "Amastan, Gwafa and Izem, I will speak the ritual binding words in my language and interpret them so you will know what I say as I take Safia into my keeping."

Her heart jumped. She shook her head. *Don't do this. Not yet. I'm not ready.*

You will never be ready, sívamet. You insist on scaring yourself. I will answer your questions, and we will work past your fears once this is done.

It won't work.

You know it will, or you would not look as though you are about to faint.

Safia would rather fight another vampire than face this. She had driven him to this. Aura had warned her, and yet she'd still pushed him. *I don't want this. Not yet.* Could she be close to a panic attack?

I warned you I was not capable of giving you up. Your heart needs to follow the rhythm of mine. Breathe with me.

"*Te avio päläfertiilam.* You are my lifemate." Petru's voice was soft but very firm. *Éntölam kuulua, avio päläfertiilam.* I claim you as my lifemate."

Safia instantly felt the fusion as tiny threads connected them deep inside. Not a few but hundreds. Instantaneously. Rapidly. There was heat, embers smoldering, threatening to burst into flame. She wanted to tell him to stop, but she couldn't speak, couldn't look away from his eyes, that intense heated silver.

"*Ted kuuluak, kacad, kojed.* I belong to you."

Did he? Did he belong to her? Did she want him to belong to her? He sounded like he meant the words. She wanted to reach up and brush strands of his silvery hair from his face and claim him with her fingertips. At the same time, she wanted to run for her life. She had the feeling that if he continued, she would never be able to get away from him. Arrogance was carved into every line of his face. He was hard. Masculine. He truly could be every inch the controlling dictator she feared.

"*Élidamet andam.* I offer my life for you."

Those words sank into her. He had sacrificed so much two thousand years earlier to save so many others. She didn't understand how much he'd suffered, but she knew he had. She'd caught glimpses of his desolate life, more than he would have allowed had he known. She feared she would never measure up. Never be good enough.

A small part of her knew the vampire had programmed her to believe her own family had chosen life over her and he had given her up to save them. Was he really offering his life for her, or were the words simply recited through conditioning and meant nothing? She wanted to belong. She wanted Petru to be that person in her life who was truly her partner.

"*Pesämet andam.* I give you my protection." For the first time, a faint smile touched his face. *You will not always appreciate my way of protecting you, but we will negotiate terms.*

Petru made her want to smile. There was such intimacy in speaking telepathically with him. He seemed to brush her mind with caresses, making her feel special despite her fear of him.

"*Uskolfertiilamet andam.* I give you my allegiance."

The strange liquid quality in Petru's eyes had formed pools of swirling silver that she found mesmerizing. She found herself drowning there, caught by the words of his ritual, his compelling voice and the pull of the threads binding them together.

"*Sívamet andam.* I give you my heart."

The moment Petru uttered that vow to her—and Safia knew it was a promise he meant to keep—her heart responded with a leap. An instant recognition, welcoming him with joy. The things he said might mean nothing to anyone else, but she felt each solemn promise branded into her very bones. Even deeper. They sank into her, becoming part of her cells, her DNA, impossible to ever erase.

"*Sielamet andam.* I give you my soul."

That was the moment he bound them together irrevocably. She felt the lock snap tightly in place, the two halves coming back together, fitting perfectly. If she hadn't been convinced before that she was his lifemate, now there was no denying it.

She had caught brief flashes, tiny vignettes of his life when she'd been with him before. With their souls bound together, she saw far more. Raised ugly scars, dark and terrible, as well as the torn and tattered places worn from the centuries of battles in a lonely gray void.

Her heart and soul wept for him. She had always been an empath, deeply feeling the emotions of those around her. Bound as she was to Petru, the feelings were amplified so much stronger.

"*Ainamet andam.* I give you my body."

The moment he uttered that promise, color swept under her skin, covering her entire body. Tiny little flames flickered in her belly, where a knot the size of his fist formed.

"*Sívamet kuuluak kaik että a ted.* I take into my keeping the same that is yours."

It was impossible not to recall the sensations his fingers had created. It was all she could do to stand still under the blazing heat of his eyes. It was difficult not to sway toward him, to turn her face up to his, knowing he was remembering the exact scorching moments together that she was.

You cannot tempt me with everyone so close, sívamet. I am no angel. A fallen one, perhaps, but I have little control when it comes to you.

She was grateful she wasn't alone in her lack of control.

"*Ainaak olenszal sívambin.* Your life will be cherished by me for all time."

I like the word "cherished." She had never been shy, but admitting that to him made her feel even more vulnerable than knowing he was aware of how much she desired him physically.

Have no fears, Pelkgapâd és Meke Pirämet. You are cherished.

What is that you called me?

Fearless Defender. Sometimes I call you Demon Slayer. Sívamet *is* "*of my heart.*" *Or* "*my love.*"

She moistened her lips, unable to speak.

"*Te élidet ainaak pide minan.* Your life will be placed above mine for all time."

When Petru stated that vow, he said it as if he meant it. Safia wondered why the man swore the vows and the woman simply listened. She knew that they were bound together and that when he had told her the ritual binding words would seal them, he spoke the truth. But why would only the man have to commit to these vows? There were so many unanswered questions.

"*Te avio päläfertiilam.* You are my lifemate."

She knew *lifemate* to Petru meant his spouse. His wife but more.

"*Ainaak sívamet jutta oleny.* You are bound to me for all eternity."

Her heart clenched hard in her chest. Eternity was a very long time. He would live for eternity. She would grow old and die. What would happen to him then? After all the dire warnings about him not being able to be without her, what would happen to him? Aura's mother had lived a half life without her husband. In fact, she had all but abandoned Aura once he was gone. She didn't want that for Petru. He'd suffered so much already.

"*Ainaak terád vigyázak.* You are always in my care."

The last words had a finality to them. She was married to Petru Cioban. For eternity. Always in his care. A shiver went down her spine. She wasn't certain if she loved the idea or was absolutely terrified.

A slow, brief, all-too-sensual smile lit Petru's eyes. He tugged at her wrists until she stepped forward, so close her hands lay against his chest. With exquisite gentleness, Petru cupped her face between his palms and bent his head to hers. She watched him come to her, those lines carved deep, the epitome of sensuality.

There was desire in his eyes but not lust. He looked tender. Almost loving. His lips brushed hers. One corner. The other. Her stomach did a roll. He kissed the dimple he seemed a little obsessed with. Just a brief touch of his lips, but it was enough to send her pulse into overdrive.

His tongue ran along the seam of her lips, and then his teeth nipped her lower lip. The sting was barely there but enough to make her gasp. He took advantage, parting her lips, sliding his tongue along hers, pouring the hot masculine taste of him into her mouth and down her throat. Instantly, glittering embers spread through every vein and artery, carrying tiny sparks, igniting a wildfire until flames seemed to be leaping through her body and racing to her core.

Petru lifted his head and pressed his forehead to hers while they both took a moment to get their breathing under control.

Amastan cleared his throat. "Did this ritual satisfy both of you that Safia is your lifemate?"

"I never had a single doubt," Petru said and straightened. Turning to face her family, he retained possession of her hand. "The ritual bound us together. In the eyes of my people and mine, she is my wife."

The three men who had always meant the most to Safia regarded her carefully. She gripped Petru's hand, terrified at the consequences of what had just occurred. She had stepped off the proverbial cliff. She did her best to keep fear from showing on her face, but she was trembling, and that was difficult to hide. The last thing she wanted was her family feeling as though they needed to fight for her. They had no chance of winning a battle against Petru and his traveling companions.

Petru stepped slightly in front of her, helping to keep her family from seeing the shaking she couldn't quite control.

"And you, *Yelli*," Amastan asked, his voice very gentle. "Do you believe you are Petru's wife? That you belong with him?"

Had he not tacked on the last sentence, Safia could have easily answered honestly. She moistened her lips and looked up at Petru. Her hand would have been crushing his if he hadn't been so strong. As it was, her knuckles were white. His thumb began to glide back and forth over the back of her hand soothingly.

"Yes, *Jeddi*. There is no question anymore in my mind that I am his lifemate." She left it at that.

"We have many issues to work out," Petru said. "Safia has raised questions she deserves answers to. I wish to take her somewhere private where we will not be interrupted. I want her to feel free to ask me questions without reservations. If she has objections, she needs to be able to voice them without feeling as if she is betraying our union. We can only accomplish that if we're alone."

"Forgive me, Petru," Gwafa said. "I know she is your wife, but we have little knowledge of you, and Safia is very beloved. These circumstances are highly unusual."

"You worry for her safety."

Safia was relieved that Petru didn't force her father to have to state his concern. That would have been an insult to the Carpathian, and they couldn't afford to keep offending him. She was very sure when they talked together, she was going to be doing enough of that for her entire family.

"I can only give you my word of honor that she will be safe with me, and I will return with her tomorrow evening. In the meantime, to keep your farm and family safe, the brethren will weave safeguards against demons and vampires."

"Do you think it wise for the two of you to go off alone with vampires and demons coming out at night?" Amastan inquired. "We can provide complete privacy for you here on the farm. We have guest quarters. Two of them are a distance from the main house."

Safia tried not to give a sigh of relief. That was the perfect answer. Trust her grandfather to think of it. That was why he was their leader. He was wise and diplomatic. He was well aware she was uncomfortable and not at all sure of the situation.

Petru gave her family a slight bow. "I thank you for the offer but must decline the invitation. We will take our leave now but will return tomorrow eve."

The pressure on her to move left her with no choice but to lead the way toward the heavy front door. It appeared as if she were taking the initiative when it was Petru. Amastan and Gwafa trailed after them, her father not bothering to hide his anxiety.

Izem had both hands on his hips as he strode right outside as if he might attempt to stop them. Petru ignored them, swept Safia into his arms and took to the sky, preventing any interference if that had been her brother's intention.

Safia pressed her lips together to keep from voicing a protest, wrapped her arms around Petru's neck and buried her face against his shoulder. She didn't want to see the family farm fading into the distance.

How did you discover the brethren were close to you?

Safia remained silent, clutching at his shoulders. The tips of her fingers touched his thick, silvery hair. It felt like silk to her. She had the unexpected urge to bury her fingers in it.

Safia? When I ask you a question, I expect an answer.

She sighed. *I don't think it best to discuss this while we're this high in the air.*

Why not? No one is around, and you can voice your objections in any way you desire.

That's just the problem. Every time I think of you sending those three to spy on us, it makes me so angry I'd like to show you just how my grandmother used to tweak our ears if she didn't like something we did.

Tweak your ears? he echoed. *I have never heard of this. Is this some kind of medieval torture? I thought I knew of them all.*

Yes. She proceeded to show him, twisting his earlobe with a bit more enthusiasm than her grandmother had ever used.

He burst out laughing. *I must try that on a vampire, although his ear would most likely fall off. They rot from the inside out, and body parts tend to come loose in an alarming fashion.*

She couldn't help but laugh with him. He had an atrocious sense of humor. Aura was the only one she could secretly laugh with over outrageous things that would shock her family if they knew she said or did them. The thought of Aura sobered her. She'd been hurt needlessly.

Aura has led a terrible life. She has lived for the same two thousand years you have, Petru. You had no emotions. While that was horrible for you, she had no family other than her mother, who lived with one foot in this world and one with her dead husband. She barely spoke to Aura. She certainly didn't counsel her in Carpathian ways.

There must have been other Carpathian families nearby. Males to watch over her.

No. She was five when the war took place. My family became her family. She grew up with us. Over and over, she grew up with us and trained the next generation, century after century. When a guardian for the gate was needed, she volunteered because she was here. She learned to fight vampires and did so alone because no one else was here to do it. Often, she was horribly wounded. She knows more of our culture than her own. You have no right to come here and treat her as an outsider. She is my sister. My family. The things we say to each other are private between sisters.

She felt fiercely protective toward Aura, and she didn't hold back that feeling from him. He might as well know how she really was. He wanted her for a wife. He said they were compatible. He needed to know whom he was dealing with. She wasn't going to back down for him or be afraid of telling him how wrong he'd been.

Aura is courageous beyond measure. She's gifted. Without her, I would have had no training. She's the one who taught me your language and worked with me on my weapons skills. In fact, she's the one who taught my mother and my grandmother.

Petru was silent for a long time. She raised her head to peek at the land below them. She didn't recognize where they were. The sky was clear, although the night was cold. She was surprised that she wasn't cold. Clouds drifted above their heads, but very few. There seemed to be a million stars looking down at them.

I have never known a Carpathian woman to be so isolated. This is an unusual situation. I will apologize to her. I've sent word of her situation to the others to better understand. We've met two other guardians. They were independent, but they were versed in Carpathian ways. She is fortunate in that she was not killed by a vampire.

Safia liked that he immediately said he would apologize and sounded sincere. He also was considering the best way to help Aura. He didn't like that she'd been so alone and had no real knowledge of her people or customs.

I should have asked you about her before I assumed she was raised as all other Carpathian women. Nothing here is as it was supposed to be.

She caught the hint of conflict in him, and self-doubt crept in despite her resolve not to allow the things imprinted on her by the vampire to get to her. She refused to feel less than Petru. Wasn't that one of her worries over their relationship? That he was so certain his species was superior to hers?

I do not think my species is superior to yours, Safia.

She slipped one hand from his neck to his shoulder. *You shouldn't be listening to my thoughts. That's an invasion of privacy. You notice I'm careful not to invade your privacy.*

Sívamet. There was a hint of amusement in the caress in her mind. *We are talking intimately, mind to mind. It is impossible to speak telepathically without being in your mind and seeing your thoughts. You can easily see mine.*

I'm not looking because I'm polite. She wasn't looking because she had already caught so many glimpses of his past, and it was all so sad, she didn't dare have any more sympathy for him until she had talked out every issue. *I don't invade your privacy without permission.*

Below them was a forest of trees. She had only traveled to the protected park a couple of times alone. By car, it was a distance, and she had so much to do, but Aura had taken her there to practice with weapons at night. When she looked down at the canopy of trees swaying in the breeze, there didn't appear to be breaks in the thick forest, but she knew there were clear meadows, some large and others small, but ones they could use when they wanted to practice unobserved.

P etru found himself amused by the little snippy note in Safia's voice. He hadn't known happiness, and she gave that to him. Even now, when he knew he was walking through a minefield, he felt the brightness in her that had passed to him. He wanted to do everything right with her, and so far, that hadn't happened. There was more about him and his people she wasn't going to like. It was important to get everything out in the open between them.

Once he'd met Safia and realized she hadn't been given any information about him or his claim on her, or about Carpathians, he felt her family had betrayed him. Still, he believed that Safia could handle the truth, and he intended to go forward being as transparent as possible with her. The bottom line was that the end of his days were near, and he was holding on by a thread. If this was going to work, she had to comply. He wasn't safe until they were completely merged together and she had accepted their relationship. He sensed she was a long way from that reality.

You have my permission to invade my privacy. I brought you here to clear up issues between us. I want you to ask questions, and I'll try to answer as openly as possible.

There was a buildup of rock forming a gorge where water ran down in a tall, narrow steady stream over misshapen smaller boulders. The water fell down the steep slope to pool below in a canyon no more than ten feet at its widest point. The gorge ran for several yards before a sharp bend took away sight of the rapidly moving current.

Close your eyes. I'm going to take you behind the water. There's a thin crack in the rocks. I'll widen the crack enough for us to get through and close it behind us. Once inside, I'll light the way so you can see. I'll have to weave safeguards to prevent the undead from entering.

Her heart accelerated and he thought she might protest, but she managed to slow her pulse to normal. *I should ensure no demon can find us as well.*

Her voice was steady despite her fear of being alone with him. They were far from her home, and she would be trapped inside the cave with no way out until he allowed it. The more he was with her, the more he admired her. The universe had been extremely good to him when he didn't in any way deserve her.

That is an excellent idea.

He widened the crack in the rock just enough to allow them to pass through. Ordinarily he would have forced their bodies to be paper thin. He didn't think she needed to have any undue stress. She was going to be facing enough of that with the things he would have to reveal to her.

Waving his hand to light sconces on the walls of the cave, he closed the crack behind them and set her on her feet. She clung to him to steady herself, but only for a moment—just as long as it took to ensure she had her balance. His lifemate was independent.

"I brought your coat and backpack just in case we ran into demons you had to destroy. I was uncertain of what you would need since we hadn't discussed it, so I brought as much as possible." He gave her a brief smile. "I didn't intrude. I probably should have."

He turned back to the entrance to weave safeguards, treating the situation as matter-of-factly as possible.

Safia followed his example, going through the backpack he had placed on the dirt floor beside a massive rock. "That was thoughtful of you. Thank you."

She didn't look at him but kept her gaze on the weave he was building to ensure nothing would disturb them. "Would you mind if I add to your safeguard? I often added to Aura's. When we wove strands together, mine kept demons from entering, but it would also confuse vampires."

Petru stepped back and indicated for her to proceed. He found her fascinating. She asked his permission, but she was already forming the proper guards in her mind with complete confidence. He studied her without seeming to. Even her demeanor had changed. She was serious, just as she had been when she was defending Aura. She *was* the defender. She'd been shaped into that role from the time she was born. He realized that was who she was and would always be. He might want to put her in a safe locked room where no harm could ever come to her, but she would never be happy. Never.

This was his lifemate. This woman standing beside him confidently adding to the safeguards he'd woven. It wasn't that she didn't trust him to take care of her. She wasn't defying him or in any way fearing he wasn't able to keep her or those around them safe. She would fight every single battle to keep those around—and him—safe because that was her true nature.

Could he accept that in her? He had watched her die. He had watched a vampire rip her heart from her chest right in front him. He hadn't protected her. He hadn't saved her. That moment was forever burned into his brain. Now that the memory was uncovered, there was no putting it aside. He knew he had failed the most important person in his life. She knew he had abandoned her. There was no taking that back.

Petru had thought that this time around, given a second chance, he would ensure her safety every waking minute. He would keep her by his side, and if he couldn't be with her, his most trusted brethren would be. He could see that further soul-searching would have to be done for him to be a better lifemate to his woman. He couldn't change who he was and wouldn't want her to ask him to be different. That meant he couldn't demand it of her.

She glanced up at him, her green eyes softening into a beautiful jade. "You're really seeing me for the first time."

"Not the first time. I didn't want to see what I'm seeing now," he admitted. "Carpathian women are rarely on the battle lines. It did not occur to me that you would need to be at the front of the battle."

He let her finish her weave, and then while she was consecrating the ground and ceiling and all four directions, he finished his safe-guards. Looking ahead to the chamber where he thought it was best to do their talking, he fashioned the room as a close version of her family room at the farm. He wanted her to be as relaxed as possible.

Petru led the way through the maze of tunnels to the chamber. It was wide and round with a high ceiling. He'd fixed sconces high up on the walls to light the room. The gems and crystals embedded in the rocks glittered, casting various colors throughout the space. The small rock fireplace with the low rolling flames was an illusion. There was nowhere for the smoke to go, and he wouldn't want it to be released into the air to give their position away. Still, it would feel to her as if it warmed the room and give her comfort.

"This is beautiful, Petru," Safia said, her eyes lighting up. For a brief moment, there was joy on her face as she looked around the chamber. She went straight to one of the chairs positioned in front of the fireplace. "Thank you for thinking of it."

Amastan had mentioned to him several times that family and Safia's home were very important to her. Her reaction to the small gesture of comfort proved her grandfather correct.

"I'm glad you like it." He took the chair opposite her and regarded her over steepled fingers. On the small table beside her, he'd added a bowl of fresh fruit and a glass of clear water, although he knew she would have trouble drinking or eating. She would have to come to realize that on her own.

"Before we get started and you ask your questions, will you tell me how you were aware my brethren were with you? It's important. If you could find them, it is possible a vampire or some other creature Lilith sends could as well. They are uneasy and your explanation wasn't log-ical to them."

Safia's jade green gaze drifted over his face. She leaned her chin into her palm, one eyebrow going up. "Not logical? Everyone, even Carpathians, has electrical charges in them. Energy, if you will. Granted, all of you have the lowest energy I've ever come across, lower even than Aura has. Hers was even lower than her mother's. Still, it's there. Once I spend time with someone, I can identify them."

She gave a little shrug as if that said it all. It didn't. He was tempted to get inside her head and pull out the memory of the moment she had found his brethren, but he'd promised himself he would attempt to talk things out with her. She wasn't trying to withhold data from him; she was trying to explain what came naturally to her.

"If you knew I was close but you couldn't see me, do you think you could locate me?"

"Yes. It would be very easy."

"Because of our blood tie?" He didn't think she located anything through a blood tie.

She gave him that little frown he had fallen hard for. "No, I told you. Energy. I would follow the energy trail. I can feel you and connect with that trail."

He was tempted to ask her what kind of energy he had but thought better of it. No doubt it was quite violent. "I would understand better if I could see the moment you found the brethren," he admitted. He made no demands on her, just waited to see if she would voluntarily allow him deeper into her memories.

Safia's green eyes moved over his face again, a slow perusal. He wasn't certain what she was looking for, because he knew he didn't give much away, but she nodded and immediately opened her mind, pushing the memory of becoming aware of the brethren in the grotto with Aura and her. He studied the way she had alerted to the presence of the brethren. Both women had become uneasy, but it had been Safia who had confirmed that his traveling companions were close. He moved in her mind, attempting to discern how she had identified they were close.

Instinct. She had the instincts of a hunter. They were bred into her, just as they were into him. She'd been born with a sixth sense; he was certain of it. It wasn't taught to her. She had known the brethren were there because she sensed they were.

She had been stealthy in the way she stalked them. Nicu first. She found him through a pattern she recognized. Then she found the others. They hadn't been aware of her touch. That was worrisome. Although he was immensely proud of her, his companions were ancients. They should have known the moment she'd locked in on them. He would have to speak with the others about her abilities. He'd never run across a human—or any other, for that matter—who could do what she had done.

"Thank you for allowing me to look into your memories. That helped me to understand the process."

Safia nodded. "Why were you upset with Aura for answering me when I asked her about Carpathian rituals?"

"It is customary for lifemates to answer questions. At that time, I believed Aura was aware of that. Obviously, that is not the case."

"What is it that I'm unaware of? It isn't something trivial. I could sense Aura was concerned I would be very upset if I knew what you were doing."

"I told you what the exchanges meant and why they were necessary. I was very honest with you." Petru chose each word carefully. One didn't lie to one's lifemate. This was coming very close. "Did you find the exchange with me repugnant?"

"You know I didn't. You didn't force me. You didn't take over my mind as you could have. I made certain Aura knew you gave me free will. She was still uneasy. That meant there was more to what we did than you were telling me. You omitted telling me something important, didn't you?"

He didn't take his gaze from hers. They had gotten here much faster than he had wanted. "I didn't think it was necessary to tell you everything at once. You hadn't been told about me until the night we met. You'd fought a vampire—amazingly well, I might add—but you'd lost blood and needed aid. I was a shock to you. I thought it would be good to try to get to know as much as we could about each other in the little time we had. But you were doing your job, defending the town of Dellys against demons, our second meeting."

"We're sitting here now," she pointed out. "What is the significance of the blood exchanges that you haven't told me?"

"It takes three blood exchanges to bring a human into the Carpathian world." He gave her the information in the same low, casual tone he tended to deliver all news. As if it were unimportant, just another fact, when it would change her life for all eternity.

She frowned, rubbed at her lower lip, and then gave a slight shake of her head. Reaching for the glass of water, she hesitated and then allowed her hand to drop into her lap. "I thought the binding words married us. Isn't that bringing me into your world? We're attempting to blend our customs. I'm trying to get the concept of exchanging blood. I do accept that I would need to give you blood if you were injured. Isn't that all part of being in your world?"

"You must come fully into my world."

Her lashes swept down, veiling her expression, and then she was looking at him with emerald eyes. "I think you need to be very clear with me, Petru, because I'm not sure what you're saying."

"When we exchange blood for the third time, you will begin the transformation from human to Carpathian. My blood will convert your cells and organs to those of a Carpathian. Essentially, you will die and be reborn Carpathian."

He heard the leap of her heart, but she controlled the swift acceleration. Her chin lifted and the green eyes deepened in color. "When did you plan on telling me about this? Before or after the third blood exchange?"

"I would have told you before." He was honest. He would have, not that it would make any difference. He was going to give her his blood and take hers. He had no choice but to bring her fully into his world. Not if he wanted to ensure everyone's safety.

"No. Absolutely not. I am Imazighen. I have always loved being one of the free people. I will always be Imazighen. There is no reason why I cannot be with you and stay who and what I am."

She didn't yell or become hysterical. If anything, she spoke in a low, casual tone, just as he did. He heard the utter resolve in her voice. Her gaze was steady on his. Her mind was closed on the subject.

12

P etru pushed down the dominant Carpathian male attitude and regarded his lifemate, attempting to see the situation through her eyes. His life would remain unchanged while hers would be completely different. She was the one giving up everything familiar to join her life to his.

"*Sívamet.*" He leaned toward her and used his most compelling voice, a brush of velvet over her skin. "Why would you think you would not remain Imazighen? That is who you are. The best part. Nothing can change that."

"You told me your blood would reshape my internal organs. Make me like you." There was uncertainty in Safia's voice. She was struggling to understand him.

Petru knew it was a difficult concept to grasp. "Your body isn't you, Safia. It isn't your heart or your mind. Your character is wholly Imazighen. Nothing will ever change who you are," he reiterated. "Certainly not the blood of a Carpathian. It will enhance your speed. You will have other abilities. You will be better able to defend your family, but you as a person will remain the same. You will always be Imazighen."

She looked unconvinced. "Will I have to survive on blood?"

"Yes. And you will have to sleep in the ground with me."

She shook her head before he finished speaking. "No. That will leave my family unprotected during the day. I can't do that. Lilith sends demons during daylight hours. If she became aware there was no protection for my family, or even Dellys, she would send as many demons as possible to wreak havoc and turn neighbor against neighbor."

"Lilith made a mistake when she waited for so long. She thought everyone would forget. There was no written history of what really happened two thousand years ago in the war. She didn't count on your ancestors, Safia. She didn't realize that your family would retell the stories and honor the promises Kahina and her husband made to me. For centuries, your family has trained to fight demons and vampires. When there was no war, they still didn't forget. They continued to prepare. Consequently, they began to be born with the skills of other generations that came before imprinted on them. Not all but most."

"My brothers and sisters have skills, but they cannot defeat demons without me."

"That may be true, Safia, but with our combined skills, Aura, my brethren and the two of us can weave safeguards and consecrate the ground and air so that she is unable to send her demons to do mayhem until we rise."

He didn't take his gaze from hers, needing to read her reaction. She had courage, his woman. She knew she had been promised to him long ago, and she was honorable. She also knew she was destined for him. The ritual words tying them together had convinced her. Still, he was asking a lot of her when she didn't yet trust him.

"I'll need time to think about what you're asking of me, Petru. This is no small thing. I hadn't ever conceived of it. It's quite terrifying, actually."

The tip of her tongue moistened the curve of her lower lip, drawing his attention to the full bow of her mouth. She had a beautiful mouth. He could fixate on her mouth if he allowed himself the luxury. Full.

Soft. He knew if he kissed her, he would taste a mixture of desire, jasmine and fear. He didn't want her to fear him.

The more he sat there with her in that remote cave, far from her family or anyone else she knew, offering her little in the way of comfort, the more he understood what the vows he made to her meant.

The color slowly leeched from under her skin. She twisted her fingers together in her lap. "You don't mean to give me any time to process this, do you? You brought me here to make the third blood exchange and intend to whether I agree or not."

There was no denying her charge. She knew his ruthless character just from the few glimpses she had into his past. She would be giving up everything for him. He had to give her something in return, even if it would damn him forever in her eyes. He wanted her respect more than that of any other, yet once he admitted his greatest weakness and shame—and he knew he had to give that to her—she would never look at him the same.

Petru forced his gaze to continue to meet hers. Her eyes had changed color from jade to a lighter emerald than he'd ever seen before. She looked different. Softer. Less frightened. She didn't speak but held his gaze, waiting for his response.

"Safia, I am aware that as your lifemate, I have failed you in every way. If I could, I would make the choice to allow you to live as a human if that was your wish. I would grow old with you and die when you did. Unfortunately, that is not a choice either of us have. That is my failing, not yours."

Her lashes swept down and then came back up, but her gaze was steady. The pulse in her neck beat strong, matching the rhythm of his. "Is that a possibility?"

"For some. Not for us."

"Because you're too close to turning? Aura tried to explain to me what that meant. Becoming a vampire if you're not anchored by your lifemate? I thought if your soul was restored, you would be safe."

Safia sounded genuinely concerned. That surprised him. He was in her mind, monitoring her reaction to see just how much of a rejection he was going to get from her. Instead of pulling away from him, she seemed to be listening and trying to understand. There was no judgment on her part—yet.

"You said the failing is yours, not mine, but if that isn't so, Petru, I'd rather you tell me the truth. Is it possible I lack in some way?"

He rubbed the bridge of his nose, trying to choose his words carefully. He wanted to be as honest with her as possible. She deserved to understand what was happening to him. He never wanted her to feel she lacked in any way. The vampire had planted that seed in her, undermining her self-confidence, hoping that if this day came and they were able to reunite, there would always be doubt in their relationship.

"The failing is mine, Safia. Carpathian males always put their lifemates first. Before any other. You heard our vows. We mean them. We have a code of honor, and we hold to that. In the history of our existence, I am the only one who has ever broken that code. I betrayed you. You were a helpless child counting on me, and I allowed you to die a hideous death."

Safia's heart clenched in her chest. She felt Petru's gut-wrenching agony in that moment when he had made the decision to save the others and turn the tide of the war. It wasn't contrived. He wanted to look away from her, feeling shame. More than shame. *He* felt unworthy of her. From the moment his memories had been restored, he had replayed his decision over and over. Each time the stain on his soul grew darker, the scar thicker and his sin more unforgivable in his eyes.

He watched the vampire rip the child's heart from her chest. Felt her terror. Felt the child's torture, tried desperately not only to get to her but to spare her the pain, to take it on himself, but was unable to do so.

"Don't look at my memories," Petru said.

"I blocked you. I cut the tie between us," Safia said. "The vampire didn't. Lilith didn't. I was the one who blocked you. You *had* to make the choice to save the others. If you had saved me—us—everyone would die. I knew that. Even as a child, I understood that. I didn't want my entire tribe dead. It wasn't only your decision, Petru."

Petru leaned back in the chair, his eyes glittering that peculiar liquid silver. "You were five. Powerful, yes, but still a human child. You have no idea of the power I wielded then. Or do now. Or how ruthless I can be. I don't have your compassion. I didn't have emotions back then. I hadn't claimed you. I knew you existed only because you touched my mind. Once I knew, it was my duty to protect you, and I failed. I allowed you to suffer and die one of the worst possible deaths."

Although she knew Petru didn't want her to see or feel his emotions, it was too important for her to pull back. She allowed his true feelings to flood her mind, tapping into the emotions before he could distance them from her or dull them. She realized he had done that earlier. He wasn't going to hide what he felt from her, but he didn't want her to pity him. He thought her too compassionate. He also didn't want her to think he was manipulating her, using her empathy against her.

Petru's nature demanded he protect her. He hadn't done so when she was a child all those centuries ago, and the guilt would never leave him. He couldn't forgive himself. The first time she felt his painful memories, he'd cushioned them, sparing her. They'd been endless agony for him. Every moment he was awake. No matter what he was doing unless he was with her.

This time she refused to allow him to spare her. The suffering he experienced had been horrific between his mental anguish, the physical pain as he'd fought vampires to get to her and sharing her pain as Eduardo tore out her heart. She couldn't imagine having to go through it over and over.

"I will forever carry the shame of failing my lifemate. Even now, I fail you. The one thing you ask for is time to process what is needed to be with me. That is not unreasonable, even with the coming war, yet because of my failure, I cannot give that to you."

Safia let her breath out slowly. She was unsure how to reach him, how to make him understand that she had been part of that decision so long ago. She had helped to influence him. His Carpathian family had influenced him. Her family had. The tribe had. Other Carpathians had. He'd had less than a few seconds to make up his mind.

"None of those people matter," he stated, making it known he was as much in her mind as she was in his. "I'm *your* lifemate. My first duty is to you. In my heart, in my soul, I chose you. My instinct was to choose you, yet somehow I was already attacking Lilith. I knew if I could remove her, we had a chance. A thousand times since I've recovered my memories I've wondered if I was so arrogant, I thought I could make it to you in time to save you."

"Petru, think back. You believed your life would end. You thought you would have no chance and intended to destroy as many vampires as possible before you died. I read your intentions as you fought your way toward me. You were so far away, and there were so many enemies between us. They surrounded you, tore the skin off you with their teeth and claws, tried to get at your heart. Still, you came for me. We both knew you couldn't make it in time. Eduardo deliberately taunted you."

He scrubbed his hand down his face, trying to wipe the sight of her from his mind, but it was etched, that small child with her large eyes fixed on him, not one sound escaping, not even when the vampire sank his teeth into her.

"You believed, because you hadn't claimed me, I would marry within my tribe and be happy when I was reborn. You didn't think I would remember you. You are not to blame." She knew it was impossible to remove his guilt. The demands of being a Carpathian lifemate were bred into him.

He gave her a faint self-loathing smile. "Do you understand how I am once again failing you by forcing you to become what you fear so quickly because I do not dare take the chance of waiting? You worry that I made a poor bargain with my lifemate. In reality, you are the one who has done so."

"What exactly does it entail to become Carpathian other than exchanging blood? I didn't find that in the least revolting, as you well know." Safia didn't believe for one moment that erotic exchange was all there was to it. "You very casually mentioned dying. That doesn't sound too fun to me."

"The conversion is very painful. I can help. The others will. I will ask Aura to aid us. But we can only help so much. No one can keep you from experiencing pain as your body is ridding itself of toxins and reshaping organs. The moment it is safe to do so, I will send you to sleep. You will finish the conversion while you are unaware."

There was no expression on his face or in his voice. His features could have been carved in stone, but she was in his mind, and he couldn't hide his emotions from her. He didn't feel as if he had anything to offer her. Nothing at all. She found that interesting. She felt that way. He felt that way. Both felt unworthy of the other.

"Do you suppose, Petru, that the suggestion was planted in *both* of us, not just me, that we should feel shame? Or guilt? Or not worthy of the other? If Lilith could find a way to drive a wedge between us, even one of our own making, that would be a win for her, wouldn't it? You might be distracted. You would be continually proving your loyalty to me rather than thinking of each battle. I would be wondering if you were going to sacrifice me again for the greater good. That would be her ultimate goal, right?"

The silvery liquid in Petru's eyes heated and became the color of mercury. His gaze sharpened. Instantly, she felt pieces of a puzzle clicking into place in his brain. The speed at which his mind worked fascinated her.

"Interesting. I was certain Lilith had Eduardo imprint on you feelings that not only I but your family had abandoned you because you weren't good enough. You're just too extraordinary not to realize your self-worth. You have confidence in your fighting skills. You must be aware of the gifts you were born with, and yet you still have moments when you feel as if you aren't worthy of being my lifemate."

Safia couldn't deny that was a fact. She nodded.

"It didn't occur to me that Lilith managed to imprint on me that I was unworthy of you. It is the truth. I am the only Carpathian who has betrayed his lifemate in the history of our world. I am guilty. I am still leaving you without choices, even though I want to give you everything you deserve. Even if Lilith did manage to find a way to get to me, there is no way to deny that I am guilty."

"All she had to do was know how a Carpathian male thinks. Aura explained to me that the vampire was once Carpathian. Wouldn't Lilith know about Carpathian lifemates through her association with vampires? All she would need to do is find a way to amplify your feelings of guilt and shame, Petru."

"What purpose would she have?"

Safia was in his mind and knew he already had ideas but wanted her opinions. She liked that he valued what she might think.

"It is possible you would take me far from here rather than risk losing me again. Or you might not want me to fight with you to destroy demons while you hunt vampires. There could be any number of reasons. If you held too tight and I was used to freedom."

Petru nodded, his demeanor thoughtful. "You bring up very good points. I am uncertain how a vampire or even Lilith could imprint on me. That is not arrogance. I just do not see how they could get into my mind—unless . . ." He looked at her.

Safia realized immediately what he was thinking. "Through me. I opened a pathway to you, and they took advantage in that short time."

"It's the only way I can think of that they might have been able to accomplish such a thing."

"I'm sorry, Petru." She spread her hands out in front of her. "I had no idea of the consequences when I connected with you. You were this larger-than-life hero, and I was so drawn to you. I remember it was such a compulsion to reach out. But I found it hard to resist everything I wanted to know more about, even before the war. Animals, people, the land, flowers, trees, rocks—everything. I was a very curious child. There was no resisting connecting with you to see what you were like."

"Do not wish you hadn't. I see that in your mind, *Ku Tappa Kulyak*."

His voice was velvet soft, sending a shiver of desire down her spine. She liked the way he called her *Ku Tappa Kulyak*. "Demon Slayer" might not be sweet and syrupy, but it made her feel as if they were partners and that he respected her. That was what she wanted above all else in a relationship.

"I believe everything happens for a reason. You were meant to be my lifemate. I cannot imagine having another, and I would not want any other woman."

She heard the sincerity in his voice. More, she felt it in his mind.

"Your answer will not change my intention to go through the conversion, although to be honest, I need to work up courage to do that and ask a few more questions, but your answer to this question is very important to me."

Petru's gaze held steady on hers. "This is the time for us to get to know one another, Safia. It is important we trust one another as much as possible in the short time we have. It will be the two of us the others depend on to get them through the coming war with Lilith. I believe that you're right, that she sought to drive a wedge between us. We can't allow that to happen."

"Do you plan to take me from my family once the war is over should we survive?"

His gaze drifted over her face. The hard lines softened until he looked almost tender. "*Sívamet*, you would be unhappy if we spent too much time away from your family. I meant every word of my vows to you. No, I have no intention of taking you away from your family. I know that Aura has a commitment to guard the gate and that she needs help. She counts on you, the defender, the one to keep the demons at bay. There are duties enough here to keep us busy. There might be times we are called to other places, but this will be our home until your family passes and you wish to move on."

She had to look away from him when she unexpectedly felt tears burning behind her eyes. It was impossible for him to lie to her when she was in his mind. At least she was almost certain it was. He might be powerful enough to keep the truth from her, but she doubted it.

Safia swallowed the lump in her throat. "I appreciate that. I love my family and can't imagine living apart from them. I thought I would have to go with you to your home."

"Someday we will travel to the Carpathian Mountains. I would like to show you many things, but we have time to visit the various lands and forests I would enjoy seeing through your eyes. First, I would like to learn the ways of your people. Amastan has been instructing me in the little time we have had together, as have your brother and father."

Her heart leapt. He had taken the time to try to understand a little of her culture. That meant a lot to her.

"It's important to note that I don't do well when you boss me around," she felt compelled to point out. "If we're getting to know one another, I prefer to discuss anything important."

His eyebrow went up. "It's just as important to note I'm not good with arguments. When I say something, it's for a reason, not just to hear myself talk. That's where trust in your lifemate comes in."

She rolled her eyes. "Perhaps taking the time for an explanation would be a good idea. I do have a brain and can understand anything you have to say."

"There might not always be time to explain, Safia."

She frowned and rubbed at her lower lip. "All right," she conceded. "I can see that and will agree, but you'll have to agree it goes both ways."

"What does that mean?"

She was very careful not to show triumph that she'd trapped him.

"I might not have time to explain to you what I'm doing, and you'll have to take things on trust as well."

"I can see that I'm going to have to work very hard to stay one step ahead of you in all negotiations."

She laughed. She couldn't help it. He hadn't gotten upset when she'd turned the tables on him. "Is that what we're doing? Negotiating?"

"It would seem so." A hint of underlying humor edged his voice.

"I don't want to sleep in the ground," she blurted out. "I mean, I can do it, but I don't like the idea. What if I wake up and you're not there?" Her heart accelerated at the thought. "It would be the same as being buried alive."

He didn't just dismiss her fear as she worried he might. "That's a normal reaction. I will teach you how to open the earth, and you can practice until you are certain you can do so by yourself. The only time you will need me to do it for you is the first time you rise, and I'll be right by your side. The earth will already be open for you before I allow you to take your first breath."

Safia liked the sound of that. She wanted to be independent. "What else will I need to learn?"

"Clothing yourself when you rise. You will decide what you want to wear, picture the detailed outfit, and as you emerge, you will be wearing the garments you decided on. When I say 'detailed,' I mean everything, from underwear, if you desire it, to shoes and jewelry."

She couldn't help liking the idea. That sounded amazing. She wasn't a designer like Farah, but she could ask Farah to help her design some nice blouses and skirts. Layla's wide belts were popular with tourists, and Safia particularly loved to wear them with her skirts. Often, Layla would make belts that could double as weapons. She would ask Layla to design a couple in great detail that Safia could duplicate when she was dressing as she emerged from the ground.

"I will also teach you to use the air. You're extremely fast already, and being wholly Carpathian will increase your speed. Your hearing will be so acute it will hurt at first, but you'll learn to turn down the volume. Your eyesight will be even better than it is now. Every gift you have will be enhanced. We'll practice becoming as small as an insect or a bird or a cheetah, whatever you wish to be. You can be part of the fog."

"You'll teach me to fight the undead?" Safia kept her gaze steady on his. She stayed in his mind.

He didn't flinch, but she knew the idea of her fighting vampires went against his protective nature. "Yes." There was reluctance in his answer. "I reviewed the way you fought and destroyed your first vampire step by step several times. I considered the best ways for you to defeat the undead should you find yourself in a position to have to do battle with them."

The fact that Petru had spent time thinking of ways for her to improve her skills in combat made her feel especially good. Her lifemate might be against her fighting vampires, but he was going to ensure she knew what she was doing.

"I really appreciate you," she said sincerely. She couldn't help looking at him with a little bit of hero worship. He had superior skills when it came to hunting and destroying the undead. She wanted to be just half as proficient as he was. A quarter. Enough to survive if she had no choice. She wasn't going looking. Her expertise was in fighting demons, but she knew Lilith would send vampires after her, and she wanted to be ready.

"Fighting the undead is always a risk, even for an experienced hunter. A newly turned vampire can get lucky. I never want you to chance taking on the undead if there is any other option. When you told me Aura has fought them alone, the idea was very unsettling. All of us were disturbed by that revelation. The undead are cruel and will use any means to win. They will take the children and assault them in front of you in horrific ways. They turn living beings into flesh-eating puppets. You cannot conceive of the vile things they do. I do not want you exposed to them if there is any way I can prevent it."

As he stated his objections, his fingers closed into a fist, and he rubbed it over his chest, directly over his heart. At the same time, her heart convulsed with an unfathomable piercing ache. She let herself connect deeper with him, feeling the sudden agony of a vampire clawing at his heart with sharp talons. Or was it her heart? The bluish-white spiderweb of scars surrounding her heart pulsed with pain.

"You have to stop doing that, Safia," Petru reprimanded gently.

"I don't always know I'm reaching for you or even why. In this case"—she tried to be honest—"I knew I had to connect with you on a deeper level but didn't know why." She frowned, trying to explain it to herself as much as to him. "It feels like a compulsion I can't resist."

"The same as when you were a child?"

The question was mild, but she glanced at him sharply, feeling reprimanded, as if she couldn't control her impulses. Faint color stole into her cheeks. She hated that he was right. She was supposed to have learned discipline over the years, but she was still that curious little girl, unable to stop herself from connecting with the creatures that intrigued her.

"That is not the way I meant the inquiry," Petru said, his voice once again that gentle brush of velvet in her mind and over her skin. "I must learn to communicate better with you so you do not feel as if I'm making accusations when I'm merely seeking knowledge for us. We have so little time to figure these things out. I believe they're important."

"Or maybe I could be a little less sensitive," Safia conceded. It made sense to figure out how she had gotten into him so quickly. As a child, she was the one to find her lifemate and, by doing so, had jeopardized the entire war. She had put Petru in a terrible position whether he wanted to admit it or not. They couldn't afford for such a thing to happen again. She had to know what was happening and how so she could prevent mistakes when Lilith's army attacked.

"You were not to blame," Petru objected. "We have to stop playing the blame game with one another. We are past that. We must build trust between us. You have a brilliant mind when it comes to tactics, and I'm counting on that. I don't want to have to wonder what you're doing; I'll know, just the way I know with Benedek and Nicu because I've fought beside them so often. I'm still learning with the triplets. The three of them have battled vampires together for hundreds of years and have their own unique methods."

Safia couldn't help but be elated that he so casually stated that she had a brilliant mind for tactics and he was counting on her. She loved that he planned on treating her as his partner in every way. She nodded to show she agreed with him about not blaming herself, although acknowledging he was right might be much easier than actually dismissing her doubts.

"To answer your question, the compulsion was stronger than when I was a child. I *needed* to connect with you."

"Did you feel my physical pain before the need?"

Had she? For Safia, everything felt as if it had occurred simultaneously. But it hadn't, not when she went over the memory, breaking it down. The effects had been fast, brutally fast, less than a second, but still there was an order to the steps.

"Memories flooded into my mind. Your memories of battles of vampires tearing open your chest, ripping at your heart, morphing into the memory of you watching my heart being ripped out. Mental anguish, I think first."

Petru pressed his fingertips to his eyes. "This presents a problem, as I do not feel emotions most of the time. I don't recall having memories in my mind. If I'm unaware of feeling pain, emotional or physical, how can I keep either from you? This is probably the same thing that happened when you were a child. I've heard other women state they felt our emotions when we did not. It was difficult to believe, although I heard the truth in their voices."

"If you don't know you still feel pain or emotion because you're too compartmentalized or because for all those centuries you were unable to connect with either, there is little you can do about it, Petru. I should be able to. The bond we're forming is new and very strong. I've never had any relationship with a man. I've not felt desire or fear like I have being around you, so it is much harder to control compulsions when it comes to you, but now that I know what is happening and we can't afford it, I'll find a way to adjust."

"It seems that you have to be the one to do all the adjusting."

She sent him a brief smile. "I thought we weren't going to play the blame game. It is what it is. We both have a few little shortcomings. Frankly, I'm glad, too. You're a larger-than-life hero, and having to live up to that would be exhausting."

He sent her a small, brief smile. She was certain he didn't often genuinely smile, so it felt a little like a victory. "I'm glad I can provide you with a few flaws to make you happy."

He gave her a courtly bow from his waist, long strands of his silvery hair falling around his face, giving her the impression of a beautiful fallen angel.

He lifted an eyebrow. "The things that come into your mind are such nonsense. A fallen angel? There is nothing angelic or beautiful about me."

Safia couldn't help laughing. He was beautiful whether he wanted to believe it or not. "A fallen angel can be quite sinful, and when you kiss, believe me, there's a lot of temptation and thoughts of doing things I'd never considered before."

He sent her a smoldering look. "I believe you're the one tempting me. I've lived over two thousand years and never once been tempted by a woman, and yet I get close to you and discipline is gone."

"Never once?" That was very hard to believe.

He shook his head. "For most Carpathian men, there is only their lifemate. Some men, before they lose their emotions, or if they are close to their lifemate and feel her but have no idea she is near, feel those urges. I was not one of those men. I felt nothing."

"But you seem so experienced," she objected.

He sent her another brief grin. This one was deliberately sinful. "Just because I didn't have urges doesn't mean I didn't want to know every way possible to please my lifemate when I found her, and I was determined to find her."

She narrowed her eyes at him. "What does that mean?"

"Two thousand years is a long time to study sex and all the different ways men and women can pleasure one another."

"Did you spy on people?"

"How else was I supposed to learn?"

"That's called voyeurism, and it's so wrong."

"I suppose it could be if I was aroused, but I wasn't. I was acquiring knowledge. I didn't lust after the woman or the man." He shrugged.

"You could share your knowledge with me the way you do the skills you acquired learning to fight various types of vampires. That way I would be as experienced as you."

He shook his head. "That wouldn't be nearly as much fun for us. I think I will like surprising you. Come here to me, *Ku Tappa Kulyak.*" He widened his thighs and pointed to the spot between them.

He sounded all at once dangerous and far too sensual. Safia's breath caught in her throat. Her heart began to pound in trepidation. She studied his masculine features. Hooded eyes. The carved lines in his face. Was he going to take her blood? Give her his? She had made up her mind to do this, but it was terrifying. At the same time, she could already taste him.

Come to me. Choose me the way I have chosen you.

His voice brushed at the inside walls of her mind like velvet, filling her with him. She shivered at the sensual desire building in her veins.

Did you choose me, Petru? Or did fate force me on you?

I would have chosen you for myself the moment I felt the heart of you. Your courage. The beauty inside you. The moment your soul touched mine.

etru's gaze drifted over Safia. She was so beautiful. He didn't know what standards other men judged beauty by, but she met every single one he had. She seemed to shine from the inside out. Sometimes when he looked at her, he could barely draw air into his lungs.

Settling his hands on her hips, he drew her closer between his thighs. The trembling of her body was so slight it was impossible to see, but he could feel it.

Shockingly, she leaned into him and brushed her fingers through his hair. "I'm very afraid, Petru. I'm counting on you to get me through this."

His heart clenched hard in his chest. She had no real reason to trust him. If anything, it was just the opposite, yet she'd made up her mind to commit totally to becoming fully Carpathian. She humbled him completely. He tightened his fingers on her hips and urged her to take another step closer to him.

"You will always be safe with me, *Pelkgapâd és Meke Pirämet.*" He kept his gaze steady on hers so she could see he meant it. "I give you my word of honor."

"If I didn't believe that, I wouldn't be doing this," she admitted.

He heard the note of strain in her voice. She was fearful but determined.

"I call you *Pelkgapâd és Meke Pirämet* because you are my fearless defender. You defend everyone you love. I have no doubt that when you love me, you will defend me with every breath in your body." Petru pushed strands of silky hair from her face as gently as he could. "I will do no less for you. You will always be my world, Safia."

Her jewel-colored eyes didn't leave his. Her fingers tightened convulsively on his shoulders as she nodded, as if giving him permission to continue.

"Straddle me." Now his voice was strained, but for an altogether different reason. He had to be careful. He had promised himself he would follow the customs of her people as much as he could. That meant he could bind her to him, which he'd done. He could convert her, which he intended to do, but when she rose Carpathian, he would return her to her family so they could be married in the way of her people. Until then, he couldn't make love to her in the way he wanted, solidifying their union.

It was a risk, but she was conceding so much to him, and he needed to give her something in return. He was learning the customs of the Imazighen as quickly as possible by reading the minds of those around him. He meant what he'd said to her—they would live with her family if they survived the coming war. Or at least as close to her family as possible.

Safia slipped over his thighs, her legs on either side of his. She slid her palms up his chest to circle her arms around his neck. Petru knew she was seeking comfort. He wrapped his arms around her and held her to him, whispering softly to her in the ancient language of his people. He could only try to assure her that he would treasure her above all else. Actions spoke much louder than words, and he intended to show her rather than talk about how much he was willing to do for her.

"We should do this fast before I chicken out," she whispered, her voice muffled against the heavy muscles of his chest.

He pulled back just enough that he could frame her face with his large hands. Her oval-shaped face felt delicate, fragile even, her skin so soft it was like satin beneath his rough palms. His gaze searched hers even as his mind touched hers intimately. She was determined but very frightened of the consequences of her decision.

"*Pelkgapâd és Meke Pirämet,*" he murmured. He brushed feather-light kisses from her temple to the corner of her left eye and then over her eyelid. "You are fearless when you defend your people. It was one of the many traits I respected and admired in you when we met. You faced demons and vampires for them without flinching. It is the reason I often call you *Pelkgapâd és Meke Pirämet.* Fearless Defender. There is no other like you."

He brushed kisses over her other eye and then trailed more along her high cheekbone, taking his time, memorizing her beautiful bone structure. His heart was pounding nearly as hard as hers. "Think of me as one of your people. Count me as one of your people. That is what you're doing right now, defending me when I need it most."

He had started out encouraging her, but in the end, he realized this woman was the key to living. To finding joy. Happiness. He didn't think in terms of finding affection. Of him falling in love. He didn't know what that emotion was when he'd started on his journey to find her. For two thousand years, he'd observed others, and he'd never really understood the concept. He knew sacrifice. But he hadn't *felt* it.

Safia reached up and ran her fingers through his hair, her touch so light it was barely there, but it was so powerful, compelling, just that gentle butterfly brush sinking deep, becoming a brand of ownership.

"I made my commitment to you, Petru. I don't give my word lightly. My first loyalty will always be to you, and that makes you not just one of my people. You're my *first* person."

Her eyes had gone that perfect shade of jade as she looked directly into his so that he would see her sincerity. He hadn't doubted her for a moment. How could he? She was showing him the way to an emotion he hadn't believed existed. Not just one emotion—several.

Safia didn't do anything by halves. She lived her life to the fullest. She loved that way. She battled demons, committing herself completely to the fight. Petru knew she would give herself to him that same way—entirely. Without reservation. The only way she would ever stop is if he screwed things up. He had no intention of doing so.

"I don't know how the universe gave you to me," he admitted. He trailed kisses from the tip of her nose to the corner of her mouth. "But I have no intention of giving you up for any reason."

Her breathing changed subtly as he breathed warm air against her full lower lip. He nipped at the curve with his teeth.

"I'm a little obsessed with your mouth, Safia. I'll confess my discipline doesn't hold up very well when I look at you. I start getting fixated." He caught her lip between his teeth and tugged, then used his tongue to ease the sting. He didn't stop there, kissing his way down to her chin and then back up to her mouth. His kisses were brief. Light. Barely there.

"We are married." There was seduction in her voice. She chased after his mouth.

His body tightened. It was impossible to stay disciplined when she was in his lap, and he could read the growing desire in her mind. She wanted him and thought seduction was far better than conversion.

"We are," he agreed. "In the way of my people." He kissed his way down to her chin again and then back up to her intriguing dimple. He had grown very fond of that dimple.

"Don't you think it would be a good idea to . . ." She broke off, her body flushing with heat as he slid buttons open on her blouse.

He did it slowly, unwrapping her like a gift, because that was what she was to him.

"A good idea to what?" He encouraged her, allowing his knuckles to brush the swell of her breasts and her soft, amazing skin as his lips wandered down the side of her neck.

"Well, you know. Before we even think about the conversion, shouldn't we complete the marriage?"

There was a hopeful note in her voice. A little shiver went through her, and once again, her hand was at the nape of his neck. Her fingers slid into his thick hair, sending streaks of white-hot lightning crashing through his veins, heating his blood. There was no keeping that reaction from her, so he didn't bother to try.

"It is necessary to stay in control. The sight of you, your incredible fragrance, the memory of your taste, you are already too much of a temptation, Safia." He had to give her something.

Her eyes darkened into the jeweled color he loved so much. "Aren't I supposed to be a temptation?"

She tipped her head to one side and leaned into him to press little butterfly kisses down the side of his neck. Each one burned like a brand. Her tongue lingered over his pulse, and his heart nearly stopped beating. His cock swelled at an alarming rate, letting him know his woman had more power over him than he'd like.

"*Ku Tappa Kulyak*, you're too much temptation, when I promised your grandfather and father I would return you tomorrow evening for the Imazighen marriage ceremony."

She pulled back a few scant inches to look up at his face. "You did what?"

"I had a long talk with Amastan and Gwafa, and both felt very strongly that you should be married in the custom of your people. They understood that we had to follow the customs of mine as well, so they knew you would be staying overnight, but they were adamant we do not consummate the marriage."

"You should have explained how necessary it was for you to complete your ritual. In our custom, the bride and groom cannot consummate the marriage for two days."

She sounded very anxious, her frown catching at him in a way he didn't expect. He realized, although she wanted him and she was doing her best to delay the conversion, her anxiety was for him, for completing the ritual to keep him safe. She was unsure what he needed. Her fingernails scraped along his scalp in a slow massage, sending more heat spiraling down his spine. She was slowly winding her way around his heart.

"It is our custom to invite our entire tribe. The marriage ritual can go as long as seven days, Petru, although that is much rarer in these times. While I love that you would give me such a beautiful gift, I don't believe it is safe for you. We should do what is right for the two of us. If Lilith strikes at us and we're not fully prepared for her, we could endanger everyone."

Petru wanted to admit she had a point, but he knew he would only be doing so for selfish reasons. He desired her with every breath in his body. Truthfully, his motives weren't all physical. He had no idea if being lifemates had added the tremendous pull to his emotional need of her. This wasn't all about lust; it was about the way she wrapped herself around his heart when he hadn't known it was possible.

He honestly didn't know what love was. He felt that emotion through her. The way she loved her family. She extended that same sentiment to Aura. When he touched on her feelings for him, there was passion. Intrigue. Fascination. Admiration. The beginnings of affection. He knew he wanted her to feel that emotion others called love for him. He wanted that unswerving loyalty for himself. The strange thing was, he was feeling those emotions toward her.

"As much as I desire to make you wholly mine, Safia, the conversion will ensure we are safe. I gave my word to your family, but more importantly, I want this for you. I have so little to offer you, and following the customs of the Amazigh people is one of the few ways I can ensure you feel you are still in your world."

"Once you assured me I would always be Imazighen, I was satisfied, Petru. You're right, nothing will ever change who I am. I love being Imazighen. I love that you recognized that being close to my family was important to me. Marrying someone from a different land with such unusual customs is frightening, but you've eased quite a lot of my fears."

"I haven't been able to take away all your fears. I wish I could, but it's impossible when you're being forced to marry a stranger on a promise given two thousand years ago."

Her fingers massaged his scalp, a soothing yet stimulating caress that made him feel more connected to her than ever. She seemed to cast her spell so easily. She smiled at him, her dimple showing, her eyes lighting up. His heart lurched in his chest. He understood chemistry, his cock leaping to life, but not the way his heart stuttered or his stomach tied into knots. Those were new experiences, ones he would have to take out and consider when he was alone.

"When you were born, apparently your soul was split in two, and somehow one half found its way into my keeping. That decision was never in your hands, unless I misunderstood how things work in your world."

"You didn't," he admitted.

"You believed you would die in the war, and you should have. Am I correct?" She persisted.

The problem with having an intelligent woman, one able to recall every detail, was she could turn around faster than you could argue with her. He nodded. He should have died. The remaining Carpathians had been in bad shape and couldn't have saved him. It had been Kahina who had saved his life, and he had needed to be in the ground for months. Aura's mother and Kahina had provided blood for him.

"There are no official written records in our family," Safia said, "but every night after dinner, it is tradition to tell stories. The warrior saving our people is legendary. That was you. Of course, to us it was a story that set our hearts pounding. We loved hearing it told in various ways. There were many such tales of demons and vampires and other mythical creatures. Reasons we learned to use strange weapons and the art of defense. Each generation became more proficient. The promise to you of marriage to me was made because Kahina saved you against your will. She knew you would have to return to save our people once again. If you didn't come back, she believed Lilith would win."

"I told her I wouldn't survive knowing you were in the world and

I couldn't get to you." He remembered that much, but it had taken him this long to remember. There had been a reason he had refused to give up on life, even when he knew he was long past his time.

"I am still your lifemate. You were never responsible for anything that happened, any more than I am."

He kissed his way from her chin to the top of the enticing curves of her breasts. "No matter how you want to put it, *Pelkgapâd és Meke Pirämet*, I didn't get to you in time to save you." He traced the bluish-white scar surrounding her heart and then pressed a kiss over it.

"If you insist on taking blame, then I must, too. I am not being forced against my will. If you need to know one thing about me, Petru, no one can force me to do anything I don't want to do, not even a lifemate. Search my mind and see if I am being coerced. What I am doing with you is entirely free will."

He kissed his way along the curves of both breasts. "I did search your mind, Safia. It was very important to me to know how afraid you were and if your family had in any way threatened you. I wanted you to come to me on your own."

He lifted his head because he had to be honest with her, his eyes meeting hers. He was an ancient and ruthless. Most of the time, merciless. He had cared nothing for the emotions of others—until Safia. "If you search my mind, you will see had you not come to me eventually of your free will, I would have forced you."

He expected her to look outraged. Instead, she gave him the sweet curve of her bottom lip that brought her fascinating dimple to the forefront. He couldn't stop his reaction. He leaned into her, sweeping his tongue into the dimple and then blowing warm air over the little indentation before nibbling at the sensual curve of her mouth.

"Just how did you intend to do that?"

The laughter in her eyes was an unexpected shared intimacy. Safia was a mystery he might never solve. He'd been on earth a very long time, and yet she didn't have the reactions he had come to expect from humans.

"The Imazighen are a people of honor. I would have appealed to your code first. I cannot imagine that you would have neglected to uphold the word of your family."

"I see."

"It would have worked." He spoke with absolute confidence. He kissed his way down her neck. Her throat. Her pulse was a steady, strong beat that beckoned him. His heart matched the rhythm of hers.

"Yes," she agreed. "When I was first told, it felt as if my father and grandfather had betrayed me. The thought of leaving my family and going with a stranger to a foreign land was not only a shock but horrifying. I felt like that little child, once more thrown away for the good of everyone else. On some level, I knew it wasn't logical."

"Of course it was logical."

"My father and grandfather have always treated me with love and kindness. It wouldn't be logical that suddenly I wouldn't matter to them. I didn't want to hear their explanation. I just wanted to run away and hide. I knew I would honor the agreement, but at the moment, when I was first told, I was so shocked and frightened at the thought of losing everyone who mattered, I wanted to strike out at my father and grandfather. I didn't want to hear what they had to say."

Petru didn't like the slight hint of guilt in her mind. "*Pelkgapâd és Meke Pirämet*, it is only natural to need time to process a shocking revelation. You were prepared to marry the man your grandfather chose for you. I saw that intention in your mind."

He blazed a trail of fire back up to her lips, needing to distract himself. The scent that was hers alone had filled his lungs. Her taste was in his mouth. The addiction was beginning to consume him, the craving for her blood.

"I wasn't prepared to marry a stranger," she admitted.

"But you would have."

The drumbeat of her pulse called to him. Just like needing time to process the idea of marriage to an outsider, she needed time and persuasion to accept the conversion. He knew there was a great deal of pain involved. He wanted to ease her into her new life, not throw her into a panic. There was no easing when his lifemate would suffer with excruciating pain. He couldn't shoulder that burden for her.

He was already asking so much from her. Changing her way of life. She would need to learn to take blood from humans to survive. She would sleep beneath the ground with him. She would live in the night, not walk in the sun. Every so many years, she would have to change location so as not to arouse suspicion because they didn't age. Or they would need the appearance of aging and dying to be reborn as another couple. She would watch her family die until the sorrow would be so much, he would be forced to take her from all that she knew.

"Stop," she whispered.

"What do I have to give you in return? Why do all Carpathian males have such a belief they can make their lifemate happy?"

"Why do you feel as if you have nothing to give me, Petru?"

"I do not understand emotion." He had tried. Emotion wasn't logical. The things he felt for Safia made no sense at all. Her reactions to him made no sense. She should despise him, and yet she laughed at the things that should make her furious. He had been prepared for a woman far different. She'd disarmed him. Cast her spell. In order to cope with her, he found himself either shutting off emotion to study her or having to continually adjust the way he was thinking about himself and his species.

"I think you're learning at an alarming rate of speed. I'm never going to catch up. I don't know what the women in your society are like at all."

Petru cupped the back of her head. She fit into the palm of his hand. "You're the one learning at an alarming rate of speed. Each time you slip into my mind, you pull out battles with vampires to learn fighting techniques. Or you look for social norms within the Carpathian society. There's no need for that." He swept back stray strands of hair from her face. "I wouldn't trust my memory on social details of

Carpathian life anyway. We don't have to be like anyone else. What we make of our relationship is for us to decide."

Petru could see that what he said pleased her. He found himself smiling at her. Or at least, he hoped it was close to a smile. He hadn't smiled in a very long time—if ever.

"I think we're going to be just fine," she said. "The key to a good relationship is both parties putting in the work and being determined to make it. I think we've got that covered."

Her gaze fixed on his mouth, her breath hitching in her throat. His fist caught at the silky mass at the back of her scalp and tilted her head. Her lips parted in a gasp, and he took full advantage, his mouth coming down on hers.

Safia lost her ability to think. She lost her ability to breathe. There was no reasoning, only feeling. The earth moved beneath them, so much so that she was instantly dizzy, as if the planet were rotating far too fast. Her ears roared with thunder, drowning out all sound. There was only Petru, turning her into a living flame. Pouring himself into her.

She'd always felt a little apart from everyone. Just a little lonely. Different. With Petru, the moment he shared her mind, every lonely place was filled with him. When he kissed her, she felt completely and utterly accepted and bonded to him. More, it was as if she melted into him, and they shared more than their minds. It was such an intimate experience, as if they were skin to skin when she knew both were clothed.

Maybe clothed. She felt the cool of the cave on her bare skin. In contrast, his mouth was a living flame moving from hers and over her lower lip, teeth tugging and nipping, his tongue hot as it traced the curve and then returned to pour more flames down her throat. His hands wandered over her breasts, cupping the weight of them, thumbs sliding over her aching nipples. Along with his teeth tugging and nipping at her lower lip, his fingers found her nipples and matched the same rhythm, rolling and tugging until she was on fire with need, unable to stay still.

He kissed his way down to her chin, leaving her breathless, her body on fire. She was desperate for the taste of him. For his hands and mouth on her. She wanted to feel his teeth sinking into her, connecting them together.

"Petru." There was an ache in her voice. A note of desperation. She didn't care that he knew how she was feeling. "You're going too slow."

"Slow is good, Safia."

"It isn't," she denied. She was going to burn up. The flames seemed to be licking at her insides, beginning to roll through her veins and spreading like a wildfire out of control.

"It is. Trust me, *Ku Tappa Kulyak*, slow is so much better for now."

Whenever he called her Demon Slayer or Fearless Defender, she found herself glowing on the inside. She couldn't help herself. That only added to the magical feelings Petru produced in her with his hands and mouth. She would never get enough of him. His teeth nipped at her chin and then moved to her throat, lingering over the pulse beating there. Her entire body shuddered in reaction.

She couldn't sit still, her legs restless, her hips bucking. Deep inside, she felt that endless coiling, the pressure tightening into a heavy fist of desire. Her breasts felt heavy and achy. Her entire body was far too hot.

Petru. The only appropriate means of communication was the far more intimate telepathy. She could barely breathe his name.

His lips continued their wandering exploration. Slow, as if he were savoring every inch of her skin between her throat and the swell of her breasts. The more he explored, the faster her heart beat. He had to do something soon, or she was going to implode.

Petru kissed first her left then her right breast, feasted at one, then the other, while she cradled his head to her and arched her back to give him better access. Safia threw her head back, trying to stay still, trying not to beg him to take her blood. In her wildest dreams, she never believed she would crave such a thing, but she was nearly out of her mind, desperate for the feel of his erotic bite.

His teeth scraped back and forth over her pounding pulse just on the upper curve of her breast, right over the spot he'd taken her blood before.

I'm not going to survive this.

For a moment, it flashed through her mind that her statement was ironic. She wasn't going to survive. At least not being the same exact person. Once he took her blood and she took his, she would die and be reborn Carpathian.

Safia's breath caught in her throat. She would be like Aura. Like Petru. No longer able to walk in the sun.

I will always be with you. Always cherish you. You will always be in my care. Stay with me, Pelkgapåd és Meke Pirämet.

Petru's voice was temptation itself. He named her Fearless Defender. An equal. His tongue slid over the spot where his teeth teased and nipped. Her entire body reacted.

I will show you the night as you have never seen it before. Believe me, you will love it as much as you do the sun.

He sank his teeth into her. The pain was every bit as exquisite as the pleasure bursting through her. The two sensations mingled together until they became impossible to separate. She was aware of every cell in her body arcing with electrical, sensual energy. She felt his every reaction. The dark craving for her blood. His need of it. His reaction to it. For him, her blood was an aphrodisiac. Deeply addicting.

Petru was as aroused as she was, maybe even more so. He reached for her hand and pressed it over the long hard length of him. A dark thrill shot through her as she felt the hard, pulsing shaft beneath her palm. He curled her fingers around the hot steel pole. Immediately, her temperature rose even higher. Instinctively, she smeared the pearl droplets over the wide head, wishing she could use her mouth to get the shaft wet.

Instantly, because he was reading her mind, he accommodated her. One of his hands surrounded hers, tightening his fingers in a fist around hers, showing her how to pump his cock. She felt pleasure radiating through him. *Pleasure* was an insipid word for the ecstasy rushing through his veins, spreading like a wildfire out of control. His euphoria fed hers.

Safia wanted to climb over the top of his cock and slide down on top of him. She didn't know what she was doing, but that didn't matter. There were dozens of erotic images in his mind, and she wanted to try every one of them with him.

Then he was lifting his head, his tongue sliding over the throbbing spot on her breast where he'd taken her blood. His eyes were twin flames of absolute lust. He looked the epitome of carnal sensuality, every line carved deep. It was impossible not to catch fire with the same dark passion.

The heavy muscles of his bare chest drew her like a magnet. Her mouth watered. The need to taste him magnified to the point she could barely think of anything else. Her pulse sounded like a drum beating so loud in her ears that it drowned out every other sound. Or maybe it was his heartbeat. She couldn't tell. Their hearts seemed to pound with the same escalating rhythm.

Retaining possession of her hand pumping his cock, his other hand cupped the back of her head to encourage her toward the line of ruby-red beads of blood welling up in invitation. She leaned into him, her tongue sliding over the crimson drops, pulling them into her mouth. The taste was even more erotic than she remembered.

Safia heard him groan. The sound seemed to echo through her entire body. With her tongue, she felt her teeth sharpen. Petru guided her to the vein and instinctively she hooked in. The moment she did, he threw his head back and roared. In her fist, his cock was so hot she feared it would burst into flames. It jumped and pulsed as she drew his blood into her mouth. His blood was just as hot and spicy of an addiction as she remembered. She couldn't possibly control her need of it.

She knew she was spiraling out of control, her body desperate for his. The more of his blood she consumed, the more desperately she needed him.

Petru, do something. She didn't care if she was pleading with him, something she was fairly certain she said she wouldn't do. Nothing seemed to matter but to be closer to him. For him to stop the tension and pressure forever building in her.

Slow down, Safia, you're always trying to move too fast.

His voice whispered along the inside of her mind, stroking caresses with a velvet brush, adding to the need in her. The fist surrounding her hand didn't slow down at all. If anything, it tightened and sped up. For some reason, that added to the rising sensual excitement in her. Her lashes swept up so she could watch as his cock grew larger. The sight of him was terribly erotic.

Petru. You're so beautiful.

Close the laceration with a sweep of your tongue, Pelkgapâd és Meke Pirämet. You have taken enough for a true exchange.

I am unable to close the wound as you do. To be honest, she was distracted and very fascinated by the way his body reacted to the way she was pumping his shaft faster and harder. His breathing was far more ragged. The pleasure escalated rapidly.

It was Petru who closed the laceration on his chest when she reluctantly disconnected from the vein. All the while, he shared the way she made him feel with the way she was working his cock. Each scorching stroke sent streaks of fire racing through him, through her.

Don't stop, Safia.

She wouldn't have stopped for the world. Her breathing found the pattern of his. Her core was so hot she feared she might detonate any moment. Her nipples were twin flames burning, as out of control as Petru was. The worst was the building tension deep inside her core. She needed. Desperately needed.

Then his fingers were there, right where she needed them to be, stroking gently, then harder, matching the rhythm of her fist curled around his cock. He seemed to know exactly where to press, to tug and flick. One moment he would fill her, then the next he would circle her clit until she was driven nearly out of her mind. Just before she found release, he pressed into her again, curling his finger to hit the bundle of nerves that caused her to explode. When she did, he did, erupting like a volcano.

The ripples in her body swelled to rolling waves, each as strong and lasting as the next. They seemed to soar together until she felt as if they'd been flung out into the universe with a million stars. Was that in her mind? Or his? It didn't matter, only that they shared the beauty of it. She dropped her forehead against his shoulder and clung to him as he slowly brought her back to reality.

Safia became aware of him murmuring to her softly in his own language as he rubbed her back gently. His mouth was against her ear, his warm breath teasing her into relaxing into him.

"Tell me what to expect." She didn't move away, snuggling closer to him.

"Just stay right here. The others, including Aura, have been informed you are prepared to undergo the conversion, and they are waiting to aid you in your journey. Aura has clearly given you blood on several occasions. I am hoping that helps ease you into our world, but no matter what happens, Safia, I will be with you."

"Can something go wrong?"

"Nothing will go wrong. You're strong, *Pelkgapâd és Meke Pirämet.* I believe the conversion will begin immediately and be over quickly. You must give yourself over to it. Don't fight it."

She nodded, believing him. She was in his mind, but more than that, already she was uneasy, the blissful feeling fading to be replaced by a hot glow stealing into her stomach. "Do you feel that, Petru?" She started to pull away from him.

Petru tightened his arms around her. "Stay with me a little longer. I'll take us to the floor and make you as comfortable as possible."

She didn't see how it was possible to wait, but she held on to him as the heat blossomed into a blowtorch, striking at her internal organs. She gasped and bit down on his shoulder.

"Breathe with me."

Safia felt him surround her, anchor in her mind, and move through her body, monitoring what was happening even as he eased both of them to the floor. The soil was rich with minerals and felt cool on her overheated skin. She heard the echo of voices raised in a chant spoken in the ancient Carpathian language.

Waves of pain, one after another, began. Endless. Merciless. It was agony. There was no getting around that, but through it all, even as her body seized, lifted and was slammed down, convulsing, Petru never left her, staying with her, breathing with her, shouldering as much of the pain as possible. When her body expelled toxins, he instantly cleared them away and left behind a clean, sweet-smelling environment.

She clung to his mind, hiding herself there, wholly dependent, trusting that he would see her through this terrible crisis. She had committed herself to this path, and she didn't fight it, breathing through each wave of agony to try to rise above it, staying as relaxed as possible and letting Petru guide her into his world.

"You're there, *sívamet*. I'm sending you to sleep. Your body will do the rest," he whispered. "You've been so brave."

She felt the brush of his lips on her forehead, and then sweet oblivion took her.

14

aughter erupted all around her, and Safia exchanged a shared look of amusement with Aura. The bride's home had been declared to be her brother Badis and Layla's house. The two had transformed it into a festive setting fit for any bride and her henna ceremony. Only family attended the ceremony with the exception of Aura, but Aura was considered family.

The women and six-year-old Tala arrived in a procession of horse-drawn carriages that made Safia so happy, tears threatened. They carried gifts as they approached the house, playing the bendir, a wooden-framed drum, as they sang songs. Safia knew they couldn't stick exactly to tradition, but they followed as best they could under the circumstances.

Layla greeted the women and her niece before serving the traditional drink of og milk, dates, honey and butter. This was an important day and one Safia had looked forward to her entire life. When she was a little girl, she would lie with her sisters and talk about the time she would have her henna ceremony on the first day of the celebration of her marriage.

On the days honoring a milestone, such as when she graduated classes, she lined up with the other young girls dressed in her finest kaftan, eager for her turn to have her henna tattoo on her hands. The tattoo was so beautiful and always made her feel grown-up and accomplished. She complimented Tala on her party dress and the henna on her hands, which Lunja had carefully applied for the festive occasion.

The women had Safia sit while they prepared her hands and feet for the application of the henna design. Each symbol was well thought out and placed on her for a reason. She was the defender of their people and therefore thought to be far more at risk than any other bride might be. The women were even going to sprinkle henna in her shoes on the night of her wedding to ward off any demons who might accost her.

"I think someone has been biting your neck," Amara observed, peering at Safia's skin as she stood over her, braiding her hair. She leaned down for a closer look. "Yes, I would say that's definitely a love bite."

"What's a love bite?" Tala asked, looking up at her mother.

"Insect bite," Safia corrected, clapping a hand over her suddenly pounding pulse and glaring up at her impish sister-in-law. "This is an insect bite."

"Ha!" Layla disputed. "Everyone knows insects don't bite you."

"Let me see." Safia's older sister, Lunja, clicked her tongue and shook her head. "I knew you shouldn't have gone off with that man. He's far more experienced than you."

Safia turned a bright shade of red. Lobster red. She felt the deep color rising despite every effort not to allow it. Even Aura burst into laughter.

Tala looked at her wide-eyed. "What man?"

"Petru, baby, the groom," Lunja explained to her daughter.

"He was a perfect gentleman." Safia was compelled to defend Petru. Another round of laughter went up and she glared at her family. "He was."

"I'm sure he was, considering you sound so disappointed," Farah said.

It was Safia's turn to laugh. "Well, in all honesty, I was *terribly* disappointed. He can kiss like you wouldn't believe. I had no idea what I was missing out on." Deliberately, she glared at each one of her sisters-in-law and then her sister. "Aura, when you get the chance, kiss the man you're attracted to. And if he happens to have a code of honor, don't let him talk to *Jeddi* or *Baba*. They won't allow him to be with you before the marriage ceremony."

"Safia." Lunja tried her best to sound outraged but looked as if she were going to fall over laughing. That made everyone else erupt into laughter again.

"Well, it's true," Safia groused. "Petru is obsessed with honor."

"That's a good thing, Safia," Layla insisted.

"I'd much rather he be obsessed with me."

"I think he is," Aura joined in the discussion.

It was Farah they trusted with the designs for the henna on her hands. Each symbol represented something of great importance to her. Her family. Petru. Crystals and rocks of significance. The Amazigh people.

Henna grew in abundance in the Mediterranean area. After the leaves were ground to a fine powder, it was often mixed with water to form a thick paste. Farah had added jasmine oil to give it fragrance, since they would be there a long time and she wanted them to enjoy the experience. A true henna is red, and Farah preferred to paint her intricate patterns on with several artist brushes of various sizes. At times, she used a thin stick to create the lines she wanted.

When Farah was finished, she would mix sugar with lime or lemon and drizzle it over the henna designs to seal them and enhance the colors. When it hardened and cracked off, the designs would stay for several weeks. The fragrance of the henna was very pleasing. It was a long process for the women to apply the elaborate artwork to both hands and feet. Farah had incorporated the symbols of the Imazighen as well as those designed to bring the couple getting married good luck. She had added in the name given to the legendary ancient Carpathian warrior in the telling of their stories. In their language, Farah had woven *amnay icheqqan n wayur* into jasmine vines. That meant "fierce knight of the moon." Aura had given her a similar name in his language. It had been difficult, but Farah had managed to add *Kuŋe kont ku votjak*, which was "moon knight" in Carpathian, under the name in Tamazight representing Petru.

They watched Farah for a few minutes as she meticulously continued her work, and then Safia asked for advice.

"Amara," she ventured cautiously. "You must have been so frightened when your family agreed to the marriage when Izem made an offer for you."

Amara ducked her head for a moment and then nodded. "My family is very different from yours. We were not allowed a say in anything. Izem is older and appeared very stern to me. He came to our home with your parents and sat with my parents to make the offer. I listened from the other room and tried my best not to cry. I knew they were going to accept him. My parents are older. I am the youngest, and as you know, I am not very graceful or quiet. I tried to be, but I was punished often for being too loud. They didn't think anyone in our tribe would make an offer for me."

It would have been impossible not to hear the hurt in her voice. Lunja wrapped an arm around her. "We're all so lucky you caught Izem's eye," she said. "You're very loved, and you bring so much joy to our family."

Tala, always empathetic, hugged Amara's waist. "I love you, too, Amara. You make us all laugh, and anytime we're hungry, you stop to get us food. Charif and Igider are *always* hungry."

Amara kissed the top of her head. "They are growing fast, little dove."

Safia nodded her agreement with Lunja. "Amara, I hope you will share with me how you were able to make such a good marriage with my brother. I want to do the same. You had to adjust to our customs and ways, which must be so different from yours, and yet you've managed to fit in so perfectly. I could use as much advice as possible. You've made Izem so happy."

Amara beamed at her. "I'll admit it wasn't easy at first, mostly because I was so afraid. Izem made it easy for me. It was really him in the beginning. I would cry whenever I was alone, but he seemed to know it, and he would seek me out and be so understanding and sweet. He kept telling me to trust him, that he would take care of me. He never once hit me. Not one single time, even when it was my turn to cook dinner for everyone and I ruined it."

Safia was horrified. "You expected him to beat you?"

Amara nodded. "Of course. I made him look bad. I ruined the meal and destroyed all the ingredients. Instead of being upset with me, he helped me cook. And you"—she looked around the room at the other women—"all of you were so understanding and kind, you helped me as well. No one ever made fun of me. Even Charif and Tala whispered they would help me learn." Once again, she kissed the top of Tala's head.

Tears glistened in her eyes for a moment, but she blinked them away. "I fell in love with Izem and wanted his happiness above anything else. I became determined to put him first in all things. I quit thinking about me and what I wanted or what I feared and just thought about what I could do to make his life as good as possible. I found the more I put him first, the more he gave to me. It never seemed a fair balance as much as I tried."

Lunja nodded. "I understand what you're saying completely, Amara. Zdan made an offer for me, and I couldn't believe it when *Jeddi* and *Baba* accepted the offer without asking me if I wanted to marry him. They asked Illi when Kab made an offer for her, so I was really upset that they didn't do me the same courtesy. Zdan is very handsome, but his ways are different, and I thought he was arrogant and overbearing. And his aunt was so condescending. She made it clear she despised me and thought our family beneath hers. I would have said no had *Jeddi* and *Baba* asked me. That would have been so terrible, and I would have lost out. Zdan is the best thing that's ever happened to me."

Safia had to agree with her. Zdan was loving and kind and very protective of Lunja and their three children. Safia had grown to love him as a brother.

"I did the same thing, Safia," Lunja admitted, turning to her younger sister. "I cried often and was afraid of how he might treat me when no one was looking or when we were alone. I went with him to see his aunt, and no matter how hard I tried to please her, she would make very cutting remarks. I tried not to let it show that she hurt me, but when I thought I was alone, I would fall completely apart. I never had anyone say the things about me or our family that she did."

Tala took her mother's hand. "We're not supposed to ever say bad things about people, especially family, but she is very mean."

It said quite a lot that her mother didn't admonish her gently.

"Lunja," Safia said, nearly getting up to put her arms around her sister to comfort her. Farah hastily pulled her down. Amara put both hands on her shoulder. Safia subsided but looked like a warrior about to go into combat.

"You should have told me. I would have done something."

"What could you do?" Lunja asked. "She still despises me. She thinks *Jeddi* has allowed us to be too outspoken."

Safia's gaze met Aura's.

"I know what you're thinking, Safia," Aura cautioned, but her voice was filled with laughter. "You wouldn't dare."

"I might. Lunja, when was the last time that old battle-ax made you cry?"

The women gasped. Tala giggled.

"Safia," Lunja protested, but weakly. "Last time I took the children. She was just as mean to Tala. She's only six, but when she tried to share what she believed would help with joint pain, Zdan's aunt cut her off and told her she should know her place. She told Zdan that was what came from marrying beneath him. He told her in a very quiet voice that he would not bring his wife or children back to her home and he would only come when necessary. He didn't want us treated like that."

Tala nodded. "*Vava* was very stern with her." She was very proud.

Lunja gave Safia a watery smile. "Like Amara, very early in our marriage I realized how lucky I am to have Zdan, and I decided I would devote myself to his happiness. I put him first in my thoughts as much as I could. I watched him closely to see what he liked. I tried to find out what was important to him. What foods he liked." She blushed. "I tried to learn to be very good in the bedroom. I knew I was never going to be a perfect wife, but I wanted him to be happy. I think that's the key. I did my best, even though sometimes I was embarrassed to talk to him about everything, and to my surprise, he wanted me to communicate with him."

Amara nodded. "Izem sets aside time every evening for us to talk. He makes it a priority. At first, I was so afraid. It felt like a trap to me, but then I finally realized he really did want to hear what I had to say, no matter how trivial."

"Zdan wanted his children raised very differently than he had been raised. He'd watched our family for a long time," Lunja said. "I was very shocked when I realized it was communication that mattered so much to him."

Farah nodded her head as she bent over Safia's hand, meticulously drawing out the patterns on her skin. "He often has long conversations with *Jeddi*."

"Because he wants to be a good father," Lunja said. "That's another thing his aunt complains about. She doesn't like the way he is with the children."

Safia's breath escaped in a long slow hiss, like that of a snake. "That woman." She narrowed her eyes at Aura. "Don't shake your head. You know she deserves a little payback."

"You shouldn't have told Safia that, Lunja. You know she's always been the defender of the family," Aura protested.

"Against demons," Layla, the peacemaker, pointed out.

"Zdan's aunt is a demon," Safia said. "She made my sister cry, and Lunja is the sweetest woman in the world. She was mean to Tala. She's six years old. There's no excuse to be ugly to a child, especially since Tala was trying to help her."

"What are you planning to do?" Lunja asked, her voice filled with suspicion.

Safia did her best to look innocent as the room fell quiet and her sisters-in-law, Tala and Lunja, regarded her carefully. "I'm pondering."

"When we were children," Lunja said, "we found out very quickly we didn't dare play tricks on Safia. Not even the boys. She always retaliated—and in a big way. Sometimes it was impossible to tell she was the one who played the prank on us, but we all knew it was her."

"Did you ask her in front of *Jeddi*?" Amara asked. She looked as if she were holding her breath.

"If she was asked outright, she would have admitted it, but we never did that, because we didn't want to get her in trouble, since we had played a trick on her first. She was just more inventive than we were," Lunja admitted, laughing at her memories. She indicated Aura. "I think Miss Aura, who is looking very innocent over there, helped her sometimes."

Aura pressed her lips together and widened her eyes. "I have no idea what you could possibly mean."

"You mean which time I'm talking about," Lunja corrected.

"That too," Aura admitted, laughing.

It occurred to Safia that this was the most she'd ever heard Aura laugh. She seemed more relaxed than she'd ever seen her. She had seemed so leery of the Carpathian males at first, and yet now she appeared to have accepted their presence. Was it because Safia had been converted and she was no longer the only Carpathian there in Dellys? Had her responsibilities been weighing her down?

I'm so sorry I didn't help you more, Aura.

Petru has promised me that he won't take you away until your family passes and it's necessary. He has been very good about keeping me apprised with what is happening, and he apologized for throwing me out of the house. There was a hint of laughter in Aura's voice. *Apparently, you were very angry with him.*

I was. It is your home.

Lunja gave Safia a little nudge in the shin with her toe. "You'd better not be conspiring with Aura. You've got that look on your face that makes me think you're up to no good."

Safia widened her eyes in innocence. "I was just thinking how I should practice controlling insects. I've been neglecting my training lately."

Lunja drew in her breath swiftly. "Don't you *dare*, Safia."

"Safia, this is the night before your wedding. We're dancing and singing. It's very traditional to be with your sisters, not practice for demon slaying," Farah said.

"Oh, you sweet innocent woman," Lunja said. "Safia intends to send a plague of insects to torture Zdan's aunt."

Again, there was a collective gasp, and then silence fell in the room. It was broken by Amara's giggle. She hastily cut it off by clapping her hand over her mouth, but her eyes were bright with merriment.

Farah peeked up from under a fan of dark lashes to look at Safia's face. Safia caught a glimpse of amusement before her sister-in-law hastily looked down at her work.

Layla suddenly became very interested in studying the patterns Farah had drawn out for them to choose from to apply to Safia's feet. It was obvious she was rubbing her lips to keep from laughing.

"Do *not* encourage her," Lunja commanded. "I love my little sister, but she can be very naughty when she's defending family."

Safia stuck her chin in the air. "It's my duty to defend all of you. I won't send stinging bugs, I promise. Nothing that can harm her. You know I wouldn't do that. More like stinky ones."

Tala clapped her hands. "Really stinky ones."

"*Tala.*" Lunja objected but found herself laughing. "Don't encourage naughty behavior in your aunt."

"It wouldn't be so naughty, would it?" Tala asked, grinning at Safia.

"She'd just make me do the cleaning," Lunja said. "Otherwise . . ." She broke off, pressing her hand over her mouth. "I didn't say that."

"If she dares call Zdan to have you come clean, you promise me that you'll be too sick to go over there," Safia said after the others finished laughing at Lunja's blunder.

"I can't lie to him." Lunja looked horrified.

"The plague will have to be sent tonight, then. You can't miss your sister's wedding. I'll count on you to set everything up for me. If you do get a mild stomachache, I didn't do it. Aura did."

"You wouldn't dare." Lunja glared at her.

"I said I wouldn't. You're my sister. Besides, I must behave. Farah's going to all the trouble of keeping me safe from anything wicked. I can't bring the evil eye down on me by harming my own sister."

"I think it best if you just behave for once, Safia. I doubt your poor husband-to-be has any idea what he's getting himself into," Lunja said. "Perhaps one of us should take him aside and warn him."

Aura sounded like she muffled laughter. "Have you seen that man up close, Lunja? He makes your Zdan look like a teddy bear. He's as dangerous as they come. I can't even talk when I'm around him. I try to fade into the background. I don't know how Safia stands up to him."

"I saw him," Amara whispered. She looked around her as if he might be spying on them. "And one of his friends. Believe me, Lunja, you don't want to just go up to one of them alone. They're scary men."

"Petru's very kind." Safia intervened before the women became too alarmed. "He looks dangerous. And I suppose he is. He has to be. He has devoted his entire life to hunting vampires all over the world. But with me, he's very gentle and thoughtful."

"And too honorable," Amara added mischievously, instantly dispelling all tension in the room.

"Well, yes, that too," Safia conceded with an exaggerated sigh, bringing back the laughter.

Aura knelt beside Safia and lifted her left foot. "I would like to try, Farah, if you don't mind. I've been studying the way you apply the henna. I've practiced for a long time, and I believe I can do a very good job. I wanted to do this for Safia ever since I first learned of the tradition. I loved it and had Safia's mother and grandmother show me. They both worked with me. I'm not nearly the artist you are, but I can copy your designs."

A lump developed in Safia's throat, nearly choking her at the thought of Aura learning the art of applying henna just so she could participate in Safia's marriage ceremony. It felt like such a loving tribute. She had to flutter her lashes several times to keep from crying.

You're amazing, Aura. You know I love you. But you can't make me cry.

Instantly, there was a stirring in her mind. Petru poured into her. Warm. Confident. A man she could always count on. The moment he was with her, she realized how much she had missed him.

He had awakened her gently, the soil already open when the sun set. He fed her, all the while showing her how to remove the earth. He had her go over the mechanics many times in her mind before he covered them again, without burying her head. He had her practice eliminating the soil from over their bodies until she was flawless at it.

She loved that he knew the one thing she feared the most. That was the first thing he addressed, teaching her how to open the soil so she could do it on her own. She had replayed the steps in her mind dozens of times since then, determined that the process would become automatic.

Sívamet? What is causing the tears? You are supposed to be happy. Should I come to you?

He was *such* a good man. Safia was very sure she had gotten lucky. *Happy tears, Petru. Thank you for thinking of this. I always looked forward to this ceremony. It marks the time when a girl makes her transition into becoming a woman. The women give advice to the bride, and we laugh, sing and tell stories. It's just such a wonderful bonding time.*

"I would love for you to help," Farah invited Aura.

Aura glanced up at Safia. The look in her eyes was loving. *Sisar,* she whispered into Safia's mind, calling her sister. She bent to begin the meticulous work of drawing the pattern Farah had designed on Safia's foot.

"What about you, Layla? Do you have advice for me? You're so good with my brother. I know Badis adores you. Was there a period of adjustment for you?" Safia asked.

Layla appeared to be very confident. She was always kind to everyone. She had a calm, serene personality. While Amara made beautiful jewelry, Layla made leather-and-silver belts. Safia thought their love of the craft gave the two women a special bond. Even though the two women were close in age, Layla seemed far older and wiser and was good for Amara.

Layla thought carefully before replying, as was her way. "There's always a period of adjustment in any relationship, Safia. You're two different people from two different environments. I knew the moment I laid eyes on Badis that he was the man for me. I was fortunate in that he felt the same way. We first saw each other at the market. He didn't speak to me, but we both looked for a long time. I wasn't surprised when he came with your parents to my home to offer for me."

Her voice was very soft in the way she had that spoke of a tremendous love. "When we married, I was determined to make him very happy. My grandmother often told me I was too proud, an overachiever, and men didn't like a woman who appeared as if she could do everything. They wanted her to be good at chores but not look as if she were. I am not the type of woman to pretend. I am who I am. I did fear Badis would think I had an inflated opinion of myself."

Safia frowned. "Why is it wrong to be good at the things you do? I'm not sure I understand. Wouldn't your partner be proud of your accomplishments?"

"I'm fortunate in that Badis is. But no, not all partners are."

"Why would that be?" Safia honestly didn't get it. She'd grown up with loving encouragement. She was surrounded by it, from both the men and the women in her family.

Aura looked up again, pausing in her work. "It has been my observation that some people can become jealous, and others feel inferior. This makes them petty and mean-spirited. Having a woman look strong and capable can threaten their authority. Fortunately, the men in your tribe do not appear to be that way."

"In any case, I promised myself I would only show Badis the true me." Layla smiled at Safia. "Your brother was gentle and caring. He showed me patience and understanding and that he was always proud of me no matter what I did. He liked the way I cooked. He loved the belts I made. When I didn't know about caring for the sheep but was able to learn quickly, he praised me. I especially liked that he was encouraging when he was teaching me to use weapons. I hadn't done anything like that before and really wanted to learn. When I asked him if it would bother him if I took extra lessons in the late evening hours to work with you and Aura, he said right away that it was a good idea." Layla's smile was serene, but her eyes glowed with love.

Safia was very happy for her. "Does he ever dictate to you? When I was a child, all my brothers were bossy and tried to tell me what to do."

"Notice she used the word 'tried.'" Lunja laughed. "If they got too bossy, Safia retaliated by having the hens lay eggs in their beds."

The women erupted with laughter.

Tala doubled over, clutching at her stomach. "I would like to have the hens lay eggs in my brothers' beds sometime."

"Maybe it would be best not to do that," Lunja said.

"There were times when her retaliation was far worse than that," Aura murmured, keeping her head down.

"Don't tell them anything else," Safia protested. "I was a child, and my brothers were always telling me what to do."

That wasn't entirely the truth. She sighed. "Well, most of the time, they weren't. Only when they thought I was doing something dangerous."

"You were always doing dangerous things," Lunja pointed out.

"I was learning how to be a defender," Safia said. Then she grinned. "Sort of. I did like to try things."

"Such as?" Farah asked.

Safia found it hard to sit still. She was someone always in need of action. It took great discipline to sit without moving to allow Farah and Aura to create the patterns on her skin. She knew the women were helping to distract her with their advice. Lunja's tales from her childhood added to the diversion, as did the occasional outbursts of song.

Safia glanced at her older sister. "It was a long time ago," she hedged. "Izem caught me trying to leap over fences. Very tall fences. They were close to the bluff. He gave me a very stern lecture that time." She made a face.

"You were five, Safia," Lunja pointed out. "The fence was there to keep the sheep from falling onto the rocks. You would have broken your neck if you'd jumped too far out or the cliff crumbled."

"I realize that now," she conceded. "But then, it was just fun to push my limits. I could barely contain all the adrenaline building up in me all the time. Izem was really upset with me. He didn't yell, but he made it clear there was to be no more leaping over those fences."

"What did you do to him?" Amara asked.

Safia groaned. "Don't make me tell you, especially since he was so sweet and built a series of hurdles, each one higher than the next, for me to practice jumping over."

"You were five," Amara pointed out.

"I know, but I was awful." She would have liked to cover her now very red face with her hands, but she had to hold still. Safia sighed. "I had salamanders crawl up the outside of the house and come in through his window. He always opened the windows at night and didn't have a screen. He should have, but he had given up the screen for one of the houses we were working on, and other materials hadn't come in yet."

"She does have a bit of a temper, doesn't she?" Layla said, amusement creeping into her voice. "She isn't the only one in the family. Badis has one as well." She rubbed her rounded belly. "I told him if our child inherited that little part of him, he will be dealing with it, as I have no idea what to do."

"What do you do when Badis loses his temper?" Safia asked.

Layla pressed her lips together for a short moment, her eyes lighting up again. She shook her head. "He makes me laugh. I try very hard not to, because he's very serious, but it feels so out of character for him. He never gets upset with me; it's always at an object. Like one of the building projects, and the wall isn't going up the way he wants. He particularly likes to create pottery, and when he's at the wheel and things go awry, he is not happy. The wheel gets an earful. That's why I know if our child takes after him, it will be difficult for me to even gently attempt to correct the behavior."

"It's probably a good thing he doesn't know how to direct insects and reptiles," Lunja said. "Otherwise, who knows what would be happening on our farm?"

"I'm beginning to fear for poor Petru, no matter how warrior-like or legendary he is," Farah said. "We should sing his song for him every time he comes around. He'll need his courage."

"Don't encourage him with singing his praises," Safia objected. "If you think any of your men are the bossy type, you haven't met my man. He may be sweet and kind, but he has no problem taking over. He hasn't done it yet, but it's coming. I can feel it. So no songs to encourage him."

Another round of laughter went up. It felt good to laugh so much. She enjoyed being with her family. The women began to make up lyrics for the legendary warrior who had saved their people with his brilliant tactics.

She groaned. *"Don't call him brilliant."*

Another round of laughter was interspersed with more lyrics, mostly to tease Safia, some wondering if he would be a legendary lover to match his warrior skills.

She loved them all so much.

Thank you, Petru, for promising me you won't take me away from my family. I love them so much.

There was a small part of her that was still a little afraid he might insist she leave her home with him. So many husbands wanted their wives to go to their land and embrace their customs. Zdan was the only man she knew who had come to their family willingly and stayed.

There was no hesitation in Petru's mind. When he came to her, pouring into her mind, she felt that same confidence, the same conviction and self-assurance that set him apart.

The things important to you are the things important to me, Safia. You wish to stay here, so we stay. I will learn to fit in.

Not only did she hear the truth in his declaration, but she felt it. He meant what he said, and she hugged the knowledge to herself. *Maybe you should have a song after all.*

She heard his male amusement in his mind. *Many songs have been sung around fires telling of my battles with the undead.*

Safia tried to detect bragging, but he was stating fact. *Well, you certainly don't need any more songs to add to your ego.* She liked that she could make him feel a sense of humor when he didn't think he had one.

Do I have an ego?

Male amusement definitely increased. She was getting the hang of this relationship thing just from watching her brothers and sisters and their marriages and the advice she'd been given so far. Her parents and grandparents had set a high standard as well.

It's hidden, but I'm certain you do. I've been studying you. You have that kind of edge to you, the one that says everyone will obey you in all things.

There was a brief pause while he conveyed deliberate puzzlement. *Shouldn't they?*

Safia burst out laughing. She couldn't help it. Color swept up her neck and into her face when the song the others were singing came to an abrupt halt.

"It's the song. Stop with the legendary lyrics. No more of that," she hastily improvised.

I knew it was going to happen," Safia declared. "We aren't even officially married, and you already think you can tell me what I can and can't do."

Petru found himself looking down at his lifemate's upturned face. Her winged brows were drawn together with what he considered the most adorable little frown in the world. He struggled not to smile and to keep amusement out of his mind. That would deepen that frown. The more he was with her, the more he understood what happiness meant. Happiness was a woman.

"I have no idea what you're talking about. We are officially married. *Te avio päläfertiilam.*" Deliberately, he used the Carpathian language to remind her she was his lifemate. His wedded spouse. He put the slightest touch of arrogance in his voice just to get her reaction. Safia was always unpredictable.

Her eyes changed color from jade, deepening to more of an emerald. Petru loved when that happened, when her eyes suddenly gave away her mood. She was such a miracle to him. He noticed the smallest detail about her. He caught a glimpse of her enticing dimple and had to resist the urge to taste her soft skin. The intriguing indentation was far too close to the full curve of her lower lip, and he knew he wouldn't be able to resist biting that tempting bow. The moment he did, he would be kissing her. Once he was kissing her, it would be impossible to stop.

"You aren't getting away with suddenly becoming a tyrant by distracting me with sex. I know better. There's no follow-through since you gave your word to my grandfather and father, not to your supposed wife. I say there is no marriage without consummation. Therefore, no dictator telling said spouse what to do." She raised her eyebrow in challenge.

He supposed there was some merit to what she had to say. They hadn't consummated the marriage. He had given his word to Amastan and Gwafa, and he couldn't go back on it. That was a matter of honor. He was certain, as much as she acted annoyed with him, she wouldn't respect him if he did.

"You are my lifemate," he reiterated. "There is no getting around that, even if there is a very small part of me that might be a tiny bit tyrannical."

She leaned back against his arm, tilting her chin in challenge. "Small? Tiny bit? I think your true colors are glaring. You couldn't even wait until after the ceremony today. I knew this was going to happen. It's because you were secretly listening to the women singing your praises and you got a big head. That's what happened. You know all those stories you heard about me retaliating when my brothers tried to boss me around?"

He didn't bother to deny he was listening. "The hens laying eggs in their beds? The salamanders climbing through the windows? Incidentally, did you send a plague of stink bugs to Zdan's demon aunt?"

"Naturally." Safia looked at him as if he might be a little bit slow-witted. "I waited until it was close to dawn and knew you were coming for me. Lunja had already put Tala to bed and climbed in with her. No way would Zdan get her up to help his nasty, mean aunt. He'll want Lunja to sleep for as long as possible before she helps with the wedding party."

Just the way Safia delivered the statement as if it were a foregone conclusion made him smile despite his every effort not to. He had to look away and clear his throat. The woman was an absolute menace. He'd lived far too long in the world, and yet she was giving him experiences he'd never had.

"I doubt stink bugs or hens laying eggs in our bed will deter my tyrannical nature."

"Probably not," she agreed readily. "I've been giving serious thought to the problem."

It was far more difficult not to laugh than he'd ever imagined it would be. Her arms were around his neck, the tips of her fingers at his nape, idly playing in his hair while she was giving him hell.

"You have?" The way she touched him moved him in a way that was another first for him. Every nerve ending came alive, was aware of her. He felt his heart shifting in his chest.

Sofia brushed back strands of hair he'd deliberately left loose. "Since last night, when the women were making up ridiculous songs singing your praises. I knew it would go to your head. I had to be prepared for your nonsense. As attractive as I find you, and I'll admit at times you're remarkably sweet, I can't have you believing you can boss me around like you do everyone else."

"I don't intimidate you?" He knew he did. Just a little. Not enough. His defender wasn't a woman to be afraid of very much, certainly not her lifemate.

She hesitated. "If you do, it's even more reason for me to stand up to you. I've practiced opening the soil hundreds of times in my mind, and now you're reneging on your promise of letting me do it."

"Why do you think I'm refusing you, Safia?" He knew the color of his eyes reflected his sobering mood. He knew they went from mercury to a piercing silver. His vision changed whenever his senses expanded.

Her long lashes fluttered. She hesitated, her frown returning, her brows coming together. She didn't look away, studying his features, then looking into his mind. "Honestly, I hadn't thought about it. I reacted. The idea of waking beneath the ground is frightening to me. I went over opening the soil hundreds of times so I wouldn't be afraid. I wanted to do it myself, not have you do it for me."

"You're still afraid." He made it a statement, using a very low tone. He wasn't going to give in on this subject. He made that very clear just with his tone.

She might believe she was ready. He knew she wasn't. If the soil closed over her head, she would panic, believing she was buried alive. She might not see that in herself, but he saw it very clearly. Once that happened to her, it would be even more difficult for her to overcome her fears. If she waited longer and continued to practice, as she was doing, she would become accustomed to the idea.

Safia didn't argue with him. She went quiet again, searching first his mind and then her own. Petru found he respected and admired her even more for the way she carefully thought things through. She didn't hurry. She really examined every angle and possibility before she sighed.

"I really don't like the fact that I jumped to conclusions about your motives. One of my worst traits has always been not accepting someone telling me what to do. Just like when Izem was fearful of me going over the cliff, but I insisted on jumping fences as a child. I wanted to defy him, mostly to show him he couldn't order me around. I thought I was over that."

Petru wished he hadn't been so quick to clothe her as he brought her to the surface and awakened her, but he knew she was too much of a temptation, especially when he fed her. He brushed kisses into her thick dark hair.

"*Hän ku vigyáz sívamet és sielamet,*" Petru murmured, rubbing his chin over the mass of hair so that the silky strands tangled with the bristles along his jaw. She was the keeper of his heart and soul. It had happened fast for him.

"You shouldn't be so nice to me when I misjudged you, Petru," she reprimanded very gently. "It wasn't fair to you for me to jump to conclusions."

He had been trying to puzzle out the meaning of emotions. Trying to find a way to make feelings fit into logic. When the sensations he felt for Safia became not just physically passionate but undeniably about who she was, causing him to question everything he thought he understood about lifemates and relationships, he would simply distance himself from all emotion.

After being with her even for a short period of time, he realized he looked forward to every moment he could spend with her. It didn't matter what the meaning of emotions were or what caused them. He liked the way she made him feel. He wanted to smile. She made him see the world differently than he'd ever seen it. He saw her family through her eyes. She loved effortlessly. Unconditionally. There was joy in her. He wanted Safia to be every bit as invested in him as he was in her.

"I'm invested," she said, proving she was in his mind, just as he was in hers.

"You're invested in our relationship," he corrected gently. "You have committed your life to mine wholly. I see that. You've given yourself to me. Your loyalty and your trust. You are determined to do everything to make the relationship work. That is your character and who you are. You still haven't quite made up your mind about me."

"I'm feeling a bit of a failure," Safia admitted, not bothering to deny his charge.

His hand came up to massage the tension from the nape of her neck. "*Sívamet*, I have had two thousand years to find my lifemate. I know what I wanted and needed. I acquired as much knowledge about you as fast as possible, not only from you but also from your family. It is second nature to me. I do so with everyone around me, you especially. I learned who you were and what you were like, everything from the moment you were born until now."

"You did?"

"A man wants to know who he is going to marry," he said.

"I don't know how I feel about that."

"It is just what we do. Our way of life. It is easier than long conversations where people do not give the information you are looking for. You have been on this earth a short time. I am used to sharing minds and gaining information. You did so with Aura, but only to acquire knowledge of fighting techniques. You haven't yet acquired the skill to investigate my memories and find out the details of my earlier life. Clearly, you're capable because you have done so accidently."

She had seen horrific things in the memories of his past. He hadn't blocked her when she looked, but she knew he'd been uncomfortable, mostly when she felt any pain of past wounds.

"What you need is time to get to know me. Tonight is the night we marry in the way of your people, but we have time before I take you to the farm. I want to teach you some of the things I know you will enjoy doing. We should also take some time to look at the areas you think Lilith may attack first. Benedek and the others have familiarized themselves with the surrounding terrain, but you know it best."

"We have to sign the marriage contract." Her emerald eyes looked straight into his. "Even with my hideous temper, are you certain you want me?"

Petru couldn't believe she still would have that little niggling of doubt in her mind. "That's Lilith and Eduardo talking, not my woman. There is no doubt in her mind that I believe she is a true miracle. When our enemies intrude, we banish them immediately. We agreed on that already."

Once again, he brushed kisses over the top of her head into the softness of her silky hair. The feel of those strands tangling with the bristles on his jaw seemed to melt something hard inside him. She was taking him over, and while he might have been resistant before, now he welcomed the invasion.

"You're really quite brilliant, aren't you?"

He kept his features as serious as possible under the circumstances.

"I am always right. That is why many songs about me are sung around the campfires at night. You have only to follow my every command, and you will be fine."

She burst out laughing, just as he'd hoped. He loved the sound. More, he was beginning to find his own ability to laugh.

"I walked right into that one, didn't I?"

"Yes." He kissed his way from her temple to the corner of her mouth to the dimple he loved so much. It took discipline, but he lifted his head and looked into her green eyes, needing to see how she would react when he asked his next question. "Are you ready to learn to shift?"

Her pulse jumped. Her long lashes fluttered. She gripped his wrist. "Shift? I'm not certain what you mean by that."

"Haven't you ever seen Aura shift?"

She shook her head, her gaze never leaving his. "You can teach me to shift my shape?" Her eyes widened. The shade of green darkened to a deeper, almost mossy forest green. "I could become a bird?"

"If that is what you would want to be."

"Fly? On my own?" Her voice filled with excitement. "I love birds. They soar in the sky and look so beautiful with the wind in their feathers. Sometimes they look peaceful, other times so fierce. I've always thought it would be incredible to be able to fly across the sky the way you did over the valley when you were coming for me."

Petru couldn't help stroking his palm down the back of her hair. She sounded so admiring of him, when each time he thought of that particular moment, the sense of guilt and despair assailed him that he couldn't get to that extraordinary child in time to save her from the vampire's cruel tearing out of her heart. They each viewed the same moment from two different perspectives, as was often the case. She viewed him as a hero, while he viewed himself as a failure. He needed to take his own advice and forget guilt.

"Shifting is dangerous if you can't keep your concentration, Safia," he warned. "Until you are adept at it, you must follow every step and hold a very detailed image in your mind at all times. One mistake could cost you your life."

She nodded. "I understand. I had years of practicing to attain the skills I have to defeat demons. I'm still practicing. I know when you're acquiring that type of knowledge, it must become automatic. Your muscles have to have those memories, just as your body does when walking or talking. I rehearse in my head, going over and over the steps to open the soil so that hopefully when I practice for real, I can do it without making a mistake."

"You will do everything I say when I tell you, Safia," he warned. "If you don't, I will take over. If I give you a command, there is a reason for it. I will give you that reason after, but at the time, it is imperative you obey without question. Is that understood?"

He waited in her mind, making it clear with his tone that he meant exactly what he said. She'd told him she had trouble with anyone telling her what to do. She would have a difficult time with that side of his personality, but he was not ever going to take chances with her life. Not when he could keep her safe. It was necessary for her to learn how to shift. How to open the soil. All the things a Carpathian could do, especially when she would need certain skills for the coming battles against Lilith's army, but he would make certain she was safe while she learned.

"I'm fully aware it's necessary to acquire the skills and talents to become as you are. I want to learn them, Petru. I also know that most of those abilities are dangerous, and it will take time to get them down. I don't have that time, so it will be extremely important not to go off on my own as I did when I was a child. I am quite logical despite the behavior I've shown you."

Petru hadn't realized how tense he was until relief swept through him. "Since your preference is to be a bird, the little owl is a good choice. Are you familiar with it?"

Safia nodded. "I've seen it quite often. It's tiny and fierce. There is a pair claiming the farm as their territory. They defend it quite fiercely."

She shared her memories of watching the owls and how much she enjoyed them.

"Study their appearance and behavior. That's extremely important. When you're in the owl's body, you must be an exact replica. Anyone observing you must believe you're an owl. If a vampire is close, he can't suspect your spirit is inside the body of that owl. Anything hunting you can't suspect, or anyone or anything you're hunting can't suspect. You must submerge yourself so completely that you're using the senses of the animal you've become to do the hunting for you."

The green in her eyes was so bright with excitement he found the color fascinating. It seemed she had several different shades of green, depending on her mood. He was going to enjoy learning every single one of them. He'd gone from a gray world to one of vivid brightness, so much so that at times, he had to mute the colors.

Petru shared a detailed picture of a female little owl in Safia's mind. "Notice how plump and compact she is. Her head is flat on top, and the tail is short. Really study her plumage and the various shadings and patterns on her feathers. She's grayish brown with streaks, spots and bars of white. Underneath she is pale and streaked with darker feathers. I think they are beautiful little birds. Long legs for their size, white eyebrows over their yellow eyes. They have very stern and fierce expressions."

Safia clenched his wrist in excitement, but she studied the image of the little owl from every possible angle. She was meticulous, taking her time, going over and over the tiny raptor to make certain she didn't miss anything about its appearance.

Petru had spent time studying Safia's approach to learning the necessary skills for fighting demons. She had been training since she was very young, almost before she could walk. She never missed a single day and would practice for hours. Her family used games at first, as did Aura, but Safia took it further after the training session ended. She would go over the instructions in her mind, just as she was doing now with her approach to learning how to open the soil above her head.

She'd been a child practicing skills, but even then, she had been using the method of mental repetition to sink the lessons deep into her brain.

While she worked on the farm, no matter what task she was doing, a part of her brain continued to go over the skill she had been learning. Step by step, she processed the way to use new and unfamiliar weapons. When she was introduced to hand-to-hand fighting, she did the same thing, going over each move in her head until her body knew the action without her thinking about it.

"Little owls are most active during early morning hours and at dusk," he continued. "They like higher perches so they can swoop down on their prey, and they are carnivores. Keep in mind, you may have no choice at times to emulate that behavior and eat earthworms or bring a mouse to a nest."

"Ugh." She wrinkled her nose, but her dimple was very much in evidence, her sense of humor overcoming her distaste. "If I ever have to carry around a mouse in my beak or eat an earthworm, I'll have disgusting tales to tell Charif and Igider. They'll love them."

Petru's heart contracted. She thought in human terms. Naturally, she would want to share amusing tales with her nephews. She was used to telling funny stories. He had looked into the memories of her family members, and with all of them, their favorite times were gathering together and sharing stories.

Safia didn't yet understand that Carpathians were secretive. They didn't allow humans to know of them. Although Aura was considered a part of their family, she hadn't told all of them the circumstances of her birth. Only the grandparents were aware of who she was. She was allowed into their home and presented as a playmate for their children. She grew as they grew. That cycle was repeated time after time.

Aura had taught the ancient language to Safia because Safia was Petru's true lifemate. She'd given her more facts on the Carpathian people only because she recognized that Safia guarded the soul of one of their own.

Safia suddenly leaned into him and rubbed at his lips. Her touch, no matter how light, always seemed to burn through his skin straight to his heart. Her eyes met his in a blaze of brilliant green. "You always have that very stoic look, Petru. You look intimidating and dangerous. Definitely the legendary warrior that led the way to victory against the underworld. But inside, I can feel your worry for me. It isn't for yourself. You never seem concerned for yourself; it's always about me. I know your fear doesn't have anything to do with my ability to learn to shift. I can see you have absolute faith in me. It's something else."

"At times, I wish I could have grown old with you in the human way. It is a gift I would have wanted to give you, Safia." He took her hand and pressed a kiss into the center of her palm. "You deserve more than this short time we have, cramming lessons that should be leisurely and fun into minutes because a war is coming. You should be spending months getting to know me. I should be doing the same with your family."

"I have no complaints, Petru. I'm excited to learn shifting. I might be a little bit frightened, but anything new can be intimidating. Opening the soil is exciting; being buried in it is terrifying. I know I can get used to it, because I already am adjusting to the idea in my mind."

"Our people have so many secrets, Safia. We have them for many reasons, but most of all because we wouldn't be accepted if humans knew of us. They declare war on one another over differences in beliefs. You can imagine what they would do if they knew of us. They believe us to be myths. We prefer it that way. It must remain that way."

He willed her to understand what he was saying without him having to spell it out for her. She was very intelligent, and her mind worked fast, but this was really about her family, and she might not want to comprehend the enormity of what he was telling her.

Her hands came up to frame his face. She leaned her forehead against his for a brief moment, as if taking strength from him before she sat up straight again. "Petru, I can't be the only human lifemate who loves her family the way I do. There must be others. We're just starting out. There are answers. We'll find them. *Jeddi* always would tell us not to worry about things that haven't occurred yet. I am going to enjoy every moment I have with you. I love learning new things. Shifting sounds amazing. I can't wait to learn. I have no doubt that you'll come to love my family, and they'll love you."

Petru felt the storm in his heart settle. Safia was right. She wasn't the only human lifemate with a family. The De La Cruz brothers, all Carpathians, owned several properties throughout South America and had human families loyal to them. One of the women who was a lifemate to a De La Cruz had siblings, a boy and girl, who were still human. They knew of the Carpathians.

Aidan Savage's lifemate, Alexandria Houton, had a younger sibling, still human. The couple had two or three humans who knew of them, devoted to caring for the boy while they slept during the day.

One of the most famous healers and one that the Carpathians depended on, Gary Jansen, had been human, but he'd known of the Carpathians for years before he'd undergone the conversion to save his life.

"There are other humans who do know," Petru assured her. "Once the war has been won and things have settled, I will send word to Zacarias De La Cruz and find out what they've done to ensure the protection of the families."

"Why would our family have to be protected?"

Just like that, she'd pierced his heart again. Calling her family *ours*. Already sharing with him the people she loved and was so fiercely loyal to was so like her. She was generous. Willing to trust him with her most precious treasure.

"Vampires can read minds. Anyone knowing about us has to be shielded. Vampires would target them. There is a society of vampire hunters who also target us. They don't care to see the difference between us. They would also torture your family members to get information from them." He despised putting the worry back in her eyes when she had been joyful just minutes earlier. "I won't let that happen."

"No, *we* won't let that happen. In any case, my family has learned to protect themselves against vampires, demons and humans far better than most. We can help them improve their skills. Aura will aid us," she added with confidence.

"No doubt she will," he agreed readily. "Just so you remember, *Ku Tappa Kulyak*, little owls are usually monogamous. The male tends to stay in the same territory and defends it vigorously. Often, the female will remain with him year-round."

Her eyes lit with feminine humor. "I detect a kind of chest-beating male warning in there somewhere. Are you expecting me to live through a winter with you? In the cold ground? Eating earthworms and mice you bring me?"

"Exactly." The woman was what he'd needed, and he hadn't known it.

She laughed. "You'd better be beyond excellent at this consummating-the-marriage business for including earthworms and mice."

"I am. Remember the songs the women were singing? Legendary. Keep that in mind." She made life fun when all he'd ever known was service. "When you read the cards for Benedek, Nicu, Mataias, Lojos and Tomas, tell them, if you can, the benefits of having a lifemate. If that is in the cards. Not just that they have a lifemate, but that she will change their life in unexpected and miraculous ways."

She sobered, her face going soft. "I'm glad I changed your life for the better, Petru."

He rose with her in his arms. "I'll take you out to the far meadow on your property where the little owl has his territory. We can practice there."

"Won't he attack if he sees us?"

She wrapped her arms around his neck, staying relaxed, giving him her trust without thought. Petru loved that about her. So far, there wasn't anything about Safia he didn't love. He found he was becoming a little obsessed with her.

"If he could see us, he would, but I'll make certain he won't. This is just for you to practice shifting. His territory is open with higher perches. You can shift and fly from stump to stump. Even if you falter, the drop won't be far. We can start with lower stumps and progress to the higher ones."

Her pulse had leapt at the word "fly." Her arms tightened around his neck, and her fingers dug into his hair at his nape. "I can't wait to be able to take to the skies myself."

Petru was happy he could give her a gift she was looking forward to. "While we're moving over the ground, study it carefully. My people and Aura have been patrolling, but Aura told us you are much more adept at spotting minute signs of Lilith's spies. She says there are times she misses them when you can see them."

"They shouldn't be able to come through the ground on the farm. They might be able to access it from another direction, but all of you wove safeguards, so I'd be surprised."

"Look everywhere, not just the farm. We protected the farm, but it was impossible to lock down the entire city. Once we're married and you have the shifting down, we can investigate the city thoroughly."

She was uncomfortable with the idea that Lilith could send her spies into the city, and she hadn't been as vigilant as she should have been. Petru had taken to the air. As he told her, he went very slowly.

No one can see us? She needed reassurance.

No. Now that she was using the more intimate form of communication, she was opening the door between them even more. She really enjoyed being in the sky, but she was concerned about the city's occupants and their businesses.

I want to practice shifting, Petru, but I'd like to go into Dellys and look around if you wouldn't mind. It's extremely important to me. I don't just defend my family.

He didn't make the mistake of hesitating. His brethren had checked the city many times for signs of vampires and Lilith's demons. Aura had as well. They had not found any indication that the city had been penetrated. Aura had made it plain to them that Safia had a sixth sense about demons and spies that she didn't, even though she was Carpathian. His brethren were skeptical, but Petru was in Safia's mind, and he caught many small suggestions that she did exactly as Aura said.

You don't need to convince me, Ku Tappa Kulyak. You are the demon slayer. If you must investigate, then we will do so.

I suddenly have this feeling.

Safia had trailed off, but he was solidly in her mind, and he caught a coiling pressure beginning to surface. The sensation was vague at first, barely there, but Petru felt the heaviness in her growing and spreading as they approached the harbor town.

Petru stayed low enough that he could easily see the more modern buildings surrounding the Casbah of Dellys. The fortress was over a thousand years old, a beautiful walled-in city, historically preserved and thriving.

Go toward the main road where the tourist section is.

Safia had ceased being polite or worrying about whether she would offend Petru. She had slipped into the mode of huntress and had become the defender of her people. Her entire being was set on ferreting out the spy. She knew there was one hiding among the people she loved so much.

Petru found her utterly fascinating. Her brain worked at an astonishing speed. Her vision and hearing were extremely acute. She didn't seem to notice the change in the way she expanded every sense.

She hissed a denial. *Oh no. I should have known.*

What is it? Petru felt the increase in the coiling pressure she felt. She was like a laser, locked on to a target. He sealed himself to that beam and followed the trail. A line of vehicles was parked around a very modern restaurant located right above the harbor. It was in a prime location. On the side overlooking the harbor was a canopied deck with several tables and benches. The front of the building had large glass windows, and inside, at least ten men were gathered around a large glowing firepit.

Lilith preys on weakness. On what people want the most.

Yes, he agreed.

Aabis Kalaz owns the restaurant. He's a good, hardworking man. He supports his parents and sisters. Unfortunately, he's asked Jeddi and Baba several times if he could marry me. He was told I was already promised to someone else, but when you didn't come, I don't think he believed them.

You believe this spy has been sent to turn him against your family.

I know it is so, she stated. *I will need my things to send the demon back to her or destroy it. I usually keep my weapons with me at all times.*

Show them to me in detail.

Safia did without hesitation. While she did, she was still concentrating on those inside the restaurant. The weapons were so much a part of her, she didn't have to think about them as she built the images of them in her mind. The descriptions were so vivid and real that her long hooded coat with the many loops and pockets was suddenly on her, filled with everything she carried with her, including her emergency medical supplies.

Thank you, Petru.

He didn't point out that she had been the one to call her weapons to her. His lifemate was more than extraordinary, and she wasn't in the least aware of it. His heart swelled with pride for her.

HOPE.
POTENTIAL.
FUTURE.

CHAPTER

16

*P*etru. There wasn't panic in Safia's voice, but something quite close to it. *They have Charif.*

He knew that had been her greatest fear. The boy was indomitable and very curious. They had safeguarded the farm, but that didn't mean those living there couldn't come and go as they pleased. Charif was known for sneaking out. He had Safia's personality when she'd been young. Curious and not one to acknowledge authority.

My family will be so frantic. Zdan and the others will already be out looking. You must let them know we'll get Charif back. If they know Aabis Kalaz and his friends are holding him captive, there will be no stopping Zdan from killing him. Tell them he encountered a demon and we are dealing with it. I cannot have any of them close, or it will be much more difficult for me.

This must have been done to draw your family outside the circle of protection, Petru said.

Perhaps, she speculated. *I believe Lilith is up to her tricks of turning friend against friend. If she divides us all, she will have the advantage of using humans against each other.*

Petru called in his brethren, uneasy with the number of men in the restaurant. More was going on than met the eye.

Have them come in very carefully. Demons sense energy, Safia cautioned.

You know they will want to exchange you for Charif.

I do not bargain with demons, Petru. I destroy them.

She was firm, both in her tone and in her mind. There was no hesitation and no room for anything else. She believed she could defeat any spy or demon Lilith sent. She would not allow them to remain. If it cost her her life, she would go down taking them with her. That resolve had been bred into her and reinforced by her training.

At least they were on the same page about trading her life for her nephew's. He wouldn't have to take command of her if she tried such a foolish thing.

I've sent word to your family. Amastan has assured me he will keep everyone home. It won't be easy. Zdan and Lunja are beside themselves with worry.

I knew they would be. Jeddi will keep them there and give us our chance to destroy the demon and keep peace. Did you tell the others to guard their energy?

They are Carpathian.

For the first time, she turned her gaze fully on him. Her eyes were completely jade, with a dark ring around them. *That is the first truly arrogant thing I've heard you say. I could feel your energy at times. If I can, they might be able to, depending on what type of demon Lilith sent.*

Benedek and Nicu were the first to arrive. They circled the restaurant before they settled to the ground beside Petru and Safia just outside under the patio cover, where they could still observe those inside through the glass.

I do not see the boy, Benedek said.

He is there. I feel him, Safia said.

And the demon? Benedek prompted, studying the men inside.

Mataias, Lojos and Tomas materialized in front of them. They too had circled the restaurant before finding their way to Petru and Safia. Clearly, they had heard the entire conversation.

Have no fear, Safia, they cannot be seen by anyone inside, Petru assured.

Aura came next, settling beside Safia. She didn't look nearly as calm as she usually did, but she was all business.

The men sitting around the fire are friends of Aabis. Aura, you've met them before. The one across from Aabis is Kadin Merabet. He owns the fishing boats that bring in the majority of fish for the other restaurants in Dellys. Although they appear to be rivals, they've always been friends. If you look closely into the four corners of the room, you will see four men in robes. Each has his face in the shadows. They are staying away from the firelight.

There was a small silence.

One of the men in the corner suddenly raised his head and looked out the window.

He is feeling one or more of you. Don't concentrate on them, Safia warned.

The man glided to the window and peered out. He seemed to be a shadowy figure, almost as if he could mask his presence. His robe was a dull gray. The air around him seemed to be gray as well, just a shade darker. He brought up his hands and began to weave a complicated pattern. As he did so, Safia matched him, her hands reversing the weave in exact time with his as if she knew what he was doing before he did it.

None of the Carpathians moved until the hooded figure turned and went back to his corner.

He's mage. There are four mages in that room, Lojos declared.

The four are demons sent from Lilith to wreak havoc, and that's what they're doing, Safia corrected. *If you give them mage status, you play right into her hands.*

A mage is a mage, Benedek said. *They are not easy to kill. Four of them present a real problem, Safia.*

If you see them as mages, you give them more power. Lilith is counting on you elevating them to that status. They are demons. They come from the underworld. I can scent a demon miles away. If you refuse to acknowledge them as mages, eventually their disguises will crumble. They will lose faith in their abilities. I can counter every move they make. You will be able to as well if you look at them as demons and not mages.

Petru was able to see into her mind. What she said made sense to her. She saw beyond the illusions and tricks of the demons Lilith had sent. These were mages long dead that Lilith now controlled. She didn't trust anyone. She'd allowed Xavier, the master of mages, to rise to the surface, letting him believe they had an alliance, but she always maintained control of him. These four had never been close to Xavier's talents, and she had lost patience with them and turned them into demons.

How did you know these things about them? Petru asked, sharing what she had learned with the others.

All but Aura and Nicu shook their heads.

Impossible to know, Benedek insisted. *Petru, you can see and feel they are true mages.*

Lojos gestured toward the restaurant. *If we go in there believing mages are something else, we could be defeated easily.*

I prefer you stay here, out of my way, Safia said. Her voice was very calm. Very matter of fact. *My nephew is in there. They will do their best to use him as a bargaining chip. I can't afford to be fighting you, mages you create and demons Lilith has sent. No doubt the moment the mages are strengthened, they will use the humans in that room to their advantage.*

She is right, Nicu said. *I have studied these demons. They are exactly as she says. Do not look with your eyes. See them with your other senses. You are seeing what you expect to see. When we get inside, they will act like mages, and that will only add to your belief if you are not one hundred percent convinced.*

How can you tell, Nicu? Tomas asked. *You and Petru are so certain, yet I cannot tell.*

She connects with them, Petru answered for Nicu. *Just as she did the sea demons, she finds the exact path into their mind and slips inside. I followed her in. Nicu did the same.*

I did as well, Aura said. *I've been doing it for many years, so it is easy for me.*

Benedek frowned. *I was being polite. Safia, you are Petru's lifemate, and I would not enter your mind without an invitation, not unless your life was at risk.*

Are you accusing me of being rude? Nicu didn't sound in the least affronted.

Everyone knows you're more animal than man, Benedek said.

That's true, Nicu agreed. *Which makes me far more intelligent, and you should have known the moment I agreed with Safia that I was right.*

How many songs are sung about you? Petru asked.

Don't get him started, Tomas said. *You're the demon slayer, Safia. Before Nicu is insufferable and starts howling like a wolf, tell us what you want us to do.*

Aura must find Charif immediately and take him to the farm. She'll need at least two of you to accompany her.

Safia looked at Petru. He knew she trusted him and wanted him to take her nephew home, but he wasn't leaving his lifemate with four demons and ten human men who might turn on her at any moment if Lilith gained the upper hand.

No. My place is by your side. Petru was implacable. There was no arguing with him, and he meant for her to see that.

I will ensure the child and Aura reach the farm safely, Lojos volunteered.

I will as well, Tomas agreed.

Thank you. When Lilith sees the first demon fall and realizes I've taken control from her, she will attempt to strike at me through Charif.

We won't fail, Aura assured her. *Charif is my family as well.*

For the first time, Petru felt a wave of relief slide through Safia as she met Aura's eyes. The two women exchanged a long look, and then Safia put her hand over her heart and nodded. Aura did the same before they turned toward the building.

When we go in, will you be able to control every human right away, Petru?

Yes. He had already examined them.

Let them talk for a few minutes so I can examine the four demons up close. I need to know which of them is the strongest. While we're in the building, Aura, Lojos and Tomas should be able to locate Charif.

It went without saying, once inside, they had to guard their energy carefully. If one demon detected them, all bets were off.

Petru lifted Safia into his arms. *I'll bring you in. We'll slip under the door without detection. Each of us will enter through this doorway or the back entrance. Just relax and trust me to get you through. The others know what they're doing, Safia. They're experienced hunters.* He wanted to assure her. She didn't know his brethren and had never seen them in battle.

I trust your judgment, Petru, she assured readily, without hesitation. *When Nicu connected with me, it was easy enough to catch glimpses of him, although I did my best not to intrude. They didn't need to give me their word. I believe they will do as I asked them.*

Petru knew she believed in the others because he did. He brushed a kiss in her hair and took her under the thin crack between the door and the floor.

The room was very warm in comparison to the cool of the night. This was the main room of the restaurant. Tables were set up, and chairs were either pushed in or set upside down on top of them. In the large foyer was the firepit where people could gather to talk. The men were seated around it, Aabis and Kadin carrying the lion's share of the conversation, with the others nodding and agreeing occasionally.

"That family has always thought themselves far above everyone else," Kadin said as they entered the room. "Any woman would be lucky to have you, Aabis. Many families have inquired if you would be interested."

A round of agreement supported the statement.

"That stubborn little boy is a prime example of what they are like.

No manners. He doesn't respect his elders," an older man said. He clasped his hands together and bowed toward the stairs leading to the offices above. "He should have been beaten like the dog he is until he knows how to speak to his betters."

Safia gripped Petru's arm. *They call him Abbot. He has always been strict, even with his own children and grandchildren. I don't see his son in the room. His son is always with him.*

Aura, Lojos and Tomas have already located Charif, Petru informed her. *They have him safe. They are building an illusion of the man who was beating him continuing to do so in case anyone goes to check.*

He showed the images of the real Charif to Safia. The boy was only seven, but he had stoically remained silent under the interrogation he'd been subjected to. Aabis and his friends wanted to know everything about Safia's intended. They wanted to know if the marriage contract had already been signed. They didn't think it had been, but it was important to know if Aabis still had a chance.

They beat him.

Yes. Petru monitored her closely. He felt the swift intake of breath. The anger that she let flow through her and then let go of.

She continued to listen to Aabis and his friends talk about her family and how she should have been more protected. Aabis insisted it wasn't her fault she was the way she was. He defended her, stating that she had a good heart, worked hard and would be an asset to him and his family once she was under his control.

The demon in the western corner lifted one hand, palm out, tracing symbols in the air. As he did, he shook his head slowly, his eyes taking on a reddish glow as if reflecting the firelight. He stared at the men gathered around the fireplace.

Abbot shook his head mournfully. "The woman must be disciplined, Aabis. Just like the boy." He looked up toward the stairs. "My son knows the right way to ensure a child or a wife is obedient in all things."

Petru kept his mind firmly in Safia's. She wasn't paying attention to what Abbot was saying. She wasn't even following the progress of

Aura, Lojos and Tomas as they took Charif toward the farm. Her entire attention was fixed on the demon in the western corner. He felt the flow of her mind moving like breath, slow and steady, a stream so light and airy it was impossible to detect. He flowed with her, as did Nicu.

Benedek waited with Mataias to take control of the human men in the room on Petru's signal. To maintain that slow, infinitely light pace was extremely difficult. Petru was used to battling the undead, striking with the speed of lightning. This kind of attack was very different but utterly fascinating.

Carpathians shed their bodies to heal. In order to do so, their species lost all ego, all sense of self, to become pure spirit. In a way, Safia was doing something similar, but she entered the mind of the demon. It was a wrenching experience. Chaos, cruelty and need for violence assailed them. There was no thought but to destroy everyone around him in as vile and brutal a manner as possible. The craving for human suffering was uppermost in the demon's mind.

His name had been Art when he'd been a mage. He could barely remember those days. Pain shredded his memory, tearing at his insides, stabbing at his head and eyes until he wanted to torture everyone around him so they would feel his pain. The knowledge flooded Petru the moment he entered the demon's mind. It came all at once, just as the agony pushed into his brain.

Petru thought to buffer Safia, but there was no need. She had expected the assault on her senses and had been prepared—if one could be. More than the pain, it was the ugliness of the creature's thoughts and needs. His only real objective was to carry out Lilith's will and bring Safia out into the open so she could be murdered. She not only wanted Safia dead but her entire family destroyed. Art's orders, along with the others, were to find Safia, kill her and burn her family alive, if possible. If not, kill them all.

Safia didn't wince at the knowledge of his orders. She continued that slow entry, filling his mind with her. Petru found the sensation was comparable to swimming through thick murky oil. As a Carpathian, he would have automatically blocked himself from the vile feeling. He could tell Nicu felt the same way.

Sensation is necessary.

Safia's advice came to him, but not in the same way as it normally did. She was more cautious than usual. The words were more felt than heard, as if she may have stroked them onto the walls of his mind with delicate brushstrokes, barely discernible.

Evil was swift and invasive, pouring into the demon without mercy, stabbing at him from every conceivable angle until his eyes and ears wept blood. He shook his head continually in a feeble attempt to rid himself of the vicious entry of his mistress.

Petru had no time to puzzle out how Safia had known Lilith was going to make an appearance. He was a very powerful Carpathian, an ancient, as was Nicu. It should have been next to impossible to mask their presence from one so evil as Lilith, but both had lived far too long and developed the scars that marked them as more beasts than men. They belonged in the underworld more than either of them belonged in the world above.

But there was Safia with her brightness and innocence. How was it that Lilith couldn't detect that shining star among the evil and brutality swirling together in the demon's mind? She had no business being there and should have stood out like a sore thumb.

"Is the woman dead?" Lilith demanded.

"No, mistress," Art responded immediately.

He clapped both hands to his mouth to prevent the scream that roared through his mind from emerging as she jabbed at his brain and eyes mercilessly with a hot poker. Petru could see the hot stick glowing bright red, retreating and then glowing again.

"Why?" Lilith snarled. "I asked two small tasks and sent four of you to get them accomplished. You were to direct the others. Are you telling me you can't control them? You can't get the others to do what you say?"

The sneer of contempt was also a promise of unrelenting retaliation. Lilith was not a forgiving person, and her torture chambers were legendary. Sometimes she forgot she sent her victims there, and they remained for years. There was no dying to escape in the underworld. The punishments went on until Lilith determined they were over.

"We'll find the woman and slay her, mistress," Art assured. He dropped his hands. Blood trickled down his face from his eyes. His expression turned sly. "We have a child, part of her family. She will come for him."

There was silence. Lilith ceased poking at him with the stick. "You may have your uses after all. Don't kill the child. Bring him to me after you manage to trap the woman. And do not fail me, or all four of you will be fodder for the games."

A shudder went through the demon. "We won't fail you, mistress," he promised.

She gave him one last vicious jab with the hot poker before she was abruptly gone. The demon spat a mixture of blood and saliva on the floor.

"What are you doing?" Aabis demanded. "People eat in here. We keep a clean establishment."

Now, Safia commanded, *take them over now. They can't see anything or be used as hostages.*

Benedek and Mataias instantly materialized, waving hands toward the ring of human males, freezing them in place so there was no possibility of them witnessing the destruction of the demons who were preying on them.

Petru allowed the four demons to see Safia and him standing directly in front of Art. Nicu continued to be concealed, their secret weapon in case they needed one.

Art appeared startled. He looked around the room to make sure the other three former mages were able to see what he was seeing— that Lilith hadn't driven him insane by her jabbing and piercing with the hot poker.

He lifted his hands to begin weaving a holding spell. "Have you come for the child?"

Safia pulled out a short black sword with an intricate hilt from the inside of her long coat. As she did, the razor-sharp blade lengthened into a crystalline sword. "There is no child here," she replied.

"You are wrong. Your curious nephew couldn't help himself when he heard your name and knew Aabis and his friend Kadin planned to set a trap for you. Little did he know, he was to be the bait in the trap."

"Again, Charif is not here. He is safe at the farm." She inclined her head, princess to riffraff. "I understand you are looking for me, so I have come to send you home. I am Safia. *Ku Tappa Kulyak*. Demon Slayer. Defender of my people."

Art frowned, glared at her and then at the air where he had woven his spell. He looked to the demon on his right. "Use a locking spell, Basil."

Basil raised his hands into the air and began the same weave Art had just used.

Safia sent Art a half smile and shook her head at him as if chastising a small child. "A demon does not know how to cast spells properly." Her voice was gentle. Sweet even. She spoke to all four demons as if they weren't quite bright enough to understand.

Art sputtered, his carefully composed image fading for a moment to be replaced by the hardened shell of dark red-and-orange armor, much like a lizard's scales. Just behind his ears, two small horns appeared, with dark hair tightly wrapped around the protrusions. The illusion was gone in the blink of an eye, almost before it registered.

"I am no demon. I am Art, and I trained with the best of masters."

"Art, you're very confused." She lowered her voice another octave. The tone reverberated throughout Art's mind. "You need Basil and your other friends to come stand beside you. You're very worn. Your mistress hurts you with that continuous jabbing pain. You've tried your best to spare the others from her cruel ways, but nothing has helped."

Petru saw the reason Safia had gained entrance to Art's mind.

She'd done so slowly and thoroughly, taking care to examine his memories. She knew him, knew his life. Lilith had him down in her torture chambers and her dungeons for hundreds of years, and she didn't know—or care to know—one single thing about him. Lilith used threats, fear and agony to demand compliance.

Safia sounded gentle and nonthreatening. Caring even. Understanding. Inside Art's mind, the brain waves were soothing. For the first time in years, the chaos had faded to the background, replaced by Safia's serenity. The low tone of her voice forced the demon to lean toward her to hear her better.

The demon was saturated with her. She'd taken him over, wrested control from Lilith without the hapless creature or his mistress aware she'd done so. She'd been quiet and stealthy, a silent invader, and for now, she had the demon tentatively under her control. Petru waited to see what she would do next.

She appeared relaxed and totally at ease. The tip of the crystal sword was pointed toward the floor, but outward, more toward the feet of the demon, although Petru could see the stance appeared natural, nonthreatening.

"Basil, come here. Colin, Arsen, come here where we can talk to Safia. She has something to tell us," Art commanded.

Petru didn't take his gaze from the former mages as they approached his lifemate from the different directions. She appeared to keep her eyes on Art, but he knew she was acutely aware of the others getting closer to her.

Charif is safe, Aura assured her. *The farm is once again safeguarded. Do you have need of us?*

No, stay there. Petru made the decision for Safia. He was far more adept at speaking telepathically, and he didn't want Safia's attention to be divided. Right now, she had Art in the palm of her hand. One misstep and she could lose him. *Guard our family. We've got this.*

He could easily slay the four demons, but he couldn't keep others like them from returning. That was Safia's gift alone. She would close that door to Lilith. The ground, the air, she was slowly shutting down portals and sealing in various forms so that Lilith's army had fewer options when they engaged with the Carpathian and Amazigh peoples.

As they approached Safia from three sides, caging her in a semicircle, the other three former mages suddenly lifted their hands in unison to attempt the holding spell. As they did, Safia lifted the crystal sword upright so it transformed into a light so hot it blazed blue. The bright flame burst throughout the room like a star, illuminating the ceiling and bouncing a shimmering glow off every window.

The demons shrieked, covered their eyes and pulled the hoods down around their heads, trying to hide from the brilliance of the revealing light.

Petru wanted to bathe in the light. The part of him covered in dark scars wanted to hide his sins from her, but in that moment, he realized that crystal blue light was literally part of Safia's essence. Whoever had forged the sword had used very unique properties, including traces from Safia herself. She most likely wasn't even aware that the fierce nature of the sword and the serenity and peace came from her own innate characteristics.

"You see yourselves now," she said gently. Her voice was angelic, almost musical, the notes in complete contrast to the grating, discordant voices coming from the demons' throats. "You see your images, what your mistress has made you into through your own greed. No longer mage. She took your power from you."

"No, no," Basil protested, his tone a mixture of a harsh rumble and high-pitched shriek that shook the building and played on nerves. "I would never do that."

Colin and Arsen echoed his objection. Just like Basil, their protests were difficult to understand. They slurred words, their voices both shrieking and rumbling so that the walls expanded and contracted. The light fixtures overhead swayed as if they would fall from the ceiling.

"But you did," she continued softly in her angelic voice. "See yourselves. Look into the mirrors in front of you. See you as she made you."

It was obvious that all four demons tried not to obey, but the compulsion was too strong. Basil covered his eyes with his hands just as Art did. The other two demons tried to cover their faces with their hoods but couldn't help dragging the material away to expose the truth. They both spread their fingers wide to peer through them. Their faces were identical with hard armor: orange, yellow and red scales. Dark gray lines were carved deep between each scale, giving the appearance of age. Eyes were hooded, with tiny spikes surrounding them. Their mouths gaped open to accommodate the serrated teeth, too wide to be human. Venom trickled continuously from the corners in thin yellowish-white streams. The long talons at the tips of their bony fingers they'd raised to cover their faces were thick, curved and pointed.

Once they had seen themselves, the four of them couldn't revert back to their forms as mages. Art tried the hardest, turning his face away from the mirror held in front of him.

"She will give us our lives back if we deliver you to her," Colin snarled, taking a step toward Safia as if to attack her. His hands came up, the long fingers twitching.

"Yes, yes," Basil agreed. His talons clicked together eagerly. "If we kill her right here, our mistress will be happy with us and will return us to our original form."

"How do we know this isn't an illusion?" Arsen demanded. "She could be tricking us into believing what we see now is real so that we turn on the mistress."

Colin tried to shuffle toward Safia, but his feet wouldn't move. He looked down at the bottom of the tan-and-orange robe he wore over his loose pants to see the feet protruding from beneath were long, skinny, bare and very hairy. There were three toes with the same thick curving talons. The armor scales were orange streaked with yellow and tan, nearly blending with his robe. He shrieked, mouth distorted, talons clicking in agitation.

Petru narrowed his eyes, and without moving, took a careful look around the room. His acute senses expanded to every corner, every crack, as he scanned for intruders. They were no longer alone. Whoever was oozing in did so slowly, determined to remain hidden. They might hide their physical presence, but there was no hiding their intent or emotions. Hatred was a living, breathing entity so malevolent the air thickened with malignant loathing. All that animosity and hatred were centered directly on Safia.

Petru stayed relaxed, still anchored in Safia, realizing she not only was fully aware of the other's presence but had also been waiting for it.

What are you doing? She is one of the most powerful beings you could imagine.

She is demon. I cannot destroy her, but I can possibly wound her as you did. You struck hard enough that she had to wait two thousand years to recover and regain her full strength. We all believed she was biding her time, hoping we would forget her, but she was diminished and had to rebuild.

Where had she gotten such a revelation? Petru took the information from her mind. Art. She had taken the demon from Lilith. His mistress no longer controlled him. He had been with Lilith the longest, and he'd been the most powerful of the four mages. Lilith had stolen the magic from all four of them. The other three were nowhere as powerful as Art had been. Art had been one of her prizes, and she'd controlled him with an iron fist and a cruelty she reserved for those she believed might someday try to revolt against her.

Art had studied her just for that purpose, believing he might escape from the underworld one day if he could just hold out long enough. Lilith had stolen his magic and mutated him, leaving him a demon, yet giving him hope that he could one day earn his mage status and magic back.

Even with the information Safia had on Lilith, it was a very dangerous move she was trying. Petru wanted to wrap her up in his arms and get her out of there, but it was too late, she'd already set the trap in motion, drawing the spider right into the web. They were going to have a very long talk about what he was going to be able to live with and what he couldn't.

His brethren were ancients, and they had their own telepathic link. He apprised them of the situation, and they waited for Lilith's opening strike.

The flames in the fireplace suddenly leapt higher. The three former mages crouched low, bared serrated teeth, held talons in front of them like claws and leapt at Safia from all three directions.

Lilith had given the command to all four demons. Petru realized Safia knew what her enemies were going to do before they attacked. As they sprang at her, she spun so fast she was a blur. In one fist was the crystal sword with its brilliant light so hot it was a blue flame. In the other was a vial of water from a sacred stream. The vial shot the water high into the air, blending with the flames, spreading in a wide circle. Drops fell like rain over the demons, hissing as they hit the armor and drove straight through them, leaving behind holes where the blue flames began to flare into a storm of fire.

Safia continued to spin, bringing the sword sideways, the blade sweeping across their necks, severing the heads, sending them rolling across the floor. At once, she buried the sword into the floor of the restaurant.

"This ground is lost to you. This form is lost to you. Any other form you sent this night cannot return to the world below. That form cannot rise to this one."

As Safia scattered the sacred water over the floor, the blue flames consumed the three demons. At first, the stench was overpowering in the enclosed building, but the fire burned bright and hot until even the ash was gone.

CHAPTER

17

Safia heard Lilith's deadly hiss, a promise of retaliation. The woman still had no idea that Safia had stolen control from her and that Art was no longer under her command.

"This is your fault, you coward," Lilith sniped, stabbing at the hapless demon's brain with her fiery poker. "If you don't kill her now, you will live for eternity in such pain as you cannot possibly imagine."

The female head of the underworld poured more of herself into the demon, taking over so she could stare malevolently through his eyes at Safia, sizing her up.

"Now," she snarled, directing Art to spring at Safia. "Tear her apart."

Safia struck with the crystal sword, piercing the demon's right eye with the blue flame, driving the sword to the hilt, withdrawing swiftly, and piercing the left with blurring speed.

Lilith's shriek was hideous, the glass shattering all around them. Petru caught Safia and thrust her behind him as Art's body exploded like a powerful bomb had gone off inside him, the blast catching the Carpathian hunter fully and knocking him backward into Safia despite the partial shield he'd managed to erect when he realized Safia's intent.

Nicu and Benedek completed a shield around the two as Petru staggered but managed to stay on his feet, facing the nearly transparent apparition, a murky pink. Both sockets were empty holes, bleeding and flickering with tiny blue flames. Lilith's hair hung in strands, with tufts bunched in places and raw patches on her scalp in others. She opened her mouth wide and spat a horde of stinging insects at Petru and Safia. The bugs hit the shield so hard they splattered against it, showing exactly where the safeguard had been erected. The insects' bodies were crushed, and yellow venom ran down the shield.

Safia started around Petru, her heart hammering. She couldn't see Petru's chest, but she felt the blast hit him. She'd also felt the explosion of pain hastily cut off. It had been true agony, much like when her heart had been ripped out of her chest when she'd been a child in a previous life. She knew the force of that blast would have killed her. He'd saved her life.

"Stay where you are."

She heard the absolute command in Petru's voice. There was no moving. Even shifting her weight from one foot to the other didn't work.

"How *dare* you," Lilith's disembodied voice intoned. "You think to challenge me with your puny skills?" Her voice began to rise to a higher pitch. "You have no power. None. You're a child playing at war." She began to shriek. "I will destroy you and everyone you love." She began to scream and curse at Safia. As she did, more insects flew from her mouth, hitting the shield. "Your Carpathian lover will lie dead at your feet, but first you will see him betray you again and again as he did in the past. You are worth nothing. *Nothing*," she screeched.

Then she was gone, leaving behind a trail of destruction.

"That was pleasant," Benedek announced. He waved his hand toward the glass, and the thousands of shards coalesced to re-form the windows.

The shield dropped. Petru burned the insect bodies and what was left of Art to a fine powder that dissolved under a white-hot flame. Mataias gestured toward one of the low-slung couches in the center of the human men who were gathered around the fire, and Petru walked over to it.

Only then was Safia free to move. Her breath left her lungs in a rush of fear when she saw Petru's mangled chest. The injury was horrendous, although he appeared stoic. She couldn't believe he had burned the insects and demon to ashes before he had gone to the couch to allow Mataias to heal him.

She had accused Petru of arrogance. At the time, she'd been half joking, but now she was terribly ashamed and embarrassed that she was the one who had been arrogant. She had believed she could incapacitate or at least constrain Lilith and drive her back to the underworld for a time.

Had she been showing off? She feared she had been. She wanted Petru to see her as a full partner. All this time, he'd been allowing her to be herself, to be the defender, but she'd been in his mind, and he was that man. The one they sang about. She might joke about it, but that song was the truth. He had turned the tide of the war and saved her people, his people, and continued to hunt evil for the next two thousand years.

She knew she couldn't measure up against his experience or the things he was capable of doing. Shifting. Soaring through the sky. Going invisible. Healing from the inside. Repairing wounds at such a rapid rate of speed. Just the way he could acquire information and absorb it so quickly was a miracle. No matter what she did, she had no hope of catching up with him and his skills.

Safia hadn't expected to like Petru so much, let alone be so attracted to him. She had no idea she would care so much about his opinion of her. If she'd thought things through, she would have made better choices, but she was too busy showing off. She knew she was good at her job, but she would never match his skills.

Mataias was suddenly back in his body, and Nicu casually offered his wrist. Benedek provided blood to Petru while Safia stood alone, her arms wrapped around her middle, hugging herself, feeling like a total failure in every possible way. That didn't mean she would stay a failure forever. That wasn't her way. This just made her more determined to overcome her flaws and be a better partner for Petru.

Safia, come to me.

That brush of velvet heat stroked inside her mind. So gentle. Almost loving. The sound and feel sent shivers of awareness down her spine. He could do that so easily—make her so acutely centered on him, every nerve ending springing to life and focusing wholly on him.

His gaze burned over her. Into her. Intent. All-encompassing in that way he had. She couldn't look at him. She was too ashamed that she'd almost gotten him killed through ego. Pride. She had to process that flaw that she hadn't been aware she had. It was a huge one.

Don't forgive me yet, Petru. I haven't begun to forgive myself. Perhaps when I know how to heal you properly, I'll be able to look at you again, but right now, I just can't.

Because she had to make certain he was going to live, she slipped deeper into his mind and did a thorough examination of the terrible wound. It was astonishing to her how much healing had already taken place from the work Mataias had done using his spirit and then more healing from the ancient blood given to him by Benedek.

This was not a request given lightly. I have need of my lifemate to come to me.

Was there an edge to his voice? She doubted it. She flicked a quick look at him, although after she did, she had to acknowledge there was little use in doing so. Petru gave little away in his stony expression.

"Benedek," she dared, once more looking away from Petru. "What will it take to heal Petru completely? I know so little about your culture."

There was no hesitation. "Soil and salvia should be packed into the wounds, and he should go to ground. Before he does, it would be good to give him more blood. It would be best if he stayed in the ground for a couple of days to ensure he is completely healed. Lilith will not wait long to retaliate."

Safia couldn't help wincing at the mention of her enemy's name. She'd never believed she could kill Lilith, but she did think she could lock her in the ground. She knew she was very, very lucky she wasn't dead or, worse, that Petru wasn't.

Sívamet. I have need of you to come to me. If you do not, I will come to you, and the others will see how weak I am. I will no longer be called Kuŋe kont ku votjak and sung in songs around campfires or told in tall tales for wide-eyed children. Instead, I will be known as Hän ku oma és gyenge.

This time there was no mistaking the trace of amusement in his voice. *You give me no choice but to come to you. I cannot have children calling you "old frail one," although I may do so occasionally.* She forced herself to join with his humor, although she didn't understand how he could find humor in the situation, not when she wanted to cry at what she had caused.

"We must get word to my family that we won't come today," she told the others as she moved around the human men she'd known all her life, standing or sitting as statues, unaware of the drama that had played out right in front of them. She barely gave them a glance, let alone a thought. "We will come to them after Petru's wound is healed."

"I gave my word of honor, *Pelkgapâd és Meke Pirämet*," Petru corrected gently. "We will go to the house of your father and grandfather, sign the marriage contract and then return to our resting place."

Safia had gotten close to him, but she stopped just in front of him. She knew the color washed from her face as she looked down at the man she had already tied her life to. She wouldn't have backed out of her commitment even if she could have. This close to him, she could see the devastation the blast had caused, even with the partial shield hastily erected and the heavy muscles on his chest. Even after Mataias' meticulous healing.

This close to him, it was impossible not to feel the pain that Petru had automatically blocked out. The moment he realized she could still feel it, he blocked it from her as well.

There is no need, Safia. He gave a mental shrug. *In a few nights, this wound will be completely gone and forgotten. I have had much worse.*

She detested the way he was so casual about such a horrific injury. "My family will understand and wait for us."   ·

"We go now," he said decisively.

Safia wouldn't argue with him, not in front of his brethren. She'd done enough to embarrass herself. In any case, she heard the single note of implacable resolve. She turned away from him, shrugging, attempting to look casual as he appeared beside her, one arm sliding around her waist, clamping her beneath his shoulder.

Look at me.

I can't. I don't understand why you're so insistent. I'm holding it together by a thread.

I need you to look at me, sívamet. See me. Look past this block you've put between us in your mind.

Around them, the other Carpathians were putting the restaurant back to the exact way it had been prior to the confrontation between Safia and the demons. They were meticulous, inspecting the entire building to ensure it was sound and free of all debris and evidence of demons or Carpathians.

The upstairs office where Charif had been held was cleaned of his blood, furniture had been put right and the human male, who had been interrogating and punishing him, had been taken downstairs and placed with the other men. All memories of Charif having been in the restaurant that night were carefully erased.

Safia watched the others setting the scene in Aabis Kalaz's restaurant back to rights as Petru led her outside.

"You will have to look at me sometime, Safia."

Why did his voice have to be so gentle? How could he affect her so easily? "I know. Just not now."

The cool night air felt good on her overly warm face. She looked up at the stars, mostly hidden by the swirling gray fog coming off the sea.

She didn't need to look at his face, that strong jaw or the lines carved so deep, purely masculine, mostly sensual to her. His eyes like crystals, so beautiful. Everything about him was beautiful. When she thought of him, she went soft inside. Safia pressed a hand to her churning stomach, feeling as if she were on the brink of a great revelation.

Despite his injury, Petru swept her into his arms and took to the air. It was astonishing to realize how safe she felt with him as they moved across the sky toward the farm. It didn't matter that his chest had been mangled and the blast had caused injuries to his heart. Aura had transported her hundreds of times in the same manner, and she'd never felt safe. She'd always remained alert for the enemy, concerned that they would be tracked by a vampire or that she wouldn't feel the presence of a demon.

With Petru, she never felt those concerns. She knew she'd made a fool of herself and he should think less of her, but she was in his mind and he didn't. He never seemed to.

Safia pressed her ear over his chest, right over his heart, listening to the steady rhythm. The moment she did, the chaos in her mind settled. The churning in her stomach lessened to the soft flutter of butterfly wings. There was such a difference in the way she felt—if she allowed herself to be open to the emotions pouring in. That door inside her inched open wider.

How many times had he whispered to her, *Come to me. See me. Come all the way to me?*

She had wanted to be his partner as a demon slayer. Had she wanted to be his partner as a wife? She felt she had something to contribute to their union because she was confident as the defender of her people. Despite the error she'd made with Lilith, she was still confident in her abilities. She'd overstepped due to arrogance, but she would remember that lesson and get back on track once the humiliation died down and she was needed.

The real question was simple: What could she give Petru that he really needed? Her people needed the demon slayer, but if she was being honest with herself, Petru didn't need the slayer. He needed a wife. Beneath her ear, his heart leapt. Or maybe that was her heart. Could it have been theirs together?

Below was the farm she'd known and loved all her life. It had always been the most beautiful place on earth and represented love and family to her. She had never wanted to be anywhere else. The sight of the family farm didn't move her in the way it had always done. That rush of affection that normally accompanied her first glimpse wasn't there.

For the first time, she wished they hadn't gotten to their destination so fast. She needed just a little more time to follow the path of reasoning that she was on. She had made her commitment to be with Petru, but she hadn't taken that last step in the way her sister Lunja had to Zdan. Or Amara had to Izem. She had the key to relationships right in front of her. Her mother and grandmother had been examples when it came to leading the way. Her sisters-in-law and sister had generously given her advice. Why hadn't she heard it?

Fear of losing who she was. Petru was that legendary hero, a larger-than-life man. She had no idea how to be a woman. Every time he kissed her, she melted into someone else, a being she didn't even recognize. Logic went out the window. She couldn't think straight. She was afraid if she gave herself totally to Petru, she would lose Safia.

Lunja had gained more when she devoted herself to her husband because he had, in turn, given her more. Not all husbands did that, but hers had. Safia didn't doubt that Petru would do his best to put her first. She didn't see him as a selfish man. He was a man living his life the way he'd done for two thousand years—without emotion. Without feeling injuries that could so easily kill him. Without taking care of himself.

That was what Petru needed most—someone to care about him. Someone to see him when others didn't or couldn't. Was that what he'd been asking for her to do all along? She did see inside of him, even uninvited. She had when she'd been that child long ago. He had no idea how to take care of himself. He wouldn't even think he needed care, but she had the best examples of how to look after him. She would know what he needed before he did.

She glanced around her again. The farm was once more coming into view. Petru had circled around while she'd been contemplating what she should be doing. She deliberately touched his mind. He'd been closely inspecting the fields and fences, looking for any breaks in the safeguards. She loved that he would think to do that. It was ingrained in him, even when his body desperately needed care.

He set them down at the front entrance, his arm sliding around her waist. For the first time since he'd been injured, she felt the slightest reaction, as if a shiver went through him. He might look steady, but his strength was waning. She looked up at him.

"Petru, will you please do me a favor? I know you want to follow this ritual as closely as possible, but for me, allow me to talk to *Jeddi* and *Baba*, explain that you need to go to a healing ground or however you want it said, sign the marriage contract and leave as soon as possible." She raised her green gaze to his deliberately as she gently moved her palm over his chest.

"Are you certain that's what you prefer to do? You'll miss out on the wedding ritual. I know you looked forward to it for most of your life."

"I looked forward to *you* most of my life," she corrected. "Once the marriage contract is signed, we're married in the eyes of my people as well as yours. Realistically, how long do you think it will take to heal your wounds?"

He shrugged. "A couple of risings."

It took a moment to realize he meant days. She was going to have to get used to the small differences in the way they spoke. It wasn't just language; it was the terms they used to describe various things.

"We will tell them we'll come back in a couple of days and celebrate then if Lilith hasn't started her war."

"She will start it as soon as she is able," Petru confirmed. "She wants her revenge."

The door was flung open, and they were surrounded immediately by the warmth of her family. Zdan stood close to Amastan, Gwafa and Izem, his eyes very serious as he regarded the two of them.

Amastan greeted them with the ritual welcoming, and both Petru and Safia responded in kind. The others followed suit. When it was Zdan's turn, he gripped Petru's forearms and leaned in to brush his mouth on each cheek and Petru's forehead, murmuring a greeting before thanking him for getting his son home safely. He did the same with Safia.

"I did incur an injury," Petru admitted, looking to Amastan. "It is nothing to worry about, but I ask that you allow us to sign the marriage contract and retreat so I may be healed in the way of my people. It may require a couple of days."

"He saved my life," Safia added. "He stepped in front of me and took the full wrath of Lilith after I very foolishly challenged her. His wound is quite severe."

Sívamet. She heard the note in his voice this time. Recognized it for what it was. Affection. She'd heard it in her father's voice when he'd sent her mother an intimate look that was for her alone.

I'm proud of you, Petru, and I want them to know what you did for me. They don't have to be proud of you the way I am, but they need to know where I stand. It matters to me that I get you to the healing ground. That matters to me more than celebrating with my family. They don't have to understand, but I believe they will.

"Thank you, Petru," Gwafa said formally.

"I appreciate that my sister is in good hands," Izem echoed.

"Please come all the way into the house," Amastan added. "I see that Safia is anxious to take care of you, as she should be."

S afia hadn't known the moon could shine so bright or the stars could look so like glittering gems. Everything appeared so much more vivid, from the leaves on the trees to the water tumbling over the rocks. Forest mist was cool on her bare skin, yet in contrast, flames burned through her veins fast, bright and hot, a wildfire out of control.

Petru's hands and mouth were everywhere, a mixture of gentle and rough so that every nerve ending was sensitized. Raw. Desperate for him. There had been no time to be afraid. She woke hungry. Craving the taste of him. The moment his mouth was on her, desire had flared out of control. He'd opened his mind to hers, and erotic images poured in, heightening the passion between them.

She might not know what she was doing, but she followed his lead unerringly, responding to every command. Every demand. Making demands of her own. Each stroke of his hands, heated pull of his mouth, tug of his teeth, sent jagged lightning streaking through her so she couldn't quite catch her breath.

He had awakened her with kisses, just brushes of his lips against hers, setting those embers smoldering for him. They lay together on a bed beneath the stars while his hands moved featherlight over her shoulder and her arm, his fingers traced her ribs and his palm shaped her hip. It was no more than a whisper of touch, barely felt, yet every nerve ending sprang to life and centered on him.

Petru kissed his way over her chin, along her jaw, up to her forehead and then along her cheekbone as if memorizing every angle of her face. He kissed his way to the corner of her mouth, found her dimple and teased it with his tongue, taking his time, as if he'd planned that luxury long ago. His mouth settled on hers, taking her breath, igniting the smoldering embers until she felt flames leaping in her bloodstream.

His hands cupped the weight of her breasts gently, the pads of his fingers stroking caresses so tenderly, but each touch burned like a brand, claiming her heart irrevocably. His mouth was a miracle, kissing her over and over until she couldn't find air and he was breathing for both of them. Until all she could do was taste him. Feel him. Want more of him. She hadn't known he could be so gentle or that it would be disarming.

She couldn't stop the moan climbing up her throat as his fingers continued their exploration, moving down the length of her body to slip between her legs. Heat rushed through her, a wild storm of desire, but his movements were languid, unhurried, as if they had all the time in the world. He explored her petal-soft folds, the slick wet reaction to his administrations. When her hips shifted restlessly, he stopped her movements with one look from his smoldering silvery eyes.

Then he was kissing her again, melting the bones in her body so she couldn't move if she wanted to. Her brain seemed to fog over when he nuzzled her neck and kissed his way to the curve of her breast. His fingers and thumb began to tug and roll her nipples, keeping even those strokes gentle, although every tug felt like a streak of lightning straight to her clit. He nuzzled the curve of her breast. Pulled her nipple into the hot haven of his mouth. She thought nothing could feel so erotic, but then he released her breast to kiss his way to that spot where her pulse throbbed and pounded in anticipation.

Petru sank his teeth deep, and Safia cried out in a kind of ecstasy, unable to hold back as she wrapped her arms around him, needing to anchor herself in him. His hands continued to move over her as he settled the length of his body between her legs, stretching them wide to accommodate the width of his shoulders.

Her breathing had given way to ragged panting. There was no control. None. One of his palms moved up and down her leg almost as if soothing her, although she found his touch more inflaming than soothing. With exquisite gentleness, he guided her leg over his back, making her feel more vulnerable than ever but also more excited and filled with stark need.

I burn for you. She should have been embarrassed to admit her loss of control, but need had been building until all at once she felt as if she might explode.

We go slow, sívamet. Your first time is slow. Your body must be prepared.

She wanted to tell him she was prepared, and there was a part of her that wanted him every bit as out of control as she was. His palm cradled the back of her head and urged her toward his chest as he blanketed her. His long heavy erection pressed hard against her inner thigh, making her wholly aware of how truly proportional he was.

Her mouth was against his bare chest. Already she had his exotic taste in her mouth. It was crazy, but she felt the slide of her teeth as she swept her tongue over his pulse. This time she needed no help connecting to his vein. He threw his head back, and his cock pulsed and jerked against her thigh. His scent surrounded her, along with that taste that was meant for her alone. It was sensual, heightening the need in her to connect them physically.

Worshipping you seems a very good idea.

Petru once more stroked his palm over her, outlining the shape of her hips and bringing his finger and thumb to her clit. She moaned, unable to contain the restless desire pouring through her body.

Petru.

Be still, Pelkgapâd és Meke Pirämet.

His whispered words stroked the walls of her mind with velvet caresses. He seemed to be everywhere. Inside her. Outside. She felt on fire. He reached between them to find his hot erection, lining the broad head up with her entrance. Safia swept her tongue across the tiny holes to stop the blood from leaking from his vein. She wanted to concentrate on every detail of their joining.

Petru didn't take her fast and hard as she expected him to. She had no idea why that was her expectation, but he proceeded very slowly, the broad head sliding into her wet heat like an invader, the tight walls of her sheath reluctantly yielding for him.

His breath hissed out of him. She could see the strain on his face, the shudder going through his body. *You're so tight, Safia. So much tighter than I anticipated.*

Good tight or bad tight? she dared to ask him. She didn't know the difference.

Feel for yourself.

He shared the exquisite pleasure with her, the way it felt to him with her silken tunnel surrounding his shaft with such heat. With such fire. He could barely breathe with the pleasure. He hit her barrier and stopped instantly when she winced.

We do not need to show bloodstained sheets to anyone, Safia. There is no need for you to feel uncomfortable. I ask that you allow me to deal with the pain of your virginity. I want your first time with me to be only pleasure for you.

How could she not fall in love with him? It was impossible not to see the man—her man—looking after her. Making certain everything was perfect for her. Her gaze moved over his face. That face. Becoming so beloved to her. So familiar to her. He thought she couldn't see beyond his expressionless mask, but she was beginning to see much more than he realized. Blinking back tears, she nodded her consent and then wrapped her arms around him in an effort to bring him even closer to her.

Petru leaned down to take possession of her mouth, kissing her lips with that same gentle fire that was just as arousing as his fierce, claiming kisses. He kissed her cheekbone and then nuzzled her silky hair away from her ear with his nose.

Warm breath sent little sparks of electricity arcing over her entire body. *"Tet vigyázam, hän ku vigyáz sívamet és sielame."*

Safia had studied his language, and granted, she wasn't the absolute best at it, but he had said, "I love you, keeper of my heart and soul." Petru wasn't the type of man to say things he didn't mean, not even in the throes of passion.

He shifted his weight again, his arms bracing on either side of her as he began to move in that slow, unhurried glide that set rockets going off in her head. She swore the earth stood still. There was no one else, nothing else, but the two of them. Each scorching-hot surge sent lashes of flames crawling through her veins, building into a rolling wildfire in her core.

He continued to share with her how it felt for him, that silken web surrounding his cock with flickering flames building hotter and hotter. He didn't want it to end. She could see he was holding on to his famous control by just a thread.

"More," she whispered. "Give me all of you, Petru."

"Too much for your first time, *sívamet*." He was tender. Implacable. So Petru. Sometimes there was no moving him, even when he wanted the same thing she did.

The fire was building between them. She felt that coiling in her growing and growing until she was desperate for release. Still, he kept that steady pace, although she swore his shaft seemed to expand, pushing at the soft tissues of her sheath, forcing her to accept him. Streaks of pleasure rode on waves of flames, leaving her gasping for breath. She couldn't tell if it was her pleasure or his, only that if he didn't take them over the edge, she might not live through it.

"Look at me, Safia."

His hips pulled back again as her eyes sought his. She was caught and held there by the intensity, that utter focus. He surged forward, one hand guiding her hips to follow his lead as he set a faster, harder pace. Her gaze clung to his, all that silver, drowning in him, while around her the world had long ago fallen away, leaving only the two of them and this magical time he shared with her.

"Know you want to be with me. That you want me for your family," he whispered aloud. "Choose me, not because you're my destined lifemate but because I'm your man."

Looking him straight in the eyes, she gave him her answer. The absolute truth. "I would never choose another. Only you."

"Come with me, Safia. We ride the sky together."

He shifted minutely, his shaft reaching some secret place inside her that took her breath, robbed her of all speech. The fire inside her blasted into a million colorful stars behind her eyes, and she found herself free-falling.

She was simultaneously aware of Petru, the shudders of pleasure exploding down his spine and the way his cock expanded in her while her body gripped, clamped down like a vise and milked with silken muscles. The dual explosion between them was so perfect a release, flinging them together into another realm, that Safia found tears burning in her eyes.

She was staring straight into Petru's eyes, and she could have sworn there was a hint of moisture in all that silver looking back at her. He lowered his body over hers, still connected to her, burying his face in her neck. She idly traced the tattoos drifting across his back, wondering why a man as heavy as he was wasn't suffocating her. She wouldn't have cared, but then it occurred to her, he was Carpathian, he could prevent that sensation. He had a way of protecting her often.

Lying out in the open, looking up at the stars, with Petru as her blanket, every movement reminding her they were joined together, felt beautiful, timeless and sensual. She wanted to stay there as long as they could, far away from the reality of their situation.

When she managed to get her breathing under control, she tried to figure out what the Carpathian letters said just by touch. Some of the words were the same.

"*Olen wäkeva kuntankért,*" he whispered against her pulse.

"Staying strong for our people," she interpreted. Her fingers went to the next line. This was far more difficult, and she couldn't quite get her arms around him to get every letter, but just moving was delicious, and in any case, he knew the lines by heart.

"*Olen wäkeva pita belső kulymet.*"

"Staying strong to keep the demon inside," she said, her lips against his chest. "You are no demon, Petru. I know them, and you are not that."

He lifted his head and looked down at her, his strangely colored eyes back to that swirling mercury. "Only because I have you," he assured her. *"Olen wäkeva—félért ku vigyázak."*

There was an instant lump in her throat. Tears burned again behind her eyes. "Staying strong for her."

Petru leaned down and brushed kisses over each eye, the tip of her nose, her dimple and the corners of her mouth.

"Hängemért."

"Only her," she whispered, looking up at him, knowing the stars in the sky were reflected in her eyes.

"Only you," he agreed and once more took her mouth.

Safia couldn't tear her gaze from the deep lines of concentration in Petru's extremely masculine features as they stood together on the bluff overlooking the sea. He was so handsome he took her breath away. He would never be the accepted sense of the word *handsome*—he was too hard-edged for that—but to her, Petru was brutally gorgeous. If she were any kind of a poet, she would secretly add to the songs sung about him.

If she were being honest about adding lyrics, she might have to add lines alluding to his prowess in other areas as well. She was certain he was every bit as legendary as a lover as he was a fighter, although that might not be the best thing to advertise in a song. Other women might get it into their heads to try to persuade him to show off his skills. She would be forced to show off hers, so no lyrics about anything but war talents.

Every line in Petru's face had been earned by the battles he'd engaged in with vicious vampires. He knew so many ways to ferret them out, no matter how adept they were at hiding. He never shirked from a fight. No matter how many vampires might be together or whether he was walking into a trap, he attacked. The lyrics to his song had to have refrains about courage. Bravery. Valor. Those were good words.

"It is not a trap if I am aware the enemy is waiting for me."

Safia had to concede that was true. She glanced up at him. The moonlight illuminated him, bathing his head in a silvery halo. He was back to looking like a fallen angel. "You don't need to stay in my head while I'm contemplating how you plan your battles."

The trace of male amusement slipping through her mind sent sparks of awareness lighting her nerve endings.

"Is that what you were doing? I thought you were dwelling on how amazingly beautiful and masculine your lifemate is."

She gave a little disdainful sniff. "You wish that's what I was doing. I'm merely interested in how to rid the world of these pesky vampires."

"Or adding lines to the songs sung in glory to your lifemate."

"I believe your hearing is faulty." She gave a little toss of her head, sending her hair flying. "That can happen when you get old."

Petru turned the full focus of his strangely colored eyes on her. His gaze drifted over her face, moved down her body and then back up to look directly into her eyes. A slow burn started in her bloodstream, little flickering embers that grew, sparked and danced, moving like molasses but wreaking havoc with her heart and lungs.

She felt his smile start in his mind and slowly work its way to his mouth. Barely there, but that faint curve of his mouth melted her heart. *Beautiful* came to mind, even though she pretended to quash the idea immediately. The moment he caught that thought, the mercury color of his eyes lit to that brilliant silver she loved so much.

"I don't believe you think there is anything faulty about my kisses."

Deliberately, she tilted her head to one side and frowned. "Kisses?" One eyebrow went up. "Perhaps your kisses aren't nearly as memorable as you believe them to be. I can't seem to recall a single one."

Petru loomed over her without seeming to move. There was not even a whisper of sound, but his larger-than-life body was against hers, arms locking her to him. He leaned his head close to hers, so she felt the warmth of his breath against the side of her neck, just below her ear, and the scrape of his silvery bristles along his jaw.

"I must have heard you wrong." His teeth nipped her earlobe. "My faulty hearing again."

His lips wandered down her chin to her throat and then back up to her bottom lip, where his teeth caught just as they had on her earlobe. He bit down, and heat rushed through her blood. Those little sparks leapt into flames as he bit down harder until there was a sting. She parted her lips, surrendering everything she was to him.

Instead of hot flames pouring into her, a wildfire out of control as expected, Petru gathered her into the shelter of his heart, placed his mouth on hers with exquisite gentleness and kissed her as if she were the love of his life. A miracle given to him. Her heart turned over. A million butterflies took wing in the vicinity of her stomach.

Safia slid her arms around his neck. Her fingers curled into the thickness of his silvery hair. *I might believe you deserve the songs they sing about you,* she admitted.

His mouth moved on hers, his tongue tangling, stroking hot flashes of fire along hers, teasing her with an emotion she didn't want to name until she wanted to crawl inside him and live there forever. The world fell away when he kissed her. There was only the two of them. No underworld. No demons. No vampires. Just feeling. Just them. She wanted just the two of them for a short while. She didn't need a lot of time—just a little.

When Petru lifted his head slightly, his eyes gleamed so bright she could have sworn they were a true silver. Instead of looking hard, they looked liquid, as if the silver had melted with passion and . . . Her breath caught in her throat—formed a lump there. Love. He looked at her with an emotion very close to love. It was more than affection. So much more.

His smile came. Slow. Taking its time. Making her wait for it before his lips curved and his eyes flickered even brighter, as if the moon were caught there briefly. He truly was beautiful.

"I may not always feel my emotions in the way others do, *Pelkgapâd és Meke Pirämet,* but what I feel for you runs deep, straight and true. You will always come first in my life. No matter that Lilith will try to drive a wedge between us in the coming days, and she will, believe me. Believe in what I feel for you."

"She's far more powerful than I ever gave her credit for," Safia admitted. She felt truly humbled by her mistake.

"Yes, but perhaps not nearly as prepared as she believes she is." He brushed kisses across her nose and straightened, taking another slow look around. "Use your senses to feel the area around you. Do it often. You're used to looking and feeling for demons. You must also be aware of the undead. You are the lifemate of *Kuŋe kont ku votjak.* The undead will try to find you. If they kill you, they kill me."

"I don't know how to search for vampires."

"You do it all the time when you search for evidence of demons intruding. You know what the undead feel like. You've felt the evidence often in my mind. Follow the path with me as I scan, and then do it yourself," he instructed.

Petru was correct in that looking for vampires wasn't really any different from searching for signs of demons. The undead gave away their presence as well. They were abominations, and any living creature, grass, shrub or tree shrank from them. If vegetation came in contact with the undead, it turned brown and eventually withered and died. When vampires took to the sky, blank spots gave their presence away. The newer vampires were much easier to spot than masters, but even the older ones were so malevolent that nature rebelled against them, shuddering and receding in an effort to avoid contact.

Safia caught on very quickly and followed Petru's example, scanning the city, the harbor, the farmlands—everywhere her senses would stretch. She found that being Carpathian gave her a longer reach and much more acute senses.

"Why did you say Lilith is not as prepared for war as she believes she is?" Safia asked.

Petru cupped the side of her face, the pad of his thumb tracing her dimple. "The belief was that she allowed so much time to go by because she wanted your family and me to forget about her. That would mean she had patience. Lilith doesn't have patience, Safia. That is not one of her traits. She is cruel and vengeful. She was defeated in a war she had invested everything in. I struck at her and damaged her severely. It took her two thousand years to regain her full strength. That's why she waited, not because she had patience."

Safia nodded. She may have been a child of five in her previous life, but she remembered that moment when Petru had struck at Lilith. The entire battlefield had gone silent, so sure that Petru would take Safia and leave them to their fate. Safia had known better. He was *Aghzen n wayur.* Moon monster. *Amnay n wayur.* Moon knight. Their savior. He had come down from the moon to fight with them, to lead the way to victory. He struck so fast he was a blur, like the very lightning he called from the sky. The devil woman had shrieked out her rage and agony, her promise of bitter, endless retaliation. Putrid smoke rose from the hole in the ground where lightning had slammed deep, and the noxious smell had tainted the entire battlefield.

"Lilith would never have waited for her revenge. She would have done her best to wipe out your entire family, Safia. She would never have taken a chance that you would be born again carrying the other half of my soul."

"Do you think she knew I would be born again?"

"I doubt she paid attention until recently. She has many schemes, and until she was healed completely, she wasn't going to exact her revenge. That's when she bothered to turn her attention this way. She didn't even use her resources to monitor your family. Had she done so, she would have seen each generation training to fight demons and vampires. That's why I said she isn't as prepared as she believes she is. Your family rose to meet the challenge, and she relied on her power."

Safia was proud of her family's skills. "They're excellent at utilizing weapons specifically made to destroy vampires and demons. Demons are more difficult only in that there are many different types, and each one can require a new way of destroying them."

"Just the fact that your family developed weapons that would destroy a vampire is impressive. I've studied their memories, and it's clear that they were born with information imprinted from generations who came before them. Even fighting skills were passed on."

Safia lifted her lashes to study his eyes. "You believe she'll come at us with everything she has now, don't you?"

He nodded slowly, not looking away from her. Not flinching. "I do believe she will make that mistake, yes."

"You think that's a mistake on her part?"

"It will be her downfall." Petru spoke complacently.

Safia instantly shook her head. "Don't do what I did. Don't underestimate her. You believe you can outthink her. She's been planning this a long time."

He bent his head to brush his lips gently across hers. Featherlight. Just enough of a touch to set her stomach rolling with anticipation. She resisted pressing a hand to her fluttering belly. They were discussing serious business. She couldn't be distracted just because he had long eyelashes and firm, cool lips. Or because his breath was always perfect and his mouth hot and addicting.

"I don't believe that. I think you brought her attention to you again, and now she's livid. She won't be thinking straight enough to plan much strategy. She wasn't brilliant at tactics. She repeated the same ones over and over because they worked for her in the beginning. Once I caught on to her pattern, it was easy enough to anticipate the movements of her various armies."

She narrowed her gaze at him. Had there been the tiniest bit of amusement in his voice? Was he reading her mind again? "You better stay out of my mind."

For the first time, his smile turned into a lopsided grin, almost as if he didn't quite know how to form that kind of spontaneous smirk. Her heart gave a funny little flip inside her chest. Even with all those years he'd spent on earth, there had been so much in his life he'd missed out on. She couldn't help herself; she reached up to rub her palm along his strong jaw.

"I don't really care if you are reading my mind, and you know what I think about you, Petru. You really are extraordinary, and not because you sacrificed yourself for everyone else, although that's a good reason. Not because you're very good-looking. At least *I* think you are. Not even because you probably are the best lover on the planet."

He waited, his eyes drifting over her face, taking her in, claiming her with just that look.

"It's because you're truly a good man. Inside, where it counts." Safia meant it.

Unlike her sisters and sisters-in-law, who had gone into their marriages without any real advantage in getting to know their husbands, Safia was able to merge her mind with Petru's. She was aware he was very compartmentalized, but even then, she saw glimpses into those areas of pain and battles and an endless gray void of an emotionless world of shadows and death. In that world is where she saw her husband, where his true self shone the brightest. His honor. He didn't realize that brightness because he saw only the tatters and the thick scarring on his soul from the many times he'd taken lives throughout the long centuries he'd been alive.

"I'm so grateful you were chosen to be my husband."

His smile faded from his expression to be replaced by an emotion altogether different, nearly blinding her with adoration. This time there was no denying the love in his eyes. She hadn't expected to ever see those lines, carved so deep, soften into that particular expression— one just for her alone.

"Carpathians don't dream. At least few of us do. I've heard of one or two where it has happened. But you, I've dreamt of you many times, Safia. Always when I began to feel there was no hope. The creed of the ancients staying at the monastery is carved into my back. It saved my sanity on more than one occasion."

"The tattoos."

That faint smile returned, the one that turned her heart over.

"If you can call those lines tattoos. We had to scar them into our skin, or they wouldn't stay. Even then, it was extremely difficult because unless we have a mortal wound, we don't scar easily. It was worth the effort it took."

She had traced the lines reverently and even kissed a couple of the words written in his ancient language. She thought the tattoos beautiful and eloquent. "I'm grateful the thought of me helped you in some small way when you needed it most."

"Not in a small way, *sívamet*," he corrected. "You saved my honor many, many times over the centuries."

Safia loved the idea that even though she hadn't been physically present, she'd been with him, helping him through the worst of times. It meant she'd been a partner to him, maybe more of one then than she was now. She'd managed to anger their enemy and turn her wrath on them, maybe before they were ready for her.

"You did hurt Lilith, Safia," Petru said suddenly. "She was looking at you through Art's eyes, and you blinded her when you struck at her. You realize she had no idea you had taken control of Art. She still doesn't know you had taken him away from her. She doesn't know you have that kind of power, and that's one more weapon in our arsenal."

Safia replayed the memory of Lilith in Art's mind. She'd avoided thinking about it, but now she needed to remember every detail. Had Lilith been aware she'd stolen Art from his mistress? Lilith had berated him severely, accusing him of being a coward. She believed he just hadn't attacked Safia when the others had because he feared retaliation from Petru. That had been uppermost in Lilith's mind. Safia had been so caught up in her plan to strike at Lilith that she hadn't thoroughly read her. The facts were there in her memory to access, but she hadn't done so until now.

She'd always been thorough when she was facing an opponent, making certain she'd examined every aspect of the demon she was going to destroy, yet she hadn't. Why? She needed to answer that question.

"She didn't know I'd stolen Art from her. She hadn't realized I'd taken control of the sea demons she sent."

"Lilith wasn't really paying attention. She believed she would easily retake this region, that after all this time, no one would remember. She was healed and at full power again."

Safia's frown deepened. She shook her head. "She wasn't, though, Petru. At least if she was at full power, she wasn't utilizing it. I could feel her energy, and yes, it came off her in waves, this tremendous feeling of supremacy, but not nearly what I would expect from someone capable of commanding armies in the underworld."

Petru's expression was inscrutable, but she felt his presence in her mind as he moved through her memories, assessing each one frame by frame, studying Lilith through Safia's eyes. She found Petru interesting, in that his manifestation was every bit as formidable or even more so than Lilith's but extremely low-key. It was almost as if the power he carried was so much a part of him, he was barely aware of it.

Safia knew she could study him for eternity and never get close to having his knowledge. How had she ever thought him arrogant? He truly didn't consider himself anything special. He simply was.

His gaze came back to hers with that hint of amusement. "*Ku Tappa Kulyak*, you persist in thinking such things of me I cannot possibly live up to."

"You'll live up to them." She was utterly confident.

"And when I start dictating?" He traced her dimple.

"I'll remind you in a way you're certain to remember that a dictatorship will never be worth it between us."

The hint of amusement turned into a brief flash of laughter that left her feeling triumphant.

"We have a little time to work on shifting." He continued to stroke the pads of his fingers over her dimple and then traced her lips. "You've got clothing down no problem. Let's try the little owl. You must be very detailed, and a bird that small will come in handy. You can master flight at the same time. Once you feel confident inside the owl's body, you will be comfortable in any form—large or small."

Her heart accelerated before she could control it. She was very excited. As far as she was concerned, shifting was one of the huge perks of being Carpathian. This time she didn't want anything to interrupt the lesson. She opened her mind to his to show him she retained all the information he'd given her on the little owl, down to the smallest detail.

Once again, Petru was meticulous, examining her owl from every angle, ensuring she had gotten every element right. He flashed a small smile at her. "This time we'll go straight to the owl's territory, no side trips, unless you think your nephew is up to no good again."

"It's impossible to keep Charif down for very long," Safia admitted, sobering. "Although if Zdan showed disappointment in him, that would curtail his activities. None of the children want Zdan to be disappointed in them."

"For the moment, he's safe at your farm."

Petru gathered her close to him and took to the air without further discussion. When he did that, Safia always lost her ability to breathe, just for a moment. The miracle of soaring across the sky was secondary to the closeness of their bodies. She loved these moments together, with the moon looking down at them and the clouds feeling close. Flying was always going to be one of her most favorite pursuits—other than making love.

I'm certainly glad that is higher on the list. I would have been worried I was doing something very wrong.

I'm certain there's always room for improvement. The more practice, the better you'll get at it. She poured comfort into his mind as if he needed it. It was extremely difficult to keep the laughter out of her voice. *I do realize that in certain circles, you are referred to as Hän ku oma és gyenge. I know I'm not the best at your language, but I do believe that means "old frail one."*

The smallest of giggles escaped. She clapped a hand over her mouth with one hand while the fingers of her other dug into his shoulder to keep from falling. She didn't believe he'd let her fall, but she never giggled. That was for schoolgirls.

He didn't drop her, but he did growl. As growls went, it was a fantastic rumble, much like a clap of thunder but only for her ears. That turned her giggle into a full laugh. The looming war should have ruined their day, but instead, he made the night seem fun and exciting. Just being with him was fun. She snuggled closer to him.

"As old frail ones go, you're not bad, Petru." She nuzzled his shoulder with her chin, sharing not only the feeling of fun with him but her growing need and love for him. Sometimes both emotions would suddenly be overwhelming.

He turned his head and focused solely on her, the intensity of his look causing an instant fluttering in her stomach, a clenching in her feminine core, heat rushing through her veins and little sparks of electricity dancing through her nerve endings. She'd never felt more alive.

His answering smile was brief, but it was there just for her, before he turned his attention to settling them down at the furthermost corner of her family farm. This was one of the most remote areas, hilly and covered with more trees than any other section. The forest crept close to the fence, sliding over and under it, occasionally forcing the family to cut down the extending branches of trees and brush reaching to reclaim the land.

"We talk about clearing this section for the sheep, but we never do," Safia explained. "We like the wildlife close. The predators leave our flock alone for the most part. We're vigilant, and there's easier prey."

She was nervous now that she was going to try shifting into something as small as the little owl but excited as well. To her, this was the ultimate challenge.

"You're making it far bigger than it really is, *sívamet*. You're already adept at your clothing. You're getting close to being able to move the soil without fear. This is a small thing when you are so good at detail."

His tone steadied her. He would never allow anything to happen to her, but more, he had such complete faith in her. She had to admit, she could use a little of that herself when she pictured the detailed image of the little owl in her mind. It was so small.

"It is only your spirit entering the owl. The essence of who you are, not your physical body," Petru pointed out. As always, he kept that same calm tone. No judgment.

Safia knew if she said she wanted to wait, he would do so, and he would never judge her. Where had she gotten it into her head that he and his brethren looked down on everyone else?

She threaded her fingers through his. "I'm ready."

The pad of his thumb slid over the back of her hand. "This is for fun. I call you *Pelkgapâd és Meke Pirämet* for a reason. You are my fearless defender. This is nothing in comparison to what you do every day. This is simple and fun. Once you do it, you will be able to take any shape you desire. You can run with wolves or cheetahs, soar with hawks or eagles. You will have the ability to utilize whatever you wish just for fun or to aid you in combat."

While he spoke, he held the image of the little owl in her mind. The patterns in the feathers were imprinted on her now. She knew the tiny bird, the way it looked and moved. Its mannerisms, the notes of its call.

"Let go of yourself as you do when you're going to heal someone. You've seen the brethren do it. Become only spirit, and keep the image of the owl in your mind. Don't allow anything else to enter. Not fear or ego. Only the little owl. It is tiny, so it may be frightening at first, but know I'm with you. Trust in me and in yourself. I know you can do this, Safia."

Safia took a deep breath and concentrated on every detail of the little owl, allowing her physical self to slip away. For a moment she felt completely disoriented and adrift. She found herself seeing with re-markable clarity, although colors were dull. She could see in three dimensions: height, width and depth perception were increased. Along with that, she was seeing close to a hundred times better than she had been. It was astonishing to see with the little owl's vision.

I'm keeping us hidden from the little ones in this territory. I don't want a fight, but you need to be very familiar with this section from above, and this is the best way to view it.

She loved the way Petru's voice was perfectly steady in her mind. He was her rock, keeping her absolutely calm. She might feel trepida-tion being so small and lost inside the little owl's body, but he was right there.

Tell me what to do.

You must step back and allow the owl to be in charge of the actual flying. That will be the most difficult part. Letting go completely. You are still there, observing, but she will fly. You will direct her to the places you wish to go.

I'm not learning to fly on my own? She knew her disappointment showed. The female owl took several tentative hops in the grass and unfolded her wings.

Patience. This is how you learn.

She heard the trace of amusement in his voice and couldn't help the answering laughter bubbling up. She felt like a child at the market for the first time, staring at all the wonders around her, eager to get a special candy she'd never had before.

The owl flapped her wings, took two hops and then was in the air. The bottom of Safia's stomach dropped away. She hadn't been prepared for the little female's sudden flight. When she settled, she found it wasn't much different from when she took control of a bat or a bird. She was utilizing all the animal's senses. And soaring across the sky. She loved the sensation. *Loved it.*

Pay attention to what you're doing. Petru's voice held a stern note, pulling her up short, making her instantly aware of her surroundings.

You are in the owl's body, but you are not the owl. You must always keep that image uppermost in your mind.

Safia was tempted to give him sass and remind him he'd said to *be* the owl so that if a vampire was in the vicinity, the undead wouldn't be able to detect the difference, but he was right, she'd almost forgotten to keep the image in her mind. She would have fallen right out of the sky.

Petru had her land on the ground, which wasn't nearly as smooth as she thought it would be. Her little owl tumbled over in a somersault, squawked in ruffled annoyance and glared at her mate.

Now shift back into you, fully clothed.

Safia had no problem with that order. She stretched, grateful to be back to her original form.

Shift into the little owl, but faster, Safia. Petru's voice was clipped. No arguing with it. He meant business, and she automatically obeyed him without thinking. *Get into the air quickly.*

She followed the male bird as it rose, barely taking the mandatory hop. She did look around to ensure there were no predators close. There hadn't been undue urgency in his tone, only the need for speed. They circled the farm again and returned to the same site to land, coming in faster this time.

Each time, Petru had her practice shifting faster and faster, following him into the air until he seemed satisfied with her speed. Then he moved slowly across the sky, quartering back and forth, studying the land beneath him. She was in his mind, following his every thought. He committed the terrain and everything on it to memory, mapping it out and recording it.

Petru noticed the smallest detail: shrubs, trees, caves, rocks, placements of roots and whether they were twisted or not. He knew where every fence was, every break in a fence. She found his brain amazing, the way it mapped out and filed information so rapidly. He shared his knowledge automatically with her, his brethren and Aura.

Finally, Petru signaled to her to drop to the ground in the farthest corner of her family's farm, in the middle of the little owl's territory, indicating they would meet others there so she might want to be fully clothed when she shifted. Safia followed him down, keeping the rules for landing uppermost in her mind. Knowing others were near made her nervous. Shifting still didn't come that easily. She'd practiced in her head hundreds of times, but it wasn't the same thing as flying through the air in the small body of a bird, retaining all the raptor's natural traits and simultaneously trying to learn battle strategy from her lifemate.

She had to let go of Petru's mind to concentrate fully on her landing, coming in feetfirst to hit the perch just right and not overshoot her mark. The little owl rocked for a moment, using its wings to keep her stable, and then she let herself feel a moment of triumph before attempting to shift back into her true form.

Being Safia was so much easier than being a little owl. She knew exactly what she looked like, and it was easy to be herself. She chose the spot where she wanted the owl to become Safia again, and she reappeared, dressed in her comfortable, familiar clothes. She was becoming adept at clothing herself. She certainly knew her wardrobe and what she liked to wear.

She had taken to flying more easily than opening the soil. She wasn't adept at that yet, and Petru wasn't allowing her to try on her own. She was learning so many other skills, she didn't mind.

Her father and grandfather were there with Zdan and Izem, clearly representing the Amazigh people. Benedek waited with Aura. Nicu leaned against the fence, studying the interior of the forest on the other side. Tomas and Lojos had wandered away from the others and were peering up at the cloud formations while Mataias was in the center of her family, his expression serious as he nodded his head, listening to their conversation. Safia was thankful that Mataias took the time to engage with her family.

Petru took her hand, and as they strolled up to the group, she sent the Carpathian male a warm smile. *Thank you. I appreciate you taking the time to make my family feel as though they mean something to you.*

Mataias turned toward her and gave a slight courtly bow. *You are family, Safia, as are they.*

For a moment, a lump blocked her throat and tears burned behind her eyes, but the other Carpathians had taken a sudden interest in her, and she lifted her chin and widened her smile.

"Let's get to it so we have time to celebrate our marriage with the family," Petru said. He crouched down as the others circled around him. "Lilith will most likely send her sacrificial pawns along these lines," he said, drawing in dirt to show the outer banks of the farm. "She'll throw a very heavy line of disposable vampires and demons at us to weaken us and kill as many of Safia's family as possible."

Aura frowned as she studied the area Petru had chosen. "Why would she choose that line? It seems to me she would have far more success if she approached the farm from the southern side and took out all the smaller homes first. I was concentrating our line of defense there."

"Or go straight up the middle," Mataias said. "Divide them. Cut the families off from one another." He sent a quick look to his brothers. "I've seen Petru do this before."

Lojos nodded. "It makes no sense, but he never fails to be right."

Nicu looked down at the map in the dirt. "He studies his enemies and reads the way they think. In this case, he's engaged with her on more than one occasion, which is bad news for her."

"Her goal is no longer to win the war," Petru announced. "She is vindictive and vengeful. What she cares most about now is punishing Safia and then destroying her. Safia managed to inflict damage on her. She dared to challenge her. Lilith's attention has been diverted from her original goal, although she sees it as the same thing. She can't conceive of a human family defeating her, even with the help of a few Carpathians."

"She's brought in vampires," Aura reminded. "I feel their presence." She rubbed at her arms.

The brethren followed the path her palms took, clearly not liking that Aura had fought vampires on her own.

"Why doesn't Lilith attack us while you're underground?" Zdan asked.

"Vampires can't attack," Tomas explained. "They would fry in the sun. They could send their puppets, humans they've converted to flesh-eating monsters that do their bidding, but those puppets cannot get through the safeguards we've woven around your farm, and she knows that. It would be a waste. Unless that curious child gets loose again."

"He won't," Zdan assured. "It is good the decision was made to allow him to retain most of his memories for the time being. I have spoken to him at length. His grandfather and great-grandfather have as well. All three of us were sterner than we have ever been with him, showing him he endangered not only himself but his entire family. He left us open to these monsters that are threatening to destroy us. He knows to stay close."

The brethren nodded. Safia became aware through a common path the brethren shared of an order left behind in her nephew's head to obey his father's directives. She pressed her fingertips to her lips and glanced at Mataias, who studiously avoided her gaze. Fortunately, the order was more of a soft suggestion that would wear away over time, but it would serve its purpose during the tense dealings with Lilith and her retaliations.

"The most Lilith has is her demons during the day, and they can't penetrate the farm," Petru added. "They could wreak havoc in parts of the city, but she isn't certain Safia has been converted. She won't want to risk losing any more of the forms she has to her."

Safia found it interesting that not only did Petru speak with complete confidence, but it was there in his mind. He had studied his enemy, gathered information over the centuries and filed it away. In particular, he had learned a lot about Lilith in the last few months while being in Siberia. He'd had numerous encounters with her demons and armies. His brethren, also battling them with the demon fighter there, had shared information. Petru seemed to soak up knowledge of his enemies the way a sea sponge might soak up water.

He stood up and once more took her hand, pulling her into him. There was no mistaking the claiming gesture. He added a few more details about the lines of defense for her family to follow but then indicated that they should return to the main farmhouse.

"I believe we have a marriage to celebrate."

Her father, grandfather and oldest brother turned their heads to regard her with love in their eyes. "We do," Amastan agreed.

The moment she awakened, Safia felt the difference in Petru. He was all business. He had shifted from the man who wore an aura of danger to the knight the moon had sent down to defend its chosen people.

She was in the company of *Aghzen n wayur.* In the stories and songs told or sung about Petru, he was sometimes called "moon monster." This was the monster of all monsters. The one the moon had sent to defeat the terrible monsters cruelly destroying the Imazighen.

Usually, the stories were about the fierce knight of the moon. Night after night growing up, she had eagerly waited to hear the story of the battles between the demons, vampires and her people fighting so valiantly to survive. Then came the mysterious people who were able to fight the vampires when the Imazighen had no way of knowing how. Why they took the side of the free people, no one knew, but they were grateful. Still, it didn't save them, and all could see the war would be lost.

They called to the moon to send them aid. They needed a fierce knight. More than a knight. As a child, Safia had sat with the other children, her heart beating fast even though she'd heard the story hundreds of times. Like the other children, she'd waited, holding her breath until Amastan had delivered her favorite part of the story.

Ayur uzend aghzen addigh imagh. Moon sends the monster to fight with us. She gasped as all the other children had. Petru, the monster sent by the moon. *Her* monster. The ancestors had named him so to Amastan, and they'd been misunderstood. That side of Petru was very much needed in this war, and she was grateful she was looking at him now, even though just doing so sent shivers creeping down her spine. Petru was always dangerous, but this version of him was cold, calculating and every bit as cruelly brutal and merciless as those they would be fighting.

Petru had risen before her, seeking blood for both of them as he did each rising. He'd scouted for signs of the enemy and consulted with his brethren before returning to her. The sun had barely set when he'd parted the soil to rouse and feed her. The risings before, he had made slow beautiful love to her, cuddling her and focusing his entire attention on her. Now he was remote, his demeanor completely different. Even his mind was different, so she might not have known him had she not been so familiar with every aspect of him.

He was closed off to everything but the coming battle. Lilith had already begun her opening moves. She saw those clearly in his mind. It was as if he were orchestrating a battle on a field already, his brain countering her.

Petru suddenly turned and framed Safia's face. His large hands felt rough against her skin yet so gentle when he touched her. His eyes were pure silver staring directly into hers. This wasn't her loving partner; this was the monster the moon sent. Their commander.

"There will be no sacrifices this time, Safia. If you die, it is over. We will have lost. Everyone dies. There can be no bargaining with Lilith. If she takes your father or grandfather. If she takes the children or your sister and tortures them in front of you, there is no exchange. If she has me, you cannot exchange your life for mine. You believe the outcome of this war depends on me, but in truth, it depends on you.

You must stay alive. No matter what else happens, what pretty lies she tells you, you hold to the course. Do you understand?"

She understood it was a decree. She could see the ruthless, merciless side of him stamped into those lines carved so deep. For the first time, she read it in his soul. He was laying down an absolute law, and if she didn't agree, if she tried to go against this one absolute, he—and his brethren—would stop her.

"I understand completely, Petru." She did. In the short time they'd been together, the one thing that had become very clear to her was the danger Petru would become to every species should something happen to his lifemate. There would be no going back for him. He was a man of honor, but the scars marking the passage of time with too many battles and taking of lives well past his time had already decided his fate for him.

"Lilith will throw everything she has at us to end the war as fast as possible," he said. "We are very few in number."

She nodded, swallowing the lump in her throat. She'd read the cards. She'd seen the odds against them. They weren't good.

"We have no choice but to even the odds, if possible. The way to do it is risky, but if we counterattack swiftly and hit back hard and precisely, as I believe we can if everyone follows the plan, we have a better chance."

"Risky?" she echoed. She had no idea what he was talking about. It wasn't like they could rush out and get reinforcements at this late date. Whatever he had planned, there was no going back. It was clear in his mind that it was the only path open to them if they were going to defeat Lilith. He had hoped an entire tribe would be backing them, not just the members of her family.

Petru hadn't complained. He never once considered leaving them to their fate. It never even entered his head. He simply planned out his battle using what little resources they had.

"Benedek is capable of using a very ancient and powerful technique, or magic if you prefer. It is unknown to mages or vampires. As far as I'm aware, only his lineage can do it or even knows of it. He needed the consent of a few of your family members."

Her heart dropped. Whatever he was about to tell her, she wasn't going to like. He had used the word "risky." This hadn't been discussed with her.

"Essentially, what Benedek does is put pieces of himself into pieces of someone else. In this case, while your entire family volunteered, Amastan was too old, Layla pregnant, Lunja and Zdan parents, so it was determined Gwafa, Izem and Usem would be the participants. They will be divided into many individuals. They won't be illusions but real thinking, breathing, fighting men with their capabilities as well as Benedek's."

She could see the drawback immediately. She didn't need Petru to point it out to her. Should any of them fall—and the chances were enormous that some would—the individual and Benedek would be significantly weakened unless that part of them could be retrieved before death.

She didn't voice her distress. No one would take such a risk unless the circumstances were dire, and theirs were. "The toll on Benedek will be terrible."

Benedek's risk was the highest, as a part of him would be in all the replicas of the men, and yet he did so without hesitation. She was coming to see that Carpathians lived a life of sacrifice.

"Your family didn't hesitate to volunteer, even after the risks were explained to them," Petru said. "It was the first time I observed discord between Izem and his spouse. She insisted on also volunteering, and Izem forbade her from participating."

"Amara never goes against Izem," Safia said, a little shocked. She dressed herself in the clothes she wore to slay demons. The long coat with the many pockets and loops holding various weapons and emergency medical supplies felt familiar as it settled around her shoulders.

"She did. She was insistent that if he took such a risk, she would, too."

Safia caught the hint of respect for her sister-in-law in his mind.

"Izem forbade it, as did Usem with his spouse. We've set up a station to replenish blood when needed, and we'll need it, most likely often. I gave Charif the task of overseeing that and the wounded to keep him occupied. His father reinforced that he was to always stay right there and see to the wounded coming in. He was shown how to treat Carpathian wounds with soil, and a fresh bed was set up at his station."

"What blood?"

"We brought in humans from town. Quite a few to supply us. They are compliant." He didn't add any other information.

Safia hadn't considered that they would need a large supply of blood, but of course there would be wounds. She had her memories of the first battle when she'd died as a child. She'd seen those gaping rips in Petru's chest where the vampires had clawed and bitten at him in an effort to extract his heart.

"There will be losses, Safia, but you must keep fighting no matter what happens. Grief can be acknowledged later. We have only one real chance at winning this war, and that's if we do so quickly."

She had read the cards. She was very aware Petru had tried to give them all hope when there wasn't nearly as much of a chance as he made it seem.

"I will be wounded numerous times. Close your mind to me. That's imperative. Lilith can't use us against one another. If I need you, I will call to you."

She nodded without looking at him. It wasn't easy to know that very soon, her entire world was going to be turned upside down.

Petru wrapped his arms around her and pulled her against his chest, holding her tight. "*Tet vigyázam.* I love you, Safia, with my heart and soul. We will see this through, and we will prevail, because there is no other option."

He lifted her chin very gently, his eyes searching hers. She found love there. Reassurance. Belief in their ability together. Belief in her family and his brethren. The knots in her stomach loosened and she nodded. They could do it. Their chances might be slim, but they could defeat Lilith if they stuck to the plan and struck hard and fast. She believed in Petru. They all did.

A slow smile touched his glittering silver eyes, and then he lowered his mouth to hers. His kiss was heat and fire but so incredibly gentle, so tender, he took her breath away. She felt his love. In that moment, he was all Petru, the man, her lifemate. Her spouse.

He lifted his head and ran the pad of his finger across her bottom lip. "We'll go to your family home so you can see your loved ones. You're there to give them hope, Safia."

She knew what he was telling her. Just as he had given her hope, her family had to believe they could win the war against Lilith. She also knew he was giving her the opportunity to say goodbye should she lose any of her family members. She pressed her forehead against his chest for a brief moment, and then she straightened her shoulders and stood upright.

"Let's get this done."

"I'm going to take you to the farm, Safia. I know you're capable of getting there on your own, but I need to hold you close to me."

He didn't wait for her to reply, he simply swept her up and launched himself into the air. Safia wrapped one arm around his neck, fingers sliding into the thick hair at his nape.

The wind fluttered against her skin, bringing the touch of the sea with it. Along with the sea, she caught the scent of evil. It was vague and far off but foul. The undead were answering Lilith's call. The wind shifted, moving inland to sweep through the forest and across the meadow. With it came a faint burnt smell that set off alarms.

What is that?

She's releasing the hellhounds. His voice was grim.

Safia drew in her breath. The farm was just below them. It looked so peaceful. So familiar. The animals weren't out the way they normally would be, but she knew every acre of the terrain and position of the houses, barns and coops. She knew the fields of grass, wheat and crops they grew for their animals and members of the tribe. One touch from a vampire's foul hand, and it all could be destroyed.

We stick to the plan, Ku Tappa Kulyak.

Petru set them down at the front door of the farmhouse, reached around her and pushed it open, certain of their welcome. It was clear he had informed her grandfather they were coming. He was there to greet them, drawing her into his arms and holding her close.

"We're ready," he said in his calm, steady voice—the one she'd known and counted on her entire life.

Safia hugged him hard. "Yes, we are," she agreed.

She followed him into the family room where everyone was gathered. They were dressed in loose clothing, clearly prepared for war. Charif had his arms around his sister and brother. He stood as tall as possible in front of his father. She noticed how much he looked like Zdan. Safia hugged each child and asked Charif where the medical station was located. He looked very important when he told her. The younger children would be with him, but locked away where they would be safe.

She knew that meant they would be asleep where Lilith and the vampires would have no knowledge of their location. That way, their enemies couldn't attempt to repeat the actions of the war crimes of two thousand years earlier, burning the children while their helpless parents watched.

Amara clung to Izem, but there were no tears. She stood almost defiantly, dressed in combat clothes, ready to fight. Farah kept blinking back tears as she hugged Safia, but she didn't shed them. She stayed very close to Usem, holding his hand and attempting to smile at him when he looked at her.

Safia stood within the circle as they prayed together. They kissed one another. She spent time with Amastan, the man she'd looked up to all her life. She felt overwhelmed with love for her family. She felt that love reciprocated.

She saved her last goodbye for her father. While standing in front of him, the man who had taught her so much about farming, memories flooded her. Never once had he complained when she'd followed him everywhere. All the times he'd carried her on his shoulders when working in the fields. The way he'd carefully showed her how to shear the sheep and harvest the wool. So many lessons. They had always shown affection in odd ways, but it was there between them.

"*Baba,*" she whispered.

He shook his head. "You're ready, *Yelli.* You were born for this day. I knew it the moment I saw you. So small when you were put into my arms but looking up at me with those green eyes. You knew too much already the day you came into this world. You're ready."

He said it with complete conviction. Hearing him, the way he uttered the words to her, there could be no doubt in anyone's mind that he believed what he was saying.

"You are so certain."

"The only thing I doubted—and I was wrong—was the choice of husbands. You and *Aghzen n wayur* will lead us to victory. You were meant to be together all along. The ancestors knew far more than I did. He was the right choice for you."

She smiled her agreement. "He is that."

"What have I always said to you, Safia?" Her father's faded blue eyes looked down into hers with love. "How do I know you and Petru will prevail?"

She lifted her chin. "Because there is no other alternative. Petru said nearly the same thing to me. There is no room for doubt. We will do this."

Her father kissed both cheeks, then her forehead, and they held each other tight before she turned and looked at her family all together for what she knew would most likely be the last time. Petru stepped up beside her, circled her waist with one arm and took off.

They split up, taking to the sky, searching for the enemy while their army waited for the assault on the farm. The ground trembled. Small insects erupted from beneath the soil just outside the fence, but none penetrated the safeguards.

An older woman approached the gate, looking small and frail, her face lined with age, gray hair covered with a scarf Safia recognized Lunja had made and gifted to Zdan's aunt, Raashidah. The scarf was a beautiful piece of artwork, hand dyed and carefully woven. Raashidah was forced to stop at the gate due to the safeguards.

She called out for Zdan, whining in a high-pitched voice for him to come to her. "It is your duty to take care of me. Open this gate and let me in," she demanded.

Zdan sighed. "Great time for her to decide she wants to join us."

Lunja wrapped her fingers around her husband's arm when he would have stepped out of the shadows. "She wouldn't have come unless something compelled her, Zdan. You can't open the gates. If you do, you allow the enemy in."

"I can't leave her out there when we know Lilith is sending vampires and demons here."

The foul stench of evil increased, along with the ominous sound of growling. The trembling of the ground grew stronger, as if an earthquake were growing in strength. Behind Raashidah, in the distance, three men dragged themselves toward the farm. They couldn't seem to pick up their feet, stumbling and falling, crawling through the dirt and grasses until they could make it back onto their feet.

Puppets, Petru identified for her. *They eat the flesh of humans and Carpathians. Do not allow Zdan to open the gate.*

Zdan was aware of the danger to his aunt. He shook off Lunja's restraining hand and began to run toward Raashidah, gesturing to her. "You must get away from here. Go back home and lock your doors."

Raashidah pursed her mouth stubbornly. "It is your *duty* to take care of me, Zdan. Open the gates and allow me in."

"She keeps telling him to open the gates," Lunja said. With great reluctance, she moved into position to take the shot should Zdan's aunt threaten Zdan. "Is she possessed?"

Safia came up on the right side of Zdan. The three puppets were close enough to see the trails of slobber coming from the gaping holes in their cheeks. Serrated teeth were black, stained with blood. Their red-rimmed eyes were fixed on Raashidah and Zdan.

"She's been programmed, Zdan," Safia said firmly, her stomach lurching at what was to come. Puppets weren't demons. Vampires had made them, not Lilith. They would devour the woman alive. "Step back. She's lost to us. There is no way to save her. It is best if you do not witness this."

"There must be a way to save her, Safia. That's what you're supposed to do." Zdan pleaded with her, but at the same time, he was resigned, turning away. He knew his aunt was lost to them. She wasn't acting the way she normally would have in the least.

Raashidah shook the gate and continued to harangue Zdan in her shrieking voice. She didn't look at the puppets as they drew closer. Instead, she tore at her skin, screaming at her nephew that he owed it to her to look after her.

Abruptly, her voice turned sly and cunning. "Lunja is seeing another man. I know who he is. Come closer, Zdan, and I'll tell you who he is. She meets him at the market."

Crows flew from the forest, so many the sky turned black, blanketing even the clouds. A noise much like thunder rumbled ominously, accompanied by the shaking of the ground as the hellhounds' hooves pounded and their massive bodies slammed into trees in a blind attempt to get to their destination.

Thick stalks burst from the soil, rising like towers, writhing like snakes with gaping mouths and spiny stems leaking poisonous drops as they swung back and forth hungrily, looking for prey. They formed a six-foot-deep perimeter around the front of the farm property, enclosing those inside.

Raashidah's high-pitched shriek turned to agony as the first puppet gripped her in clawed hands and dragged her to him, sinking teeth into her bony shoulder, tearing a strip of flesh from her. The second puppet reached her from her other side, jerking her head toward him, clumsily attempting to pull her from the first one.

"Petru was right," Zdan whispered, lifting his gun. "This is the distraction he said Lilith would send to us." His voice was as steady as his hands as he took aim and pulled the trigger. His aunt crumpled to the ground. He swallowed hard, but there was no expression on his face as he turned toward Safia.

"Keep well back from the fence, and whatever you do, don't allow anyone to open the gates," Safia cautioned. "You have to make Lilith believe we think the main attack is here."

Zdan nodded. "How do we kill those things?"

Even as he asked the question, lightning sizzled through the dark clouds, lighting up the sky in an ominous display behind the heavy screen of crows. Three jagged bolts slammed through the screen of crows and drove down onto the three puppets' heads. The bolts continued straight through them to the ground underneath.

There was no doubt that the lightning had Petru's stamp all over it. There was no way for Lilith, or anyone else, to tell that he was a distance away and not right there, believing Lilith was sending her army straight at them.

Safia drew her crystal sword and raised it toward the clouds, the flame burning blue-hot as hundreds of dead crows, their blackened carcasses falling from the sky, landed on the greedy stems with their grisly mouths gaping wide.

The venomous vines slammed at the fence repeatedly and tried to burrow under it. They had snaked their way toward Raashidah's body, their mouths snapping and lunging in a vicious attempt to grab her. Tongues licked at the blood pooling on the ground. When the bolts of lightning struck the puppets and incinerated them, flames leapt to Raashidah's body as well and reduced it to ashes, burning many of the tongues of the demonic vines.

Safia kept her focus on the vicious snakelike creatures eager to gobble up the burned carcasses falling from the sky. The dead crows passed through the crystal light of her luminous sword. Instantly, tiny blue flames could be seen glowing beneath the charred feathers.

She pulled the vial of water from the sacred stream from her pocket and, with one hand, unsnapped the lid to toss the water into the air as she spun. The water spread through the air and began to rain down, the drops hissing as they fell fast onto the charred birds, just before the reaching vines gobbled the crows whole, blackened feathers and scorched carcasses.

She spoke softly, using the same perfectly pitched tone she'd been taught from the time she was a child. "Hear me, demons sent by Lilith, queen of the underworld. You cannot enter these gates or break through these safeguards."

The vines opened their mouths, screaming and thrashing. They slammed their thick bodies against the fence and ground while their red malevolent eyes fixated on her. The rain continued to pour down on them. The hissing grew louder, and tiny holes began to appear in the stalks and shoots. Inside the holes, little blue flames flickered and glowed.

Close to the fence, she plunged the blade of her sword deep into the soil. The snakelike vines shrieked in fury and fear. The holes in the stems grew larger, as if the woody stems were tearing apart from the inside out.

"This ground is lost to you. This shape is lost to you. Each form she sent from the ground will be lost to her as this ground is consecrated." She scattered more liquid above her head and then in the four directions and onto the ground.

Blue flames burst through the ever-widening holes in the thick stems, and the gaping mouths vomited blackened feathers and strangely colored blood. The stems collapsed on the ground, withering. The fire inside began to roar, turning an even brighter blue, escaping through the large holes and rushing over the stems to devour them.

That is enough for Lilith to believe we are both there and have fallen for her deception. We need you here now.

Petru's voice in her mind was a command.

Safia didn't hesitate or wonder if she would be able to shift and hide her presence from the enemy. She had practiced as much as she was able in the short time she'd had. She had no choice, she would have to shift and get to the real site of the invasion without tipping off Lilith or any of the enemy.

She went for it, putting the image of a little owl in her mind, the one creature she was certain of. The moment she did, she felt Petru with her. Not only Petru but Aura and Nicu. Tomas, Lojos and Mataias. She almost laughed, certain Benedek would have been crowding in as well had he not been occupied with the much more important job of managing an army.

There is no more important job, Benedek corrected, *than ensuring your safety.*

She should have known he was monitoring the situation. A war was being fought, but every Carpathian was ensuring she stayed safe while shifting and donning that cloak of invisibility in the way they had.

The moment she came to the western side of the farm, where Petru had deliberately allowed a tiny flaw in the weave of safeguards to draw Lilith's army into an ambush, she saw the full extent of the chaotic scene below her. This was a real battlefield. So many of the enemy. They were everywhere.

There were demons in every form imaginable. She knew the hierarchy and how difficult some were to destroy. Vampires of every rank, too many to count. They seemed to be coming out of the clouds and diving toward Petru's head while others rushed him from every direction. Land. Trees. Air. It appeared to her as if the vampires were all converging on him, concentrating their attacks directly on him.

Petru seemed to be everywhere, moving so fast he looked a blur. She could barely take her horrified gaze off him. She knew she shouldn't fixate on him. It was the one thing he'd cautioned her against, but he didn't even try to avoid the vile creatures coming at him. Already he was covered in blood, his chest torn. There were tears in his shoulder, one particularly jagged wound near his neck where teeth had come far too close to his artery.

She tore her gaze from him and looked over the battlefield. Lilith had thrown everything at them, pouring her army of demons and vampires into that narrow valley Petru had chosen to allow them to invade.

Benedek had created what were real fighters, not illusions, men combating the demons and vampires using the skills they had learned over the centuries, imprinted from ancestors and practiced diligently, along with what Benedek had shared with them, but demons were difficult to kill. Vampires even more so. Those men were slivers of her father and brothers with a part of Benedek inside each of them—a very dangerous thing to do.

Find the generals, Safia. We must destroy the chain of command fast.

Petru gave the order to her just as he was leading the others. She could hear him directing the Carpathians from one place to another as if he knew in advance where the worst of the vampires were suddenly going to appear. All the while, he continued to advance straight through the melee, fighting his way toward some unknown destination. It wasn't difficult to see why he'd earned the name *Aghzen n wayur.* Moon monster. It was nearly impossible to tell him apart from the monsters he destroyed, other than that he was faster and much more vicious.

Safia shut out the sounds of the battle, the sight of the various demons and vampires, even the man she was married to. She had to find Lilith's generals. That was the job Petru had assigned to her. She was in the form of the little owl and, at the moment, still invisible to those on the battlefield. That gave her an advantage.

She reached out, expanding her mind, keeping her energy low, avoiding the disturbing foulness of hatred, the need to destroy and feast on blood. There had to be some intelligence receiving orders from Lilith and directing the army of demons to carry them out.

It took more time than she wanted, although it was not more than a few minutes, but she discovered four of the demons she had been taught to call Valk. In the hierarchy of demons, they were at the very top, reigning over the others and extremely difficult to kill. Most lesser demons never got in their way or dared to oppose them. Fortunately, there were very few of them, mostly because they were so powerful, Lilith likely feared them banding together against her. She had proven to be as paranoid as she was narcissistic and evil.

The four generals had positioned themselves at the four corners of the battlefield, readying themselves for a massive strike. To Safia's dismay, they were seated astride hellhounds. Behind each one was a pack of the two-headed beasts.

She touched the mind of each of the generals, a very delicate entry. Their orders were to wait until the demons and vampires had killed as many of the farm's defenders as possible and then release the hellhounds, driving them straight into the remaining men who were alive. In the narrow valley, few would live through that stampede.

Safia passed the orders along to Petru.

Stop them.

There was complete confidence that she would. Her stomach clenched. She took her gaze from the hellhounds to her right and once more looked at her husband. It defied all reasoning that he was even alive. There didn't seem to be a place on his body that wasn't torn and bloody, but it didn't seem to matter. He appeared larger than life. Indestructible. Even as she watched, he literally tore out one heart, tossed it in the air and called down the lightning as he was driving his fist through another vampire's chest while two others leapt on him.

She couldn't watch Petru and do the task given to her. She took another deep breath, let go of doubt, dismissed Lilith's generals and studied the hellhounds. Technically, they were creatures. They might be from the underworld and totally terrifying, but they were still animals. She was very, very good at connecting to all sorts of animals, even feral ones.

Very slowly and with great care, she stretched her mind toward the hellhound the general to her right was astride. It stood to reason that if the general chose that one to sit on, that hellhound controlled the pack. She found that some animals, particularly pack animals, often shared the ability to communicate.

Her touch as she entered the hellhound's mind was extremely light. She flowed in cautiously, careful to keep her presence light so that her entrance was undetected and the animal's hatred and the centuries of torture this animal had endured wouldn't paralyze her empathic nature to the point she wouldn't be able to function.

The hellhound had a ferocious temperament. Hundreds of years of being subjected to cruelty and pain had only added to its hatred of humans. It loathed demons even more. The beast despised the demon on its back but knew if it dared to throw him off, it would be subjected to months of a bullwhip biting into its flesh and even longer of starvation.

The general's name was Bos, and the demon particularly enjoyed jabbing its spurred feet into the hellhound's sides. The Valk were immune to any poison the hellhound salivated and took special delight in driving the animals to the brink of insanity with their cruelty.

When Safia had adjusted to the hellhound's vicious nature, innate cruelty and eagerness to kill, she began to flow through its mind, spreading out until she encompassed the entire brain. She matched the rhythm of the snorting, pawing beast, its heartbeat, the way it continually sent out silent messages to the rest of the eager pack to hold back when they wanted to charge. This particular hellhound was powerful and held sway over the others. She hoped that would be the case with the ones the other generals had chosen to sit on.

She turned her attention to the hellhound on her left. That general was named Shock, and he seemed even worse than Bos. He was so eager to send the hellhounds smashing into the army in the valley, he continually raked at the hound he was astride with his spiked feet to keep him agitated.

Again, Safia took time to slowly enter the hellhound's mind. She couldn't assume that because she'd managed to ensnare one creature, she could gain control of another. This hellhound was so tense and frantic to charge, its mind in utter chaos, it was seeing red. She had to be extremely careful as she entered its brain. She couldn't make the least wave. It took effort to bring calm and center the animal, to bring it under her control.

Hidden with the smallest pack of hellhounds, the demon who had managed to make his way deepest into the interior of the farm was named Rupert. He seemed in charge of everyone, including the other three Valk. He was the one receiving direct orders from Lilith and passing them on to the others. He was much more alert than either Shock or Bos.

Cautiously, Safia reached out to the hellhound Rupert sat astride. Like the others, it was eager to get into the battle and kill. This beast wasn't nearly as agitated as the others simply because the demon on its back wasn't focused on keeping it riled up. Rupert was busy describing the battle to Lilith. He wasn't just using his own vision but was relying on the hellhound's as well.

She had to be very, very careful as she encompassed the hellhound's mind. Lilith hadn't known she had taken over the sea creatures. Lilith hadn't recognized Safia as being in control of Art at the restaurant. It hadn't occurred to Lilith that Safia was powerful enough to wrest control of any of the queen of the underworld's creatures from her. Still, Safia kept her energy very low as she wove her mind through the hellhound's, privy to everything in his brain and that of Rupert's.

Lilith was blind. She needed Rupert's eyes to see the battlefield. She also needed his expertise. Petru had called it. She wasn't the brilliant strategist she'd been given credit for. She was essentially trying to use the same tactics she had before to win her war against them. Mostly she was attempting vengeance against Safia by destroying her family and home. Her hatred was palpable. The hellhounds were programmed specifically to target anyone of her bloodline.

The last general was Grog. He was hidden in the forest with his pack of restless hellhounds, waiting to close the trap on those on the farm. They would shut the door on all escape so everyone could be killed. His hellhounds snorted and pawed the ground, eager to rush into the fray, but like Rupert, Grog didn't antagonize the pack waiting behind him. He was second-in-command and kept close watch on the battle in the valley.

The hellhound he sat astride was the most resistant of the four she'd penetrated. It was difficult not to feel the pressure of time passing while the fight raged between Benedek's army and the demons and vampires. Twice she had to withdraw, take deep breaths, reset and start over again, blocking out what was happening around her. She couldn't think about her family. She couldn't smell blood. She had to concentrate on taking over the hellhounds so she was in complete control of them. Once that was done, she would have the task of destroying Lilith's generals. She didn't dare think about that until she had accomplished taking over the hellhound Grog sat on.

It is done. She gave Petru the news that she had the hellhounds under her control.

20

Already they had suffered too many injuries. No one had died yet, but it was only a matter of time. Aura had carried the wounded back to the medical station for treatment and blood over and over and then brought them back to the fight. Often, she'd had to give blood right there, or they would have lost one of their men. Benedek was everywhere, not just in those other men fighting but also in his own form, getting torn up just like the other Carpathians. He was carrying more than his share.

Petru knew they couldn't keep up the battle much longer. They had to score their victory and do it very decisively. The toll on Benedek was unimaginable. All the Carpathians felt his fatigue, but they couldn't do anything to help him. Lilith had enlisted an army of master vampires to aid her, and they brought various levels of servant vampires with them. The vampires craved the blood of the ancients, but most importantly, this was their best chance to destroy six of the foremost hunters in the world.

Safia had uncovered Lilith's generals. She had discovered that the underworld's leader had been blinded when Safia had attacked her. Lilith was dependent on her generals to show her the battlefield. If they could destroy those generals, Safia controlled the hellhounds.

They could have a decisive victory if they struck hard and fast. It was absolutely necessary for her to figure out how to destroy the Valk before the Imazighen and Petru's army could make their final move. Petru knew he couldn't hurry her, but the odds were stacking up against them rapidly.

Petru's body was wearing out. He'd lost too much blood and needed to resupply. He couldn't stop to do that. He needed to continue his forward momentum, driving down the middle. He knew Lilith had something big waiting. He had to force her to show them what that was. He kept hoping Safia would manage to uncover Lilith's surprise weapon when she was testing the demons for their weaknesses.

Keeping his eye on the battle Benedek was conducting, Petru respected her family more than ever. Although all the men appeared different, through Benedek, Petru was aware which ones were part of Izem, Usem or Gwafa. Usem and Izem did their best to take the brunt of the fighters to protect their father as much as possible.

Izem took on the worst of the vampires, but he was smart about using different men each time so that when he was wounded, and that was often, he wasn't risking the same version of himself too many times. Occasionally, he'd had to send one of his men to the medical station, or Aura had treated his wounds right there to save him. That didn't deter him from stepping in front of his father or his younger brother if he could do so. He even did his best to protect Benedek, knowing the Carpathian was more important than the three Imazighen. Without Benedek, all the fighters would fall, leaving them without anyone to fend off the demons and vampires raging against them in the valley.

Demons in the shape of green-and-red-striped toads with serrated teeth, standing about a foot high, dotted the ground. Some already lay dead or dying, killed by the Carpathians or Benedek's army, but many leapt on the Imazighen, viciously biting at their legs, injecting a paralyzing poison. With each bite, they croaked loudly to signal to the other toads. The other amphibians rushed at the victim, biting and tearing at their flesh to bring them down to the ground, where more toads could inject their paralyzing venom so there would be no way to fight back.

Izem was growing weak. He didn't quite understand that the continual wounds, although spread among the various men, were all wounds to pieces of him and would collectively take a toll. Because he often took the brunt, fighting the most experienced vampires from the shadow world, the wounds were life-threatening. As he weakened, his speed became slower, as did the speed of every one of his replicas.

The toads seemed to sense that Izem was the weakest. Even as the green-and-red-striped demons targeted Safia's oldest brother, Petru caught sight of a dark shape slipping through the taller grasses toward Izem. Gwafa must have spotted the same threat to his son as well, because he began fighting his way toward him.

Petru put on a burst of speed, meeting two of the four vampires stalking him head-on, catching them before they were ready. He slashed the neck of one while he drove his fist through the chest of the second one, gripping the heart and tearing it out before the vampire even knew he had been touched.

The remaining vampire's head listed to one side as the creature shifted, choosing the image of a giant toad and croaking horrifically to summon the toads on the ground to his aid as he leapt on Petru's back. The vampire-demon sank its serrated teeth into the back of Petru's neck and shoulder, tearing chunks of flesh out as he injected the paralyzing venom. With every penetrating bite, he sent out a hideous croak, calling to those toads on the ground to rush to his aid. He had a chance to vanquish their greatest enemy.

Petru felt glee and triumph pouring off the vampire as dozens of toads leapt over their dead and dying companions to join the vampire trying to devour Petru alive. He blocked out the pain and concentrated on keeping his feet under him. The venom spread rapidly through his body as more of the vile toads bit into his calves and chewed their way up his thighs.

"The great Petru Cioban," a voice drawled. "I was told you were impossible to kill, yet here you are, your blood the fodder for these foul amphibians." There was pure loathing in the voice, as if just the thought of the toads sickened him.

"Draven Dubrinsky." Petru acknowledged what once had been Mikhail Dubrinsky's elder brother. He had been first in line to become the prince of the Carpathian people. The sickness and need of power had rotted his brain until his intelligence had narrowed to that of a selfish, cunning, narcissistic evil vampire. He had long ago given up his soul. Gregori, Mikhail's second-in-command, had dispatched him to the land of shadows. Clearly, he had made a deal with Lilith.

It wouldn't have been impossible for Lilith to draw so many vampires to her or even command them. When vampires were destroyed, they went to the shadow world and were given a chance to redeem themselves. Few took that opportunity. Lilith's demons were often there, tempting them or sometimes punishing them if they agreed to serve her and didn't respond fast enough to her liking. The majority of those they were fighting had to be taken from the realm of the dead.

Most of these vampires were those already destroyed, recruited from the shadow world, and probably given the empty promise of life again on earth should they serve Lilith and win this war for her. Vampires rarely told the truth. Why they would believe anything Lilith promised them, Petru had no idea, but she seemed able to convince demons and vampires alike of her sincerity, even when they witnessed her renege on her word over and over. That only went to show her power.

A blue light burst over the battlefield, illuminating the valley. Petru didn't glance up, and neither did his enemies. His ancient blood was far too valuable of a prize, and all attention was riveted on the richness flowing freely from his terrible wounds.

With casual ease and without looking at his prey, Petru reached over his shoulder with one hand and yanked the enormous toad from his back. As he did, he punched through the toad's back to find the withered heart. Yanking it free, he tossed it into the sky. Several lightning bolts struck it. The toad's mouth gaped open as the body flopped over and hit the ground.

Petru's eyes, a penetrating silver, had never left the undead facing him. Draven stood what he considered a few safe feet away. He couldn't conceal the greed on his face as he stared at the blood covering Petru's body.

"I have only to wait until you bleed a little bit more. Your strength will be gone." He grinned, indicated the toads doing their best to eat through Petru's legs. "Soon, their venom will paralyze you, and you won't be able to fight me. I may keep you alive just for your blood."

The blue light seemed to pulse in the air, and a low musical voice chanted softly. The toads suddenly pulled back from Petru in alarm, leaping from his legs to the ground, lifting their heads and looking in all directions. They began to utter loud, obnoxious croaks in counterpoint to the soft melodious chanting.

I am behind you, Petru, Aura said. *I am keeping the illusion of your body covered in blood but am healing your wounds while you push the venom out.*

I fear there is going to be an attack on the shortest member, which is Izem. I will be able to destroy this vampire. He is too sure of himself, Petru informed her.

Nicu sent me to give you blood. He said if you do not take it and allow me to heal you, he will come save you himself and never allow you to forget it. He said to remind you, eternity is a long time.

Unfortunately, that sounded exactly like something Nicu would say. Aura was already healing him. Beneath the illusion Aura provided, Petru pushed the paralyzing venom from his body and took blood from Aura's wrist. While he did so, he assessed how exhausted Safia was.

Safia was expending tremendous amounts of energy holding the hellhounds in place, keeping the generals and Lilith from realizing she had taken control of the beasts and searching for a way to destroy the demons. Destroying the toads while carrying that load would drain her further and was extremely risky. She would need to expend energy. If that energy was felt by Lilith or the demon generals, everything was lost.

Touching her mind, seeing through her eyes, Petru only felt her confidence. She was *Ku Tappa Kulyak*, his demon slayer. She was *Pelkgapâd és Meke Pirämet*, his fearless defender. She was calm as she assessed the toads, unfazed by their sheer numbers or size. She paid no attention to their hideous serrated teeth or their venom. She didn't appear to look at the damage they did to her family, to his brethren or to him. She simply was the demon slayer.

He turned his attention back to Draven. The vampire was waiting for him to fall, his cocky grin still on his face. Petru didn't have time to waste, not when his lifemate was under such pressure and something was stalking Izem through the continual clashing of vampires, demons and toads. Time was against them. Draven might think he was still the heir to the Carpathian throne, but he had never been more than a pompous traitor.

The moment Aura was safely away, Petru charged forward with his incredible speed. He struck Draven with the force of a runaway train, fist driving through the chest wall. The vampire's eyes went wide with shock and horror as Petru's fingers wrapped around his withered heart and began to extract it.

Draven tore at Petru's chest with his claws in an attempt to stave him off, but Petru was too fast and too experienced. He swung Draven around easily, as if he were a rag doll, ripped the heart entirely from the chest and shoved the body from him into the middle of the frenzied toads. The heart was instantly incinerated as it met the lightning bolt sizzling across the sky.

Toads scrambled in all directions to get out of the bluish light that seemed to illuminate the entire valley. Drops of water rained down, as if the clouds had broken open. As the water hit the toads, holes began to appear in the bodies of the amphibians. A hissing sound erupted along with columns of bluish-gray smoke from hundreds of the toads as they tried to out-hop the pouring rain. The water fed the blue flames erupting from the holes rather than putting out the fire.

Above the screams and shrieks of the vampires and demons his brethren dispatched and the clash of weapons between demons and the Imazighen, Petru was tuned to the melodious perfect pitch of Safia's voice chanting, sealing the ground against the shape of toads, consecrating it, and closing it off so that those above could not return and no others could be sent.

The water was destroying the toads at a faster rate than the fighters had been able to. Along with the toads, other demons, depending on their shape and hierarchy, were also experiencing the brutal repercussions of the drops on their bodies as they rained down on them, mingling with the blue light.

Petru continued his forward drive, seeing the battle already forming in his mind. He couldn't send his brethren; they were engaged. Aura transported two injured men, both made up of Izem and Benedek. Izem was stretched far too thin. He'd protected his father, his brother and even Benedek and endured too many major wounds. Both men Aura took to the medical station were in bad shape.

You cannot afford to continue as you're going, Izem, Petru cautioned. Even as he warned Safia's eldest brother, he was again forced to slow his forward momentum as he was closed in on from three sides by the undead.

Two leapt into the air, flying at him from either direction, while the third confronted him directly. A fourth, hidden, threw spinning spears wrapped in razor-sharp steel at him.

Hidden in the shadows, a vampire that had been stalking the shorter version of Izem suddenly sprang at the Imazighen fighter from behind, but Gwafa inserted his body between the undead and his son. The fist struck Gwafa hard, driving through his chest, while the vampire's teeth tore at his shoulder, removing flesh all the way to the bone.

Izem instantly attacked the vampire, throwing him off Gwafa. A fountain of blood spurted from Gwafa's chest while more formed a river at his shoulder, running down his arm, back and chest.

Aura. Need you now. Benedek's call was calm, but the underlying urgency was felt by everyone.

Through Benedek, Petru knew it was too late to save Gwafa. The wound was mortal.

Retrieve the part of you in him from all replicas, Petru commanded Benedek as he knocked the spinning spears from the sky with a clash of his own spinning swords, which he wielded with the ease of centuries of expertise.

Petru felt Safia and her brothers go very still inside. They continued to fight, but they were all too aware of what that command meant for their father. There was no way to save him. None. Aura couldn't repair those wounds or give him enough blood. They couldn't chance losing Benedek.

If I do, all replicas of Gwafa go down at once. Our illusions of fighters will be gone.

Gwafa's voice trembled with his waning life, but he showed his courage as he had done in saving his son. *I will hang on long enough to have the men appear to be naturally killed.*

Petru recognized the vow, and Gwafa had always kept his word. That didn't mean he wasn't human, and his body would give out before his spirit. They knew they wouldn't have much time. That meant, as Petru fought off his attackers, he would have to orchestrate the battle below so that every one of Gwafa's replicas would be attacked and fatally injured, one after another. Benedek would have to be close enough to retrieve his sliver from the injured and dying replica. The enemy would believe they were winning the war.

Baba, Safia whispered. *No.*

At once, all four packs of hellhounds reacted, stomping restlessly, heads swinging from side to side. They roared aggressively in protest.

Some had more than one head. They were larger than bison, and their heads were enormous. The eyes glowed sometimes a malevolent yellow and other times a bloodshot raging red.

It was often said that hellhounds were the heralders of death and anyone who looked directly into their eyes would be overcome with plague and sickness. They carried the plague in their teeth and claws, or whatever the mage aiding Lilith had put in place when they were sent to do her bidding. Their fur was short, dark and spiked, the bristles standing up all over their bodies like barbs. Great claws hooked into the ground when they ran, tearing up the earth and throwing clods of dirt they had fouled behind them.

Every part of a hellhound was venomous. Weapons and one's body had to be coated in hyssop oil to be able to combat the creatures. The only way to kill them was to shoot them directly in the eyes with an arrow coated in hyssop oil. Petru had prepared Safia's family for the event that Lilith might use hellhounds against them. She had done so in the past. He didn't think she was a very imaginative woman, tending to rely on what she thought had worked for her before.

Focus, Petru demanded firmly. *If you do not, we will lose everyone.*

He couldn't blame Safia. She was losing her beloved father. She had known they would suffer losses. He couldn't comfort her, not when he was fighting for his life and the lives of the rest of her family. He had to get her to concentrate on helping him. He needed her.

We must take down the generals now. Have you found their weakness?

He couldn't lose Safia at this crucial point. Gwafa was hanging on long enough to allow Benedek to recover the parts of himself keeping Gwafa's replicas moving through the battlefield fighting demons and vampires, but they would be going down very soon. That would be a good thirty men gone.

One of the vampires coming at Petru from the sky ripped at his back with the claws of a grizzly, tearing through flesh and muscles before he could spin around and rip its throat out, flinging it away, whirling back fast enough to slice through the second vampire rocketing through the sky straight at him. The bottom half of the body dropped away from the top half, and black blood poured to earth, scorching the ground below.

Petru followed the torso as it tumbled, slamming his fist through the chest wall and extracting the heart. The first vampire desperately tried to retrieve his throat through the onslaught of spinning spears that were still coming toward Petru from the direction of a small group of trees. Several pierced the vampire's body as he tried to outrace Petru, who was in pursuit.

The sword flashed again, cutting through the back of the vampire's neck, beheading him. The head fell forward, and black blood poured out in all directions. It was acidic, and everywhere the blood splashed on him, it burned through skin to the bone. He tore the heart from its chest and threw both hearts toward the clouds, calling lightning at the same time to incinerate them and then the bodies.

There was a rush of adrenaline when fighting now, a by-product of the scars forming on his soul from so many kills. He felt a predator's joy rising in direct proportion to the number of vampires he was tearing through. That wasn't a good sign, and he pushed the emotion away. It hadn't done much good for Aura to give him blood when he was already bleeding from so many wounds again. He parried the spinning spears and smacked a lightning whip down on the tree in which he was certain the vampire was hiding, allowing the tail to curl around the limbs and trunk.

Seven of Gwafa's men had gone down, and through Safia, he could feel the glee of Lilith's generals. Rupert reported to Lilith, although he was having difficulty controlling his mount. The beast had two heads and swung them continually, his large body shaking with rage as he pawed the earth and stomped. Rupert was forced to divide his attention between the battlefield and the pack leader.

Lilith hissed her anger at him. *Settle him down. Can't you control him? He'll give your presence away before we're ready. All the hellhounds will stampede if he does.*

Eight more Gwafa replicas died on the battlefield. Three were mortally wounded. Lilith's triumph was so tangible it could be felt throughout the valley.

Petru waited a heartbeat for Safia to pull out of her grief enough to get the hellhounds settled. It took only a few seconds, and the packs calmed to the level they'd been before. She'd timed the lead hellhound's response to Rupert's reprimand. The demon general clearly considered himself superior, lording it over the three generals when their hellhounds subsided after his did.

These demons have few places one can harm them.

Petru was aware. He'd studied them through Safia even as he ran the battle. He'd hoped she would see something he hadn't. He hadn't found a chink in their armor. Lilith had designed them as near to perfection as possible. Even if he managed to penetrate the armor plates on their bodies, he hadn't detected a heartbeat. He had no idea where to find the heart in order to rip out the organ to kill them.

He stilled inside, waiting, even as he flew at the tree, spinning swords to block spears flying his way. Safia hadn't sounded defeated. She was onto something.

The spears were wobbly, not at all as they had been. Petru's opponent had been shaken by the lightning whip. At the last moment as Petru approached the tree, he disappeared, coming in from behind. He was bleeding from half a dozen places, and he'd deliberately left the scent of his blood everywhere.

Ancient Carpathian blood was tantalizing to the vampire—a temptation the undead would never be able to resist. Petru circled the tree fast, winding up the trunk, splashing droplets of blood along the blackened tree branches and outer leaves, just a few feet from the splitting trunk.

Poison seeped from the crack in the trunk. The vampire couldn't keep his presence hidden from nature. All things living recoiled from the abomination of the undead. The vampire had to be hiding inside the trunk of the tree, but Petru knew he would be unable to resist the lure of ancient blood.

A long lizard-like tongue escaped through the crack in the trunk, seeking the air, looking for those droplets of blood. Tentatively, a bulbous head emerged, the undead freezing in place to look warily around before he tilted his rotting chin toward the branch overhead, where a few drops of blood clung to a cluster of withered leaves. The vampire couldn't quite reach the blood without moving more of his body outside the protection of the tree trunk.

Petru deliberately stirred the breeze to float more of the enticing scent to the creature. He was starved for blood. He'd been in the tree, waiting to spring his trap, and had been smelling blood from the battlefield for some time. He was extremely anxious to feed on the blood and couldn't keep his mind on anything else. Saliva hung in streams from both sides of his mouth.

He stuck his head out further, gave a cursory glance in both directions and then turned his head up toward the branch as his torso emerged. Petru struck with violent force, punching through the back of the undead as the vampire stretched as high as he could, concentrating wholly on reaching the droplets of ancient blood.

Petru ripped through muscle and bone to grasp the shriveled heart. The vampire roared and tried to twist, but the tree held him prisoner, allowing Petru to extract the heart. Lightning met the shrunken organ in the air. Petru dragged the shuddering body from the tree and tossed it to the ground so the bolt could incinerate it.

He dropped to the earth and continued his forward momentum, right down the valley, as if he knew they would be victorious even though six more of his men had fallen. Six more and it was over for them. Once those men went down, Lilith would order the hounds released, and she would discover they were under Safia's control. Before that happened, he had to know how to destroy her generals.

For these demons to be created, and they were, there must be one place on them that is a birthmark, much like where an umbilical cord would have been. At least one vulnerable spot.

She was musing to herself. Had she been able to, he knew she would have been pacing. He didn't hurry her, although the sense of urgency was on all the fighters, and she had to feel it. So much pressure on her shoulders.

They sit astride the hellhounds. They oversee the packs of hellhounds. Only they handle them. They seem to be completely impervious to them. Immune to their venom.

Part of Petru kept looking through Safia's eyes. Not only was she meticulously studying Rupert, using her enhanced vision, but she was using the hellhound's vision and going through his memories as well. He couldn't give up enough of himself to speculate on what she was onto. He was too busy sending out his men ahead of Lilith's army and fighting off her demons and vampires.

Three more replicas went down. That left only three fighters representing Gwafa left. Petru felt a small hint of relief sweep through Safia's mind. She found something that she was confident she could use against the demon generals. She showed a small indentation on Rupert's thigh. It was a light spot in his armor. It appeared as a discoloration, almost a golden stain. That one small scale glistened as if it had oil on it.

He has rubbed hyssop oil just on that scale. No others. He's vulnerable to the hellhounds right there. If a horn or a claw penetrated that spot, most likely he would be infected immediately with whatever Lilith has had the mage place in the venom. I would have to introduce the flame of the crystal into him through that opening and destroy him from the inside out.

Petro's heart skipped a beat. He'd promised himself he would trust her to do her job. She was the demon fighter and very skilled. To do what was required of her, she would have to approach each demon while she was entirely invisible, stay undetected and remove the oil from the scale without them noticing.

The Valk had acute senses. If she moved the smallest amount of air or her energy got away from her, there were so many things that could go wrong. He shut his mind to the hundreds of possibilities. He just had to know one thing.

Can you do this when we lose your father?

Not *if* they lost him; *when* they lost him. And that time would be very soon. It was a brutal thing to ask of her and entirely unfair, but he had to know. They all had to know they could count on her. Her father was suffering, dragging out the end of his life as long as he was able in order to give Safia the chance to destroy the four demon generals.

The Carpathians ordinarily would have taken on Gwafa's pain, but they were stretched too thin, fighting too many battles on too many fronts. She would be attempting to destroy the highest-ranking, most lethal demons Lilith had in her arsenal, and she would be doing it most likely as her father died.

I am ready.

That was his only warning. She was in his mind, just as he was in hers. She felt the last of the men fall. Thirty dead or dying. Rupert relayed the information to Lilith. She screeched her triumph loud enough that it echoed through the valley. The sound was so disturbing it once more set off the hounds. They lifted their massive heads and bayed and howled wildly. Animals and night raptors took offense, shuddering and protesting with squawks and cries. Insects buzzed and crackled, chirped and whined, adding to the cacophony of noise.

Safia took advantage of the unrest, entering straight into Rupert's personal space, so close she nearly brushed against the sidestepping, baying hound. Rupert had all he could do to control the two-headed beast. The massive animal continually shook its heads, each going in the opposite direction, causing the broad back to sway and buck, nearly unseating Rupert.

For the first time in his centuries of fighting vampires, Petru found he was distracted, part of him concentrating on Safia as she moved in carefully, not expending energy to draw attention to herself as she polished that one scale on Rupert's thigh to remove the hyssop oil before backing away and flying across the valley to her right to get to Shock and remove the oil before the chaos was quelled.

Petru felt her subtly feeding the hellhounds' unrest. Not just the hellhounds but all the animals, including raptors and insects in the vicinity. Once she had polished the scale on Shock's thigh, she shot across the valley to the left side to do the same to Bos. He was quite vicious with his hellhound, raking at the beast with his spiked feet and punching at its hide with a curved spear until blood stained its side. The animal was almost mad with pain.

Safia increased her speed, trying to suppress her energy as she did so, flying across the valley to the last remaining general, Grog, who waited just out front to close the trap. She barely had time to clean the oil off his scale before Lilith was screaming her orders at Rupert to release the hounds.

Kill them all. Kill everyone. I want them all dead. Every single member of her family. Order the beasts to the farmhouse and tear them all apart, Lilith commanded.

Safia sent her own orders to the hellhounds. *Get the Valk from your backs. Attack their thighs; there is an open scale you can penetrate. I will aid you. Attack all demons on the battlefield and destroy them. Do not touch any of those with my blood or those belonging to this land.* She visualized the instructions clearly to them, showing them how to attack the generals.

The hellhounds reacted instantaneously, as if they'd been waiting a lifetime for just such a command. The leader of each pack began to bay, a peculiar, different note in the voice, all the while whirling wildly and pitching much like an untamed stallion. Steam rose from its nostrils, and the eyes glowed an evil yellow-orange.

Rupert and the other generals began to utter foul curses as they struggled to stay on the backs of the brutish hellhounds determined to unseat them. Members of the packs slammed into them, nearly driving the leaders off their clawed feet and shaking the Valk generals from their perches.

The second hit sent Rupert tumbling to the ground. Instantly the hellhound sank its massive jaws around his thigh, one razor-sharp tooth penetrating deep, right through the open scale. The same thing happened with each of the other generals. They were pinned to the ground by a hellhound crushing their thigh and holding them there.

Safia materialized, standing out in the open, making Petru's heart pound. She raised her crystal sword toward the sky, and instantly the dark was pierced with light. She looked like an angel, with her dark hair falling around her shoulders and her face illuminated by the crystal.

Rupert, I can't see what's happening, Lilith said sharply. *Let me see.*

The hellhounds had done their work, stomping on the demon generals, goring while using their massive jaws and teeth to crush the thighs and open the scale to the blue flame of Safia's sword. They rushed the demons in the valley, turning on them. Petru's army doused themselves with hyssop oil to avoid any contact and pulled back to allow the hellhounds to attack the demons on the battlefield.

Safia began to chant, her voice musical, a perfect pitch as blue flames began to flick around her sword.

"What are you doing, my dear?" a voice asked. "Surely you aren't going to aid the man who betrayed you. He left you to die. Why would you help him?"

Petru stopped moving and stared at the master vampire as he emerged from the shadows. Eduardo. This, then, was Lilith's surprise. She had sent the very vampire who had ripped Safia's heart from her body when she'd been no more than a child.

"He told you he killed me, didn't he? He is a deceiver. Here I stand, alive and well. He lied to everyone so they would believe him a hero. Their savior. In truth, he is the ultimate betrayer." Eduardo took a few more steps toward Petru, his long, bony fingers continually moving because he was so restless for blood, he couldn't quite control himself.

Petru didn't look at Safia. She'd had to contend with so much already. Now here was the vampire who had bitten into her neck, taken her blood and torn the heart from her chest. It would be easy enough to believe him when he stood there in front of everyone looking immaculate in his three-piece suit when Petru was torn up all to hell.

Who looked like the monster? Eduardo's hair was trimmed neatly, and his face was clean-shaven. He looked handsome, as if he had never done violence to anyone in his life. Would Safia think her memories of her past had been planted?

Don't be silly. Lilith would love for us to doubt one another. He is a demon. I am a demon slayer and recognize them very easily.

The knots in Petru's gut unraveled that easily. *Sívamet.* He poured love into her mind. He could give her that in the midst of all that happened this night.

"He hasn't claimed you, has he?" Eduardo continued, watching Safia.

She hadn't paused in her chanting. The blue flames flickered and grew inside the bodies of the Valk. The flames began to roll out of the one open scale and over the top of the squirming bodies. She didn't look at the vampire but continued her ritual, sealing the ground against that form of demon so no others could find a portal to pass through, and they couldn't return to Lilith should they survive.

Impatience was ugly on Eduardo's features, but he carefully smoothed the lines over. He took a moment to survey the battlefield where the hellhounds had dispatched the last of the demons and were stomping on the bodies. The blue light crept over the valley, infiltrating the darkness there.

Petru stood tall and straight, his body bleeding bright crimson blood—the blood of an ancient from so many places, facing Eduardo across the space between them. It was nearly silent, all eyes on them. He knew where the brethren were—guarding his back and watching over Safia—but Eduardo seemed unaware of them. Lilith no longer had eyes on the battlefield, and no one other than Eduardo was reporting to her.

Petru began searching for signs of her beneath the ground. *Do you know where she is?*

Yes, Safia answered. *She hasn't moved. She is staying very still, trying to gather information from Eduardo, but I am confusing him by allowing him to see in hints of color.*

Very clever. Perhaps he should begin to feel remorse. Worry for you. Confusion. Vague emotions or he won't be able to believe it. Feelings will have to creep in.

The temptation of ancient Carpathian blood found its way into the air, drawing the surrounding vampires closer. Petru didn't deign to notice. Eduardo had six lesser vampires with him. He hadn't been allowed to bring many from the underworld. Lilith trusted no one.

The master vampire's servants salivated, strings of drool escaping their open mouths. Tiny parasites crawled through the drool or clung to the sides of their rotting flesh. They swayed and stamped their feet, eager to start the pattern that they were certain would lock Petru in their circle, preventing him from fleeing the master vampire.

Petru lifted an eyebrow. "Why would you think I would attempt to convert her? She does not belong to me. She never did. She was never my lifemate. I was not the one to betray her, Eduardo. I did not rip her heart from her body. I did not betray my code of honor and choose to give up my soul."

Eduardo's long bony fingers twitched, the thick curved nails that had grown into wicked razor-sharp talons. He sniffed the air, glanced at Safia and then pulled his gaze away with effort.

"Do you not see color when you are around her? At least a hint of color? Do you not feel something?" Petru taunted. "You did even then, when she was a child."

Eduardo shook his head, his eyebrows coming together. He looked around him at the forest, then once more at Safia. She turned her attention from the ashes of the demons to the hellhounds now baying in distress.

I hate to destroy them.

They are suffering, sívamet. You must put them out of their misery.

I know they wish it, but there is so much death. I see what's been done to them, and there is no way to fix it. After they helped us, I feel as if I'm betraying them.

He wanted to gather her into his arms and hold her close, shelter her against his heart, but the lesser vampires swayed and danced, creeping closer despite Eduardo's orders to stay still. The smell of the ancient blood drove them mad. Any moment, they would attack, and Eduardo would be forced to do the same.

The Carpathians were gathering their strength, pooling energy to strike at Lilith. They had to be precise in their attack to end her raids on the Imazighen, at least for another two thousand years. She needed to turn her attention elsewhere.

There is no betrayal when you are being merciful. They suffer, sívamet.

Safia struck at the hellhounds fast, making their deaths as quick and painless as possible. The hounds dropped to the ground, shocking the vampires. They turned their attention to the valley floor long enough for the brethren to combine their power with Petru's. He gathered the energy, and once again, as Benedek opened the ground above Lilith, Petru slammed the lightning bolt directly on her.

All the Carpathians contributing their power and energy were ancients, and the combination was lethal. The ground shook so hard it buckled, and large cracks appeared in several places. Everywhere a crack opened, black-and-orange smoke poured out of the ground, rising toward the clouds in a high column. The gas was foul-smelling and toxic. The moment it touched the blue crystalline light, the odor neutralized, and the noxious gas dissipated as if it had never been. It had to have been a direct hit. Lilith hadn't made a sound. The bolt had struck her with enough force to damage her, most likely knock her out completely.

Even as the ground rolled and buckled, and smoke poured from it, blue flames burst from the demon bodies on the valley floor. The flames leapt high, burning bright over the hellhounds. The massive bodies appeared like blue sparkling diamonds dotting the landscape.

Eduardo's six lesser vampires teetered on the pitching ground. From behind them, Aura, Tomas, Lojos, Benedek, Nicu and Mataias materialized out of the sky, not even slowing down as they rocketed toward the undead circling Petru. They were on them before the vampires could warn one another.

Simultaneously, Petru rushed Eduardo, breaking through the line of his guardian vampires, now occupied with fighting for their own survival. Eduardo heard a soft voice as he tried to keep his feet.

It's impossible to defeat him. He is Amnay icheqquan n wayur. He is the fierce knight of the moon. He is Aghzen n wayur. Moon monster. Even now, you are too slow. Look how fast he is. A blur. You are wading through sand. The moon sent this monster to fight with the Imazighen. You cannot defeat him.

Eduardo felt heaviness invading his arms and legs. He screamed his protest against that insidious voice, but it was relentless. Sweet, like an angel. Pure. A perfect pitch. The sound hurt and scraped at the insides of his head, throwing him off-balance.

Petru hit him, strike after strike. Each blow rocked him. Petru shared that voice, heard the song start as a whisper of tribute, but it swelled in volume, so no matter what Eduardo did, he heard the lyrics coming at him from every direction, even from inside his mind. The vampire slammed his hands over his ears to drown out the sound, an impossibility, but it left his torso wide open to attack.

Petru tore his heart from his body, ignoring the acid blood burning through his flesh as he tossed the heart into the sky to meet the lightning. He stood for a moment, bowing his head as the last body fell, and he allowed it to burn to ash before he bathed away the burns on his own body from the vampire acid.

Safia materialized beside him, swaying with weariness but inspecting his wounds. "Petru. These look bad."

"Easy enough to take care of," he assured. "I know you're exhausted, *Ku Tappa Kulyak*, but we must finish this before we can rest and heal our wounds. There are demons at the gates of your farm. The members of your family must also be fatigued holding their positions."

Safia looked him over, her expressive eyes sad as she lifted her gaze to take in her brothers and grandfather. "This war cost us much, but without you and your friends, we wouldn't have survived. Thank you. Perhaps you should go to ground, and I can deal with the demons."

"*Sívamet*, we do this together, and then we both will go to ground and heal—body and spirit. The brethren will aid your family and then us should we have need before they seek the healing earth. Benedek must go now. He is at his limit."

Safia didn't protest. She simply went to her brothers and grandfather, touched her lips to each cheek and forehead, murmured her love of them and came straight back to Petru, nodding that she was ready.

T
hree weeks of mourning had taken a toll on the Meziane family, but it was impossible to keep them down. Petru found he respected them more and more with each rising. They were gentle with each other and allowed every family member the space to grieve in their own way while fully supporting one another.

Petru and Safia had stayed in the ground for two weeks to heal their wounds before joining the family. Benedek took more time than the other Carpathians, but he was out and restless, declaring he needed to continue his journey to find his lifemate.

Petru was gentle with Safia, waking her each rising and making love to her, giving her lessons in shifting before taking her to the family farm to be with her loved ones. They patrolled the harbor and town of Dellys, along with surrounding farms and forests, for any signs of Lilith's return but found none.

Several times the Carpathians went with Aura to the gate, but Justice hadn't been anywhere near it recently. Petru could tell that worried Aura. She felt he was testing the strength of all four gates and had devised some plan to escape. The gate appeared weak in some places, but the ancient wood was still holding. Something or someone had been chipping away at the safeguards and making headway, but it was a slow process.

Petru and the brethren added their weaves to Aura's. Safia didn't have the necessary skills yet to build safeguards, but she could consecrate the ground to keep demons from entering. That was the best they could do when there was no sign of the beast and they couldn't assess accurately what was going on.

"I've got to go now. This evening," Benedek insisted when they'd returned from the gate to the farm. "I feel a sense of urgency and I can't ignore it."

Petru glanced at him sharply. "*Feeling?* That's an emotion, Benedek. You don't feel emotion unless you're feeling it through Adalasia or Vasilisa, and we're too far from either of them."

Benedek gave him a cool look from his midnight black eyes. "I am well aware."

Benedek was a big man, light on his feet and lethal as hell. Petru had spent more time with him than any other being. There was no stopping Benedek from leaving once he made up his mind—and he was determined.

Petru touched his mind. Benedek didn't block him. The urgency was there. A growing sense of danger and the need to be somewhere to stop it. Petru would have left as well. There was no doubt that emotion was tied to Benedek's lifemate, just as Petru's had been tied to Safia when he'd started out on the journey to find her.

"It is your lifemate calling to you," Petru said with conviction.

"I believe she has need," Benedek said. "I don't know if it is her calling to me, but she has great need. There is fear."

Nicu cleared his throat. "My lifemate may be close to his. I feel that same urgency and fear as well. A premonition of great danger, as if we're running out of time."

"Safia, I would greatly appreciate a reading from your tarot cards before I set out on my journey," Benedek said. "Hopefully, the cards will give me direction, although I am already feeling a sharp pull."

Nicu nodded. "I am also feeling a sense of urgency and the need to travel with you, Benedek. If you do not mind, Safia, I would like to know what the cards have to say as well."

"Of course."

Safia agreed readily, but Petru felt her hesitation. It didn't show on her face, but still, it was there.

What is it, sívamet?

They have given so much for us and done so selflessly. I feel that same sense of urgency for both. I fear what I will see in the cards for them. I don't want to be the one to give either of them bad news. Benedek is still quite weak. He would never admit such a thing, but if he faces more battles, and I fear he will, he will not be at full strength.

Petru knew she was right. He had given Benedek blood numerous times and tried to persuade him to spend more time in the ground. Benedek had refused but hadn't given an explanation until now. Petru could see the need to leave was weighing on him. To find out Nicu felt the same urgency, and now Safia admitted she did as well, set alarms off. It was entirely possible Safia, being so empathic, was simply feeding off the two men, but Petru doubted it.

"We will travel with Benedek and Nicu," Mataias announced. "We have heard the cards are capable of telling us if our lifemates are alive in this century."

"And possibly the direction where they might be located," Lojos added.

"I would be happy to give each of you a reading. It is little enough to do in return for what you provided for my family," Safia said. She glanced up at Petru, seeking comfort.

Her unease didn't show at all, but she needed his support. The last thing she wanted to do was provide a negative reading for any of the Carpathians who had risked their lives for her family.

"Before you start," Aura said, settling into one of the comfortable chairs in the family room across from the small table where Safia would lay out the cards. "I need to make a confession. It is something

I never told Safia but should have. You will need this information, Benedek. At least I think it will be pertinent to your journey."

"You believe my lifemate is guarding the last gate." Benedek made it a statement. "Or that she is the demon slayer."

Aura nodded. "I do."

Petru had to agree. "We set out on this journey with Sandu. Siv found his lifemate and I found mine. Each has been a demon slayer or the guardian of the gate or both. It stands to reason that your lifemate would be at the gate."

Aura took a breath. "Safia is also a gatekeeper. I didn't tell her because I knew she was Petru's lifemate and would have to train harder than any other to be the demon slayer. If I felt I couldn't handle the gate myself, I would have asked for her help, or if the society members seeking the tarot cards came, I would tell her about them, but she didn't need distractions. I'm sorry, Safia, so much was put on your shoulders already, and you didn't need to worry about being attacked from so many fronts."

"I'm not sure I understand," Safia said.

"The holder of the tarot cards guards the gates. Each gate can only be opened by a specific alignment of the tarot cards. Only one of the four decks can make the alignment, and it must match the proper gate. That was Adalasia's ancestor's idea when she asked to make the cards and was given permission by your ancestors, Safia. I guarded the gate with you and fought off vampires."

Instantly, there was a stirring of protest from the Carpathians. Aura smiled at them. "Believe me, none of us left behind guarding those gates wanted any confrontation with vampires. We only did it out of necessity. Fortunately, we were able to share information, or I would have been in trouble. I wasn't given very much in-depth history on our people."

Petru kept his opinion to himself on the way Aura's parents had left her alone without giving her the education she needed. It wouldn't have been that difficult to share with her by simply transferring the information mind to mind, but her mother had clearly been more in the shadow world than in the real one with her daughter.

"There were a few times the gatekeepers traveled to visit one another, so I do know the way to the last gate," Aura continued. "It is necessary, Benedek, that you don't discount this society of humans that are after the tarot cards. They may be human, but they date back centuries and are quite violent. They hunt us, just like vampire hunters, and they're relentless. Lilith wants to control the beast. These humans want him. And he wants out. If he escapes, we don't have a single hunter, ancient or not, who can take him down alone. It would be a catastrophe if he escapes."

There was a small silence while Safia went to the table she had been using for years to read the tarot cards. Petru stood behind her, hands on her shoulders to steady her. Even the familiar setting hadn't helped calm her churning stomach. Safia was certain she was going to find the cards foretelling misfortune for one or more of the Carpathians, and she didn't want to deliver bad news to any of them.

"Tora guards the fourth gate," Aura continued. "Like me, she's Carpathian. I think Justice has been weakening all four gates with the idea he will force one open. All gatekeepers have reported weak spots in the wood that shouldn't be there. Tora guards the gate with the demon slayer and wielder of the tarot cards." She hesitated, looking troubled. "We've always managed to find a way to stay in touch. I haven't heard from Tora in the past month, but then I've been busy with what's gone on here. It's just that there's been no messages from her to any of us. I asked the others, and they haven't heard from her."

That sounded ominous to Petru. Tora was a Carpathian woman, and if she was like the other women guarding one of the four gates, she was without aid from other Carpathians. Anything could have happened to her. Aura's revelation only added to the urgency Benedek and Nicu were feeling.

Benedek indicated for Lojos to go to the table first. "Nicu and I have had the cards read twice for us. We know our lifemates exist in this century. At least we have hope to continue."

Lojos sat across from Safia. Petru knew the goddess wouldn't react to Lojos as the cards had reacted at his prior readings. Aura knew Lojos, and Safia knew him; therefore, the cards would have already judged his character.

She handed him the cards and told him to shuffle and then divide the deck into three piles as he thought of what he wanted the cards to answer for him. He was to take a card from each pile and place it face up on the table. Lojos did so without hesitation. He kept his gaze fixed on her face as if she would give something away to him. Petru knew she was too experienced to read anything she personally felt. She did her best to step back from the cards and allow them to answer his question.

"You have a lifemate, Lojos," Safia said.

She made a little moue with her lips, tempting Petru to kiss her. He felt the laughter in her mind. "She is not a woman to take lightly. She waited long for you, gave up on you coming for her, and will soon go her own way. Pointing you in a direction is useless when she is unpredictable. However, I see that your paths will cross if you continue the course of service you have set for yourself."

Lojos glanced up at his brothers. "Unbelievable. It really works." He stood up while Safia gathered the cards.

"Give me a minute," she said as Tomas sank into the chair across from her. "I like to cleanse the cards before the next reading." She stood up and stretched, taking the cards with her.

Do you have an idea who Lojos' lifemate is? Petru asked.

Safia shook her head. *She is strong-willed and a warrior. She will fight by his side or not accept him. The cards said that very clearly.*

She will have no choice if he binds her to him.

We will see. Safia sat across from Tomas and handed him the cards, murmuring the same instructions.

Tomas took his time shuffling the cards. He was very methodical as he divided the deck into thirds and very precisely pulled three cards from the center of each of the piles, turning them face up.

Safia's lashes fluttered, and her palm pressed over her heart where the goddess card lay beneath her clothing. Tomas had very different cards from his brother. Petru tried to read Safia's mind before she spoke, but she was allowing the deck to interpret for her, as the cards could be read in several ways. She wanted his question answered in the way he asked it.

"You have a lifemate as well, Tomas. Your lifemate is somewhere in South America. Your journey will be dangerous, and you must go first with your brothers to follow their path." She frowned and studied the three cards, gave a slight shake of her head and continued. "It is important that you are together on these journeys. Your lifemate is not alone, and the danger to her grows over time. Someone important will not be saved if Lojos, his lifemate and Mataias are not with you."

She looked up at him, gathering the cards as she did so. "I hope that answers your question."

"Perfectly. Thank you." He stood up, gave her a slight bow and moved away so Mataias could take his place.

That sounded as if Tomas should leave for South America right away, which is a big place, by the way. Petru watched her cleanse the cards. *I would have a difficult time knowing my lifemate might be in danger and I needed to wait for my brother to secure his lifemate first.*

I don't know why it is important for Lojos to find his lifemate first, but it is. Safia returned to the table and faced Mataias. She moistened her lips, touched her palm to the goddess card beneath her clothing and glanced at Aura. Aura gave her an encouraging smile. Petru knew both women had a fondness for Mataias.

He took the deck and shuffled. Mataias handled the cards with grace, the way he did most things. He seemed to be a completely self-less man. There was an innate gentleness about him. He treated the tarot deck with respect as he divided it and chose a card from each stack, turning them face up.

Safia waited for the cards to speak to her, to answer whatever question Mataias had asked. The answer puzzled her, not making sense to her. She looked up at Petru. "I was born two thousand years after I died and held your soul. Is that normal? I don't understand how it works."

"A lifemate can be reborn if she is unclaimed and dies in some way, such as a vampire kills her. The soul can be passed to another if the situation is dire. It doesn't happen often, but it can happen. Once, that we know of, the female was murdered, but Mother Earth held her spirit for three hundred years, and then she was born anew, a daughter of the earth. When she was born, a male Carpathian was also born, his soul splitting so that she became the keeper of his soul. There are many ways."

Safia rubbed her temples. She had the beginnings of a headache. Petru could tell his answer didn't clarify anything in her mind. He put his palms on either side of her head and removed the ache.

"You have a lifemate, Mataias. She lives, but she is young. There will be danger to her and many others. Again, you must journey with your brothers after you complete this task with Benedek and Nicu to ensure your lifemate survives. I'm sorry I can't tell you much more."

"You've told me I have reason to continue my existence," Mataias pointed out as he rose.

Safia's heart pounded as she cleansed the deck. This time she turned to Petru for comfort, wrapping her arms around him and laying her head on his chest.

I want this to go well. I feel such danger surrounding them.

We should offer to accompany them, Petru said carefully. He had promised to keep her there with her family. Now, more than ever, since she'd lost her father, he knew she would want to stay close to them, but they owed Benedek. Petru was a master battle planner. If he was needed, he should go.

We will offer, she agreed, *but they will not accept. And we are not meant to go. I read the cards myself to ask if we were to leave with them.*

He should have been with her, but he'd been out getting blood for her. She still didn't go hunting, and he didn't push her. They had plenty of time for her to learn everything she needed to survive. She'd been through so much and she'd done amazingly. He couldn't ask for more.

Safia straightened her shoulders and pulled away from him. Petru stopped her, gently taking her face between his palms and tilting her head up so he could capture her mouth with his. It was brief, a kiss of encouragement and love. He brushed the curve of her bottom lip with the pad of his thumb.

"*Tet vigyázam*, Safia."

"I love you, too," she whispered back.

The light brush on his jaw reminded him of that first butterfly touch of her fingers on his skin. Every time he felt he couldn't love her any more, he found himself overwhelmed all over again. He followed her back to the table. This time Nicu sat across from her.

He'd known Nicu for centuries. The man was very different, but he was a good man and had served the community his entire existence. He deserved a life of happiness. Petru wanted this reading to be one filled with answers just as much as Safia did. She took several breaths, clearing her mind before she handed the deck to Nicu.

Nicu didn't look at the cards as he shuffled and split the deck into three stacks. He simply turned the top card over, still not looking at the faces. He kept his gaze on Safia.

She moistened her lips, listening to some inner voice. Once again, her palm pressed against her heart. She nodded her head. "There is avoidance and fear. That fear is growing. There is good reason for it. She believes she isn't in danger from those around her. Although she walks on a tightrope of vulnerability, the fear isn't that she will be harmed. She fears you will find her and she will lose control."

She looked up at Nicu, her gaze meeting his. "She's wrong about the danger. She's right about the loss of control. The answer to the second question is 'You know the truth.' I have no idea what that means, but the goddess card believes you know the truth. Your soul knows, and you must believe in your instincts because they are always correct."

Nicu nodded, his features grim. "Thank you, Safia. I appreciate the reading." He indicated the cards. "They are a tremendous help. Thank your goddess for me." He stood up and waved Benedek to the chair.

Safia cleansed the cards carefully. She was exhausted. She hadn't done so many readings at one time, especially ones that were so important.

Do you need me to give you blood?

I just want this over. Benedek is last. I want to know as much as he does, that his lifemate is alive and well. I must be very careful not to mix my questions with his. I'm going to do a little meditation to clear my mind before I go to the table so that I give him the best reading possible.

Petru was very proud of her as she moved away from all of them into the next room. Benedek touched one of the rocks embedded in the table.

"Is she all right?"

Petru nodded. "She's tiring and very determined to give you the truest reading possible. She doesn't want her questions to interfere with yours. She cares very much for all of you, and this has been difficult for her."

"I feared it might be," Benedek said. "Still, I had to ask her. The cards can give insight when needed. I've come to believe in them when before I thought they were a child's game."

Petru sent him a smile. "I will admit I felt the same."

Safia returned to the room and took the seat across from Benedek, immediately handing him the deck.

"I thank you, *sisarke*. I need this information, or I wouldn't have asked." Benedek took the cards and began to shuffle before she could reply.

He seemed to be more careful and meticulous, as if he were hand-picking his cards, although that would be impossible. He divided the deck into thirds, laid each stack precisely and then drew a card from each pile, leaving them face down on the table.

"I've asked my questions."

"Turn them over."

Benedek looked at the cards for what seemed several minutes before he turned the first one over slowly, then the second and third. Safia took a long breath and let it out. Petru could have sworn her face paled. He moved closer to the back of her chair and wrapped his long fingers around the tops of her shoulders while pouring strength into her mind.

Tell him, sívamet. He already knows or he wouldn't have risen this early and insisted on leaving now, when he knows he still needs the healing earth. Anything you give him will help.

The room remained eerily silent. At some point during Tomas' reading, Amastan and Izem had joined them, but they stayed in the back of the family room and were quiet, listening to Safia's interpretation of the cards for their Carpathian allies.

"There is trouble coming from every direction. Above. Below. East, north, west, and south. I see injuries. Chaos. There is no one to trust but those you bring with you."

Safia hunched over the table to study the three cards as if, by staring at them, she could discern so much more. Find more details for him.

"Benedek, our world appears to be shaky and under attack from all directions. It isn't just your lifemate in danger. It could be all of us."

"The answer to my second question?" he persisted, his voice calm and steady, strictly neutral.

Petru felt her heartbeat accelerate, but she forced it under control.

"The cards say you have a chance to get to her. Follow your instincts. Trust yourself. Trust your brethren. No one else," she emphasized again. "Only those you know to be true friends."

Benedek nodded. "Thank you, *sisarke*." He put his palms on the table to push up.

She laid her hand over his. "I thought we should stay here, but I think you have more need of us with you."

Benedek shook his head. "I believe Justice is going to make his try, and we don't yet know which gate he will choose. He's powerful, and he will create chaos. He was a brilliant man. A brilliant tactician. And now he's a cunning beast. He has an escape plan that he's been working on for centuries. If he's about to implement it, every gate must be guarded. You and Petru are needed here."

Safia removed her hand and stood as he did.

Amastan and Izem came forward. "You fought beside us, Benedek," Amastan said. "We would go with you now and aid you. Safia and Petru along with Zdan and Lunja will be fine caring for the farm. The others will be given a choice to stay or help you."

Benedek stepped forward to grip Amastan's forearms in the way of respect from one Carpathian warrior to another. "Thank you for the offer. You may be needed here. If Justice attempts to break free here, few, if any, will be able to stop him. Be safe. I am honored to have fought beside you."

Benedek did the same with Izem. Nicu followed suit.

Petru faced Benedek. They'd been together for centuries, watching each other's backs, ensuring they stayed strong and never breaking the code. "It feels wrong that I won't be there to fight for your lifemate."

"I know this is how it has to be," Benedek assured him, gripping his arms tightly. "Stay strong. We will meet again soon."

Petru nodded, unable to say what was in his heart. He regarded Benedek as a brother, and letting him go into a nightmare situation without backing him up was difficult. He understood that if Justice chose the gate in Dellys to attack, he would be needed to try to stop him, but he also knew Benedek was heading straight into trouble.

They said their goodbyes, and through it all, Petru found that having emotions wasn't always a good thing. Aura transferred the map in her head to Benedek and the others so they knew the exact location of the fourth gate.

There was a long silence after the Carpathians left. Safia turned to Petru and wrapped her arms around his neck, leaning her body into his. He knew she was comforting him, not the other way around.

Amastan and Izem moved in close. It was Amastan who broke the long silence. "You have good friends, Petru. A man with the kind of friends you have is wealthy beyond measure."

Petru gathered Safia closer as he lifted his head to take in Aura, Amastan and Izem. "A man with friends like my brethren and family like I'm privileged to have right here truly makes me wealthy beyond measure. Thank you for welcoming me the way you have."

He meant it. He felt a part of them, and he was grateful. Mostly, he was grateful for the woman holding him so close. For her understanding. For her love. She gave him that unconditionally, something he thought he would never really have.

She lifted her head and looked at him. "I do love you beyond measure, my old frail one," she teased.

He found himself laughing with the others despite the melancholy that had settled on him. This was what it was like to have a lifemate and a family. He felt whole. Complete. It was everything.

The Goddess

أنتمي إليك ... أنت رفيق ...

أسعى ... ى بحياتي من أجلـ

أفدي بقلبي من أجلك أهدي لك ولائي

أعتبر كل ما تملك ملكي وأسعى للحفاض عليه

حياتك ستكون دئما سعيدة وستفتخر بها بفضلي

حياتك ستكون دائما من بين أولوياتي و هم فوق همومي

أنت مرتبط بي إلى الأبد   أنت رفيق دربي

CARPATHIAN HEALING CHANTS

To rightly understand Carpathian healing chants, background is required in several areas:

1. The Carpathian view on healing
2. The Lesser Healing Chant of the Carpathians
3. The Great Healing Chant of the Carpathians
4. Carpathian musical aesthetics
5. Lullaby
6. Song to Heal the Earth
7. Carpathian chanting technique

1. THE CARPATHIAN VIEW ON HEALING

The Carpathians are a nomadic people whose geographic origins can be traced at least as far as the Southern Ural Mountains (near the steppes of modern-day Kazakhstan), on the border between Europe and Asia. (For this reason, modern-day linguists call their language "proto-Uralic," without knowing that this is the language of the Carpathians.) Unlike most nomadic peoples, the Carpathians did not wander due to the need to find new grazing lands as the seasons and climate shifted, or to search for better trade. Instead, the Carpathians' movements were driven by a great purpose: to find a land that would have the right earth, a soil with the kind of richness that would greatly enhance their rejuvenative powers.

Over the centuries, they migrated westward (some six thousand years ago), until they at last found their perfect homeland—their *susu*—in the Carpathian Mountains, whose long arc cradled the lush plains of the kingdom of Hungary. (The kingdom of Hungary flourished for over a millennium—making Hungarian the dominant language of the Carpathian Basin—until the kingdom's lands were split among several countries after World War I: Austria, Czechoslovakia, Romania, Yugoslavia and modern Hungary.)

Other peoples from the Southern Urals (who shared the Carpathian language but were not Carpathians) migrated in different directions. Some ended up in Finland, which explains why the modern

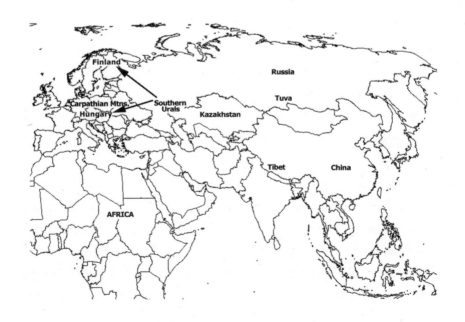

Hungarian and Finnish languages are among the contemporary descendants of the ancient Carpathian language. Even though they are tied forever to their chosen Carpathian homeland, the Carpathians continue to wander as they search the world for the answers that will enable them to bear and raise their offspring without difficulty.

Because of their geographic origins, the Carpathian views on healing share much with the larger Eurasian shamanistic tradition. Probably the closest modern representative of that tradition is based in Tuva (and is referred to as "Tuvinian Shamanism")—see the map on the previous page.

The Eurasian shamanistic tradition—from the Carpathians to the Siberian shamans—held that illness originated in the human soul, and only later manifested as various physical conditions. Therefore, shamanistic healing, while not neglecting the body, focused on the soul and its healing. The most profound illnesses were understood to be caused by "soul departure," where all or some part of the sick person's soul has wandered away from the body (into the nether realms) or has been captured or possessed by an evil spirit, or both.

The Carpathians belong to this greater Eurasian shamanistic tradition and share its viewpoints. While the Carpathians themselves did not succumb to illness, Carpathian healers understood that the most profound wounds were also accompanied by a similar "soul departure."

Upon reaching the diagnosis of "soul departure," the healer-shaman is then required to make a spiritual journey into the netherworld to recover the soul. The shaman may have to overcome tremendous challenges along the way, particularly fighting the demon or vampire who has possessed his friend's soul.

"Soul departure" doesn't require a person to be unconscious (although that certainly can be the case as well). It was understood that a person could still appear to be conscious, even talk and interact with others, and yet be missing a part of their soul. The experienced healer or shaman would instantly see the problem nonetheless, in subtle signs that others might miss: the person's attention wandering every now and then, a lessening in their enthusiasm about life, chronic depression, a diminishment in the brightness of their "aura" and the like.

2. THE LESSER HEALING CHANT OF THE CARPATHIANS

Kepä Sarna Pus (**The Lesser Healing Chant**) is used for wounds that are merely physical in nature. The Carpathian healer leaves his body and enters the wounded Carpathian's body to heal great mortal wounds from the inside out using pure energy. He proclaims, "I offer freely my life for your life," as he gives his blood to the injured Carpathian. Because the Carpathians are of the earth and bound to the soil, they are healed by the soil of their homeland. Their saliva is also often used for its rejuvenative powers.

It is also very common for the Carpathian chants (both the Lesser and the Great) to be accompanied by the use of healing herbs, aromas from Carpathian candles and crystals. The crystals (when combined with the Carpathians' empathic, psychic connection to the entire universe) are used to gather positive energy from their surroundings, which is then used to accelerate the healing. Caves are sometimes used as the setting for the healing.

The Lesser Healing Chant was used by Vikirnoff Von Shrieder and Colby Jansen to heal Rafael De La Cruz, whose heart had been ripped out by a vampire, as described in *Dark Secret*.

Kepä Sarna Pus (The Lesser Healing Chant)
The same chant is used for all physical wounds. "Sívadaba" (into your heart) would be changed to refer to whatever part of the body is wounded.

Kuñasz, nélkül sívdobbanás, nélkül fesztelen löyly.
You lie as if asleep, without beat of heart, without airy breath.

Ot élidamet andam szabadon élidadért.
I offer freely my life for your life.

O jelä sielam jörem ot ainamet és soŋe ot élidadet.
My spirit of light forgets my body and enters your body.

O jelä sielam pukta kinn minden szelemeket belső.
My spirit of light sends all the dark spirits within fleeing without.

Pajńak o susu hanyet és o nyelv nyálamet sívadaba.
I press the earth of our homeland and the spit of my tongue into
   your heart.

Vii, o verim soŋe o verid andam.
At last, I give you my blood for your blood.

To hear this chant, visit christinefeehan.com/members/.

3. THE GREAT HEALING CHANT OF THE CARPATHIANS

The most well-known—and most dramatic—of the Carpathian healing chants is **En Sarna Pus (The Great Healing Chant)**. This chant
is reserved for recovering the wounded or unconscious Carpathian's
soul.

Typically a group of men would form a circle around the sick
Carpathian (to "encircle him with our care and compassion") and begin
the chant. The shaman or healer or leader is the prime actor in this
healing ceremony. It is he who will actually make the spiritual journey
into the netherworld, aided by his clanspeople. Their purpose is to ecstatically dance, sing, drum and chant, all the while visualizing (through
the words of the chant) the journey itself—every step of it, over and
over again—to the point where the shaman, in trance, leaves his body
and makes that very journey. (Indeed, the word *ecstasy* is from the Latin
ex statis, which literally means "out of the body.")

One advantage that the Carpathian healer has over many other
shamans is his telepathic link to his lost brother. Most shamans

must wander in the dark of the nether realms in search of their lost brother. But the Carpathian healer directly "hears" in his mind the voice of his lost brother calling to him, and can thus "zero in on" his soul like a homing beacon. For this reason, Carpathian healing tends to have a higher success rate than most other traditions of this sort.

Something of the geography of the "other world" is useful for us to examine in order to fully understand the words of the Great Healing Chant. A reference is made to the "Great Tree" (in Carpathian: *En Puwe*). Many ancient traditions, including the Carpathian tradition, understood the worlds—the heaven worlds, our world and the nether realms—to be "hung" upon a great pole, or axis, or tree. Here on earth, we are positioned halfway up this tree, on one of its branches. Hence, many ancient texts referred to the material world as "middle earth": midway between heaven and hell. Climbing the tree would lead one to the heaven worlds. Descending the tree to its roots would lead to the nether realms. The shaman was necessarily a master of movement up and down the Great Tree, sometimes moving unaided and sometimes assisted by (or even mounted upon the back of) an animal spirit guide. In various traditions, this Great Tree was known as the *axis mundi* (the "axis of the worlds"), Yggdrasil (in Norse mythology), Mount Meru (the sacred world mountain of Tibetan tradition), etc. The Christian cosmos, with its heaven, purgatory/earth and hell, is also worth comparing. It is even given a similar topography in Dante's *Divine Comedy*: Dante is led on a journey first to hell, at the center of the earth; then upward to Mount Purgatory, which sits on the earth's surface directly opposite Jerusalem; then farther upward to Eden, the earthly paradise, at the summit of Mount Purgatory; and then upward at last to Heaven.

In the shamanistic tradition, it was understood that the small always reflects the large; the personal always reflects the cosmic. A movement in the greater dimensions of the cosmos also coincides with an internal movement. For example, the *axis mundi* of the cosmos corresponds with the spinal column of the individual. Journeys up and down the *axis mundi* often coincided with the movements of natural and spiritual energies (sometimes called *kundalini* or *shakti*) in the spinal column of the shaman or mystic.

En Sarna Pus (The Great Healing Chant)
In this chant, ekä ("brother") would be replaced by "sister," "father," "mother," depending on the person to be healed.

Ot ekäm ainajanak hany, jama.
My brother's body is a lump of earth, close to death.

Me, ot ekäm kuntajanak, pirädak ekäm, gond és irgalom türe.
We, the clan of my brother, encircle him with our care and
    compassion.

O pus wäkenkek, ot oma śarnank, és ot pus fünk, álnak ekäm ainajanak,
    pitänak ekäm ainajanak elävä.
Our healing energies, ancient words of magic and healing herbs bless
    my brother's body, keep it alive.

Ot ekäm sielanak pälä. Ot omboće päläja juta alatt o jüti, kinta, és
    szelemek lamtijaknak.
But my brother's soul is only half. His other half wanders in the
    netherworld.

Ot en mekem ŋamaŋ: kulkedak otti ot ekäm omboće päläjanak.
My great deed is this: I travel to find my brother's other half.

Rekatüre, saradak, tappadak, odam, kaŋa o numa waram, és avaa owe
    o lewl mahoz.
We dance, we chant, we dream ecstatically, to call my spirit bird, and
    to open the door to the other world.

Ntak o numa waram, és mozdulak; jomadak.
I mount my spirit bird and we begin to move; we are underway.

Piwtädak ot En Puwe tyvinak, ećidak alatt o jüti, kinta, és szelemek lamtijaknak.
Following the trunk of the Great Tree, we fall into the netherworld.

Fázak, fázak nó o śaro.
It is cold, very cold.

Juttadak ot ekäm o akarataban, o sívaban és o sielaban.
My brother and I are linked in mind, heart and soul.

Ot ekäm sielanak kaŋa engem.
My brother's soul calls to me.

Kuledak és piwtädak ot ekäm.
I hear and follow his track.

Saŷedak és tuledak ot ekäm kulyanak.
I encounter the demon who is devouring my brother's soul.

Nenäm ćoro, o kuly torodak.
In anger, I fight the demon.

O kuly pél engem.
He is afraid of me.

Lejkkadak o kaŋka salamaval.
I strike his throat with a lightning bolt.

Molodak ot ainaja komakamal.
I break his body with my bare hands.

Toja és molanâ.
He is bent over, and falls apart.

Hän ćaδa.
He runs away.

Manedak ot ekäm sielanak.
I rescue my brother's soul.

Alǝdak ot ekam sielanak o komamban.
I lift my brother's soul in the hollow of my hand.

Alǝdam ot ekam numa waramra.
I lift him onto my spirit bird.

Piwtädak ot En Puwe tyvijanak és saγedak jälleen ot elävä ainak majaknak.
Following up the Great Tree, we return to the land of the living.

Ot ekäm elä jälleen.
My brother lives again.

Ot ekäm weńća jälleen.
He is complete again.

To hear this chant, visit christinefeehan.com/members/.

4. CARPATHIAN MUSICAL AESTHETICS

In the sung Carpathian pieces (such as the "Lullaby" and the "Song to Heal the Earth"), you'll hear elements that are shared by many of the musical traditions in the Uralic geographical region, some of which still exist—from Eastern European (Bulgarian, Romanian, Hungarian, Croatian) to Romany ("gypsy"). These elements include:

- the rapid alternation between major and minor modalities, including a sudden switch (called a "Picardy third") from minor to major to end a piece or section (as at the end of the "Lullaby")
- the use of close (tight) harmonies
- the use of *ritardi* (slowing down the pace) and *crescendi* (swelling in volume) for brief periods
- the use of *glissandi* (slides) in the singing tradition
- the use of trills in the singing tradition (as in the final invocation of the "Song to Heal the Earth")—similar to Celtic, a singing tradition more familiar to many of us
- the use of parallel fifths (as in the final invocation of the "Song to Heal the Earth")
- controlled use of dissonance
- "call-and-response" chanting (typical of many of the world's chanting traditions)
- extending the length of a musical line (by adding a couple of bars) to heighten dramatic effect
- and many more

"Lullaby" and "Song to Heal the Earth" illustrate two rather different forms of Carpathian music (a quiet, intimate piece and an energetic ensemble piece)—but whatever the form, Carpathian music is full of feeling.

5. LULLABY

This song is sung by a woman while a child is still in the womb or when the threat of a miscarriage is apparent. The baby can hear the song while inside the mother, and the mother can connect with the child telepathically as well. The lullaby is meant to reassure the child, to encourage the baby to hold on, to stay—to reassure the child that he or she will be protected by love even from inside until birth. The last line literally means that the mother's love will protect her child until the child is born ("rise").

Musically, the Carpathian "Lullaby" is in three-quarter time ("waltz time"), as are a significant portion of the world's various traditional lullabies (perhaps the most famous of which is Brahms's Lullaby). The arrangement for solo voice is the original context: a mother singing to her child, unaccompanied. The arrangement for chorus and violin ensemble illustrates how musical even the simplest Carpathian pieces often are, and how easily they lend themselves to contemporary instrumental or orchestral arrangements. (A wide range of contemporary composers, including Dvořák and Smetana, have taken advantage of a similar discovery, working other traditional Eastern European music into their symphonic poems.)

Odam-Sarna Kondak (Lullaby)

Tumtesz o wäke ku pitasz belső.
Feel the strength you hold inside.

Hiszasz sívadet. Én olenam gæidnod.
Trust your heart. I'll be your guide.

Sas csecsemőm; kuńasz.
Hush, my baby; close your eyes.

Rauho joŋe ted.
Peace will come to you.

Tumtesz o sívdobbanás ku olen lamt3ad belső.
Feel the rhythm deep inside.

Gond-kumpadek ku kim te.
Waves of love that cover you.

Pesänak te, asti o jüti, kidüsz.
Protect, until the night you rise.

To hear this song, visit christinefeehan.com/members/.

6. SONG TO HEAL THE EARTH

This is the earth-healing song that is used by the Carpathian women to heal soil filled with various toxins. The women take a position on four sides and call to the universe to draw on the healing energy with love and respect. The soil of the earth is their resting place, the place where they rejuvenate, and they must make it safe not only for themselves but for their unborn children, as well as their men and living children. This is a beautiful ritual performed by the women together, raising their voices in harmony and calling on the earth's minerals and healing properties to come forth and help them save their children. They literally dance and sing to heal the earth in a ceremony as old as their species. The dance and notes of the song are adjusted according to the toxins felt through the healers' bare feet. The feet are placed in a certain pattern, and the hands gracefully weave a healing spell while the dance is performed. They must be especially careful when the soil is prepared for babies. This is a ceremony of love and healing.

Musically, the ritual is divided into several sections:

- **First verse:** A "call-and-response" section, where the chant leader sings the "call" solo, and then some or all of the women sing the "response" in the close harmony style typical of the Carpathian musical tradition. The repeated response—*Ai, Emä Maye*—is an invocation of the source of power for the healing ritual: "Oh, Mother Nature."

- **First chorus:** This section is filled with clapping, dancing, ancient horns and other means used to invoke and heighten the energies upon which the ritual is drawing.
- **Second verse**
- **Second chorus**
- **Closing invocation:** In this closing part, two song leaders, in close harmony, take all the energy gathered by the earlier portions of the song/ritual and focus it entirely on the healing purpose.

What you will be listening to are brief tastes of what would typically be a significantly longer ritual, in which the verse and chorus parts are developed and repeated many times, to be closed by a single rendition of the closing invocation.

Sarna Pusm O Maγet (Song to Heal the Earth)

First verse
Ai, Emä Maγe,
Oh, Mother Nature,

Me sívadbin lañaak.
We are your beloved daughters.

Me tappadak, me pusmak o maγet.
We dance to heal the earth.

Me sarnadak, me pusmak o hanyet.
We sing to heal the earth.

Sielanket jutta tedet it,
We join with you now,

Sívank és akaratank és sielank juttanak.
Our hearts and minds and spirits become one.

Second verse
Ai, Emä Maye,
Oh, Mother Nature,

Me sívadbin lańaak.
We are your beloved daughters.

Me andak arwadet emänked és me kaŋank o
We pay homage to our mother and call upon the

Pōhi és Lōuna, Ida és Lääs.
North and South, East and West.

Pide és aldyn és myös belső.
Above and below and within as well.

Gondank o mayenak pusm hän ku olen jama.
Our love of the land heals that which is in need.

Juttanak teval it,
We join with you now,

Maye mayeval.
Earth to earth.

O pirä elidak weńća.
The circle of life is complete.

To hear this chant, visit christinefeehan.com/members/.

7. CARPATHIAN CHANTING TECHNIQUE

As with their healing techniques, the actual "chanting technique" of the Carpathians has much in common with the other shamanistic traditions of the Central Asian steppes. The primary mode of chanting was throat chanting using overtones. Modern examples of this manner of singing can still be found in the Mongolian, Tuvan and Tibetan traditions. You can find an audio example of the Gyuto Tibetan Buddhist monks engaged in throat chanting at christinefeehan.com/carpathian_chanting/.

As with Tuva, note on the map the geographical proximity of Tibet to Kazakhstan and the Southern Urals.

The beginning part of the Tibetan chant emphasizes synchronizing all the voices around a single tone, aimed at healing a particular "chakra" of the body. This is fairly typical of the Gyuto throat-chanting tradition, but it is not a significant part of the Carpathian tradition. Nonetheless, it serves as an interesting contrast.

The part of the Gyuto chanting example that is most similar to the Carpathian style of chanting is the midsection, where the men are chanting the words together with great force. The purpose here is not to generate a "healing tone" that will affect a particular "chakra" but rather to generate as much power as possible for initiating "out-of-body" travel and for fighting the demonic forces that the healer/traveler must face and overcome.

The songs of the Carpathian women (illustrated by their "Lullaby" and their "Song to Heal the Earth") are part of the same ancient musical and healing tradition as the Lesser and Great Healing Chants of the warrior males. You can hear some of the same instruments in both the male warriors' healing chants and the women's "Song to Heal the Earth." Also, they share the common purpose of generating and directing power. However, the women's songs are distinctively feminine in character. One immediately noticeable difference is that while the men speak their words in the manner of a chant, the women sing songs with melodies and harmonies, softening the overall performance. A feminine, nurturing quality is especially evident in the "Lullaby."

THE CARPATHIAN LANGUAGE

Like all human languages, the language of the Carpathians contains the richness and nuance that can only come from a long history of use. At best we can only touch on some of the main features of the language in this brief appendix:

1. The history of the Carpathian language
2. Carpathian grammar and other characteristics of the language
3. Examples of the Carpathian language (including the Ritual Words and the Warriors' Chant)
4. A much-abridged Carpathian dictionary

1. THE HISTORY OF THE CARPATHIAN LANGUAGE

The Carpathian language of today is essentially identical to the Carpathian language of thousands of years ago. A "dead" language like the Latin of two thousand years ago has evolved into a significantly different modern language (Italian) because of countless generations of speakers and great historical fluctuations. In contrast, many of the speakers of Carpathian from thousands of years ago are still alive. Their presence—coupled with the deliberate isolation of the Carpathians from the other major forces of change in the world—has acted (and continues to act) as a stabilizing force that has preserved the integrity of the language over the centuries. Carpathian culture has also acted as a stabilizing force. For instance, the Ritual Words, the various healing chants (see Appendix 1) and other cultural artifacts have been passed down through the centuries with great fidelity.

One small exception should be noted: the splintering of the Carpathians into separate geographic regions has led to some minor dialectization. However, the telepathic link among all Carpathians (as well as each Carpathian's regular return to his or her homeland) has ensured that the differences among dialects are relatively superficial (small numbers of new words, minor differences in pronunciation, etc.), since the deeper internal language of mind-forms has remained the same because of continuous use across space and time.

The Carpathian language was (and still is) the proto-language for the Uralic (or Finno-Ugric) family of languages. Today, the Uralic languages are spoken in northern, eastern and central Europe and in Siberia. More than twenty-three million people in the world speak languages that can trace their ancestry to Carpathian. Magyar or Hungarian (about fourteen million speakers), Finnish (about five million speakers) and Estonian (about one million speakers) are the three major contemporary descendants of this proto-language. The only factor that unites the more than twenty languages in the Uralic family is that their ancestry can be traced back to a common proto-language—Carpathian—that split (starting some six thousand years ago) into the various languages in the Uralic family. In the same way, European languages such as English and French belong to the better-known Indo-European family and also evolved from a common proto-language ancestor (a different one from Carpathian).

The following table provides a sense of some of the similarities in the language family.

Note: The Finnic/Carpathian "k" shows up often as the Hungarian "h." Similarly, the Finnic/Carpathian "p" often corresponds to the Hungarian "f."

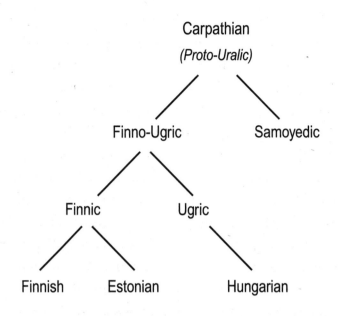

Carpathian
(Proto-Uralic)

Finno-Ugric — Samoyedic

Finnic — Ugric

Finnish — Estonian — Hungarian

Carpathian (proto-Uralic)	Finnish (Suomi)	Hungarian (Magyar)
elä—live	elä—live	él—live
elid—life	elinikä—life	élet—life
pesä—nest	pesä—nest	fészek—nest
kola—die	kuole—die	hal—die
pälä—half, side	pieltä—tilt, tip to the side	fél, fele—fellow human, friend (half; one side of two) feleség—wife
and—give	anta, antaa—give	ad—give
koje—husband, man	koira—dog, the male (of animals)	here—drone, testicle
wäke—power	väki—folks, people, men; force	val/-vel—with (instrumental suffix)
	väkevä—powerful, strong	vele—with him/her/it
wete—water	vesi—water	viz—water

2. CARPATHIAN GRAMMAR AND OTHER CHARACTERISTICS OF THE LANGUAGE

Idioms. As both an ancient language and a language of an earth people, Carpathian is more inclined toward the use of idioms constructed from concrete, "earthy" terms rather than abstractions. For instance, our modern abstraction "to cherish" is expressed more concretely in Carpathian as "to hold in one's heart"; the "netherworld" is, in Carpathian, "the land of night, fog and ghosts"; etc.

Word order. The order of words in a sentence is determined not by syntactic roles (like subject, verb and object) but rather by pragmatic, discourse-driven factors. Examples: *"Tied vagyok."* ("Yours am I."); *"Sívamet andam."* ("My heart I give you.")

Agglutination. The Carpathian language is agglutinative; that is, longer words are constructed from smaller components. An agglutinating language uses suffixes or prefixes whose meanings are generally unique and that are concatenated one after another without overlap. In Carpathian, words typically consist of a stem that is followed by one or more suffixes. For example, *sívambam* derives from the stem *"sív"* ("heart"), followed by *"am"* ("my," making it "my heart"), followed by *"bam"* ("in," making it "in my heart"). As you might imagine, agglutination in Carpathian can sometimes produce very long words, or words that are very difficult to pronounce. Vowels often get inserted between suffixes to prevent too many consonants from appearing in a row (which can make a word unpronounceable).

Noun cases. Like all languages, Carpathian has many noun cases; the same noun will be "spelled" differently depending on its role in a sentence. The noun cases include nominative (when the noun is the subject of the sentence), accusative (when the noun is a direct object of the verb), dative (indirect object), genitive (or possessive), instrumental, final, suppressive, inessive, elative, terminative and delative.

We will use the possessive (or genitive) case as an example to illustrate how all noun cases in Carpathian involve adding standard suffixes to the noun stems. Thus, expressing possession in Carpathian—"my lifemate," "your lifemate," "his lifemate," "her lifemate," etc.—involves adding a particular suffix (such as "*-am*") to the noun stem (*"päläfertiil"*) to produce the possessive (*"päläfertiilam"*—"my lifemate"). Which suffix to use depends on which person ("my," "your," "his," etc.) and whether the noun ends in a consonant or a vowel. The following table shows the suffixes for singular nouns only (not plural), and also shows the similarity to the suffixes used in contemporary Hungarian. (Hungarian is actually a little more complex, in that it also requires "vowel rhyming": which suffix to use also depends on the last vowel in the noun, hence the multiple choices in the table, where Carpathian has only a single choice.)

	Carpathian (proto-Uralic)		Contemporary Hungarian	
person	**noun ends in vowel**	**noun ends in consonant**	**noun ends in vowel**	**noun ends in consonant**
1st singular (my)	-m	-am	-m	-om, -em, -öm
2nd singular (your)	-d	-ad	-d	-od, -ed, -öd
3rd singular (his, her, its)	-ja	-a	-ja/-je	-a, -e
1st plural (our)	-nk	-ank	-nk	-unk, -ünk
2nd plural (your)	-tak	-atak	-tok, -tek, -tök	-otok, -etek, -ötök
3rd plural (their)	-jak	-ak	-juk, -jük	-uk, -ük

Note: As mentioned earlier, vowels often get inserted between the word and its suffix so as to prevent too many consonants from appearing in a row (which would produce unpronounceable words). For example, in the table on the previous page, all nouns that end in a consonant are followed by suffixes beginning with "a."

Verb conjugation. Like its modern descendants (such as Finnish and Hungarian), Carpathian has many verb tenses, far too many to describe here. We will just focus on the conjugation of the present tense. Again, we will place contemporary Hungarian side by side with Carpathian because of the marked similarity between the two.

As with the possessive case for nouns, the conjugation of verbs is done by adding a suffix onto the verb stem:

Person	Carpathian (proto-Uralic)	Contemporary Hungarian
1st singular (I give)	-am (andam), -ak	-ok, -ek, -ök
2nd singular (you give)	-sz (andsz)	-sz
3rd singular (he/she/it gives)	— (and)	—
1st plural (we give)	-ak (andak)	-unk, -ünk
2nd plural (you give)	-tak (andtak)	-tok, -tek, -tök
3rd plural (they give)	-nak (andnak)	-nak, -nek

As with all languages, there are many "irregular verbs" in Carpathian that don't exactly fit this pattern. But the table is still a useful guide for most verbs.

3. EXAMPLES OF THE CARPATHIAN LANGUAGE

Here are some brief examples of conversational Carpathian, used in the Dark books. We include the literal translation in square brackets.

It is interestingly different from the most appropriate English translation.

Susu.
I am home.
["home/birthplace." "I am" is understood, as is often the case in Carpathian.]

Möért?
What for?

csitri
little one
["little slip of a thing," "little slip of a girl"]

ainaak enyém
forever mine

ainaak sívamet jutta
forever mine (another form)
["forever to-my-heart connected/fixed"]

sívamet
my love
["of-my-heart," "to-my-heart"]

Tet vigyázam.
I love you.
["you-love-I"]

Sarna Rituaali (The Ritual Words) is a longer example and an example of chanted rather than conversational Carpathian. Note the recurring use of *"andam"* ("I give") to give the chant musicality and force through repetition.

Sarna Rituaali (The Ritual Words)

Te avio päläfertiilam.
You are my lifemate.

Éntölam kuulua, avio päläfertiilam.
I claim you as my lifemate.

Ted kuuluak, kacad, kojed.
I belong to you.

Élidamet andam.
I offer my life for you.

Pesämet andam.
I give you my protection.

Uskolfertiilamet andam.
I give you my allegiance.

Sívamet andam.
I give you my heart.

Sielamet andam.
I give you my soul.

Ainamet andam.
I give you my body.

Sívamet kuuluak kaik että a ted.
I take into my keeping the same that is yours.

Ainaak olenszal sívambin.
Your life will be cherished by me for all my time.

Te élidet ainaak pide minan.
Your life will be placed above my own for all time.

Te avio päläfertiilam.
You are my lifemate.

Ainaak sívamet jutta oleny.
You are bound to me for all eternity.

Ainaak terád vigyázak.
You are always in my care.

To hear these words pronounced (and for more about Carpathian pronunciation altogether), please visit christinefeehan.com/members/.

Sarna Kontakawk (The Warriors' Chant) is another, longer example of the Carpathian language. The warriors' council takes place deep beneath the earth in a chamber of crystals with magma far below it, so the steam is natural and the wisdom of their ancestors is clear and focused. This is a sacred place where they bloodswear to their prince and people and affirm their code of honor as warriors and brothers. It is also where battle strategies are born and all dissension is discussed, as well as any concerns the warriors have that they wish to bring to the council and open for discussion.

Sarna Kontakawk (The Warriors' Chant)

Veri isäakank—veri ekäakank.
Blood of our fathers—blood of our brothers.

Veri olen elid.
Blood is life.

Andak veri-elidet Karpatiiakank, és wäke-sarna ku meke arwa-arvo,
  irgalom, hän ku agba, és wäke kutni, ku manaak verival.
We offer that life to our people with a bloodsworn vow of honor,
  mercy, integrity and endurance.

Verink sokta; verink kaŋa terád.
Our blood mingles and calls to you.

Akasz énak ku kaŋa és juttasz kuntatak it.
Heed our summons and join with us now.

To hear these words pronounced (and for more about Carpathian
pronunciation altogether), please visit christinefeehan.com
/members/.

See **Appendix 1** for Carpathian healing chants, including the *Kepä
Sarna Pus* (The Lesser Healing Chant), the *En Sarna Pus* (The Great
Healing Chant), the *Odam-Sarna Kondak* (Lullaby) and the *Sarna
Pusm O Mayet* (Song to Heal the Earth).

4. A MUCH-ABRIDGED CARPATHIAN DICTIONARY

This very-much-abridged Carpathian dictionary contains most of the
Carpathian words used in the Dark books. Of course, a full Carpathian dictionary would be as large as the usual dictionary for an entire
language (typically more than a hundred thousand words).

Note: The Carpathian nouns and verbs that follow are word **stems**. They
generally do not appear in their isolated "stem" form. Instead, they usually
appear with suffixes (e.g., *andam—I give*, rather than just the root, *and*).

a—verb negation (*prefix*); not (*adverb*).
aćke—pace, step.

aćke éntölem it—take another step toward me.

agba—to be seemly; to be proper (*verb*). True; seemly; proper (*adj.*).

ai—oh.

aina—body (*noun*).

ainaak—always; forever.

o ainaak jelä peje emnimet ŋamaŋ—sun scorch that woman forever
(*Carpathian swear words*).

ainaakä—never.

ainaakfél—old friend.

ak—suffix added after a noun ending in a consonant to make it plural.

aka—to give heed; to hearken; to listen.

aka-arvo—respect (*noun*).

akarat—mind; will (*noun*).

ál—to bless; to attach to.

alatt—through.

aldyn—under; underneath.

alə—to lift; to raise.

alte—to bless; to curse.

amaŋ—this; this one here; that; that one there.

and—to give.

**and sielet, arwa-arvomet, és jelämet, kuulua huvémet ku feaj és
ködet ainaak**—to trade soul, honor and salvation for momentary
pleasure and endless damnation.

andasz éntölem irgalomet!—have mercy!

arvo—value; price (*noun*).

arwa—praise (*noun*).

arwa-arvo olen gæidnod, ekäm—honor guide you, my brother
(*greeting*).

arwa-arvo olen isäntä, ekäm—honor keep you, my brother (*greeting*).

arwa-arvo pile sívadet—may honor light your heart (*greeting*).

arwa-arvod—honor (*noun*).

arwa-arvod mäne me ködak—may your honor hold back the dark
(*greeting*).

aš—no (*exclamation*).

ašša—no (before a noun); not (with a verb that is not in the imperative); not (with an adjective).

aššatotello—disobedient.

asti—until.

avaa—to open.

avio—wedded.

avio päläfertiil—lifemate.

avoi—uncover; show; reveal.

baszú—revenge; vengeance.

belső—within; inside.

bur—good; well.

bur tule ekämet kuntamak—well met brother-kin (*greeting*).

ćaδa—to flee; to run; to escape.

čač3—to be born; to grow.

ćoro—to flow; to run like rain.

csecsemő—baby (*noun*).

csitri—little one (*female*).

csitrim—my little one (*female*).

diutal—triumph; victory.

džinõt—brief; short.

ећi—to fall.

ej—not (*adverb, suffix*); *nej* when preceding syllable ends in a vowel.

ek—suffix added after a noun ending in a consonant to make it plural.

ekä—brother.

ekäm—my brother.

elä—to live.

eläsz arwa-arvoval—may you live with honor; live nobly (*greeting*).

eläsz jeläbam ainaak—long may you live in the light (*greeting*).

elävä—alive.

elävä ainak majaknak—land of the living.

elid—life.

emä—mother (*noun*).

Emä Maγe—Mother Nature.

emäen—grandmother.

embε—if; when.

embε karmasz—please.

emni—wife; woman.

emni hän ku köd alte—cursed woman.

emni kuŋenak ku aššatotello—disobedient lunatic.

emnim—my wife; my woman.

emninuma—goddess.

én—I.

en—great; many; big.

en hän ku pesä—the protector (literally: the great protector).

én jutta félet és ekämet—I greet a friend and brother (*greeting*).

en Karpatii—the prince (literally: the great Carpathian).

én maγenak—I am of the earth.

Én olenam jelä—I am the light.

Én olenam teval it—I am with you now.

én oma maγeka—I am as old as time (literally: as old as the earth).

En Puwe—The Great Tree. Related to the legends of Yggdrasil, the *axis mundi*, Mount Meru, heaven and hell, etc.

enä—most.

engem—of me.

enkojra—wolf.

és—and.

ete—before; in front of.

että—that.

év—year.

évsatz—century.

ewal—sweet; tender.

fáz—to feel cold or chilly.

fél—fellow; friend.

fél ku kuuluaak sívam belső—beloved.

fél ku vigyázak—dear one.

feldolgaz—prepare.

fertiil—fertile one.

fesztelen—airy.

fü—herbs; grass.

gæidno—road; way.

gapâd—free; idle; unoccupied; easy; petty; small; trifling.

gond—care; worry; love (*noun*).

gyenge—weak; frail; slight; infirm.

hän—he; she; it; one.

hän agba—it is so.

hän ku—prefix: one who; he who; that which.

hän ku agba—truth.

hän ku kaśwa o numamet—sky-owner.

hän ku kuula siela—keeper of his soul.

hän ku kuulua sívamet—keeper of my heart.

hän ku lejkka wäke-sarnat—traitor.

hän ku meke pirämet—defender.

hän ku meke sarnaakmet—mage.

hän ku pelkgapâd és meke pirämet—fearless defender. (*Pelkgapâd és Meke Pirämet*: "Fearless Defender" used as a nickname.)

hän ku pesä—protector.

hän ku pesä sieladet—guardian of your soul.

hän ku pesäk kaikak—guardians of all.

hän ku piwtä—predator; hunter; tracker.

hän ku pusm—healer.

hän ku saa kuć3aket—star-reacher.

hän ku tappa—killer; violent person (*noun*). Deadly; violent (*adj.*).

hän ku tappa kulyak—demon killer. (*Ku Tappa Kulyak*: "Demon Killer" used as a nickname.)

hän ku tuulmahl elidet—vampire (literally: life-stealer).

hän ku vie elidet—vampire (literally: thief of life).

hän ku vigyáz sielamet—keeper of my soul.

hän ku vigyáz sívamet és sielamet—keeper of my heart and soul.

hän sívamak—beloved.

hängem—him; her; it.

hank—they.

hany—clod; lump of earth.

hisz—to believe; to trust.

ho—how.

ida—east.

igazág—justice.

ila—to shine.

inan—mine; my own (*endearment*).

irgalom—compassion; pity; mercy.

isä—father (*noun*).

isäntä—master of the house.

it—now.

jaguár—jaguar.

jaka—to cut; to divide; to separate.

jakam—wound; cut; injury.

jalka—leg.

jälleen—again.

jama—to be sick, infected, wounded or dying; to be near death.

jamatan—fallen; wounded; near death.

jelä—sunlight; day, sun; light.

jelä keje terád—light sear you (*Carpathian swear words*).

o jelä peje emnimet—sun scorch the woman (*Carpathian swear words*).

o jelä peje kaik hänkanak—sun scorch them all (*Carpathian swear words*).

o jelä peje terád—sun scorch you (*Carpathian swear words*).

o jelä peje terád, emni—sun scorch you, woman (*Carpathian swear words*).

o jelä sielamak—light of my soul.

joma—to be underway; to go.

joŋe—to come; to return.

joŋesz arwa-arvoval—return with honor (*greeting*).

joŋesz éntölem, fél ku kuuluaak sívam belsö—come to me, beloved.

jŏrem—to forget; to lose one's way; to make a mistake.

jotka—gap; middle; space.

jotkan—between.

juo—to drink.

juosz és eläsz—drink and live (*greeting*).

juosz és olen ainaak sielamet jutta—drink and become one with me (*greeting*).

juta—to go; to wander.

jüti—night; evening.

jutta—connected; fixed (*adj.*). To connect; to join; to fix; to bind (*verb*).

k—suffix added after a noun ending in a vowel to make it plural.

kać3—gift.

kaca—male lover.

kadi—judge.

kaik—all.

käktä—two; many.

käktäverit—mixed blood (literally: two bloods).

kalma—corpse; death; grave.

kaŋa—to call; to invite; to summon; to request; to beg.

kaŋk—windpipe; Adam's apple; throat.

karma—want.

Karpatii—Carpathian.

karpatii ku köd—liar.

Karpatiikunta—the Carpathian people.

käsi—hand.

kaśwa—to own.

kaða—to abandon; to leave; to remain.

kaða wäkeva óv o köd—stand fast against the dark (*greeting*).

kat—house; family (*noun*).

katt3—to move; to penetrate; to proceed.

keje—to cook; to burn; to sear.

kepä—lesser; small; easy; few.

kessa—cat.

kessa ku toro—wildcat.

kessake—little cat.

kidü—to wake up; to arise (*intransitive verb*).

kim—to cover an entire object with some sort of covering.

kinn—out; outdoors; outside; without.

kinta—fog; mist; smoke.

kislány—little girl.

kislány hän ku meke sarnaakmet—little mage.

kislány kuŋenak—little lunatic.

kislány kuŋenak minan—my little lunatic.

köd—fog; mist; darkness; evil (*noun*). Foggy, dark; evil (*adj.*).

köd alte hän—darkness curse it (*Carpathian swear words*).

o köd belső—darkness take it (*Carpathian swear words*).

köd elävä és köd nime kutni nimet—evil lives and has a name.

köd jutasz belső—shadow take you (*Carpathian swear words*).

koj—let; allow; decree; establish; order.

koje—man; husband; drone.

kola—to die.

kolasz arwa-arvoval—may you die with honor (*greeting*).

kolatan—dead; departed.

koma—empty hand; bare hand; palm of the hand; hollow of the hand.

kond—all of a family's or clan's children.

kont—warrior; man.

kont ku votjak—knight.

kont o sívanak—strong heart (literally: heart of the warrior).

kor3—basket; container made of birch bark.

kor3nat—containing; including.

ku—who; which; that; where; which; what.

kuć3—star.

kuć3ak!—stars! (exclamation).

kudeje—descent; generation.

kuja—day; sun.

kule—to hear.

kulke—to go or to travel (on land or water).

kulkesz arwa-arvoval, ekäm—walk with honor, my brother (*greeting*).

kulkesz arwaval, joŋesz arwa arvoval—go with glory, return with honor (*greeting*).

kuly—intestinal worm; tapeworm; demon who possesses and devours souls.

küm—human male.

kumala—to sacrifice; to offer; to pray.

kumpa—wave (*noun*).

kuńa—to lie as if asleep; to close or cover the eyes in a game of hide-and-seek; to die.

kuŋe—moon; month.

kuŋe kont—moon warrior.

kuŋe kont ku votjak—moon knight.

kuŋe s3c3—moon monster.

kunta—band; clan; tribe; family; people; lineage; line.

kuras—sword; large knife.

kure—bind; tie.

kuš—worker; servant.

kutenken—however.

kutni—to be able to bear, carry, endure, stand or take.

kutnisz ainaak—long may you endure (*greeting*).

kuulua—to belong; to hold.

kužõ—long.

lääs—west.

lamti (or lamt3)—lowland; meadow; deep; depth.

lamti ból jüti, kinta, ja szelem—the netherworld (literally: the meadow of night, mists and ghosts).

lańa—daughter.

lejkka—crack; fissure; split (*noun*). To cut; to hit; to strike forcefully (*verb*).

lewl—spirit (*noun*).

lewl ma—the other world (literally: spirit land). *Lewl ma* includes *lamti ból jüti, kinta, ja szelem*: the netherworld, but also includes the worlds higher up *En Puwe*, the Great Tree.

liha—flesh.

lõuna—south.

löyly—breath; steam (related to *lewl*: spirit).

luwe—bone.

ma—land; forest; world.

magköszun—thank.

mana—to abuse; to curse; to ruin.

mäne—to rescue; to save.

maɣe—land; earth; territory; place; nature.

mboće—other; second (*adj.*).

me—we.

megem—us.

meke—deed; work (*noun*). To do; to make; to work (*verb*).

mić (or mića)—beautiful.

mića emni kuŋenak minan—my beautiful lunatic.

minan—mine; my own (*endearment*).

minden—every; all (*adj.*).

möért?—what for? (*exclamation*).

molanâ—to crumble; to fall apart.

molo—to crush; to break into bits.

moo—why; reason.

mozdul—to begin to move; to enter into movement.

muonì—appoint; order; prescribe; command.

muonìak te avoisz te—I command you to reveal yourself.

musta—memory.

myös—also.

m8—thing; what.

na—close; near.

nä—for.

nâbbŏ—so, then.

ŋamaŋ—this; this one here; that; that one there.

ŋamaŋak—these; these ones here; those; those ones there.

nautish—to enjoy.

nélkül—without.

nenä—anger.

nime—name.

ńiŋ3—worm; maggot.

ńiŋ3 ködak—shadow worm.

nó—like; in the same way as; as.

nókunta—kinship.

numa—god; sky; top; upper part; highest (related to the English word *numinous*).

numatorkuld—thunder (literally: sky struggle).

ńůp@l—for; to; toward.

ńůp@l mam—toward my world.

nyál—saliva; spit (related to *nyelv*: tongue).

nyelv—tongue.

o—the (used before a noun beginning with a consonant).

ó—like; in the same way as; as.

odam—to dream; to sleep.

odam-sarna kondak—lullaby (literally: sleep-song of children).

odam wäke emni—mistress of illusions.

olen—to be.

oma—old; ancient; last; previous.

omas—stand.

omboće—other; second (*adj.*).

ŏrem—to forget; to lose one's way; to make a mistake.

ot—the (used before a noun beginning with a vowel).

ot (or t)—past participle (*suffix*).

otti—to look; to see; to find.

óv—to protect against.

owe—door.

päämoro—aim; target.

pajna—to press.

pälä—half; side.

päläfertiil—mate or wife.

päläpälä—side by side.

palj3—more.

palj3 na éntölem—closer.

partiolen—scout (*noun*).

peje—to burn; scorch.

peje!—burn! (*Carpathian swear word*).

peje terád—get burned (*Carpathian swear words*).

pél—to be afraid; to be scared of.

pelk—fear (*noun*).

pelkgapâ—fearless.

pesä—nest (*literal; noun*); protection (*figurative; noun*).

pesä—nest; stay (*literal*); protect (*figurative*).

pesäd te engemal—you are safe with me.

pesäsz jeläbam ainaak—long may you stay in the light (*greeting*).

pide—above.

pile—to ignite; to light up.

piŋe—little bird.

piŋe sarnanak—little songbird.

pion—soon.

pirä—circle; ring (*noun*). To surround; to enclose (*verb*).

piros—red.

pitä—to keep; to hold; to have; to possess.

pitäam mustaakad sielpesäambam—I hold your memories safe in my soul.

pitäsz baszú, piwtäsz igazáget—no vengeance, only justice.

piwtä—to seek; to follow; to follow the track of game; to hunt; to prey upon.

poår—bit; piece.

põhi—north.

pohoopa—vigorous.

pukta—to drive away; to persecute; to put to flight.

pus—healthy; healing.

pusm—to heal; to be restored to health.

puwe—tree; wood.

rambsolg—slave.

rauho—peace.

reka—ecstasy; trance.

rituaali—ritual.

s3c3—lizard; monster.

sa—sinew; tendon; cord.

sa4—to call; to name.

saa—arrive, come; become; get, receive.

saasz hän ku andam szabadon—take what I freely offer.

saγe—to arrive; to come; to reach.

salama—lightning; lightning bolt.

sapar—tail.

sapar bin jalkak—coward (literally: tail between legs).

sapar bin jalkak nélkül mogal—spineless coward.

sarna—words; speech; song; magic incantation (*noun*). To chant; to
sing; to celebrate (*verb*).

sarna hän agba—claim.

sarna kontakawk—warriors' chant.

sarna kunta—alliance (literally: single tribe through sacred words).

śaro—frozen snow.

sas—shoosh (*to a child or baby*).

satz—hundred.

siel—soul.

sielad sielamed—soul to soul (literally: your soul to my soul).

sielam—my soul.

sielam pitwä sielad—my soul searches for your soul.

sielam sieladed—my soul to your soul.

sieljelä isäntä—purity of soul triumphs.

sisar—sister.

sisarak sivak—sisters of the heart.

sisarke—little sister.

sív—heart.

sív pide köd—love transcends evil.

sív pide minden köd—love transcends all evil.

sívad olen wäkeva, hän ku piwtä—may your heart stay strong, hunter (*greeting*).

sívam és sielam—my heart and soul.

sívamet—my heart.

sívdobbanás—heartbeat (*literal*); rhythm (*figurative*).

sokta—to mix; to stir around.

sõl—dare, venture.

sõl olen engemal, sarna sívametak—dare to be with me, song of my heart.

soŋe—to enter; to penetrate; to compensate; to replace.

Susiküm—Lycan.

susu—home; birthplace (*noun*). At home (*adv.*).

szabadon—freely.

szelem—ghost.

ször—time; occasion.

t (or ot)—past participle (*suffix*).

taj—to be worth.

taka—behind; beyond.

takka—to hang; to remain stuck.

takkap—obstacle; challenge; difficulty; ordeal; trial.

tappa—to dance; to stamp with the feet; to kill.

tasa—even so; just the same.

te—you.

te kalma, te jama ńiŋ3kval, te apitäsz arwa-arvo—you are nothing but a walking maggot-infected corpse, without honor.

te magköszunam nä ŋamaŋ kać3 taka arvo—thank you for this gift beyond price.

ted—yours.

terád keje—get scorched (*Carpathian swear words*).

tõd—to know.

tõdak pitäsz wäke bekimet mekesz kaiket—I know you have the courage to face anything.

tõdhän—knowledge.

tõdhän lõ kuraset agbapäämoroam—knowledge flies the sword true to its aim.

toja—to bend; to bow; to break.

toro—to fight; to quarrel.

torosz wäkeval—fight fiercely (*greeting*).

totello—obey.

tsak—only.

t'śuva vni—period of time.

tti—to look; to see; to find.

tuhanos—thousand.

tuhanos löylyak türelamak saγe diutalet—a thousand patient breaths bring victory.

tule—to meet; to come.

tuli—fire.

tumte—to feel; to touch; to touch upon.

türe—full; satiated; accomplished.

türelam—patience.

türelam agba kontsalamaval—patience is the warrior's true weapon.

tyvi—stem; base; trunk.

ul3—very; exceedingly; quite.

umuš—wisdom; discernment.

und—past participle (*suffix*).

uskol—faithful.

uskolfertiil—allegiance; loyalty.

usm—to heal; to be restored to health.

vad—savage.

vár—to wait.

varolind—dangerous.

veri—blood.

veri ekäakank—blood of our brothers.

veri-elidet—blood-life.

veri isäakank—blood of our fathers.

veri olen piros, ekäm—literally: blood be red, my brother; figuratively: find your lifemate (*greeting*).

veriak ot en Karpatiiak—by the blood of the prince (literally: by the blood of the great Carpathian; *Carpathian swear words*).

veridet peje—may your blood burn (*Carpathian swear words*).

vigyáz—to love; to care for; to take care of.

vii—last; at last; finally.

votjak—to harness (a horse).

wäke—power; strength.

wäke beki—strength; courage.

wäke kaða—steadfastness.

wäke kutni—endurance.

wäke-sarna—vow; curse; blessing (literally: power words).

wäkeva—powerful; strong.

wäkeva csitrim ku pesä—my fierce little protector.

wara—bird; crow.

weńća—complete; whole.

wete—water (*noun*).